Contents

Author's foreword

In the summer of 1969 three bulky leather-bound volumes changed hands in the sitting-room of a small house in Kensington. I was not to know then that these books, crammed with indecipherable script, maps and diagrams, were to take me – almost physically at times – back into the dark, brutal and secret places of the Victorian underworld.

It is now common knowledge that these books are the coded journals of James Moriarty – the diabolically cunning, highly intelligent criminal mastermind of the late nineteenth century.

The known felon who handed the books to me, on that hot and heavy night six years ago, was called Albert George Spear, and his claim was that they had been in his family since his grandfather's day – his grandfather having been one of Moriarty's principal lieutenants.

I have already told the story, in the foreword to *The Return of Moriarty*, of how the cipher to the journals was finally broken, and how my publishers soon realized that it would be impossible to offer these extraordinary documents to the public in their original form. For one thing, they present grave legal problems, for another there are incidents contained in them of such an evil character that, even in this permissive age, they could be accounted a corrupting influence.

There is also the small possibility that the journals might just be a hoax, perpetrated by Spear himself, or even by his grandfather, who figures so largely in them.

I personally do not believe this. However, I think it quite

possible that Moriarty, the criminal mastermind, has, in writing the journals, sought to put himself in the best possible light, and with consummate cunning may not have told the entire truth. In some places the journals clash strongly with other evidence – most notably the published records of Dr John H. Watson, friend and chronicler of the great Mr Sherlock Holmes; in others with the evidence I have been able to amass from the private papers of the late Superintendent Angus McCready Crow – the Metropolitan Police officer assigned to the Moriarty case during the closing years of the last century.

Taking these things into account, my publishers very wisely commissioned me to write a series of novels based on the *Moriarty Journals*, occasionally altering names, dates and places wherever this seemed advisable.

It struck us at the time that these books, so shaped from the journals, would be of great interest, not simply to addicts of Dr Watson's memoirs of Sherlock Holmes, but also to the more general reader who might well be entertained by the many aspects of the life, times, adventures, organization and methods of the supremely devilish villain whom Holmes once called the Napoleon of Crime.

The first volume, *The Return of Moriarty*, was concerned with, among other things, the true identity of Professor James Moriarty; the structure of his criminal society; his own version of what really occurred when he met Sherlock Holmes at the Reichenbach Falls (described by Watson in *The Final Problem*); his struggle to maintain a grip on the London underworld of the early 1890s; his alliance with four of the great continental criminals – Wilhelm Schleifstein of Berlin; Jean Grisombre of Paris; Luigi Sanzionare of Rome, and Esteban Segorbe of Madrid; and the, hitherto unpublished, details of a dastardly plot against the British Royal Family.

This present volume continues the story, though it can, of course, be read as a separate entity.

Once again I have to thank Miss Bernice Crow, of Cairndow, Argyllshire, great granddaughter of the late Superintendent Angus McCready Crow, for the use of her great-grandfather's journals, notebooks, personal correspondence and jottings.

I also have to thank the many friends and colleagues who have given sterling support to this venture in ways too numerous to catalogue here. In particular my thanks go to Enid Gordon, Christopher Falkus, Donald Rumbelow, Anthony Gould-Davies, Simon Wood, Jonathan Clowes, Ann Evans, Dean and Shirley Dickensheet, John Bennett Shaw, Ted Schultz, Jon Lellenberg, and many others who prefer, sometimes for obvious reasons, to remain nameless.

John Gardner,
Rowledge,
Surrey.
1975.

When an individual's success, or his status, or his recognition is hindered or threatened, he usually thinks in terms of some person or persons hindering his success or threatening his status, or discouraging his recognition. Thus he may try to revenge himself by removing the cause – in this case, the person concerned.

The Principles of Criminology
Edwin H. Sutherland & Donald R. Cressey.

Sometime when you have a year or two to spare I commend to you the study of Professor Moriarty.

Sherlock Holmes in *The Valley of Fear*.

LONDON AND AMERICA:
Friday, 25 May 1894-Friday 22 August 1896

(Crow on the trail)

At a little before five o'clock on a Friday afternoon towards the end of May, in that chilly spring of 1894, a hansom drew up outside 221B Baker Street and deposited a tall, craggy man, straight of bearing and with that authoritative stamp about him which marks a person who has spent his life with either the military or the police.

In this case it was the police, for he was none other than Inspector Angus McCready Crow of the Criminal Investigation Department of Scotland Yard.

An hour or so earlier, Crow had stood at his window in the Police Office, looking out across the busy river, a telegram stretched tight between the thumbs and forefingers of his hands.

The message was brief and to the point –

I would be grateful if you could call upon me at five o'clock today.

The signature was that of Sherlock Holmes, and, as he read the missive, Crow reflected that there was only one subject he wished to discuss with the great detective.

His hands trembled slightly – an emotional reaction of hope. Crow mistrusted emotion, especially when he was a prey to it. His business stood or fell by facts, logic and the law. Logic told him now that, though Holmes expressed a desire to see him, it was not certain they would talk of Professor James Moriarty.

On the last occasion the two men had spoken, Holmes had given Crow short shrift on that matter.

'My feud with Professor Moriarty ended a long time ago at the Reichenbach Falls,' he had said bluntly. 'There is no more for anyone else's ears.'

That was a few weeks past: before Crow had proved beyond doubt that Moriarty lived, and still ran his criminal empire from the secret headquarters in Limehouse; before he had become aware of the meeting of European criminal leaders, with Moriarty at their head; before the disgraceful business at Sandringham, when Crow had come within an ace of putting the evil Professor behind bars.

Now he stood in front of the Baker Street house, his hand reaching for the knocker. Moriarty had gone: disappeared as though he had never been, and the sense of failure and frustration at so narrowly missing the villain was constantly in the forefront of Crow's mind, often blotting out other matters – including his own forthcoming marriage.

The faithful Mrs Hudson answered Crow's knock, told him that he was expected and led him upstairs where he found the great man awaiting him in a mood of high excitement.

'Come in and sit yourself down, my dear fellow. Here in the basket chair,' Holmes said quite cheerfully, leading Crow over to the fireplace of his somewhat cluttered sitting room.

Having asked Mrs Hudson if she would be so good as to bring them some tea, the consulting detective waited until the door was closed before seating himself in his favourite place and fixing Crow with a steady gaze.

'I trust you are not inconvenienced,' he began. 'I see that you have come straight from your office.'

Crow must have looked surprised, for Holmes smiled indulgently and added, 'It is not hard to deduce, for I see that you have some specks of pink blotting paper adhering to your cuff. If my eyes do not deceive me, it is pink blotting of the type usually found on the official desks of the Metropolitan Police. It is in small details like this, Mr Crow, that we lead criminals to their rightful fate.'

Crow laughed and nodded. 'Indeed, Mr Holmes, I have come directly from my office at the Yard. Just as I know that earlier this afternoon you were at the Foreign Office.'

It was Holmes's turn to look amazed. 'Astute, Crow. Pray tell me how you deduced that.'

'Not a deduction, I'm afraid, sir. It just so happened that my sergeant, a lad named Tanner, was passing down Whitehall and spotted you. When I told him that I was off to see you, he remarked upon it.'

Holmes looked a little put out, but was soon back in his excited mood. 'I particularly wished to see you at this hour. My good friend and colleague, Dr Watson, is at present in the process of selling his practice in Kensington, with a view to moving back here before either of us is much older. He is, of course, a constant and welcome visitor, though at the moment I know he is engaged until after eight tonight, therefore he will not disturb us. You see, my dear Crow, what I have to say to you is for your ears alone and those of no other living being.'

At this point Mrs Hudson arrived with the tea, so further conversation was abandoned until the cheering brew had been poured and they had helped themselves from the array of jams and interesting cakes which the housekeeper provided.

Once they were again alone, Holmes continued his monologue. 'I have only recently returned to London,' he began. 'You may be aware that I have been occupied in the past weeks with that thoroughly unwholesome business concerning the banker, Mr Crosby. But then I do not suppose you are much interested in red leeches?'

The great detective paused for a second, as though waiting for Crow to reveal a great passion for the subject, but, as no such revelation was forthcoming, Holmes sighed and started to speak in a grave tone.

'It was only this afternoon that I became acquainted with this terrible Sandringham business.'

At this, Crow was startled, for, to his own knowledge, Holmes' name was not among those authorized to see the file.

'It is highly confidential. I trust . . .'

Holmes gestured impatiently with his right hand.

'Your sergeant spotted me leaving the Foreign Office this afternoon. I had been visiting my brother, Mycroft. His Royal Highness had consulted with him on the matter. Mycroft in turn promised to speak with me. I was shocked and more distressed than I can tell you, or, I suspect, even admit to myself. I recall that at our last meeting I told you my feud with James Moriarty ended at the Reichenbach Falls. Well, Crow, that is what the world must believe – at least for many years to come. But this monstrous act of anarchy puts a new complexion on the matter. He paused, as if on the brink of some momentous statement. 'I have no intention of being publicly associated with any investigations concerning the despicable Moriarty, but I will now give you what help I can in a private and confidential capacity. And help you will surely need, Crow.'

Angus McCready Crow nodded, scarcely able to believe his ears.

'However, I have to warn you,' Holmes continued, 'that you must not divulge the source of your intelligence. There are personal reasons for this, which, no doubt, in the fullness of time shall be revealed. But at this juncture I shall need your solemn oath that you will keep counsel and disclose to no living soul that you have access to my eyes, ears and mind.'

'You have my word, Holmes. Of course you have my most sacred word.'

Crow was so amazed at Holmes' unexpected change of heart that he had to suppress a wild desire to bombard the man with a volley of queries. But, rightly, he held himself in check, knowing this was not the way.

'Strange as it may seem,' Holmes continued to transfix Crow with a steady eye, 'I find myself somewhat on the horns of the proverbial dilemma. There are certain people whom I have to protect. Yet I must also do my duty as an Englishman – beggin' your pardon as one who comes from North of the border.' He chuckled for a second at his own little quip. In a flash the laughter was gone and Holmes was all seriousness again. 'This outrage against a royal personage leaves me scant margin for manoeuvre. I have little time for the official detective force, as you must well know. However, good Crow, my observations tell me that you are possibly the best of a bad bunch, so I have no option but to turn to you.'

There was the mildest pause, during which Crow opened his mouth as if to object to Sherlock Holmes' opprobrious remarks. Yet, before he could translate thoughts to speech, the great detective was talking again in a most animated fashion.

'Now, to work. There are two questions I must put to you. First, have you had any of the bank accounts examined? Second, have you been to the Berkshire house?'

Crow was flummoxed. 'I know of no bank accounts, and have never heard of the Berkshire house.'

Holmes smiled. 'I thought not. Well, listen carefully.'

It transpired that Holmes was a mine of information regarding Moriarty and his habits ('You think I do not know of his lurkers, the Praetorian Guard, his punishers, demanders, and the control he has over the family people?' he asked at one point). The Berkshire house, as he called it, was a large country dwelling, built in the early years of the previous century, known as Steventon Hall, and situated roughly half-way between the market towns of Faringdon and Wallingford, a few miles outside the hamlet of Steventon. According to Holmes, the house had been purchased by Moriarty some years before, and the great detective had deduced that its sole purpose was that of a bolt-hole in time of need.

'I would arrange some kind of raiding party if I were in your boots,' said Holmes without a hint of humour. 'Though I should imagine the birds have long since flown these shores.'

The bank accounts were another matter, and Holmes explained them at length. For some years he had been aware of a number of accounts, in various names, run by Moriarty in England. Also some fourteen or fifteen more abroad, mainly with the *Deutsche Bank and Crédit Lyonnais*. He had gone as far as noting the details of all these upon a sheet of notepaper bearing the letterhead of 'The Great Northern Hotel' at King's Cross. This paper he handed over to Crow who accepted it gratefully.

'Do not hesitate to seek me out when you require further assistance,' Holmes told him. 'But I pray that you will use your discretion.'

Later, as the Scotland Yard man was taking his leave, Holmes looked at him gravely.

'Bring the blackguard to book, Crow. That is my dearest wish. Would that I could do it myself. Bring him to book.'

Angus McCready Crow, a radical policeman, warmed

heartily to the attitude and brilliance of the great detective. This one meeting with Holmes strengthened his resolve regarding the Professor, and, from this time forth, the two men worked in secret harmony towards Moriarty's downfall.

Though distracted by his impending marriage, Crow wasted no time. That very night he set about arrangements regarding the bank accounts, and was also quickly in touch with the local constabulary in Berkshire.

Within two days he led a force of detectives, together with a large party of constables, in a raid upon Steventon Hall. But, as Sherlock Holmes had predicted, they were too late. There was no evidence that the Professor himself had recently been in the house, but after examination of the buildings, and some intense questioning of the local populace, there was little doubt that at least some of Moriarty's henchmen had, until a short time before, inhabited the place.

Indeed they had been almost flagrant about it; making no secret of their presence, with their comings and goings of rough-looking men from London.

In all, Crow deduced that at least five persons had been permanently quartered at Steventon Hall. Two of these had even gone through a form of marriage, quite openly, giving their names as Albert George Spear and Bridget Mary Coyle, the ceremony being conducted with all the religious and legal requirements in the local parish church. There was also a pair of men described variously as 'big and brawny'; 'smartly dressed but with a rough quality to them'; and 'like a brace of brothers. Very burly in their physique'. The fifth person was Chinese, and so much noticed in this little pocket of countryside, where people remarked upon his polite manners and cheerful countenance.

Crow had little difficulty in identifying the Chinese – a man called Lee Chow already known to him. Albert Spear was no problem either – a big man with a broken nose and a jagged scar running down the right-hand side of his face, narrowly missing the eye but connecting with the corner of his mouth. Both of these men, the detective knew, were close to Moriarty, being part of the quartet the Professor liked to speak of as his 'Praetorian Guard'. As to the other members of this elite bodyguard – the large Pip Paget and whippet-like

6

Ember – there was no sign. Crow reflected that Paget had probably gone to ground after the rout of Moriarty's organization in April, but the whereabouts of Ember worried him.

The burly pair were another matter, as they could well have been any of the dozens of mobsmen employed by the Professor before his last desperate escape from Crow's clutches.

The larder at Steventon Hall was well-stocked, a fact which led Crow to believe this oddly-assorted quintet had left in haste. There was little else of note, except for a fragment of paper upon which the sailing times of the Dover packet to France had been scrawled. Further enquiries made it plain that the Chinese man, at least, had been seen on the packet during its crossing only three days before the police raid upon the Berkshire house.

As for Moriarty's bank accounts in England, all but one had been closed and funds removed, within two weeks of the Professor's disappearance. The one account that remained was in the name of Bridgeman at the City and National Bank. The total amount on deposit was £3 2s 9³/₄d.

'It would seem that the Steventon Hall crew have departed for France,' Holmes said when Crow next consulted him. 'I'd wager they've joined their leader there. They will all be snug with Grisombre by now.'

Crow raised his eyebrows and Holmes chuckled with pleasure.

'There is little that escapes my notice. I know about the meeting between Moriarty and his continental friends. I presume you have all the names?'

'Well,' Crow shifted his feet uneasily.

He had imagined this piece of intelligence was the sole prerogative of Scotland Yard, for the men of whom Holmes spoke included Jean Grisombre, the Paris-based captain of French crime; Wilhelm Schleifstein, and Führer of the Berlin underworld; Luigi Sanzionare, the most dangerous man in Italy, and Esteban Bernado Segorbe, the shadow of Spain.

'It would seem likely that they are with Grisombre,' Crow agreed unhappily. 'I only wish that we knew the purpose of so many major continental criminals meeting in London.'

'An unholy alliance of some kind, I have little doubt.' Holmes appeared grave. 'That meeting is but a portent of evil things to come. I have the feeling that we have already seen the first result with the Sandringham business.'

Crow felt instinctively that Holmes was right. As indeed he was. But, if the Scotland Yard man wished to catch up with Moriarty now, he would have to travel to Paris, and there was no method of obtaining permission for this. His nuptials would soon be upon him, and the Commissioner, sensing that for some time there would be little work from the newly-wed Crow, was pressing hard regarding the many other cases to which he was assigned. There was much for Crow to do, both in his office and out of it, and even when he returned home to the house which he already shared with his former landlady and future bride, the nubile Mrs Sylvia Cowles, at 63 King Street, he found himself whirled around with the wedding preparations.

The Commissioner, Crow rightly reasoned, would no more listen to requests for a special warrant to visit Paris in search of the Professor, than he would grant leave for an audience with the Pope of Rome himself.

For a few days, Crow worried at the problem like the tenacious Scot he was; but at last, one afternoon when London was laced with an unseasonable drizzle accompanied by a chill gusting wind, he came to a conclusion. Making an excuse to his sergeant, young Tanner, Crow took a cab to the offices of Messrs Cook & Son of Ludgate Circus where he spent the best part of an hour making arrangements.

The result of this visit to the tourist agent was not immediately made apparent. When it was revealed, the person most affected turned out to be Mrs Sylvia Cowles, and by that time she had become Mrs Angus McCready Crow.

In spite of the fact that many of their friends knew Angus Crow had lodged with Sylvia Cowles for some considerable time, few were coarse enough to openly suggest that the couple had ever engaged themselves in any premarital larks. True there were many who thought it, and, indeed, were correct in their deductions. But, whether they thought it or not, friends, colleagues and a goodly number of relations gathered together at two o'clock in the afternoon of Friday, 15

8

June, at St Paul's Church, Covent Garden, to see, as one waggish police officer put it, 'Angus and Sylvia turned off.'

For the sake of propriety, Crow had moved out of the King Street house two weeks previously to spend his last bachelor nights at the Terminus Hotel, London Bridge. But it was to the King Street house that the couple returned for the wedding breakfast, leaving again in the early evening to spend their first night of married bliss at the comfortable Western Counties Hotel at Paddington. On the Saturday morning, the new Mrs Crow imagined, they would travel to Cornwall, by train, for an idyllic honeymoon.

Until well into the evening, Crow allowed his bride to go on thinking that the honeymoon would be in the West Country. After they had dined, Crow lingered over a glass of port while the bride bathed and prepared herself for the rigours of the night ahead; and when at last the detective arrived in the bridal chamber he found his Sylvia sitting up in bed, clad in an exquisite nightdress much trimmed and fussed with lace.

In spite of the fact that neither of them were strangers to one another in the bedchamber, Crow found himself blushing a deep scarlet.

'You set a man all in a tremble, my dear Sylvia,' his own voice demonstrating the quaver of desire.

'Well, darling Angus, come and tremble upon me,' she retorted coquettishly.

Crow held up a hand to silence her. 'I have a surprise for you, my hen.'

'It is no surprise, Angus, unless you have taken it to the surgeon since last we met between the sheets.'

Crow found himself both put out and put on by his new partner's flagrant bawdiness.

'Now hold, woman,' he almost snapped. 'This is important.'

'But Angus, this is our wedding night, I . . .'

'And this concerns our honeymoon. It is a happy surprise.'

'Our cavortings on the Cornish seaside?'

'It is not to be the Cornish seaside, Sylvia.'

'Not . . .?'

He smiled, inwardly praying that she would be pleased. 'We do not go to Cornwall, Sylvia. Tomorrow we are off to

Paris.'

The brand new Mrs Crow was not amused. She had taken great pains with the arrangements for her wedding, and, to be honest, had called the tune concerning most of the plans, including the choice of venue for their honeymoon. Cornwall was a county to which she had an immense sentimental attachment, having, as a child, been taken to several watering places along the coast. She had specifically chosen it now as their hideaway – even selecting the rented house near Newquay – because of those happy associations. Now, suddenly, on the brink of what should have been the happiest night of her life, her will and desires had been opposed.

It will suffice to state here that the honeymoon was not an unqualified success. Certainly Crow was attentive to his wife, taking her to the sights of the great city, dining her in the restaurants he could best afford and paying her court in all the time-honoured ways long tried and tested. But there were periods when, as far as Sylvia Crow was concerned, his behaviour left much to be desired. There were, for instance, periods when he would disappear for hours at a stretch, failing, on return, to explain his absence.

These missing times were, as you will already have realized, spent with various people in the Police Judiciaire; in particular with a somewhat dour officer named Chanson who looked more like an undertaker than a policeman, and was nicknamed L'Accordeur by colleagues and criminals alike.

From the nickname alone one gathers that, whatever his personal appearance and demeanour, Chanson was a good policeman with his official ear very close to the ground. Yet, after a month, Crow was not much wiser concerning Moriarty's movements or present whereabouts.

There was some evidence indicating that the French criminal leader Jean Grisombre had assisted in his escape from England. One or two other hints pointed strongly to the possibility of some of the Professor's men having joined him in Paris. But there was also a weight of intelligence, culled mainly from Chanson's informers, that Grisombre had demanded that Moriarty leave Paris as soon as his companions arrived from England, and that, in all, the Professor's short stay in France had not been made wholly comfortable.

That he had left France was in little doubt, and there were only a few added gleanings for Crow to file away in his mind and ponder upon once back in London.

By the end of the honeymoon, Crow had made his peace with Sylvia, and on returning to London became so caught up in routine, both of his marriage and work at Scotland Yard, that the immediate problems of his vow against Moriarty slowly faded into the background.

However, his continued visits to Sherlock Holmes convinced him of something he had long suspected, and indeed worked for – that the profession of criminal detection needed a great deal of specialized knowledge and much fresh organization. The Metropolitan Police appeared slow to take up and grasp new methods (for instance, a system of fingerprinting, already much used on the continent, was not adopted in England until the early 1900s), so Crow began to build up his own procedures and muster his own contacts.

Crow's personal list grew rapidly. He had a surgeon, much experienced in post-mortem procedure, at St Bartholomew's; at Guy's there was another medical man whose speciality was toxicology; the Crows would also dine regularly with a first-rate chemist in Hampstead, while in nearby respectable St John's Wood, Angus Crow would often call upon a well-trained cracksman, happily living out his latter days on ill-gotten gains. In Houndsditch he had the ear of a pair of reformed dippers and (though Mrs Crow was ignorant of this) there were a dozen or more members of the frail sisterhood who would supply information privately to Crow alone.

There were others also: men in the City who knew about precious stones, art treasures, works of silver and gold, while at Wellington Barracks there were three or four officers with whom Crow had a constant acquaintanceship, all of them adept in some field of weapons and their uses.

In short, Angus McCready Crow continued to expand his career, solid in hs determination to be the best detective in the Force. Then, in January 1896, the Professor emerged once more.

It was on Monday, 5 January 1896, that a letter was circulated from the Commissioner asking for comment and intelligence. Crow was one of those to whom the letter was sent.

It had been written in the previous December and was couched in the following terms:

December 1895

From: The Chief of Detectives
            Headquarters
            New York City Police
            Mulberry Street
            New York
            USA

To: The Commissioner of Metropolitan Police
    Esteemed Sir,

Following incidents in this city during September and November, we are of the opinion that a fraud has been perpetrated upon various financial houses and individuals.

In brief, the matter is as follows: In the August of last year, 1894, a British financier, known as Sir James Madis, presented himself to various individuals, commercial companies, banks and financial houses here in New York. His business, he claimed, was concerned with a new system for use on commercial railroads. This system was explained to railroad engineers employed by some of our best known companies, and it appeared that Sir James Madis was in the process of developing a revolutionary method of steam propulsion which would guarantee not only faster locomotive speeds, but also smoother travelling facilities.

He produced documents and plans which appeared to show that this system was already being developed, on his behalf, in your own country at a factory near Liverpool. His aim was to set up a company in New York so that our own railroad corporations could be easily supplied with the same system. This would be developed in a factory built here especially by the company.

In all, financial houses, banks, individuals and railroad companies invested some four million dollars in this newly formed Madis Company which was set up under the chairmanship of Sir James, with a board of directors drawn

12

from our own world of commerce, but containing three Englishmen nominated by Madis.

In September of this year, Sir James announced that he was in need of a rest, and left New York to stay with friends in Virginia. Over the next six weeks the three British members of the board travelled several times between New York and Richmond. Finally, in the third week of October, all three joined Madis in Richmond and were not expected back for a week or so.

During the last week in November, the board, worried as they had not heard from either Madis or his British colleagues, ordered an audit and we were called in when the company accounts showed a deficit of over two-and-a-half million dollars.

A search for Madis and his colleagues has proved fruitless, and I now write to ask for your assistance and any details of the character of the above-named Sir James Madis.

There followed a description of Madis and his missing co-directors, together with one or two other small points.

In the offices of Scotland Yard, and those of the City Police, there were many chuckles. Nobody, of course, had ever heard of Sir James Madis, and even policemen can be amused by fraudulent audacity – particularly when it is carried out with great panache, in another country, thereby making boobies of another police force.

Even Crow indulged in a smile, but there were grim thoughts in his mind as he re-read the letter and those details appertaining to Madis and his accomplices.

The three British directors of the Madis Company were named as William Jacobi, Bertram Jacobi and Albert Pike – all three coming close to answering the descriptions of men who had been at Steventon Hall. Crow was also quick to spot the irony between the name Albert Pike and Albert Spear (the man who had been married to Bridget Coyle at Steventon). That play on names was at least significant of the kind of impertinence which could well be the hallmark of Moriarty.

It did not stop there, for the description of Madis himself required examination. According to the New York Police

13

Department, he was a man of great vigour, in his late thirties or early forties, of medium height, well built, with red hair and poor eyesight necessitating constant use of gold-rimmed spectacles.

None of that meant a great deal, for Crow knew well enough that the Moriarty he had traced in London was capable of appearing in any number of guises. Already Crow had proved, by logical deduction, that the tall, gaunt man identified as the famous Moriarty, author of the treatise on the Binomial Theorem and *Dynamics of an Asteroid*, was but a disguise used by a younger person – in all probability the original Professor's youngest brother.

But one further clue was embedded in the terse description of Sir James Madis. The one fact which linked Madis with the infamous Napoleon of Crime. The New York Police Department had been thorough, and under the heading of 'Habits and Mannerisms' was one line: *A curious and slow movement of the head from side to side: a habit which seems to be uncontrollable after the manner of a nervous tic.*

'I know it is he,' Crow told Sherlock Holmes.

He had asked for a special appointment with the consulting detective on the day following his first reading of the letter, and Holmes, always true to his word, had engineered some commission for Watson so that they were assured privacy. Crow had gone with a certain amount of trepidation, for, on his two most recent visits to the chambers in Baker Street, he had been alarmed at the condition in which he found Holmes. He seemed to have lost weight and appeared restless and irritable. But on this particular afternoon, the master detective appeared to have regained all his old mental and physical vigour.*

*It would be as well to note here – particularly for those who may be unfamiliar with Dr Watson's comments on Holmes' drug addiction – that in the passage concerning cocaine in Glaister's and Rentoul's Medical Jurisprudence and Toxicology, the following observations are made: 'The stimulating effect of the drug [cocaine] is responsible for the acquired habit. When the effects wear off, however, there are irritability and restlessness... The cause of addiction may be attributed to the fact that cocaine quickly banishes fatigue and mental exhaustion, which are replaced by a feeling of mental and physical vigour.' (p. 633. 12th edition.)

'I know it is he,' repeated Crow, thumping his palm with a clenched fist. 'I know it in my bones.'

'Hardly a scientific deduction, my dear Crow, though I am inclined to agree with you,' said Holmes briskly. 'The dates appear to fit, as do the descriptions of his co-directors in crime. You have, yourself, commented on Albert Pike being synonymous with Albert Spear. As for the other two, might I suggest that you examine your records for a pair of brothers: burly built and with the surname of Jacobs. As for the Professor himself, it is just the kind of cunning trick of confidence that diabolical mind would conceive. There is another point . . .'

'The initials?'

'Yes, yes, yes,' Holmes dismissed the query as being obvious. 'More than that . . .'

'The name?'

There was a short pause as Holmes looked at Crow with a somewhat challenging stare.

'Quite so,' he said at last. 'It is the kind of game that would also amuse James Moriarty. Madis is . . .'

'A simple anagram for Midas,' beamed Crow.

Holmes' face froze into a wintry smile.

'Precisely,' he said curtly. 'It would appear that the Professor is intent on amassing great riches – for what purpose I will not speculate as yet. Unless . . . ?'

Crow shook his head. 'I do not think speculation would be wise.'

Returning to his office at Scotland Yard, Crow set to composing a lengthy report for the Commissioner. To this he coupled a request asking that he be authorized to travel to New York, consult with the Detective Force there, and give what assistance he could in apprehending the so-called Sir James Madis and identify him with Professor James Moriarty.

He also set Sergeant Tanner onto sifting the records for two brothers with the surname of Jacobs.

After instructing the sergeant, Crow gave him a dour smile.

'I think it was that Yankee poet, Longfellow, who wrote, "The mills of God grind slowly, yet they grind exceeding small". Well, young Tanner, it seems to me that we of the detective force should do our best to emulate God in this respect. I do not intend blasphemy, ye'll understand.'

Tanner left to perform the task, raising his eyes to heaven as he went. In the event he could only find one pair of brothers named Jacobs in the existing records. Some two years ago they had both been serving a term of imprisonment at the House of Correction, Coldbath Fields. As that prison had now been closed, Tanner reflected that they had probably been moved to the Slaughterhouse (the Surrey House of Correction, Wandsworth). There he left the matter, little realizing that William and Bertram Jacobs had long been spirited away and at this very moment were carrying out the first step in a plot of revenge which might well shake the whole foundations of both the underworld and normal society. For the Jacobs brothers had been elevated to that select group which had the close ear of James Moriarty.

However, Crow's report was persuasive. Two days later he was required to wait upon the Commissioner, and less than a week elapsed before he was gently breaking the news to Sylvia that he would be off to America on police matters in a month or so.

Sylvia Crow did not take kindly to the prospect of remaining alone in London. At first she smouldered with resentment about her husband's job taking him such a distance from her. But the resentment soon changed to a realization that her beloved Angus might actually be putting himself in danger by journeying to the far-off continent. From there, her active imagination took over and, during the week before Crow's departure, she awoke on several occasions, anxious and hysterical, having dreamed of her husband being surrounded by hordes of yelping redskins, each one of whom was personally intent on removing the policeman's scalp. In a muddled sort of way Sylvia Crow was in reality uncertain of the true nature of a scalp, a confusion which led to the nightmares being more terrifying though vaguely erotic.

Angus Crow calmed her worst fears, assuring her that he did not expect to come into contact with any Indians. As far as he could see, his time in America would be spent in the city of New York which, surely, could not be so unlike their own London.

16

But, from the moment Crow set his eyes on the wooden shambles of New York's waterfront, he knew that the two cities were as different as the proverbial chalk and cheese. There were similarities, of course, but the essential heartbeats of each city were of a different speed.

Crow landed in the first week of March, after a tempestuous crossing, and for the first week or more he found himself bewildered by the bustle and strangeness of this thriving city. As he wrote to his wife, 'While English is the, supposedly, common tongue, I find myself more a foreigner here than anywhere in Europe. I do not think you would care for it.'

It was the style of the place, he considered, that was so different. Like London, New York visibly mirrored a yawning gulf between opulent and impoverished: a strange amalgamation of vast wealth, vigorous commercialism and abject poverty, the whole played out in a dozen different languages and coloured by a range of complexions, as though the entire populace of Europe had been sampled, stirred in a melting pot and then tipped out into this extreme corner of the world. Yet even in those areas of the city which seemed to smell, and ever taste, of poverty, Crow noted an underlying current of hope, absent in similar parts of London. It was as though the vigour and pulse of the place held out promise, even in the most miserable quarters.

He soon discovered that the problems of policing the city were very similar to those of his own home ground, and he listened with interest, not to say understanding, to the stories of the many criminal gangs which appeared to abound in the city, and of the violent rivalry between the various racial factions. Much of the crime was but a mirror of that encountered in London, as indeed was the vice which so often spawned it. But, after a week or so, Crow found himself in contact with another breed of man – financiers, railroad barons, bankers and lawyers – among whom he would have to move if his search for the illusive Sir James Madis was to reach a successful conclusion. These people, he considered, were as ruthless in their own way as the more notorious desperadoes of the New York underworld.

With his own knowledge of Moriarty's methods and

colleagues in London, Crow was able to approach the puzzle from a fresh aspect. It was not with Madis in mind that he first questioned those who were caught up in what the newspapers were already calling THE GREAT RAILROAD SWINDLE, for at the outset, he was more concerned with descriptions and impressions of the three co-directors – Pike and the two Jacobis. Gradually, after spending many hours patiently questioning equally impatient and frustrated businessmen, Crow was able to build up a mental and physical picture of the three men, and through this, a picture of Sir James Madis. So, by the end of May, he was completely convinced that Professor James Moriarty was in truth the infernal Madis, and that Spear and two more of the Professor's henchmen had posed as the co-directors.

His search now took him further afield – to Richmond, Virginia, which had been Madis/Moriarty's headquarters for the last crucial weeks of the plot. By the beginning of July, Crow had completed yet another part of the puzzle by tracing the last movements of the Madis faction from Richmond: discovering that they had gone as far as Omaha before disappearing. After that the trail went cold. It was as though the four men had booked into the Blackstone Hotel, Omaha, on one night and then evaporated.

Crow was convinced, however that Moriarty had not left America and that this was now really a matter for the Attorney General's Office. Accordingly, Crow, together with the New York City Police Department's Chief of Detectives, travelled to Washington from whence a general alarm was put out to all law officers, asking that they should report the presence of any newly arrived wealthy man, with at least three partners and a suspected leaning towards the criminal classes.

The weeks passed and there was no news of such a man, or group. By mid-August, Crow was reluctantly preparing to make the return journey to Liverpool, home and the beauty of his wife. Then one evening a cable arrived from the Attorney General's Office which made the detective rush to Washington. There was a new, possible suspect, a wealthy Frenchman called Jacques Meunier who had, in a comparatively short space of time insinuated himself into the thriving underworld of San Francisco. Already a Special Agent had been dispatched.

The description of Meunier, and those close to him – including a Chinese – rang a whole symphony of chords in Crow's brain. Surely this time he was really close, and, with blood throbbing to the chase, and arrangements made to meet one of the Attorney General's agents in San Francisco, Crow boarded the Union Pacific's Hotel Pullman Express bound for the West coast.

There was no reason for him to imagine that he was being watched or followed, so he little knew that, skulking in another part of the train, during its long and beautiful journey across America, was one of the members of Moriarty's Praetorian Guard he had yet to track down – the short, slimy and rodent Ember.

In San Francisco, Jacques Meunier, or James Moriarty – for indeed they were one and the same – read through Ember's cable twice, a low hiss escaping from between clenched teeth as he lifted his face to look hard at the Chinese, Lee Chow, with those bright and glittering eyes feared by so many because of their mesmeristic power.

'Crow,' he whispered softly, but with almost visible loathing. 'The time has come, Lee Chow. Crow is on our trail and I curse myself for not finishing him off that night at Sandringham.'

His head moved to and fro in the strange reptilian motion which was the one betraying characteristic he could never disguise.

'I'll not stand and fight him here, nor do the morning jig for a paltry Scot.' He paused, throwing his head back in a short laugh. 'The time has come to go home and it's the devil's own luck that the Jacobs are already in London on the lurk for us. Get Spear for me, Chow. We must withdraw our investments here – America has provided an unwitting fortune for us. It's time to put it to use and wreak revenge on those who think they can betray us. Get Spear, then go quickly. We must leave within the next four and twenty hours or we'll be nibbed and meat for a lagging. Our friends in Europe will soon see what it is to cross me.'

'Po'fessor,' Lee Chow ventured. 'Last time in London

you . . .'

'That was then,' cut in the Professor sharply. 'But this time, Lee Chow. This time our treacherous European allies will come to heel, and Crow and Holmes will taste retribution. Get Spear.'

So, when Crow finally arrived in San Francisco, there was no trace of the Frenchman, Meunier – only the fact that he had disappeared overnight having made a small fortune among the alleys and lanes of the Barbary Coast and Chinatown.

Angus McCready Crow had once more failed by a hair's breadth. Almost in despair, he started to pack his bags, the only bright star on the horizon being the thought of returning to his wife in King Street, London.

He was not to know that he had already been marked down, together with five other persons, as targets for an ingenious and subtle revenge designed to place James Moriarty at the pinnacle of criminal power.

LIVERPOOL AND LONDON:
Monday, 28 September – Tuesday, 29 September
1896

(Reunion)

Moriarty could smell England, even though there was the best part of a day's steaming ahead before they would enter the Mersey. True, it was only intuition, but it entered his nostrils in a wholly physical manner, sending a thrill of expectation coursing through his body. He leaned against the rail, looking for'ard into the glistening sheet of calm sea, topcoat collar high and buttoned, one gloved hand resting on the circular life-buoy bearing the red painted inscription SS AURANIA. CUNARD.

He was not in disguise, so many would have been surprised to learn that this upright, stocky and square-shouldered figure could, through the art of make-up, so easily become the gaunt, stooping, bald and hollow-eyed man normally identified with his name – the Professor of Mathematics who, the world believed, had fallen from grace to become the most dangerous scientific criminal of his time: the very Napoleon of crime.

They would also find it difficult to believe that he was one and the same as the well-built, red haired Sir James Madis; or the distinguished-looking, powerful Frenchman, Jacques Meunier.

But these people were all one and the same: living, together with many more aliases and physical personalities, within the cunning mind and deft body of this James Moriarty – the youngest of the three Moriarty brothers, known to the

denizens of crime throughout Europe as the Professor.*

The wooden deck moved slightly under his feet as the helmsman on the bridge altered course a point or two. Moriarty reflected that he would be altering some lives a point or two once he stepped back upon British soil.

True it was all to happen sooner than he had intended. Another year would have seen his wealth doubled, but he could not really carp, for in all he had already quadrupled the amount taken from his bank accounts in England and Europe. First with the Madis Company in New York, and then among the rogues of San Francisco.

He sniffed the air again, savouring the dampness in an almost sensual manner. During this, his second exile since the Reichenbach business in '91, he had longed for England, and most particularly London with its familiar smoky, sooty odours; the noise of its cabs, the calls of the newsboys and street traders, the sound of the English language as he knew it – the argot of his people: the family people.

But the time spent abroad had been worth while. He settled his gaze firmly upon the horizon, contemplating the sea. In some ways he could think of himself as a creature of the deep: a shark, perhaps? Huge and silent, moving in for the kill.

A wave of anger ran through his body when he considered how they had treated him – those four European crime lords he had so pleasantly greeted in London barely two-and-a-half years before.

They had come at his bidding – Schleifstein, the tall German; Grisombre, the Frenchman who walked like a

*The detailed description of how and why James Moriarty the younger took up his academic brother's mantle and perfected the incredible disguise, is written in my earlier chronicle. However, on publication of that first volume of these memoirs, there were a number (happily but a small handful) of unlettered and ill-read persons who scorned the idea that there were three Moriarty brothers, each named James. For those who have neither taken the trouble to read, mark nor learn from Dr John H. Watson's masterly chronicles concerning his mentor, Mr Sherlock Holmes, I have briefly assembled facts and conclusions which can be found in the Appendix.

dancing master; the stout Italian, Sanzionare; and the quiet, sinister Spaniard, Esteban Segorbe. They had even brought him gifts and paid court to him and his dream of a great European network of criminal activity. Then, because of one small error on his part – and the work of the wretched Crow – it had suddenly changed. Only weeks after they had pledged themselves to the promotion of chaos for their own ends, they had rejected him.

Certainly Grisombre had helped him to get out of England, but it was not long before the Frenchman made it plain that neither he, nor his associates in Germany, Italy and Spain, were prepared to either harbour him or accept his authority.

So the dream had ended. Much good had it done them, thought James Moriarty, for all the intelligence he had received from that time on told a sorry tale of fights and squabbles and of no central control.

It had been while Moriarty was craftily building a new fortune as Sir James Madis in New York, and Jacques Meunier in San Francisco, that the plan had taken shape. It would have been easy simply to return, re-establish himself in London and then arrange, discreetly, for four neat, and simultaneous, assassinations in Paris, Rome, Berlin and Madrid. Then, just as easy, to dispatch Crow with a bullet, and the meddling Sherlock Holmes with a knife – for Moriarty had long realized that his final success depended on the demise of Holmes. But that would have been mere blundering retribution.

There was a better way. More cunning and stealthy. He needed the quartet of European henchmen if he was to stand astride the western underworld. So, they would have to be shown, with humiliating clarity, that he was still the only true criminal genius. With care and investment, the intricate plot would work. After that there were other plans, not for the elimination of Crow and Holmes, but for their utter discredit in the eyes of the world. He smiled to himself. Those two symbols of established authority would come to their own separate kinds of grief, and the irony was that they would be overthrown through the flaws in their own particular characters.

Running a gloved hand through his rich mane of hair,

Moriarty turned from the rail and began to make an unsteady progress back to his cabin on the boat deck. Spear was waiting for him.

On most evenings after dinner – for they dined at four o'clock on board ship – Moriarty's lieutenant would make his way up from the third-class cabins and slip, unnoticed, into his master's quarters. He now stood waiting by the Professor's bunk, a big heavily built man with a broken nose and features which might have passed for good looks had it not been for the scar which ran, like a lightning fork, down the right side of his face.

'I tarried over long on the promenade deck, Spear. Here, help me off with my coat. Nobody observed you?' Moriarty's voice was all the more commanding because of its soft, almost gentle, tone.

'Nobody ever observes me unless I wish it. You should know that, Professor. Is all well with you?'

'I cannot say that I will be sorry to get the motion of this confounded ship from under my feet.'

Spear gave a short laugh. 'It could be worse. The everlasting staircase can be worse, I assure you.'

'Well, you should know, Spear, you should know. I am happy to say that I have never made a close acquaintance with the treadmill.'

'No, nor likely to. If they ever did lay hands on you, it would be the morning drop and no messing.'

Moriarty smiled thinly. 'No doubt, and the same would go for you.' He cast aside his coat. 'Now, is Bridget well?' It was like a squire asking after one of his tenants.

'The same. Sick as a cat since New York.'

'It'll soon pass. She's a good girl, Spear. I trust you are seeing to her.'

'I jolly her along,' the laugh was almost callous. 'Some days she thinks she's dying and there's a few more like that in the bowels of this tub. The smell down there could be sweeter. Anyhow, I've lined her guts with god's juice tonight and coddled her proper.'

'Aye, my friend, there's more to marriage than four bare legs in a bed.'

'Maybe,' the bruising Spear sighed. 'But when your

buttocks itch, it's good to scratch.'

The Professor smiled indulgently. 'You have set eyes on Lee Chow in the past two days?' he asked, abruptly changing the course of the conversation.

Moriarty was, himself, travelling first class under the assumed name of Carl Nicol, described in forged letters of introduction as a professor of law from some obscure university in the mid-west of America. Spear and his wife journeyed third, giving the impression of having no connection with their leader. Lee Chow had been placed in the most hapless position of all, forced to sign on as a crew member for the duration of the voyage.

Spear chuckled. 'I seen him swabbing down the after-deck yesterday morning looking as miserable as a rat in a tar barrel. A real son of a sea cook: you'd think he was one of Mr Stevenson's pirates. You recall reading that book to us, Professor? Well, I thought for a lark I'd put pen to paper and tip him the Black Spot...'

'I'll have no daft games of that sort,' Moriarty snapped. 'There's plenty that deserve the Black Spot, but it's a poor joke to our own.'

Spear looked sheepishly down at his feet. Baiting Lee Chow was almost a hobby to him. A silence flared between them for a few seconds.

'Well, this will be my last visit to you here,' he said finally. 'Tomorrow we'll be safe on dry land.'

Moriarty nodded, 'Then others can look to their drums. Just pray that Ember got over safely and the Jacobs boys had their messages clearly given. You can get word to Lee Chow before we dock?'

'I'll make it my business.'

'If all is well, Ember is to meet him outside the dockyard once he has been paid off. They will go straight to the Great Smoke. By now arrangements should have been made there.'

'And us?'

'One of the Jacobs will be meeting me. The other will await you and Bridget. We are all to rest the night in some comfort at Liverpool. We need time to talk before going on, and the Jacobs will have the latest intelligence.'

'It'll be good to get back.'

'Things have changed, Spear. Be prepared for that.'

'I am, but it is funny how one misses the cobbles and fogs. There's something about London...'

'I know...' Moriarty appeared to be lost for a moment in private thoughts, his head filled with the street sounds of the capital, the smells, the texture of life in his city. 'Good,' he said quietly. 'Till tomorrow, then, in Liverpool.'

Spear hesitated by the cabin door, bracing himself, one foot forward against the constant roll of the vessel.

'The loot is safe?'

'As the Bank of England.'

'Perhaps they'll be asking you for it.'

'They can ask away,' the Professor's eyes strayed towards the locker which housed the big leather trunk they had brought all the way from San Francisco.

When Spear had gone, Moriarty opened the locker, suppressing the desire to pull the trunk out into the cabin, open it and gloat over the fortune it contained. He had no illusions regarding wealth. It brought power and was a bulwark against most of the pitfalls that besieged a man in this vale of tears. If wisely husbanded, wealth would in turn bring more wealth. His ventures in London – both legal and illegal – would be raped and plundered by now: Crow had seen to that. Well, the contents of this leather trunk would help rebuild his web-like empire, bring the recalcitrant foreign element to heel, and then, like some magic formula, would redouble themselves again and again.

Balanced atop of the leather trunk was a second piece of luggage: an airtight Japanned trunk of the kind used by officers and government men in India. Moriarty rested his hand on this box, smiling to himself, for it contained his store of disguise material: clothes, wigs, false hair, boots, the harness which he used to give him the permanent stoop when appearing as his long-departed eldest brother, and the corset which helped to give that lean look in the same guise. There were also the paints and powders, the lotions and all other artifacts of his armoury of deception.

Closing the locker, the Professor straightened up and looked across to the foot of the bunk and the final piece of luggage in the cabin: the big Saratoga trunk with all its trays

26

and compartments in which he carried his daily clothes and immediate needs. Crossing to it, Moriarty took out his chain and selected the correct key, sliding it into the brass lock and lifting the heavy lid.

Resting on top of the first neatly arranged tray lay the Borchardt automatic pistol – one of the very first of its kind – which had been given to him by the German, Schleifstein, at the meeting of the continental alliance two years before. Below the weapon lay two oblong leather-bound books, and above it a small wooden stationery cabinet containing quantities of notepaper (much of it bearing the letterheads of various hotels or businesses, all filched as the opportunity arose, for who knew when they might have a use or purpose?), blotting, envelopes and a pair of gold-mounted Wirt fountain pens.

He drew out one of the books and a pen, closed the lid of the trunk, and walked with the roll of the ship to the small armchair which was bolted to the cabin floor.

Making himself comfortable, the Professor leafed through the book. The pages were closely filled in a neat copperplate hand, interspersed with occasional maps and diagrams. The book was about three-quarters full, but any stranger glancing at the writing would have made little sense of it. There were, for instance, breaks in the writing only when a capital letter was required. Apart from these capitals, the longhand flowed on and on, sometimes for two lines or more, as though a gifted penman was engaged in an involved copybook exercise. Nor were there any readable words, either in standard English or any foreign tongue. This was, of course, Moriarty's cipher: a cunning poly-alphabetic system based upon the works of M. Blaise de Vigenere* to which the Professor, with his active

*The French cryptologist who published his *Traicté des Chiffres* in 1586 and is famous for what has been described as 'the archetypal system of poly-alphabetic substitution and probably the most famous cipher system of all time'. In spite of the clarity with which he expounded his system, Vigenere's cipher fell into disuse and was forgotten until it was reinvented and once more entered the mainstream of cryptology in the 19th century. Moriarty made use of Vigenere's original autokey system and not the standard alphabet system which is generally known as the Vigenere cipher today.

cunning, had added a few intricate variations of his own.

At this moment Moriarty was not concerned with the bulk of the book. He allowed the leaves to ripple between finger and thumb, letting the last quarter of blank pages fall free until he came to the final ten or twenty leaves. These, like the first part of the book were covered with writing, though incomplete and with a single word heading every third or fourth page.

These single words, written in block capitals, when transcribed into plain text and then deciphered into clear, were names. They read: GRISOMBRE. SCHLEIFSTEIN. SANZIONARE. SEGORBE. CROW. HOLMES.

For the next two hours, Moriarty sat engrossed in these personal notes, adding a line here, making a small drawing or diagram there. For most of the time he worked on the pages dealing with Grisombre, and anyone who was blessed with the skill and ingenuity required to decode the cipher would have noticed that the notes included the constant repetition of several words. Words like *Louvre, La Gioconda, Pierre Labrosse*. There were also some mathematical calculations and a series of notes which appeared to indicate a delicate time scale. They read:

Six weeks for copy.
Substitute in eighth week.
Allow one month to pass before approaching G.
G must complete within six weeks of accepting the charge.

To this the Professor added one final note. Deciphered it read: *G must be faced with the truth within one week of success. Have S and Js to hand.*

Closing the book, Moriarty smiled. The smile turned into an audible chuckle, and then to a laugh in which one could almost hear the discord of wickedness. In his head the plot was hatching against Grisombre.

The elevated railway which ran through the Liverpool Docks was known locally as the dockers' umbrella, because of the shelter it afforded dock labourers on their way to and from their places of employment. It served this secondary function well on the morning of 29 September 1896 when a lengthy period of dry weather was broken by a warm gentle drizzle.

In spite of this inclemency, the sprawling outline of the gigantic port and docks – second only to London – was a welcome sight to the passengers of the *SS Aurania* as they crowded the boat and promenade decks.

From the shore, the 4000-ton vessel seemed strangely alive, sighing steam, her red funnel flecked with white seaspray, as though breathing hard with fatigue and relief at having reached a haven after its arduous journey.

She docked a little after noon. By then the drizzle had eased away and the overcast sky became ragged with streaks of blue, as though someone had taken a claw across the clouds.

Bertram Jacobs arrived at the berth just in time to see the *Aurania* tie up, watching with undisguised interest as the gangways were swung up and the first pieces of baggage began to be hoisted ashore.

Bertram's brother, William, also watched, but from a vantage point some hundred-and-fifty yards distant, for the pair had set out separately that morning, obeying Moriarty's instructions to the last letter.

They were well set up young men who would obviously be able to look after themselves if called upon. Dressed neatly with little trace of flamboyance, they could have easily passed for sons of a middle class, respectable, family; even, in certain circumstances as rich young men about town. They both had clear blue eyes and features in which there was neither trace nor blemish inherited from their somewhat rough and ready antecedents – for their background had been stolidly lower criminal class (their father had died in jail, a forger of unmatched talent, while they boasted two uncles who had been rampsmen of considerable brutality). The Jacobs boys had, in fact, been close family people since childhood, working first as skilled toolers and later becoming mobsmen of some importance. They were both extremely valuable to Moriarty, who had personally seen to their training, making sure that they were taught not only the rudiments of their craft, but also the more unusual subjects ranging from speech to etiquette, for he saw these intelligent lads as a considerable asset.

Neither of the brothers had any doubt as to where their

loyalties lay. If it had not been for Professor James Moriarty they would not have had such a good start in life and, more recently, might have still been passing their day in the Steel, the Model* or the Slaughterhouse – where in truth the blue boys fondly imagined they were both held at this very moment.

Bertram hung back at the edge of the crowd, now growing and excited as the ship began to disgorge her passengers. Friends and relatives greeted one another raucously, joyfully, with tears or simple sober handshakes. One Holy Joe went down on his knees making public thanksgiving to the Almighty for a safe return. Yet, in the midst of all this, Bertram Jacobs noticed, with a sly smile, that there were not a few young women on the fringes of the crowd who were obviously on the naughty, looking for likely fellows – passengers or crew – ready to spend freely. Young Jacobs wished that he was carrying cash for some of these ladybirds, for they looked tasty enough in a gaudy manner.

William Jacobs, eyes peeled for Spear and Bridget, caught sight of Lee Chow assisting a portly, black-coated traveller with his baggage. Their eyes met, but Lee Chow registered no flicker of recognition.

Passengers were coming off thick and fast now, and a large pile of bundles, trunks, bales and packing cases was starting to build on the quayside. Sailors and porters were everywhere, some not too careful with their luggage, taking little notice of protests from more refined ladies and their companions. Carts and cabs, a steam van, numerous drays, hansoms and growlers – the four-wheeled cabs – were pulled up on the dockside, coming and going the whole while. All was noise and shoving, good-natured shouts, orders, jests and activity.

Moriarty came off shortly after half-past one, looking the picture of a slightly bewildered professional man setting foot in an English seaport for the first time. He had two porters with him, carrying the luggage, and to these he kept up a constant flow of instructions, bidding them to take care, all delivered in the clipped nasal drawl of central America.

Bertram Jacobs pushed his way to the foot of the gangway,

*Pentonville Prison.

30

held out his hand and greeted the Professor quietly, leading him over to the growler which had been waiting for the past hour. He was pleased to see Moriarty flash a quick smile at the driver – Harkness, the Professor's coachman from the old days.

The porters stowed the luggage and Moriarty went through an elaborate charade, pretending not to know the right money for their gratuities. In the end, Bertram joined in the play-acting, tipping the men out of his own pocket.

It was not until they were both seated inside the cab, with Harkness urging the horses forward, that the Professor leaned back and spoke in his normal voice.

'So I am back yet again.' He paused, as though mentally examining the statement. Then – 'Where are we quartered?'

'At the Saint George's. Ember said you wanted a little luxury and no slap-bang shops. Was the journey peaceful?'

Moriarty nodded, smiling as if to himself. 'Greasy weather some of the time. Bridget Spear thought she'd be popped in her eternity box before we got here. The Saint George's is good and a little comfort will not come amiss. A day will see me back with my land legs. A day and some naked brandy.'

'And a still bed?'

'Not so still as you'd notice,' the Professor chuckled. 'I always find it hard to sleep after a sea voyage. Is Ember safe?'

'He'll take Lee Chow to London. All is arranged.'

'And your brother?'

'Bringing Spear and his lackin on to the hotel. They've a room on the same landing as yourself. Bill and me are just across the passage, so we're all grouped close for tonight. There's no whisper about you. Not anywhere as far as we can make out. And there were no jacks around when you came off the ship. It's quite calm.'

'Harkness?'

'Lodged near the hotel stables. He'll start for London tonight. We go on by rail tomorrow.'

Moriarty, his body rolling easily with the motion of the cab, peered out of the window like a man eagerly sampling the sights of a new country.

'The Pool changes little,' he said, so quietly that Jacobs could only just hear him. 'I'd swear I have set eyes on a dozen

31

judys that worked the streets when I was here as a lad.'

They were fast leaving the dock area with its teeming grog shops and colonies of whores, the delight of seamen the world over.

'A good investment, the property down here,' said Jacobs. 'It used to be said than an acre around Liverpool Docks could bring in ten times as much as a hundred acres of the best farmland in Wiltshire.'

'I can believe it. There's many a straight furrow ploughed down here.'

'And few other things,' Moriarty mused.

A few minutes later they passed into the broad and imposing Lime Street, coming to rest outside the Saint George's Hotel where porters and pages made much fuss of the arriving guest. Moriarty signed in using his fictitious name and giving his home address as some obscure academic institution in middle America.

For their leader the Jacobs brothers had reserved a large suite of rooms, comprising a drawing-room, a large bedroom and a private bathroom – the best in the hotel, tastefully decorated and nicely appointed with windows looking down onto the busy and constantly engaging street below.

The porters deposited the luggage in the bedroom and departed, pulling their forelocks as Moriarty ran the palm of his hand over the leather trunk as though it was in itself an object of great beauty.

'I have a small surprise for you, Professor,' Bertram grinned once the porters had gone. 'If you'll pardon me for a moment.'

Moriarty nodded and set to uncorking the bottle of fine Henessy's brandy which had been brought up with the baggage. He felt tired and out of sorts, the result, he presumed, of the strain and the sea voyage.

His old spirits returned quickly, when Bertram opened the door and ushered Sally Hodges into the room.

'It is good to see you back.' Sal Hodges held out her hands and moved towards the Professor, taking his hands in hers and kissing him tenderly on both cheeks.

Sally Hodges held a special place in Moriarty's society, for she had been an important member of his staff – his whore

32

mistress in charge of street women and brothels – including the famous Sal Hodges House in the West End; also a provider of young women for his personal use; and at not infrequent intervals, his favourite mistress.

Now, in her middle thirties, she was a striking woman with hair of a flame copper and a superbly proportioned figure which she always set off to the best advantage, as indeed she did at this moment in the blue velvet gown which graced her body in a manner which, while modest, gave more than a hint of the lascivious pleasures which lay beneath.

Moriarty stepped back, as though examining her, a brief smile playing on his lips.

'Well, Sal, so you have been faithful to me.'

'It has not been easy, James.' She was one of the few confidants who could call him by his first name with any impunity. 'The old days are gone. You know that. I now have only one house in London and there's been no controlling the street girls since you've been away.'

'But . . .?'

'But I shall be proud to warm your supper for you on any night you may choose.'

She took a step towards the Professor, who backed away a mite, for he did not like to show much extravagance towards women when in the presence of his lieutenants. At that moment there was a commotion in the passageway outside, heralding the arrival of William Jacobs and the Spears.

There was much handshaking, and some kissing and whispering between the women. This was followed, naturally, by the pouring of liberal doses of brandy.

When all was quiet, and Bridget Spear seated, still looking green about the gills, Bert Spear raised his glass towards the Professor.

'I give you our safe arrival,' he toasted.

As the murmur of assent died away, Moriarty looked around the faces of his small band.

'A safe arrival, he repeated. 'And triumph over those who have crossed us.'

'Amen to that,' muttered Spear.

'Confusion to them,' said Bertram Jacobs, glass poised.

'Let them pass blood and rot,' William Jacobs spat out.

33

The women nodded agreement and they all tossed back their brandy as if their lives depended upon it, Bertram refilling the glasses as fast as they were emptied.

Presently, Sal Hodges, taking her cue from Moriarty, drew Bridget Spear to one side, suggesting that they should leave the men to business.

Moriarty looked from one Jacobs brother to the other, once the women had left.

'Well,' he began. 'What arrangements have you made?'

Bertram Jacobs acted as spokesman. 'The house is ready: that's the best news I can give you. It is what they call a desirable residence, near the Ladbroke estate in Notting Hill, so it's well situated. There's plenty of room for all and a small garden and conservatory at the back. We have put it about that you are an American Professor who does not take kindly to socializing. You are here to study, though you will be spending some time on the continent.'

'Good,' Moriarty's head was oscillating slowly. 'And the furnishings are complete?'

'All you need.'

'And my picture?'

'The Greuze was exactly where Ember told us. It's hung in your new study and you will set eyes on it tomorrow.'

Moriarty nodded. 'And what of our people?'

The Jacobs brothers looked grave, the smiles fading from their faces.

'Sal's already told you her side,' Bertram frowned. 'The girls have all split up, or are working in twos and threes. The same applies in all business. Our old demanders have set up for themselves; the street people go their own way. Without anyone to control it, the best cracksmen put up their own screwings, and the fences are doing business direct. There's no order any more.'

'Then no one person has taken control?' Moriarty's voice dropped to almost a hushed whisper.

'There are several groups, but nobody big, not like in your day, Professor. Not now there is nobody to show the way.'

'You mean nobody's really putting up?'*

*'A put up job' is a phrase still in currency. To put up, here, would be to arrange a robbery or some other criminal act – in other words to

34

It was William Jacob's turn. 'Separate items have a put up. Fences do it from time to time. But it is not . . .'

'And who else?'

'There was talk of the Frenchie putting up for a screwing in Mesopotamia* a few months back.'

'And the German . . .' Bertram began.

'Schleifstein?' Sharp, angry, the voice raised for the first time.

'Yes. It is said that he is looking for something to tickle his fancy.'

'Vultures. Scavengers. What of our lurkers?'

The lurkers were a large army of beggars and snoozers whom Moriarty formerly employed to provide him with intelligence.

'Most are lurking for what they can make, for themselves.'

'How long to get them steady again?'

Bertram shrugged. 'If they was paid regular, I reckon we could get half of them back within a month.'

'Half of them?'

'It's not like it was, Professor. Some have died, others just disappeared. The slops . . .'

'Crow and his crew.'

'Not just Inspector Crow. The coppers have been most active. There's been a lot arrested. Even some of our best cracksmen have taken to living respectable.'

'And the punishers?'

'They've only ever been good for one thing – for ramping.'

'Oh, they are good for putting God's fear into people, and for drinking and whoring besides.' Moriarty sounded humourless.

'Goes with the calling, Professor.' It was the first time Spear had spoken during the exchange between the brothers

mastermind a crime, to provide intelligence and financial backing, also, probably, to arrange the fencing of the articles to be stolen. It was a term, and method, well-known to 19th-century criminals and is mentioned in *Oliver Twist* – 'It can't be a put-up job as we expected.'

* That is, Belgravia, the fashionable residential area of London, south of Knightsbridge. Also known as Asia Minor, the New Jerusalem.

and their leader. 'What about the big fella? What about Terremant?'

'Terremant's working in a Turkish baths,' Bertram answered, his face lighting up. It had been the massive, steel-hard Terremant who had been the lynchpin in the brothers' escape from jail. 'The rest of them, well, they do odd jobs for any that'll pay for their services. I should imagine a bit of mug-hunting on their own also. I do know of a cash carrier down the Dilly who used two of them against three of his girls. Wanted to set up on their own. The girls, I mean. They were dissuaded.'

Moriarty sat silent for the best part of a minute. When he spoke it was as though to himself.

'There must be order among our own people – among family people – if we are to prosper. Just as there must be disarray – chaos – in society.' The threadbare picture painted by the Jacobs brothers was bad.

He rose, stretched and walked over to the window. The sun had gone in again, now covered with cloud, dark and building into high masses. The drizzle was back, and the air hot, tangible, heavy with imminent thunder.

As though suddenly making up his mind, Moriarty wheeled around and looked straight at Spear.

'When we get back to London your first charge will be to round up Terremant and four or five more. We'll see what they can do for a regular wage. Then I'll put Ember on to the lurkers. London was my city and will be again, and I'll not have people like Grisombre and Schleifstein cracking my cribs or dipping into my people's pockets. Nor will I have the likes of Crow calling the tune.' His head flicked towards Bertram Jacobs. 'What of Holmes?'

'He carries on his work.'

Moriarty stood, like some dangerous reptile poised to strike. Then, softly –

'If we settle with individuals, the rest will come to heel. I am back for one purpose, and before long it will be revealed.'

Sally Hodges assisted Bridget Spear from her bath, wrapping a large towel around the girl's shoulders. There was nothing abnormal about Sal's sexual appetite, but she could

36

appreciate a woman's physical attractions for she had much experience of that in her line of business. Now she watched Bridget towel herself dry and start dressing.

A good face, thought Sal Hodges, good hair and teeth, a shade short in the body but strong hips and pretty legs. Bert Spear had got himself a stayer who would keep him happy for a long time to come. The girl had a natural voluptuousness, now most apparent as she drew on the short silk drawers, stockings and petticoats.

Sal Hodges had no illusions about Bridget. She was not an empty-headed chit, meat for a man's bed or as company on a cold evening. This one was as tough as old boots and, if it were required, she would not think twice about killing for her man. Sal had known that soon after first meeting the girl – when she had helped save Spear from Moriarty's rivals.

That seemed a hundred years ago, and Bridget appeared more mature now, more confident as she talked of the fripperies which were a mutual attraction for the two women. The rust-coloured gown, into which she now stepped, had, she said, been bought in New York City.

'You liked America then, Bridget?'

'Well enough. The last few weeks have been hard. But with a man like Bert you come to expect that.'

Sally laughed. 'You did not like the sea journey, I gather.'

'Oh, it wasn't just the journey,' she turned, presenting her back to Sal Hodges. 'Will you lace me into this? Not too tight. No, I would have suffered wherever we were. But don't breathe a word yet. I have still to tell Bert.'

Sally had thought her breasts were more full than she had remembered.

'How long?' she asked as though it was no surprise.

'I reckon I'm about two months gone. It'll be showing soon. Will the Professor be angry?'

'Why should he be? Bearing children is the natural enough function of a wife.'

'There's much happening, though. Oh, it's all right so long as we're with the Professor, but if I know Bert, it's but the start of a mighty brood. I don't want them to end up like my own brothers and sisters, and those of others – living off old bones and skilly, huddling in corners to keep warm, dressed in rags and dying young because they had no shoes on their feet, and their fathers strangers from the Bridewell. No, Sal, I want my children brought up right. Bert's a good man, but how long can it go on?'

'I've known the Professor for many years, Bridget, and he's always been fair to them that are straight and loyal to him.'

'I've no doubt of that. But you did not have to run, Sal. We ran from the Limehouse place; then from the Berkshire house. I thought we'd be settled in France, but no. We ran from New York and I thought, again, we'd be safe in San Francisco. I liked it there, but we had to run again. Now we're going back to London and, with luck, I'll have the child there,' she patted her stomach. 'But how will that end?'

'If I know the Professor it will end with him wreaking havoc on the foreigners. And on Crow and Holmes also.'

LONDON:
Wednesday, 30 September–Thursday
29 October 1896

(A desirable residence)

North Kensington was pitted with small redoubts of poverty. Dirty, stinking, and overcrowded pockets of misery tucked away behind the affluent building developments which had been growing and spreading in ordered rows during the last half-century. In the past four decades many grand squares and crescents had blossomed along the High Road leading from Notting Hill to Shepherds Bush, changing the character of whole areas.

The most impressive of these was the Ladbroke Estate – 'leafy Ladbroke' as they called it – secure and self-satisfied with its focal point of St John's Church, its paired villas with wide frontages, rich façades and large gardens. The natural influence of this building style was logically carried eastwards to make up that network of desirable residences around Holland Park and Notting Hill – places with addresses like Chepstow Villas or Pembridge Square. It was to a cul-de-sac in the midst of this rash of respectability – Albert Square* – that a pair of growlers brought Moriarty and his party on the hot early evening of Wednesday, 30 September 1896.

They had come down from Liverpool by rail, and Moriarty's mind buzzed with associations and memories as the cab took him across London. It had been a hot day and familiar smells pervaded the interior of the vehicle with a sharp pungency heightening the Professor's nostalgic appetite.

*The true name has been altered and it should not be confused with any existing Albert Square.

The streets were just as crowded as he remembered them, even more so now with the addition of the occasional self-acting vehicle. In the main thoroughfares the poor openly nudged shoulders with their betters, the shops still taunted the less fortunate, bulging with goods, and one could really believe that here the pulse of the Empire throbbed audibly. Moriarty also believed he could still detect the beating of his empire's pulse: not yet dead.

Hot and tired, but with a sense of great well-being, Moriarty looked out, for the first time, on his new home: 5 Albert Square, one of ten paired villas set geometrically around a small railed-in plot of grass and trees, dusty with summer, the pavement studded at regular intervals with ash saplings. A desirable neighbourhood. A small world, self-contained and smug in its calm dignity, run on the aching backs of parlourmaids and the cool subservience of cooks, butlers and nannies; as far removed from Moriarty's real world as Windsor Castle was from the sweatshops, thieves' kitchens and gin palaces.

In many ways the houses of Albert Square were pretentious. Not as large as those of the Ladbroke Estate, they still boasted wider frontages than most London homes, though the porticoed entrances and rising five storeys had an overdressed look.

'The town house of the Duke of Seven Dials, eh?'* Moriarty clucked.

Barely a mile away there were courts with one pump to a dozen hovels and not a tree in sight. But the nice folk of Albert Square would not like being reminded of that other world.

A hidden watcher on that evening would have seen the growlers draw up and notice that there were two women in the party: one tall with copper-gold hair neatly piled under a large summer hat, the other shorter, but dressed just as fashionably. Both women left the cabs without hesitation, going quickly up the steps and in under the portico. Outside, two men stood on the pavement looking up, casting experienced eyes over the façade, exchanging a word or two,

---

*A mythical peerage jocularly bestowed on persons dressed or behaving in a manner above their natural status.

smiling and nodding. One dressed in black, hat in hand. A good head of hair swept back. The American professor coming to Number Five ('I hear he is a brilliant man, but something of a recluse. Travelling in Europe and doing some important new studies in London. Is he medical perhaps?'). The other was taller, rugged, sunburned face with a livid scar. A bit of a rough diamond. Travelling companion? Or maybe a clinical assistant?

All this time two other figures, burly lads, were helping the cabbies to unload the luggage and carry it down the area steps where a smaller man waited in shirtsleeves. Among the baggage a large Saratoga trunk, a Japanned box and a big leather trunk which was treated with great care, as though it contained the crown jewels – as, in some ways, it did.

The hall was cool with the scrag end of the day's sunlight reflecting off the stained-glass door panels, red and blue quivering specks against the wall. Lee Chow stood smiling to welcome the party, bowing and grinning his constant smile at the Professor. The women, who knew their place, had disappeared into the bowels of the house.

'Your study all arrange over here,' the Chinaman's hand outstretched towards the door on the right of the staircase. Against the other wall, a small table upon which stood a bowl of flowers, the fresh remnants of summer interspersed with the first brown leaves of autumn. Lee Chow, the Professor thought to himself, never ceased to amaze. The Chinese boy would kill without conscience or scruple; would sleep sound as a babe after putting a human soul through unbearable torture, yet he cooked meals as well as any woman and was particularly good at things like arranging flowers.

So Professor James Moriarty passed through the door into his new study, the room from which he would plan and direct the matters in hand – the downfall of four continental villains and two guardians of the law.

It was an oblong room, high ceilinged with two large windows looking out onto the square. Above the fireplace, which was set in the wall facing the door, an ornate overmantle towered upwards, throwing back reflections from its seven or eight mirrors inlaid among the shelves and twists and flutes of wood. On either side of this, tall bookcases reached to the picture rail: rows of books, grave, leather-spined, silent erudition. Underfoot an Axminster of dark brown and beige. Other furnishings included four easy chairs with arms, covered in buttoned brown leather, while the centre-piece was a massive mahogany writing desk and matching chair, also with arms. On the wall behind the desk hung a solitary painting – a young woman, coy, head on hands: the work of Jean Baptiste Greuze. It was Moriarty's favourite possession.

He stood looking at the painting for a full three minutes, eyes bright, mouth firm – a hint of ecstasy, for he had not seen the work since Ember spirited it away to safe hiding before the flight from the Limehouse headquarters in '94.

Sally Hodges came in with the Professor's stationery box, and together, with Spear in attendance, they spent an hour looking around the house – dining-room, the kitchens down in the basement (Bridget Spear already making lists and sending William Jacobs off on errands, for she would be ruler of this roost as the Professor's housekeeper); the drawing-room on the first floor; the nine bedrooms; the two bathrooms; the dressing-rooms and usual offices. Downstairs again to the conservatory and morning room. Then back to the study.

'It will do very well,' Moriarty told Spear. 'We'll be snug as bugs.' He hesitated as the laughter of children floated in from the square. 'Snug as bugs, as long as there's not too much disturbance from the neighbours and their brats.'

He asked that Bridget should be brought to him and arranged for everyone to meet in his study at eight o'clock. 'We can dine late for a change.'

Half an hour was spent with Bridget, hearing her report on the kitchen facilities and what help she would need in order to run the household. Then an hour with Sal Hodges, unpacking personal clothing and their necessary items. The big leather trunk had by this time been brought up to the master bedroom and remained untouched in the middle of the floor.

'You want me to be here tonight?' asked Sally.

'Unless your business cannot do without you.'

He was preoccupied with finding the right shelves and cupboards for the disguise materials.

'As long as I can see to things tomorrow.'

'Tomorrow we'll all be out and at it early. Some of us will be in the streets tonight,' turning and smiling at her, the head quivering slightly in that strange reptilian motion. 'But not us, Sal, not us.'

At eight o'clock the curtains were drawn, the gas mantles lit, the lamps trimmed, and good sherry poured for the council that was now called to order in the study.

Using few words, Moriarty praised the Jacobs brothers for the choice of the house, then immediately started in on the business.

'You know what I wish concerning the punishers,' he reminded Spear. 'Get on with it as soon as it is convenient. For the time being they are not to come here during the hours of daylight. I will speak with them tomorrow night at ten. In all matters, remember that too much haste and flurry causes people to turn their heads and look closely. Too much commotion, sudden change, always gathers onlookers. So we move gently but not at a snail's pace. We have not all the time in the world. Nobody has.'

'They'll be here.' Spear did not need to elaborate.

Ember was the next to be addressed.

'I want no direct mention of me, you understand?' Moriarty cautioned after giving his orders regarding the re-enlistment of the lurkers. 'Yours is possibly the most important commission, for we cannot work without eyes or ears. There will be work for them directly and I want quality rather than quantity. They will be answerable to you, Ember, and you alone. As always you will be answerable to me.'

'They'll be on the streets within four and twenty hours.' Ember sniffed, an unpleasant little man – a rodent, but one whom Moriarty trusted.

'Lee Chow?'

The silent Chinese raised his head, the large eyes responding, like those of a trained dog to his master's call.

'Before we left, there was a chemist who was helpful. A chemist on Orchard Street.'

A slow grin opened lee Chow's mouth. Gold teeth showed in the small cavern.

'The one who is good frien' to Mr Sherlock Holmes,

Po'fessor?'

'The very one. The dealer in dreams. One of your special people, Lee Chow.' The Chinese had always been Moriarty's commander in that twilight world of medicines, smoke and potions so necessary to London's hundreds of dope fiends. 'You recall him?'

'Charles Bignall,' Lee Chow enunciated carefully so that the name came out as three words.

Moriarty gave a soft chuckle. 'Cocaine Charlie.'

'That what you alway' call him.'

'Like the rest of our good people in that field, he no doubt imagines that he works for others now. Or even for himself. Discourage him from those ideas, my dear Chow. A little money or a trifle of pain. Either will suffice. I must know if he is still assisting the clever Mr Holmes. Whatever the situation we wish to retain his services. Exclusively. You understand?'

'I understan'. I look aroun' other people also?'

'Softly, softly.'

'Catchee monkey. Yes. I arrange all. Mr Bignall first.'

'Do that. I need Bignall for my scheme against Holmes, just as I need punishers and lurkers for other plots.'

A dog barked somewhere in the world beyond Albert Square. Moriarty's head flicked to and fro dangerously.

'Now, all of you. We need intelligence regarding Crow. The Black Inspector Angus McCready Crow.'

'He's not yet returned from America.' Ember's smile was crooked and self-congratulatory.

'I dare say.' The Professor did not smile. 'I require more than that, though. I need to know when he is expected to return; how his marriage is progressing; details of his household; relations with his superiors and those placed under him.' He ticked the items off on his fingers. 'His past also concerns me. His record as a policeman and his career as a man – if you take my point.'

Sal Hodges gave a high short laugh, like a sudden flash of light on the surface of brooding water.

'I have yet,' the Professor continued, 'to meet with the man who has nothing in his past that he thinks worth hiding. Human frailty is the most deadly weapon we have at our disposal. It is worth a hundred men, two hundred barkers. Its

44

price is the same as that of a virtuous woman – far above rubies.'

'I know a Ruby,' muttered William Jacobs. 'She's a whore down the Chapel and *her* price is low enough.'

Moriarty froze him with a look.

'Find me Crow's frailty.'

William Jacobs looked down at his feet and there was a quick exchange of looks between the two women. Silence but for the hiss of the gas mantles.

Sal cleared her throat. 'I think you will find that we already have eyes on Crow,' she smiled at Moriarty, her eyes almost challenging.

'Good. Speak with me later. Now, regarding our erstwhile German friend, Wilhelm Schleifstein.' The Professor spat out the name as though it was bitter to his mouth. 'I understand he is looking for a pretty crib to crack. Well, I have always tried to be helpful to my brothers in law. I wish to find him something that will be a challenge. A daring screw that will bring him good rewards. Avarice is our second most deadly weapon. Trap a man with his own avarice and he is yours for life. And, bear in mind, Ember, when your lurkers are set, I need to know where Schleifstein is hiding.'

Ember gave the nod, and Moriarty turned swiftly to other matters. First to Sal Hodges who was entrusted with bringing in two good girls to help Bridget Spear with the house.

'None of your soiled doves or plucked pullets, mind, Sal. I want girls with no past and little future. Ripe for moulding.'

'You'll have slaves tomorrow,' Sal replied. She was well used to filling situations with the right women.

'Tomorrow indeed,' Moriarty nodded. 'And tomorrow, Bertram, I shall require you close to me, for working the fences. William, you can lend your hands to Spear and Ember, whichever has most need of you. But before tonight is done, there is one more name I wish to drop among you. The name Irene Adler. You may have heard of her: a lady of American origin about whom I made certain enquiries in New York. She is, apparently, in Europe and may well be travelling under her married name of Norton – though the marriage did not last long. She is now some eight and thirty years old. At one time an operatic contralto. But she has other talents. Blackmail a speciality. This is a task of the utmost importance and it is for you all. Bear Irene Adler in mind.'*

The meeting was closed and Moriarty let it be known by his manner, that he required no questioning tonight. His instructions were clear and concise and the group left the study to prepare for dinner which Bridget would serve in half an hour or so.

Alone, Moriarty idly picked up the evening paper which Lee Chow had brought in for him. Gladstone had been speaking again. He chuckled for the old politician had been in Liverpool. Talking about the Armenian massacres and pleading for isolated action by Britain. The old fool, he thought.†

The newspaper did not hold his attention for long, however. He turned his chair and looked, for a few moments, at his beloved painting, contented in the thought that within hours of returning to London he was already once more spinning his web. The sight of the Grueze prompted him to action. There was another painting in his mind's eye: world famous and priceless. Or was it? He jotted some figures onto a piece of paper. That painting was in Paris, as was Jean Grisombre. The latter's sense of avarice could be married to that priceless painting and so bring about the downfall of the Frenchman. Drawing a sheet of notepaper towards him, Moriarty began to compose a letter. On completion he read through the missive twice before sealing it within an envelope which he addressed to – M. Pierre Labrosse. The address was in the Rue Gabrielle, Montmartre, Paris. Another strand had been woven.

*A great deal more will be heard of this lady. It is well to recall, however, that she is famous for her great brush with Sherlock Holmes as recounted by Dr Watson in *A Scandal in Bohemia*, to which further reference will be made. On Dr Watson's word we have it that 'To Sherlock Holmes she is always *the* woman.'

†Which newspaper this was is not recorded. It was certainly either old or slow with the gathering of news. Gladstone's Liverpool speech – incidentally his last – took place on the 24th. During the previous month Armenian revolutionaries had attacked the Ottoman Bank in Constantinople: an action which provoked a three-day massacre.

Sally Hodges was exhausted. James Moriarty had always been a passionate and skilful lover, but tonight, back in London, it was as though some new confidence had been released within him. Sated with coupling, the Professor lay beside her, his breathing deep, rhythmic, like a man steadily rowing towards some unseen goal. Sal Hodges was not a woman to be easily disturbed by men, nor frightened by violent quirks. Yet tonight she found sleep difficult. It was as if she had touched a madness within her lover: an obsession which shrieked one word. Revenge.

Though the house in Albert Square was silent, Sal Hodges was not the only one who could not sleep. Bridget Spear also lay, alone in her unfamiliar room, wishing that her husband would return from the errand upon which he had embarked soon after they had eaten their evening meal.

She was anxious and frustrated, for she had planned to break the news to him that night. Every word had been rehearsed, all courage summoned. Then, suddenly, the opportunity was not there. She had even tried to dissuade him from going out. Tomorrow, she had argued, would be soon enough. She should have known better, for Bert Spear had always put the Professor's business before all else.

'You go on to bed, duck. I'll try not to waken you when I get back.'

He hugged her close before leaving, and she could feel the hard heavy bulk of the pistol in his pocket, pressing against her bosom. This doubled her concern. Her husband out in the city, prowling among the inhabitants of the darker citadels: and her own condition, as yet unrevealed to him. Twin frustrations making the night pass slowly.

In another part of the city, Sylvia Crow lay awake, snug in 63 King Street. Her thoughts, however, were happy and excited. Tomorrow she would be reunited with her husband, for at this very moment Angus McCready Crow was sailing into the Mersey. On his arrival in the morning, he would, in fact, catch a glimpse of the *SS Aurania*, oblivious that he had been hard on the heels of Moriarty. But Sylvia Crow's thoughts were far removed from her husband's official work or the villains which he so devotedly pursued. Tomorrow night, she dreamed, Angus would be back and she had many surprises in store for him.

The name of Faulkner was well-known in London. In some circles Faulkner's Baths had become a byword. In all, Faulkner ran three establishments. The one at the Great Eastern Railway Station was the most simple – straight-forward hot and cold baths and showers. At 26 Villiers Street things were more elaborate: 'Brill's' seawater baths were a speciality, as were the Sulphur vapour, Russian vapour and Sultan baths. The Faulkner's at 50 Newgate Street fell half-way between the simplicity of the Great Eastern and the opulence of Villiers Street. Here you could bathe for a shilling, take a plunge for ninepence, hot or cold shower for a shilling and the full Turkish bath for two and six.

Bert Spear paid for a Turkish bath but only got as far as the changing rooms, for there he saw the attendant who was his sole reason for the visit. The attendant was a huge bruiser of a man, with a damaged ear and hands the size of shovels.

'What cheer,' said Spear with a delighted grin.

'Bert Spear. Blind me, I never expected . . .'

'Well, there you are. A surprise. You still with me for a fair slice?'

Terremant did not have to think. 'Say the word.'

'I want you and five good 'uns. Men we've used before. Handy and big.'

'Done. Is it for . . .?'

Spear held up a hand in caution.

'Can you remember an address?'

'Me memory only goes duff for the Peelers.'

'Tomorrow night. Ten o'clock. Two and threes – not all in a lump. Number Five Albert Square, other side of Notting Hill.'

'A job?'

'You're hired. Permanent.'

Terremant's face broke into a broad beam and one huge fist smacked gently onto Spear's shoulder.

'Like the old days.'

'Exactly like the old days. You'll meet a lot of friends. But I want you silent. If not, you are a mouth and will die a lip.'

'I'm deaf and dumb, you know that.'

Spear looked at him hard. Terremant could have lifted and crushed him with one hand, but the big man knew that Spear was highly respected. In spite of his reputation as no mean punisher, Terremant would never go looking for trouble where one of Moriarty's Praetorian Guard was concerned.

'Tomorrow night then.'

Spear smiled and nodded and left for other haunts that were not nearly so salubrious as Faulkner's Turkish Baths.

Since the 1850s the face of London had undergone a subtle change. Building developments had altered and removed many of the teeming rookeries, those cesspools of evil, but in spite of reform and replanning, there were still streets and maze-like back alleys into which the police only ventured in pairs and the stranger only entered by foolish chance.

These areas held no fear for Ember. On and off for over thirty years he had come and gone along the darker and more notorious of the city's streets with the particular immunity accorded to those who held a special and useful sinecure within the bastions of the criminal world.

No matter that Ember had been absent from old haunts for two years and more. In some way this fact only went to enhance his journey during that night as he slipped, a thin shadow, from street to street, to taproom, lodging house and obscure kitchen. Everywhere he went in the cold and dank thoroughfare there were men and women who hailed him, sometimes as an equal, but more often as a person of rank.

He moved quickly, not tarrying in any one place, having short conversations with various ragged individuals. On occasion money changed hands, slid surreptitiously from palm to palm to the accompaniment of nods, leers and winks.

When dawn came up, heralding another bright day in that Indian summer of 1896, Ember emerged from the smoke, ripeness and clinging gin-sodden air of that nether world with the knowledge that he had relaid the foundations of the network which was once Professor James Moriarty's pride and joy: that invisible chain of intelligence which would provide the most recent and detailed knowledge regarding both champions and enemies of the underworld alike.

The sun began to climb higher and at ten o' clock on that

same morning, a group of ragged urchins hammered on the door of 221B Baker Street and were eventually led into the presence of Sherlock Holmes himself. Fifteen minutes later the street arabs left, happy and clutching silver shillings, their reward for the whispers passed on to Holmes who, for the next hour, sat in his rooms playing the violin and pondering hard on the intelligence which had been brought to him.

As the morning wore on, several connected events took place. At a little after ten, Moriarty left Albert Square in the company of Bertram Jacobs and Albert Spear, bound for a series of meetings which would turn some of the contents of his big leather trunk into coin of the realm.

In all they visited three persons: the old Jew, Solly Abrahams, with whom the Professor had conducted business on many previous occasions, and the spacious back rooms of two dingy pawn shops. One in High Holborn and the other near Aldgate.

At eleven o'clock, Sal Hodges – who had gone out early – came back to Albert Square accompanied by two thin, almost waif-like, girls who could not be more than fourteen or fifteen years of age.

In spite of their wasted and scrawny appearance, both of these girls – a pair of orphans named Martha and Polly Pearson – were bubbling with suppressed excitement as Sal prodded them down the area steps and into the kitchen where Bridget Spear was cross and hot with trying to do a hundred jobs at once.

'Well, you need fattening up and that's to be sure,' said Bridget after the girls had been made to remove their shawls and show themselves. But there was a hint of kindness in the housekeeper's voice, for she could still clearly recall the night on which she had been brought into the Professor's service: thin, filthy and browbeaten. 'You been on the streets, have you?'

'No'm.' They both shook their heads.

'Well, you've certainly never been in service and I shall have to teach you everything I suppose. Will you work?'

They nodded enthusiastically.

'You'll know it if you don't. All right, get yourselves a bowl of broth and some bread. Over there. Sit down at the table and we'll see what we can do.'

Orchard Street lay between the busy thoroughfare of Oxford Street and the grave respectability of Portman Square: a quiet tributary leading from the babbling commercial river to a placid wealthy lake.

Half-way down on the right-hand side, coming from Oxford Street, was a small chemist's shop, all neat with white paintwork and a window containing large thin-necked apothecary jars bright with coloured liquids: red, yellow, blue and green.

There were few people about and nobody in the shop when the Chinaman entered, shutting the foor firmly behind him and, with a quick movement, turning the key and pulling down the grey blind so that the word CLOSED showed towards the street.

The chemist was a small man in his early middle years, untidy in appearance with wispy hair and a pair of half-spectacles balanced precariously on his nose. He had been replacing a jar labelled Pumiline Essence on a shelf which was heavy with bottles and preparations. *Rooke's Elixir, King's Dandelion Pills, Johnson's Soothing Syrup,* and one which always amused Lee Chow, *Hayman's Balsam of Horehound.*

'How do you do, Mr Bignall?' said Lee Chow, the smile permanent on his face, his pronunciation still meticulously dividing the chemist's name into two equal parts.

For a few seconds Bignall stood, mouth open, a puzzled expression on his face, like a man who has just received bad news.

'You all right Mr Bignall?'

'I don't think I want you in the shop.'

If the chemist intended it to be in any way threatening, it was not a convincing speech, for the man's complexion had taken on an ashen shade akin to the texture of a winding sheet.

'I have not see you a long time, Mr Bignall.'

'You should leave. Go now. Before I call the police.'

Lee Chow laughed as though it was a very good joke. 'You not call police. I think you rather listen to me.'

'I run a respectable business.'

'You still have customers I bring to you?'

CR974

'I don't want any trouble.'

'You already got trouble, Mr Bignall. You make a lot of money in last two years since I not been here.'

'It is nothing to do with you.'

The Chinese appeared to think for a minute. Chemists were his stock in trade. They could provide many things that were hard to come by and some people were willing to pay well for a chemist's private services. At last he shrugged and began to turn back towards the door.

'All right. I leave you alone, but you get visits from friends soon. Good day, Mr Bignall.'

'What do you mean?'

'Just you get visit from friends. Pity. Nice shop. All clean now. Apple pie order. Soon apples go rotten and police come after that. You un'erstand?'

Bignall understood. He was a man of vivid imagination.

'Wait,' he called out. 'Wait one moment. I'll give you money.'

'I have money, Mr Bignall. I have money to give you if you do favours like before. Favours to special friends I send.'

'I . . .'

Lee Chow came slowly over to the counter and leaned towards the chemist.

'You still supply white powder to Mr Holmes?'

Wearily Bignall nodded.

'And you still keep truth hidden from his friend, the doctor Watson?'

A sigh, as though the chemist was in many ways relieved to share the intelligence with another person.

'Yes.'

'You still get opium my people send?'

Another nod.

'You have all old customers?'

'Yes.'

'And some new, perhaps?'

'One or two.'

'And you still do the surgical operations? You still get rid of babies?'

'Only when it is necessary.'

'Good. Now we talk of how things must be.'

52

It was half an hour before Lee Chow left Orchard Street, returning to Albert Square with happy news for his master. Another move had been made in the great game of revenge and retribution.

That evening, both Lee Chow and Ember reported in full to the Professor. Many of the lurkers who had been in their employ in the past were now out again on Moriarty's business: ears pricked, eyes searching, scavenging for words, hints, signs, eager in the knowledge that there was a small yet steady wage for them in return for whatever scraps or titbits they could grasp.

In particular there were men and women seeking news in St George's Street, once the notorious Ratcliffe Highway, centring much of their activity around the *Preussische Adler*, a favourite haunt of German seamen and others who did not count the police among their close friends. Their duty was to seek out news of Wilhelm Schleifstein.

But wherever they went along that evil street – to the *Rose and Crown* or the *Bell*, or, in fact, any of the sluiceries, dance and music halls, their enquiries were circumspect. The names locked in their heads included Irene Adler, the policeman – Crow – Holmes himself, as well as the other foreign villains upon whom the Professor was concentrating the main portion of his endeavours.

All day, Spear moved between Albert Square and a dozen secret places within the metropolis. Later, after dinner – served by the nervous twins, Martha and Polly, with much prompting from Bridget Spear – he too had private words with Moriarty. Already Spear had assumed tacit command of the Praetorian Guard and he brought news that in the past two hours he had spoken with a dozen or so professional men – cracksmen, toolers, magsmen, macers and demanders who were now working on their own account. His approach and progress had been careful, circumspect and not unsuccessful.

When Spear left him, Moriarty stood at the drawing-room window, a glass of brandy in one hand, looking out over the square. Out there, thought the Professor, his kingdom was once more on the move; his family people beginning to come together as his own, just as they had done before that undignified rout in 1894. Out there were also the keys that would unlock the road to disaster for the six enemies who preyed so constantly on his mind.

A slight breeze stirred the trees in the square, as though they were taking fright at the menace emanating from the drawing-room window.

Turning his attention back into the room, Moriarty looked lovingly at the piano which occupied a position of some importance – a drawing-room grand by Collard & Collard, purchased by the Jacobs brothers from a dealer who had access to these instruments, brand new, but at greatly reduced prices. The piano was a luxury which the Professor had done without for too long. As a child, music had been almost a background to his daily home life. Had not his mother given lessons? Indeed, he could remember the feeling of satisfaction it had given him at a very early age to be able to play with no small talent. He often imagined that it was the one thing which his two brothers envied ('Mrs Moriarty, young Jim should really take it up as a profession and give concerts. He is so skilful.' That was a passing comment still remembered).

It was many years, though, since he had sat at a keyboard and, since their arrival in the house he had to some extent been putting off the moment. He approached the instrument gingerly, as if it were some animal which needed taming. Once seated, he closed his eyes stretching his mind back to the time when playing was as easy to him as breathing. If Holmes could scratch his fiddle, then he could tease melody from the black and white keys. Slowly his long fingers began to move soundlessly over the keyboard, and then, as if suddenly ready and confident, he found the notes, and began a Chopin étude: the 12th – the 'Revolutionary' as it had become known.

It was no ordinary performance, but one of feeling which gave the piece a unique interpretation, as though the music was an outlet for all the pent desires and frustrations, glories and madnesses within. With the music came a kind of transitory peace, and Moriarty continued to rediscover his talent until the clamour of the bell downstairs heralded the arrival of Terremant and the first punishers.

Upstairs in their comfortable bedroom, Bridget Spear faced

her husband.

'Mr Knap's been here,' she blurted out, one hand to her stomach. It was easier for her to use this old phrase, which denoted pregnancy, than any of the more formal, coy or simpering speeches with which young women were supposed to break the news of 'an approaching little stranger' to their husbands.

Albert Spear's mouth came open and then closed again. 'Bridget. Well, I never dreamed . . .'

'Then you should have done, Bert. What do you think we was at, making pottery jugs?'

'I'm to be a father, then?'

Trust *him*, thought the girl. His first thought was that *he* was to be a father.

'And I a mother,' she said coolly.

Bert Spear's face broadened into a grin.

'I'll bet he comes into the world clutching the midwife's wedding ring an' all. It's good news, Bridget. The start of our own family. Good news, indeed. Wait 'til the Professor hears. He'll be proud as old Cole's dog.'

'He will?'

'Of course, girl. Why it's a family baby. He'll truly be its godfather.'

'Bert?' She had gone up to him, placing a hand gently on his arm. 'I only want good for the child. He won't live the life we led when we were nippers, will he?'

'With the Professor standing for him? No, girl, he'll want for nothing.'

From below they heard the liquid sound of the piano, then, far away, the ringing of the doorbell.

At the very moment that Professor James Moriarty sat down to play Chopin Angus McCready Crow was being united with his bride at his house in King Street.

The detective had particularly asked her not to meet him at the railway station. Partly because he did not altogether approve of married women being seen abroad unaccompanied, but mainly because he was forever pessimistic regarding timetables, knowing full well that betwixt cup and lip there lurked all kinds of dangers, slips, nudges and jogs.

In the event, he was at his own door almost to the minute of the calculated time, his heart considerably lighter for having survived all his journeying. As he jabbed at the brass knocker, all the frustrations concerning the Moriarty fiasco disappeared from his mind, replaced by other thoughts which swamped his whole body: for he could not deny that he longed to embrace Sylvia's ample person – and more. His desires, however, were not simply of a lustful nature. One of the things he had missed most on his travels was Sylvia Crow's good home cooking. To his mind, nobody made a steak and kidney pudding like her; nor could they produce cakes or pies more satisfying, while her jugged hare was, Crow often maintained, a taste of paradise on earth.

As he waited for his wife to open the door, Crow was assaulted by a whole cannonade of desires. Well-remembered aromas and succulent tastes combined with the deep hidden sensualities of the bedchamber, and all those titillations which Sylvia could use with such aplomb. The swell of her breast and thigh mingled attractively with images of roast potatoes and saddle of lamb.

The door opened and Angus Crow, overwhelmed by the fancy of his senses, thrust forward to embrace Mrs Crow. Home was the sailor, home from the sea, and the hunter home from the hill.

'Sylvia, ma beloved,' he crooned, eyes half-shut and accent broadening as it always did in times of emotional stress.

His hands barely connected with the woman before there was a yelp and commotion.

Crow opened his eyes to see, not his fair Sylvia, but a young woman of somewhat angular aspect, dressed in black gown, white frilled apron and cap. His first reaction was too look anxiously at the door in order to ensure that he had not mistaken the number. But there it was, plain, polished above the knocker. Sixty-three.

The young woman had recovered her composure more quickly than Crow.

'Good evening, sir,' she said, all breathy. 'Who shall I say is calling?'

'Inspector Crow.'

56

A grunt as light began to dawn. Sylvia had always had ideas. Before their wedding she had run the small house on her own, happy to cook and make beds, clean, dust and shop with never an idle moment. It was obvious to Crow that in his absence, his wife had shattered the peace of their hearth by introducing servants.

'Angus.' She had waited until the girl had opened the door to receive him, then, unable to abide by the more correct observances of society, launched herself into the tiny hall. 'Oh, Angus, you are home.' She embraced him quickly, a wifely kiss on each cheek, before holding him at arm's length and addressing the girl. 'Quick, Lottie, the master's luggage. Get it in, girl, before all the neighbours come out to have a look.'

'What is this, Sylvia?' muttered Crow.

'*Pas devant les domestiques*,' hissed Sylvia, her mouth set in a welcoming smile. Then, loudly, 'Oh, it is so good to see you. Lottie, take the bags upstairs. Beloved, come into the parlour and let me look at you.'

Crow, bewildered by events, allowed himself to be bustled through into their small parlour which, he was relieved to observe, seemed to be little changed.

'Sylvia, who is that woman?' he bludgeoned almost before the door was closed.

'A surprise, Angus. I thought you'd be so pleased. It's Lottie, our cook general.'

'Cook general, and what is that when it's at home?'

'Angus, she is our servant. After all, we have a position as a married couple, and you heading for an important post at Scotland Yard...'

'What important post?'

'Well, you are bound to be promoted and...'

'There is no reason for you to think for one moment that I shall be promoted. If you want the truth, I have failed miserably on my present assignment, and I'll be lucky if I am not pounding the beat by this time next week. What in the name of heaven made you bring anyone else into our little home. Our little...' he hesitated, 'Our little love nest?'

Sylvia started to cry. It usually worked. 'I thought you would be pleased. It raises the tone.' Sniff. 'It takes away some of the drudgery.' More sniffing and a knock at the door, at which sound the tears disappeared. 'Enter.' No quaver in her voice.

'Dinner is served,' proclaimed the geometrical Lottie.

Dinner lowered Angus Crow's spirits even further. Before going through to the dining-room, he had tried to soothe his wife by telling her that of course he did not want her to become a drudge, and that he was a little tired, what with the journey and everything. But the dinner was an unhappy experience as it was obvious from the start that Sylvia had taken no part in either its preparation or cooking. The soup was watery, the beef overdone and the greens soggy, while the pastry of the apple pie defied description.

After dinner, Crow brooded, drank a little, listened patiently to his wife's monologue regarding the problems and trials she had endured during his absence. At last, not able to bear it longer, Crow announced that it was time for bed, leaving no doubt as to his meaning and intention. At least, he concluded, she cannot have a servant to take her place in the connubial couch. Nor for that matter would she desire it. Sylvia had always been enthusiastic and knowing in that department.

Mrs Crow's eyes once more filled with tears. 'Angus, it is not my fault,' she wailed. 'I have no power over the phases of the moon. I am so sorry, my dear, but there's a padlock on the pleasure garden.'

Angus Crow could have wept. His failure to track down the Professor had been bad enough and he had successfully cloaked the reality of this with thoughts of the pleasures of his home-coming. As it was, he retired to his favourite chair in the parlour and began sorting the pile of letters which had arrived during the sojourn in America.

They were mainly tradesmen's accounts and short notes from relatives, but at the top of the pile lay one note delivered by messenger that very morning. He recognized the hand instantly and tore it open. His assumption was correct, for the heading showed that it was from 221B Baker Street. It read:

Dear Crow,
    I do not know if you have yet returned from our

erstwhile colonies. If not, this will await you. You will obviously have more recent news than I. However, certain matters not unconnected with our friends have today been revealed to me. I would, therefore, be grateful if you would get in touch with me at your earliest convenience.

Your sincere colleague,
Sherlock Holmes

'You know of Moriarty's so-called Praetorian Guard?' Holmes stood with his back to the fireplace, looking down on Crow who sat comfortably in the wicker chair.

'I do indeed.'

He had made arrangements quickly on the following day. Holmes was to be alone during the late afternoon and, at a little before five, Crow presented himself at the front door.

Mrs Hudson offered her master's apologies, saying that Mr Holmes had stepped out for a short while and had instructed her to see that the Inspector was comfortably provided for until his return.

When Holmes reappeared, some fifteen minutes later, Crow was settled with a tray of tea, muffins and a large quantity of Mrs Hudson's home-made strawberry jam.

'Pray don't stir yourself, Crow,' Holmes began the moment he entered the room. 'Good of you to wait. I believe you are a little thinner in the face. I trust your digestion has not been put out by American hospitality.'

Crow observed that he was slightly flushed, and carried a number of small parcels which he deposited on the table. One, the policeman could see, was sealed with wax and bore a chemist's label. *Charles Bignall, APS, Orchard Street.*

Holmes appeared tired and a shade nervous, explaining that he had hoped to be back before five. However, they were now together, and the consulting detective wanted to hear what progress Crow had made in America.

Angus Crow went through each stage of his investigations, ending with his abortive attempt to get the professor's collar in San Francisco, laying great stress on the frustration of being so near, and yet so far, to a capture. It was not until he had completed this monologue that Holmes asked about his knowledge concerning the Praetorian Guard.

'There were,' Holmes continued, 'originally four men who were members of this particularly evil band. A heathen Chinese called Lee Chow; a wretched, slimy little fellow known as Ember; a rampsman by the name of Albert Spear, and a rogue called Paget. Since the Spring of '94 there have only been three.'

'I know about Paget,' said Crow dryly. 'There seem now to be two others besides. Two I cannot yet put names to. Also there is little doubt that Johnny Chinaman, Ember and Spear were all with our man, at one time or another, in America.'

'Well,' Holmes regarded the detective with an expression of gravity. 'I have it on good authority that Ember, at least, is back in London. On the night before last he was seen in several places where you and I might well have to fight for our lives. I have somewhat more irregular methods of keeping an eye on such places. Ha-ha.' His laugh had little genuine humour to it.

'So.'

'It has been my experience that wherever members of the so-called Praetorian Guard go, the Professor soon follows.'

Crow could do nothing but agree with him, his frustration seeming even more pronounced, for Holmes had made no comment regarding the American adventure and it seemed plain that it had been of little use. However, Angus Crow left Baker Street light of heart. Perhaps their quarry was nearer now than he had dreamed. Tomorrow he would put a bold front on things when he reported to Scotland Yard. As for now, his heart descended rapidly, he must return to King Street and the social pretensions of his wife. He would have to be most canny if that little problem was to be solved without too much friction.

The days which followed were ones of intense activity at Albert Square. The task of rebuilding the Professor's criminal family was a slow and careful business, but not a day passed without some progress being made or some old follower discovered and brought back into the fold. It was all accomplished with much stealth and, as often as not, without the name of Professor James Moriarty being mentioned aloud.

During this crucial time, Moriarty left the daily arrangements in the competent hands of his lieutenants – now much assisted by the muscular power of Terremant and his punishers – while he spent the time issuing orders and seeing to his finances: visiting fences and creating new bank accounts in hitherto unheard-of names. He played the piano a little each evening, read the newspapers, cursed the politicians as imbeciles, and occasionally indulged in his only other hobby, the art of conjuring.

Each night he would sit for a good hour in front of a mirror, a copy of Professor Hoffman's famous work, *Modern Magic*, open on his lap and a pack of cards in his hands. He considered that his progress was fair, having mastered most of the sleights described. He could make the *pass* in five different manners, change cards, force them and palm cards with reasonable dexterity. When Sally Hodges spent the night at Albert Square she now became used to acting as a guinea-pig for new tricks with the cards before getting down to old tricks between the sheets.*

As the financial side of Moriarty's plans progressed, he dealt with several urgent and pressing matters and Sal Hodges figured prominently in these. Two more houses were purchased in the West End and, by the second week in October, Sally was herself supervising lavish decorations and a staff of elegant, enthusiastic young women. By the end of the year those investments would, the Professor was certain, be showing a profit.

Moriarty also spent long hours poring over the notes he had to hand on the four continentals, and on Crow and Holmes. The lurkers had tracked down Irene Adler quite quickly, discovering through their foreign counterparts that she was living alone, and frugally, in a small *pension* on the shores of Lake Annecy. The Professor appeared well pleased that she was short of money and within a day of the discovery ordered that a man be found who could be trusted and would pass

*Those who have read the earlier chronicle will recall that Moriarty was much taken with a stage magician he saw performing at the Alhambra Theatre and it seems that from this time onwards, the Professor took a keen interest in the art of prestidigitation.

easily as either English or French. Though he was to be used first on business uncompleted with the Adler woman.

Within twenty-four hours, Spear brought in just such a person: a former schoolteacher who had fallen on bad times and even served a stretch in the Model for theft. His name was Harry Allen, and the other members of the Albert Square household were surprised to find that the Professor insisted on his being moved into the house without delay. He was a young and personable fellow who soon made himself useful around the place and seemed to take a great liking to Polly Pearson.

On one or two occasions, Spear attempted to discover Harry Allen's purpose within his leader's overall plan – for the man had little to do, except be ready to talk for long periods with the Professor behind closed doors. However, when his lieutenant broached the subject, Moriarty would only smile knowingly and say that in the fullness of time all would be revealed.

It soon became plain that, among the European leaders, Grisombre, Sanzionare and Segorbe were snug in their own cities. There were reports that Sanzionare had visited Paris for a week or so during the summer and had been seen with Grisombre, but Moriarty's grand design for a European criminal society appeared to have come to naught.

Schleifstein, the German, however, was not in his native Berlin. The lurkers eventually located him, living with a handful of dubious villains of mixed nationality, in a quiet villa in Edmonton, not far from the *Angel*. A watch was set on this establishment and it was soon apparent that the German was casting about for a really large and impressive crib ripe for cracking.

Moriarty was already piecing together intelligence regarding one particularly lucrative possibility in the City – a bait for the avaricious villain to swallow whole.

So the last leaves on the trees of Albert Square crinkled and fell like pieces of burned paper; the winds became bone-chilling, and the days shorter. Greatcoats and mufflers, discarded during the summer, were taken out again, and in the drab back streets frequented by the underworld's rank and file, people appeared to be bracing themselves for the onslaught of winter.

Each day the fogs and mists crept earlier up the river to mingle with the soot and grime from factories and private chimneys, and an autumnal dampness pervaded the city. In the last week of October there were three days during which man was all but cut off from his fellows as a thick London 'particular' shrouded main thoroughfares, alleys and byways alike. Naphtha flares sprouted flame at corners, people carried lanterns and torches, familiar landmarks vanished in the murk only to loom up unexpectedly, like ships off course. The incidence of robberies rose, pickpockets and mug-hunters did a roaring trade, and death stalked among the sopping slums nearest to the river, where the elderly and those with chronic chest complaints went down like flies. On the fourth day a mild breeze shifted the pea-souper and the sun, weak and as though strained through a fine muslin, lit up the great metropolis once more. But those who were familiar with the city weather predicted a long and hard winter.

On the evening of Thursday, 29 October Moriarty had a visitor. He came off the boat rain at Victoria Station, a tall skeleton of a man, wrapped in a long black overcoat which had seen better days. On his head a wide-brimmed, clerical-looking hat covered an untidy clump of wispy fine grey hair, and his beard gave one the impression that it had been gnawed by rats. He carried a large portmanteau and spoke English with a rough French accent.

Coming out of the station he took an omnibus to Notting Hill and walked the rest of the way to Albert Square. His name was Pierre Labrosse. He had travelled from Paris in answer to the Professor's letter, and at his coming Moriarty's revenge was afoot.

(The art of robbery)

'Of course I am able to do it. Who else? There is nobody in the whole of Europe who could make a copy as well as I. Why would you send for me if this were not so?'

Pierre Labrosse had a wild macabre look about him, like a scarecrow marionette worked by an unseen drunken puppeteer. He lolled in a chair opposite Moriarty, a glass of absinth – which seemed to be his staple diet – in one hand, the other skinny arm gesticulating in a grandiose manner.

They had dined in private and now Moriarty had cause to question whether or not he had made a wise choice in sending for Labrosse. There were many other artists in Europe who could have done the copy equally as well, if not better. Reginald Lefty, constantly insolvent portrait painter and aspiring academician, to name but one within easy reach.

The Professor had chosen Labrosse only after much thought, having met him but once, during his period in the European wilderness following the Reichenbach business. On that occasion he had acknowledged the man's instability, at the same time recognizing his great gifts. Labrosse was, in plain truth, a self-styled genius who, had he applied himself to original creation, could possibly have made a great name for himself. As it was, the only name he had made was with the Sûreté.

The letter which the Professor had written to him on returning to London had been carefully worded, giving little hint of what he required, yet containing enough to bring the painter to England. In particular there had been guarded references to the man's great skill and reputation, and a hint

64

of riches to be earned. Yet now that he had Labrosse safe in Albert Square, Moriarty could not help having second thoughts regarding his choice. In the time which had elapsed since their last meeting, Labrosse's instability was even more pronounced, the delusions of grandeur even more marked, as though the poison of the absinth was daily biting more deeply into his brain.

'You see, my friend,' Labrosse continued, 'my talent is unique.'

'I would not have sent for you if that were not so,' remarked Moriarty quietly. Lying in his teeth.

'It is truly a gift from God.' Labrosse fingered the flamboyant silk cravat at his throat. You did not have to be a detective to tell that the man was an artist. 'A gift from God,' he repeated. 'If God had been a painter, then he would have given the world his truth through me. I would surely have been Christ the artist.'

'I'm certain you are right.'

'My gift is that when I copy a painting I do it with the greatest attention to detail. It is as though the original artist had painted two at the same moment. This is something I find difficult to explain, for to me it is as though I become the original artist. If I copy a Titian, then I am Titian; if I do a Vermeer, I think in Dutch. Only a few weeks ago I did a remarkable modern canvas. The Impressionist Van Gogh. My ear hurt the whole time. This power is frightening.'

'I can see that you are in awe of yourself. Yet you are not above performing this great work for money.'

'Man cannot live by bread alone.'

Moriarty frowned, trying hard to follow the Frenchman's reasoning.

'How much did you say you would pay for a copy of *La Joconde*?'

'We did not speak of money, but now that you ask, I will provide you with food, a man to assist you during the work, and a final sum of five hundred pounds.'

Labrosse made a noise like a cat whose tail had been trodden upon. 'I need no assistant. Five hundred pounds? I would not copy a Turner for five hundred pounds. We are talking of a Leonardo.'

'You will have the assistant. He will cook for you and report to me on the progress. Five hundred pounds. And for this I demand quality. You understand that this is for an elaborate hoax. It must be convincing.'

'My work is always convincing. If I do *La Joconde*, then it will be *La Joconde*. The experts will not be able to tell the difference.'

'In this case, they will,' said Moriarty firmly. There will be a hidden flaw.'

'Never. And never for a paltry five hundred pounds.'

'Then I must go elsewhere.'

It was doubtful whether Labrosse took heed of the icy edge which had entered into the Professor's tone.

'At least one thousand pounds.'

Moriarty rose and walked to the bell pull. 'I shall ring for the maid who will bring one of my more muscular male servants. They will then eject you, bag and baggage. It is a cold night, Monsieur Labrosse.'

'Maybe I would do it for eight hundred pounds. Maybe.'

'Then I'll have no more of it.' He tugged at the bell pull.

'You drive a hard bargain. Five hundred.'

'Five hundred and the few little extras. Including the scratching of a word on the wood – I have a piece of old poplar which I have acquired for the purpose. One word will be scratched before you begin, in the right hand bottom corner.'

'Only one thing I will not agree. I must be alone. No assistant.'

'No assistant, no money. No commission.'

The Frenchman shrugged. 'It will take a long time. To produce the exact cracks there has to be much baking during the painting.'

'It will take no more than six weeks.'

This time Labrosse caught the menace, even through the mist of his delusions. Polly Pearson was at the door and Moriarty ordered her to send up William Jacobs and then seek out Harry Allen and have him come to the drawing-room. Polly, already filling out with food and regular, though hard, hours of work, blushed crimson at Allen's name.

Jacobs took Labrosse off to his guest room, with firm instructions to see that the artist did not wander or walk in his sleep. Presently, Harry Allen came to the drawing-room and there behind a locked door, the Professor gave him instructions regarding his forthcoming sojourn with the French artist in Paris.

'When it is all done, Professor, will there be other work for me?' asked the former schoolteacher as he took his leave.

'If the job is done well, then you will be regarded as one of the household, one of the family. Bert Spear always has work for likely lads such as you.'

Ten minutes later, Moriarty went downstairs to the study and took the piece of aged poplar from a locked drawer in his desk, turning it in his hands and smiling. Within a few weeks this simple piece of wood was to be transformed into the ageless and priceless *Mona Lisa*. The bait would then be prepared for the Frenchman, Grisombre. In the meantime, Spear and Ember were about the business which would trip the arrogant Wilhelm Schleifstein.

Spear was with Ember and two of Terremant's men in the City. They crouched, in silence, in a darkened ground-floor room looking out onto the junction of roads which made up Cornhill and Bishopsgate Street, their attention focused upon the corner building, a jeweller's establishment, which appeared to be in darkness except for two tiny slits of light at eye level in the window facing Cornhill, and one similar slit on the Bishopsgate window.

'Here he comes again,' whispered Ember. 'Up Bishopsgate.'

'A good timekeeper,' smiled Spear in the darkness. 'Regular as a Swiss horizontal. He never alters it?'

No. Every fifteen minutes. I've had it watched over three weeks.' Ember hissed. 'His sergeant joins him at ten, then again at one. Sometimes at five in the morning as well, though not always. Falls in step with him and walks the beat in the same way.'

They fell silent as the uniformed policeman clumped steadily towards the junction from Bishopsgate, pausing to try the handles of each door, like a drill sergeant going through some parade ground review, his bullseye lantern throwing out a dull glow from where it was clipped on his belt.

He arrived at the corner, paused and peered through the slit in the window on the Bishopsgate side, tested the door in the shuttering and paced around the corner into Cornhill where he began to go through the same procedure. There was a rattle and sound of hooves from the direction of Leadenhall Street and a lone hansom came clattering past, heading towards Cheapside.

The policeman hardly paused, squinting in through both slits on the Cornhill side, trying the other door-handle and then continuing on his way, his footsteps echoing in the empty street, dying off until silence again fell over the area.

'I'll go over and have a peep,' said Spear, more confident; louder now the uniformed figure had gone.

The room from which they had been watching smelled musty as though inhabited by rats, and the bare floorboards creaked as Spear stepped towards the door, avoiding the workmen's rubble which littered the place. It had in fact become vacant only a month before, the lease snapped up quickly by Moriarty under an assumed name. Like the shop across the street, it too had been a jeweller's – as were many of the premises along Cornhill – and it was now undergoing 'Complete Refurbishing', as witnessed by the board fastened to the outer door.

Spear paused in the empty street, ears pricked to catch the slightest sound. It was strange, he thought crossing the road, how this could be such a busy and crowded place during the day, yet so deserted at night. Few shopkeepers lived on their premises, preferring to reside in cosy terraced houses an hour or so away by train or omnibus. Mr Freeland, whose name appeared, coupled to that of his son, in white square lettering above the windows in both Cornhill and Bishopsgate, had what they called a bijou residence in St John's Wood. Spear smiled to himself. These people never seemed to learn. One robbery would make them all wary for a while. They would have new locks fitted, perhaps even employ special nightwatchmen. But in a year or two the fear would pass and they would return to their old ways. The safe-makers even designed new safes, but the old ones were still used all over the City.

Spear reached the Cornhill front of John Freeland & Son.

No sound, not a soul in sight, the road sparkling in the lamplight as though dusted with frost. The whole angled frontage of the shop was encased in iron shutters, blanketing the windows, apart from the slits which were cut some five and a half feet from the pavement: nine inches long and two inches deep. Spear pressed his eyes to the first slit. Inside, the shop was bright with light, for the gas mantles were lit and turned up full: the counter and the empty glass display cases in the outer shop all clearly visible. The real object of these peep holes, however, was not this first room where customers daily purchased rings and watches, necklaces and brooches, or ordered stones to be set in baubles of intricate design, but the rear shop in which the real craftsmanship was carried out.

A wall separated the two rooms, access between them being maintained through a wide arch, and the squint holes being particularly designed so that a watcher could see directly through this opening, and so clearly view the one object of importance – a large iron safe, painted white, standing in the middle of the second shop floor.

Spear moved to his right and peered through the second slit. Again the main view was of the white safe, this time from a slightly different angle, but clear as day. Still with ears cocked for the first sound of the beat man's boots on the pavement, Spear rounded the corner and squinted again. The viewing slit in Bishopsgate gave yet another picture of the safe, this time ingeniously assisted by a mirror set cunningly at an angle. He nodded to himself and began to retrace his way towards the empty shop across the road. If Ember's intelligence was correct, then he would not mind being on this screwing himself, for there would be a king's ransom of booty in it.

'You are sure about the way in from the rear?' he asked Ember, back in the empty shop again.

'Certain sure. The only ones they bother about are the doors through the iron shutters; and the three locks on the safe. Why should they?' Ember gave his thin ratty grin. 'They reckon you couldn't do much even if you did get in, what with the blue boy pacing by every fifteen minutes getting his free peepshow.'

'And the dates are true?'

'True as you'll ever get. He's here...'

The beat policeman was once more pounding his sedate way up Bishopsgate.

There was a lot of whispering on the attic landing at the Albert Square house that night for Polly was canoodling with Harry Allen in the small hours.

When she finally crept back to the bed she shared with her sister, her eyes were damp and she sniffed so much that it woke Martha.

'Poll, you shouldn't, you'll get us both in trouble with Mrs Spear if you're caught. And Harry will be in the Professor's bad books. Just when we've got a good place.'

'You need not worry,' Polly sniffed loudly. 'There'll be no trouble for a long time. Harry's been sent away.'

'What? Got the boot?'

'No. Oh, Martha, I shall miss him so. He's off to France with that strange gentleman that came tonight.'

'What, old skin and bones? What larks, off to France.'

'For weeks. Not be back before Christmas he says.'

'Well, good riddance, I say,' snapped Martha who was sincerely concerned for her sister. 'That Harry's a bad influence on you, my girl. Any more of it and he'd be getting you in trouble. Then where would we be.'

'Harry's not like that...'

'Show me a man what isn't.'

'He says that he'll bring me fine things back from Paris.'

'You're getting ideas beyond your station, Poll. Don't you forget that we was cold, in rags and grubbing for food a few weeks ago. Getting this place was a miracle and I'm not having the likes of Harry Allen spoil it for us.'

'He's a gentleman...'

'A good for nothing I would say.'

Polly lapsed into her tears. 'Well, you'll be rid of him tomorrow,' a great bawl of frustration, 'and you don't care what happens to me.'

'For Christ's sake, shut your row, Poll. You'll wake the whole bleedin' square.'

Harry Allen carried the piece of poplar wood in his valise

when he left the following morning, with Labrosse. He also carried a pistol.

During the day Polly Pearson dissolved into tears when anyone spoke sharply to her, a situation which so aggravated Bridget Spear that she eventually threatened the luckless girl with a sound birching if she did not pull herself together.

'You see what you've done,' hissed Martha to her sister in the scullery. 'You'll get us both birched and I don't fancy that.'

Polly's eyes streamed again. 'I can bear it,' she blubbered, 'if it is for him.' She had much to learn about the ways of men.

At noon Ember and Spear were closeted in the study with the Professor, and instructions were given to the Jacobs brothers that they were not to be disturbed. Even Sal Hodges, who came to the house a little after one o'clock, was told that she would have to wait.

'And you're sure of the stuff?'

Moriarty sat behind his desk, papers piled neatly in front of him, a pen uncapped near his right hand. Spear and Ember had pulled two of the easy chairs near to the desk and sat, upright, not lounging, facing their leader. All three had about them the air of businessmen gravely tackling a problem of great importance to their company: Ember thrusting his ferrety little face forward, as though sniffing at a scent; Spear unsmiling, the light from the windows falling across the left side of his face, making the jagged scar show in stark relief.

'Dead sure as we'll ever be,' Ember snapped.

'The workman you got it from?'

'Boasting to one of our people – Bob the Nob – in a sluicery on payday. Showing off about what valuable stuff they handle. Our fellow left it a week, then went back for more. Said to him, 'I suppose you've got the Queen's diamonds coming in for a polish.' 'Not the Queen's,' the workman said, 'but some very fancy stuff from Lady Scobie and the Duchess of Esher.' Our bloke bought him a few more jars and got a glim of the worknote. 'I've a copy.' The paper appeared from some fold in his clothing and was passed over to the Professor.

Moriarty glanced down the list and began to read, half aloud, his voice falling often to a murmur, then rising again so that odd words came out loud, as though stressing value.

'To be brought in Monday, 16 November and be called for Monday, 23rd. Work must be completed by closing Friday, 20th.'

'There's nobody there of a Saturday,' said Spear. 'It'll all be in the safe, with his usual stock, from the Friday night to opening Monday.'

Moriarty nodded and continued to read. 'Duchess of Esher: one diamond tiara: cleaning and polishing, also test settings. One pair diamond earrings: repair hooks and make good. Diamond pendant, gold chain: repair slightly damaged link in chain, fit new ring. Pearl necklace for rethreading. Five rings. One, gold with diamond cluster of five and one: clean and secure settings of two smaller stones. Two, gold, large emerald: reset. Three, white gold with six sapphires: reset to specification and design. Four, one gold with three large diamonds: clean. Five, gold signet: clean and re-engrave.'

'They want them before the Christmas balls and parties. They're both to be guests at some grand functions.'

Moriarty did not seem to have heard. 'Lady Scobie,' he continued to read. 'Tiara, white gold with eighty-five diamonds clean and check settings. One ruby and emerald necklace (the Scobie Inheritance): new links between third and fourth stones, repair clasp. Ruby earrings: new hooks. One diamond ring, gold with large diamond and ten smaller stones (the Scobie Diamond): clean and tighten setting for large stone. There's a fortune here if it's true.'

'It's true enough,' Ember licked his lips as though savouring a mouthful of whelks.

'And there's his stock besides,' Spear chanted softly. 'Watches, rings and everything. About three thousand pounds worth. The whole lot in the safe all over the weekend.'

'And the safe?'

'Big one. Chubb triple lock. Anchored to the floor and secured on an iron bed. An old one,' he added with a smirk.

'Then wood?'

'The ordinary floor.'

'How much do you see through the peep holes?' The questions came fast, like a courtroom barrister.

'Just the safe. Hardly any of the floor.'

'And what's below?'

'Cellar. There's no problem there.'

'No bells or any of those newfangled contraptions?'

'There may be, but you only have to cut the wires once you've found the batteries. They'll have plenty of time.'

'Has Schleifstein got a good screwsman?' This to Ember.

'Not good enough for this. All his lads are brute force and ignorance. I'd have to sell him the whole thing with a screwsman.'

'You've had plenty of experience, Ember. Could you do it?'

'I could,' from Spear.

Moriarty's head moved dangerously, the reptile aggressive and ready to strike. 'I was asking Ember. Schleifstein does not know Ember.'

Spear nodded, unabashed by the sharpness of Moriarty's tone. Inside his mind, the Professor had a picture of a dog worrying a rat, then the logical process and the questioning. Could they tempt the German? Could the wretched man pull it off without getting caught – that was until he, Moriarty, was ready for him to get caught?

'Besides,' he continued to Spear, 'I shall need you for the blues. Could you do it, Ember?'

'It would take all possible time. Couldn't work by day. Go in Friday night and cut the floor, then out again and pray nobody goes in on the Saturday. In again on the Saturday night, jack the safe on the hinge side. Ten minutes working time out of every fifteen, that'd make it more difficult once we got the door off.'

'You could handle a Chubb triple lock? You wouldn't have to cut it with a blower?'

'I told you. It's an old one.'

Moriarty nodded. 'Hinges strengthened though.'

'You can still get the door off as long as there's room to get the wedges in. Once you get the wedges into the crack a screwjack will take it off like opening a tin. So long as you're patient. And as long as you don't bend the door too much and can't prop it back. If the beat man sees it off, he'll raise the alarm in no time.'

'Leave the beat man to Spear,' the Professor grinned like a gargoyle. 'You see, Ember, you are going to be caught on the way out with the swag.'

Ember grinned back. 'Of course we are, guv'nor, I'd quite forgotten.'

'You know where Schleifstein's making put-up offers?'

'One or two places.'

'You can get to him?'

Ember nodded, not over happy at the thought of working in the enemy camp.

Moriarty, as though sensing cowardice, looked at him hard, his deep eyes willing strength into the little villain. When he spoke it was in the quiet rhythmic voice, gentle and soothing, as a nurse will speak to a child.

'Go and sell yourself to him. Set him at ease, but watch his man Franz – the big one. If he gets wind of you, he will crush you with his little finger.'

When they had gone, leaving him alone, Moriarty started to do some simple arithmetic. He had been right to concentrate upon bringing the foreigners and the pair of jacks to heel, leaving the reconstruction of his rank and file to the others. It was both intellectually and aesthetically satisfying to work out the involved plots that would deal with the powers which offended him; stimulating to put them into action, and pleasurable to see the results. There was something godlike in the occupation. His genius, he knew, was in planning and guiding, and, if he recognized the truth, he found the day by day running of his criminal society somewhat humdrum. This was a supreme challenge. His nostrils twitched, for already Grisombre and Schleifstein were marked down, the train of events set in motion. Also, Crow and Holmes were oblivious to these snares being set in their paths.

But, to basics. What had it cost him from the wealth he had brought back from America? The lurkers, punishers and other individual criminals back on his strength were now being paid weekly wages, but already he was seeing a return for his money – the tribute starting to flow in from the demanders; wallets, watches, silk handkerchiefs and purses from the dippers and toolers. There was wages for young Harry Allen. They would be worth every penny, for Harry appeared to be a good boy. The running of the Albert Square house, the purchase of the house in Cornhill. The two new places for Sal. As though in answer to his thoughts, Sal Hodges appeared in the doorway, tapping lightly and entering without waiting for the Professor's call.

'I think I have a temptress for you, James.' She looked almost demure, the laces of her tight boots showing beneath the long slim skirt, the white blouse, high to the neck making the texture of her beautifully managed hair even more dazzling than usual. 'The kind of temptress you required.' The smile on her face like a cat that has swallowed all the cream in the larder. 'A temptress like a tiger.'

'Well, Sal, tigress is it? Italian tigress?'

He had spoken to her only a few nights previously, between bouts of passion at the old game, of his need for an Italian girl. His instructions, as always, were clear. Preferably an Italian girl born in England. One who had never set eyes on her true native shore. One who was a looker and right for grooming. Most assuredly one who was a tigress between the sheets.

'Hot blooded the Italians,' he had murmured at the time.

'Do you imply that we English bred girls are without hot arses?' She teased, a challenge in her upturned face while her full thighs began kneading his.

'They're not all as you, Sal. Not all have honey pots full of wasps and salamanders.'

Now she closed the door and came towards him, bending to kiss him lightly on the forehead.

'This tigress ...' Moriarty began.

'You plan to test this tigress yourself?' The smile licking at the corner of her mouth exaggerated the deep laughter curves which were set, like brackets, on each side of her lips.

Slowly, almost gravely, the Professor nodded. 'It is part of my grand design, Sal. It is necessary. No disrespect to you, my girl, but I have to train this one myself.'

'Then I'd better bring her to you. Will tonight suit, or have you other plans?'

'I have much to do. You stay tonight, Sal. This girl? Does she have intelligence? A quick wit?'

'She'll serve. Whatever your purpose, she'll serve.'

He knew she was fishing, but the Italian girl's purpose was part of the whole design wrapped in his head, and he would not rise to Sal Hodges' bait. The Italian girl was for the lecher

Sanzionare. He glanced down at the paper Ember had handed him. There was a ruby necklace on that list which would also serve for Sanzionare. Moriarty's hand tightened as though pulling on invisible strings.

Sal was sent off in search of Bertram Jacobs who came down within the quarter hour. More money was to be laid out. Again in property. This time somewhere safe within one of the hard territories. Moriarty had his eye near the river – an old stamping ground. Perhaps somewhere in Bermondsey, he suggested. It had to be secure, where they could keep a watch, where nobody could come upon them without warning. Bertram Jacobs took it all in and went off to do his master's bidding.

That evening Spear came and told him about Bridget's condition, but Moriarty showed little interest except to say that he hoped Bridget would train the two young Jemimas so that they could be trusted while she was lying in.

'I cannot afford for the routine in this household to be shuffled,' he said, and Spear returned to his part of the house feeling vaguely uneasy.

Meanwhile, Labrosse and Harry Allen were on the French railway, nearing Paris – Labrosse well drunk on absinth and Allen doing as he was told, acting as a caretaker. Back in London, Ember was banging the hoof around various hostelries which he knew were haunts of the German's crew. After a few hours searching, he sauntered into Lawson's in the naughty St George's Street. It was kept by a German, though its clientele was mainly drawn from Norwegian and Swedish seamen. The first person he spotted on entering was Schleifstein's bodyguard, Franz. All seven foot of him.

Franz sat at a table in the corner with a man called Wellborn: a name which belied the fellow's ancestry. Both were drinking cheap whisky, sluicing it down as though their guts were on fire and needed quenching.

The place was noisy and filled with smoke, while several young whores were working overtime, trying to part the men from their wages. Ember fended off a gypsy-looking girl of about fifteen, half cut, who made a hand for him before he had moved three paces into the crowd.

He pretended not to notice Franz and Wellborn, making

straight for the bar where he ordered gin, then turned with his back to the counter to peer through the dense atmosphere, trying to shut his ears to the din around him. He had seen Franz on a number of occasions, but never close to. As for Wellborn, he would work for anyone: a not over-talented snoozer by profession, but wily and never to be trusted. If the German had many like him in his crew, Ember did not think much of their chances.

He caught Wellborn's eyes and nodded, seeing him lean over and whisper something to Franz. The big man stiffened and then looked straight over at Ember. A hard man with cold eyes and arm muscles you could see bulging out of his velvet jacket. Ember coolly nodded at him, picked up his glass and began to push his way through the jostle.

'Hallo, Mr Ember what brings you down this way?' Wellborn had a rough voice, almost sarcastic in tone.

'I'm trying to trace the source of the great stench, and I think I've found it,' said Ember turning to the German. 'You speak English?' he asked, his face as an open book, a trick long learned in his trade.

'Naturally,' a clipped accent, shaped with mistrust.

Ember nodded to Wellborn. 'You work with him?'

'In a manner of speaking. I just told him you was with the Professor at one time. Not run abroad with his lot then?'

Ember cleared his throat and spat on the floor. 'I'm my own man now. Almost carried it for bloody Moriarty, didn't I?'

'He was a clever man,' said Franz in the same sharp tone. 'But not clever enough.'

'I hear your boss is putting up.'

'So? Who tells you that?'

'I'm not unknown. I got friends you know. I been around some time, Mr ...'

'Just call me Franz. What is it to you that my boss is, as you say, putting up?'

Ember needed time to think, but time had run out. He plunged.

'I might just have the very thing for him. As long as I am dealt in. It's not easy.'

'A screwing?' asked Wellborn.

77

'That would be for his guv'nor to find out.'

'You have a proposition?'

'I think you could put it like that.' He lowered his voice, 'It's a big one, Franz. It needs a good crew. Just the thing for Mr Schleifstein.'

'Herr Schleifstein,' a correction was implicit, 'is looking for something exceptional.'

'It is exceptional.'

'The spoils would ...'

'Have to be large, I know. They would be. Too big for me to handle. They'd have to be fenced off on the other side of the Channel. I want to see him, Franz. Tell you the truth, I been looking for him.'

'You cannot tell me about it?'

'Only your guv'nor.'

'You come back with me. Now.'

'I'd better be getting along,' Wellborn started to rise, but Franz leaned across and pushed him gently back in his seat.

'Mr Wellborn will also come with us.'

'I think you're very wise, Franzy boy. Wellborn has a reputation.'

'Now look, Mr Ember.'

'You just come along with Franz and me. I've said too much already and don't want you going round every flash house in the Smoke chaunting that Ember's got a prime crib.'

'I wouldn't do that. I just ...'

'Mr Ember is right. You come back with us.' Franz lurched to his feet, a good-humoured grin on his pock-marked face. 'You come or I'll snap your arms.'

Ember had already viewed the house at Edmonton when he was setting up the lurkers. When they got off the omnibus at the *Angel* and walked the few hundred yards up to the place, he spotted two of the family people – Blind Fred working the matches on the opposite side of the road, being led by that skinny little girl of his, and Ben Tuffnell doing the shivering Jemmy between a grocer's and a smart milliner's shop. Blind Fred tapped out his one-two-three to let Ember know he had seen him, which did not help a great deal. If Franz had a mind, he could have snapped Ember's neck and smashed Fred's white stick down his porridge hole quicker than kiss your fancy. Though there was not much security in it, Ember was at least happy that the lurkers were doing their job.

It was a tidy little place, the house: grey stone with two long built-out bows, one each side of the door, high windows set in them on first and second floors. A little iron gate took them up a cement path and five stone steps to the front door. There was a preposterous brass bellpull on the right, and, in the half-light, it looked green and unpolished. Franz had his own key, but as soon as they were inside, Ember knew it was a tinpot show. The furnishings were shoddy and the hall needed new wallpaper. There were also grease stains on the worn carpet. No women, he thought. Schleifstein's doing this on the cheap.

Franz led them into a dining-room to the right where two Germans were bent over bowls of fatty looking soup. One was a plump, unshaven man, dirty and mean-looking; the other a younger fellow altogether different, clean and neat as a pin. They both nodded and exchanged a few words with Franz, using their natural tongue.

'Wait,' Franz cautioned, leaving the room.

Ember heard his feet thudding up the stairs and a door opening. Then voices from above. Then another from the doorway.

'Hallo, Ember, looking for work, then?'

The newcomer was a big fellow, a nobbler from Houndsditch who had worked off and on for the Professor in the old days. His name was Evans, and Ember would not trust him with his sister's cat.

Ember inclined his head towards the ceiling. 'You work for the Prooshan cove then?'

'When he's over here. It's not like being with Moriarty, but nothing is these days, is it? You on your own?'

'Come to see him with a proposition.'

Franz was coming downstairs again. He looked huge standing in the doorway. Ember noticed that Evans the nobbler treated him with deference.

'He'll see you. Upstairs. You come with me.'

Franz's eyes slid round the whole bunch and Ember had the distinct feeling that he was not among friends.

Schleifstein's room would normally have been the master

bedroom – the first floor front. The German himself could easily have passed for a provincial bank manager – which he well might have become had he stayed on the straight and narrow path. Here, in the shabby bedroom with its iron cot, cheap wooden table and peeling wallpaper, he looked incongruous. Ember wondered if this was really a front, or whether, for some reason, Schleifstein had been ousted from his superior position in Berlin.

He was an imposing figure, clad in dark professional clothes; a man who gave off the aura of one who is born to lead; a man very much apart from those who followed him.

Indeed, Wilhelm Schleifstein had started life in banking, a fact which led to embezzlement, fraud and from thence to robbery and the flesh trade. Ember knew his reputation as a man of ruthlessness, but somehow could not equate his present position – with the deadbeat gang downstairs – with the legendary criminal overseer of Berlin. For a second he wondered why the Professor was bothering with such an elaborate plan to trap the fellow.

'Good evening, Mr Ember. I have heard much about you. Franz tells me that you have a proposition.' He spoke exceptionally good English, only a hint of accent – ts instead of ds. His large soft hands were steady on the table, and his dark little eyes unwavering. 'I can only offer you the bed to sit on, and I see that you are wondering why I should be living in this pigsty.'

'It doesn't seem to be your style.'

Ember decided that the cocky approach, though dangerous, might be the best way. Speak to him on equal terms, he told himself.

'The collapse of the previous régime has left London in some chaos, and a strong hand is needed for reorganization. Your former master was a firm disciplinarian, as I am in my natural element – Berlin.'

'I had heard.'

'Here it is different. This is something of an open market now. One I can put to good use. But one I do not desire to alert. If I put up at one of the better hotels, the police would be sniffing like dogs around a bitch. If I lie low here, make some simple reconnaissance, then perhaps people will come

80

to me. People who know my reputation. People like yourself.'

'It makes sense. I'm here, aren't I?'

'If I can put up for a grand screwing, using mumpers like those downstairs, it will possibly draw even more prime coves to me. It is better to start small, Ember, and then grow, instead of going off at half cock. What is your proposition?'

Ember looked towards Franz who still towered by the door. There was an uneasy pause during which a snatch of drunken warbling could be heard floating in from the street. Probably Ben Tuffnell letting him know that he was still there and watching.

Schleifstein spoke a rapid sentence in German. Franz nodded and, with a quick suspicious glance at Ember, left the room, his footsteps on the stairs thudding like drumbeats.

'Now,' Schleifstein relaxed. 'I know of you. I know you worked for Moriarty in a place of rank. Whether I can trust you remains to be seen. Your proposition.'

Ember had a duplicate list of the jewellery which would be in Freeland & Son's safe over the weekend of 20th – 23rd. The list did not give the company's name or address, nor the names of Lady Scobie or the Duchess of Esher. The dates were also omitted.

Schleifstein read through the list twice. Once more it was the vision of a bank manager examining a delicate account.

'A list of gems. So?'

'So they'll all be in one place at one time. And more besides.'

'This place?'

'Is in London. That's all for now.'

'And is it accessible?'

'Well, it won't be like cracking a dolls' house, but it can be done – with a good crew.'

'Of which you would be one?'

'Of which I would be the most important.'

'You are a cracksman? I had not heard.'

'I've done a little of everything. I could do this with the right planning.'

Schleifstein did not look convinced. 'Then why not do it, friend Ember? Why come to me?'

'These are big pieces, some of them well known. I need

them fenced in France, or Holland, Maybe in Germany,' he added for good measure.

'Surely there are people with whom you have worked in the past.'

'Plenty. But when these sparkling stones disappear, the esclops will be pulling down doors to get at every fence in London. You could have them away before the loss is discovered.'

'And how do you see the division of spoils?'

'You would get the lion's share. Then me. The rest divided among the crew.'

'How many in the crew?'

'It would be a four-hander. Two nights' work – and it would be hard work.'

'Give me the name of the place and the dates.'

'Sorry, Herr Schleifstein. You have to trust me and I you.'

The German looked at the list once more. 'You are certain all this will be there?'

'It will be there. It can be done.'

'Tell me how.'

For the first time, Ember detected the glint of greed in the man's eyes. He went through the plan, carefully avoiding anything which could lead the German to the exact location.

'You would be safer to make it a five-hander,' Schleifstein said when he had finished. 'An extra fellow to keep watch. Would you do it with Franz and three others?'

'Depends on the three others.'

'You have met two of my German men downstairs?'

'Yes.'

'Them, and a man called Evans who is also in the house.'

'You also have a snoozer. Wellborn, downstairs. He has a gabby mouth. If I am to do it with them, I'd want them all kept close.'

'That constitutes no problem.'

'And after we've cut the floor out on the Friday night there is a day's wait until we go back in on the Saturday. I'd want us all together during that time. Nobody wandering off on his own.'

'You would all lie up here. It's secure enough.'

'How long would you need in advance? To make your

shipping arrangements?'

'Four days. My people are in and out of London all the time.'

'I'm willing then.'

'Good,' Schleifstein mouthed the word as though biting into jam pudding. 'When will it take place?'

'A little while yet. I'll come back in three days and talk to Franz and your people. Give them their orders.'

'Your hand on it.'

Ember was about to reach out, 'We haven't really come to terms though.'

'You said the lion's share for me. Half for me, we split the rest down the middle: half for you and the remainder for my people. It is fair?'

'It will be considerable chink.'

'Your hand then.'

Schleifstein's palm felt like a piece of tripe. Ember noticed that he wiped it on his handkerchief after they had shaken.

Blind Fred had disappeared outside and Ember could not see Tuffnell, but presumed he was loitering in the shadows somewhere. There were not many people about now, but when he got to the *Angel* he saw Hoppy Jack on his crutches, leaning against the wall with a glass in his hand. There were one or two ragged urchins around, some of them sipping on tots of gin.

Ember broke into song, his hands deep in the pockets of his greatcoat – low but happy:

It's a gentleman soldier, in a sentry box he did stand,
He fell in love with a fair maid, and boldly took her hand;
He kindly did salute her, he kissed her in a joke,
He drilled her into a sentry box, wrapt up in a soldier's cloak.'

Hoppy Jack did not even look his way, but the song meant that he was to follow anyone who showed more than a passing interest in Ember.

There were no omnibuses about, so he decided to walk for a while. Within five minutes he knew there was somebody behind. Twice he stopped suddenly, in deserted lanes, and the echo of the other's footsteps continued for a split second.

Then he paused at a corner and caught sight of a figure turning at the end of the alley.

Time to give him a run, thought Ember, and began to cross and recross his own path, dodging down alleys, doubling back on the opposite sides of streets. But he could not lose the follower. It went on for half an hour or so until he was almost in Hackney. Hoppy Jack would have lost his crutches by now and was nimble enough when it came to giving a person the shadow. But that was not enough. Ember was intrigued, and a little apprehensive.

He came to the corner of a narrow, deserted alley which ran some three hundred yards into Dalston Lane. Half-way down, a lamp bracket threw out a small and diffuse pool of light. Ember paused for a moment, then took to his heels heading for Dalston Lane pell-mell, his shoes hitting the cobbles loudly, the sound bouncing from the dirty walls on either side. Past the lamp and into darkness beyond almost up to the main street. Then, turning he moved back in the deep shadow, treading quietly, listening to the rapid sound of approaching footsteps.

Ember was not naturally a man of violence. He had not the build for it, but his cunning was not easily surpassed. His right hand found the object he wanted in his greatcoat pocket – a pair of brass dusters he always carried. He stayed close to the wall, returning towards the pool of light. The other figure was coming full tilt towards him, he could hear the panting and, as the follower came level, Ember stuck out his foot.

With a choked oath the man went down, rolling forward in the half light. Ember took a quick pace towards the sprawled figure and his boot found a target. In the darkness a flash of white as the victim's face came round. The fist with the dusters connected and the man went limp.

Ember raised his head and whistled softly. Hoppy was coming down the alley.

'Here,' called Ember, using the toe of his boot to turn over the thing at his feet. The face came into the pool of lamplight. It was the nobbler, Evans, out cold in the land of nod.

Moriarty listened in a concentrated grim silence as Ember told him of the previous evening's events.

'Wilhelm is being very cautious,' he said when his weasely lieutenant had completed the tale. 'In many ways that is admirable. I would have done the same. Yet I am concerned. I would have been happier if Franz had followed you. I recall friend Evans. Brawn and balls, but little constructive intelligence. He had, if I remember aright, a certain facility with words. One who could twist. The fact that he was put to follow you indicates that he is trusted, and that smacks of the crooked cross, Ember. We must be like cats on thin ice.'

'Blind Fred got a message to me in the early hours.' Ember looked tired and jumpy. Not a good state for one who was marked to take part in a dangerous screwing. 'He says Evans got back to the Edmonton place a couple of hours after I left him. He was moving slowly. After half an hour Franz and the other two Prooshans were on the streets.'

Moriarty's head swung to and fro. 'You act innocent,' he counselled. 'Yes, somebody jumped you, but you did not stop to look.'

Ember sighed unhappily. 'I think Hoppy lifted his purse.'

Spear, who had been sitting silent in the corner of the study, looked up. 'You weren't to know who'd come sniffing around after you left.'

'There are two things,' said Moriarty. He spoke like a man using extreme care in choosing words: a man under police questioning. 'First, they are possibly looking for you. You must be looking for them. If it comes to the push, some mug-hunter was chasing you and you thought it best to tell them. If they do not disguise the fact that it was Evans, you have to be suitably outraged. You do not wish for bad blood in your crew. We all know what can happen in that situation. Second, if they have decided to watch you, they must not be led here. You'll have to keep a leary eye over your shoulder.'

'I'll have a brace of lurkers watching my back door.' Ember gave a toothy grin.

'It would be best. Make sure they're trusted ones.'

'Two that haven't been near the Edmonton house. Slowfoot and one of the women, Widow Winnie'd be as good as any.'

'It's not for long, less than three weeks now, but we must watch every angle.' Moriarty was getting into his stride, always at his best when moving the pawns in the criminal game. 'We'll need lurkers at every end – in the Cornhill, unseen, and along the route back to Edmonton. It would be a cruel blow to find friend Wilhelm changing his plans at the last moment. What of the coppers, Spear?'

'All stays normal on the Friday night. We'll put our man in on the Saturday, as late as possible.'

'And the sable maria?'

'It'll look like the real thing; and the uniforms will look natural as bread and cheese.'

'You have tools, Ember?'

'I'm borrowing them. Double enders, spiders, jack-in-the-box, brace and bit, jemmies. All the usual. Borrowing them from old Bolton. He's past it now. Lives up St John's Wood. Always willing to lend a hand, old Bolton.'

'Trust nobody, not even your shadows.' Moriarty rose from the desk, pacing to the window. 'Best say you are borrowing them for a friend. Haven't we got tools in the family?'

'You said to keep it close. Better to have stuff that hasn't been used for a few years.'

The Professor nodded. He did not particularly like Ember but he was a true and loyal man. Inside him the familiar excitement was building into almost a sensual pleasure with the knowledge that soon his shark's teeth would fasten around Schleifstein's legs. The thought was distinctly erotic. I must tell Sal to bring the Italian girl down, he reflected.

Ember went up to St John's Wood and called upon Tom Bolton, the retired cracksman, in his little cosy villa bought with the proceeds of a life-time of burglary. The reason of the visit was to collect tools.

'They're for a friend,' he explained. 'Got a little crib with an old safe out in the country.'

'They're good tools,' said the old man. His eyes were watery and he had to get about on a pair of sticks now; all his old agility gone – and him a man who could slide through impossible windows and wriggle across rooftops like a snake. 'There's none of your newfangled stuff, you know.' He seemed loath to part with them. 'None of them blow-lamps and things.'

'Won't be needed,' Ember replied cheerfully. 'I said it's an old safe.'

'It's not that I mind lending them.' He obviously did mind. 'But I'd like to know who'll be using them.'

'It's a Prooshan friend of mine. They're searching all over Germany for him and he's short of chink. Just doing the one crack here to set up for a while. Good bloke, he is. The best.'

'Well...'

'There's a hundred guineas in it for you.'

'That's a lot of money, Ember. It can't be such a small crib.'

'Ask no questions, Tom. Fifty now. The rest later.'

Reluctantly the retired burglar painfully hauled himself upstairs. Ember heard him banging about in the bedroom.

'They're on the landing,' said Bolton when he reappeared. 'I can't manage to carry them downstairs. Age and the rheumatics is a terrible thing. I once got me tools and forty-odd pounds of swag over eight rooftops, with the peelers hunting me all the way. Now it takes me an hour to get me tea. A Prooshan, you said? Would I know him?'

'Doubt it.' Ember cascaded the gold sovereigns onto the kitchen table and ran up the stairs for the bag – what they called a brief bag in a nut brown hide. 'You won't regret it,' he called out to old Bolton. 'You'll have them back before the end of the month.'

Tom Bolton had a woman who came in to see he was managing, and do his little bits of shopping. It was not charity, for he paid her odd sums and knew that she stole from the shopping money, but it was necessary. When she popped in on the following morning, he asked her to post a letter which had taken him a long while to write, the knuckles on his hands being swollen. She took it down to the corner box on her way to pick up his groceries. The letter was addressed to Angus McCready Crow, Esq., at his home address.

As he had promised, Ember returned to the Edmonton house three nights after his initial visit. In the time that passed in between, he caught only a glimpse of Franz and one of the other Germans – the clean one. They did not see him and the lurkers, Slowfoot and Widow Winnie, were certain that he had not been followed.

Franz opened the door to him and Ember immediately felt the atmosphere. In the dining-room Wellborn sat with the plump and dirty German. Evans was by the fire, his head in a sling.

'What you been up to?' Ember asked as cheerfully as he could muster.

'Douse the chat,' slurred Evans unpleasantly.

'Did you have trouble getting home the other night, Mr Ember?' Franz sounded openly unfriendly.

'Well, now you mention it, some ramper tried it on, this side of Hackney.'

'There's a lot of nasty people abroad in the streets at night. You must take care of yourself.'

'Oh, I do, Franz. I've never been a shirkster when it comes to keeping body and soul together.'

The house smelled of stale greens, an all-pervading aroma which was familiar enough to Ember who did not hold with the sentiment that cleanliness was next to godliness.

Evans muttered something from the fireside.

'When is this screwing?' asked Franz.

'When I give the word and not before.'

'You do not trust us?'

'I don't trust anyone, matey. I'll trust you, Franz, when we've done and we're away safe.'

Schleifstein came in and sniffed the stale air.

'I would like to talk with you upstairs, friend Ember.'

Schleifstein was as neat as ever, controlled and self-contained, though Ember got the impression that the German thought he carried a smell in his clothes.

'Did you give Evans a bad time?' Schleifstein asked when they were alone.

'Evans? A bad time?'

'Come, come, Ember. I asked Evans to see you home. You laid about him off Dalston Lane.'

Ember knew he was clear, home and dry. He could afford to push it now.

'It was Evans, was it? With respect guv'nor, don't ever do that to me again. Not without telling me, that is. I don't take kindly to being lurked round the streets. Makes me nervous. I have been known to chiv someone proper when I'm nervous.'

'I merely wanted to protect you.' He was suave, plausible even. 'But there is no harm done. Except to Evans' face and he will soon get over that. His pride is hurt, mind. I do not think it wise to let him know it was you.'

'No, I suppose not.'

'Nor do I think it was fair to take his wallet.'

'I didn't take no wallet.'

'If you say not, then we will remain silent. Evans will be a week on the mend. Is that time enough, or do we need another man in?'

'It's time enough.'

'Good. Then if Peter has come in, you had better aquaint them with your plan.'

'One thing,' Ember made as though to tug at Schleifstein's sleeve. 'I want it made plain that while we're inside the crib, I'm in charge.'

'It will be something like that.'

Ember thought that did not sound over-promising.

Peter was the cleaner of the two Germans. He had got back by the time they went downstairs again, though nobody volunteered intelligence about where he had been or what he had been doing. There was another person in the dining-room also: a lad of around seventeen, tall and gangly with thick hair that had enough grease in it to fry bread.

'I'll only talk to the crew,' Ember said, pitching his gaze somewhere between Schleifstein and Franz.

Wellborn and the boy were sent out and Ember began to outline the plan. He let them know that it would take place over a weekend, and that there would be two visits, though he gave no clue as to the size or layout of the premises, adhering mainly to the essential facts: how they would get in, the exact amount of work which had to be done, and who would do what. Franz tried to ask questions afterwards, but Ember only answered those that would not give anything away.

They appeared friendlier towards him before he left, though Ember remained much on his guard. In the hall he spoke to Schleifstein.

'Within the next three weeks, so keep them all at hand,' he said, conscious that it was he who now gave the orders. 'I will come here on the Monday or Tuesday before it is to take place. That will give you enough time to get your sailing orders out.' At the door he said, 'Don't have anyone look after me tonight, guv'nor. Really I can manage on my own.'

Ben Tuffnell was still across the road, a permanent figure, they would not notice him any more than the brickwork now. Two hundred yards down, on the same side as the house, Scarecrow Sim was begging in the gutter. Ember thought he had collected a lot more sores since he last saw him. They looked very real, and the good people of Edmonton appeared to be parting with a lot of chink to salve their consciences.

To set the Italian girl at her ease, Moriarty was showing her a complicated card trick involving the four aces. You put the two black aces in the middle of the pack and the red aces at top and bottom. Then you turned the pack over and there was a black ace at top and bottom and the two red aces were together in the middle. The Italian girl was impressed.

Her name was Carlotta and she had a waist which looked slim enough to encompass with two hands, jet hair and a dark, almost negroid complexion which intrigued the Professor. She also had neat ankles and her body moved beneath her gown in a manner which set raging torrents of blood bubbling through Moriarty's veins.

Sal had brought her up, told her that the Professor had some nice things to say to her; that she had to be good to him and that she was to fear nothing.

Moriarty saw Sal Hodges to the drawing-room door and she gave him a narrow-eyed smirk and whispered, 'Wasps, salamanders and lizards. We'll talk, James. I hope she is the right one.'

The Professor assured her that he thought Carlotta would be admirable for what he had in mind. He then talked to the girl, played a little Chopin to her and did the card trick which involved the four aces.

She seemed very young, perhaps nineteen or twenty summers, and had a calm manner with no sign of the violent temper which Moriarty associated with Latin women. Bridget Spear had laid out a cold collation – ham, tongue and one of Mr Bellamy's pork pies. There were also two bottles of

Moet & Chandon, Dry Imperial, the '84, and they drank one bottle between them before going to bed, where Carlotta proved to be more than a tigress.

'I understand from Mrs Hodges,' Moriarty said during a recuperative rest, 'that you have never been to your native Italy.'

She pouted, 'No. My parents do not wish to return and I have never had the time or money. Why do you ask?'

She ogled him blatantly. With a little grooming and the right clothes – she was somewhat flashily dressed – the dark Carlotta might just pass for a countess.

'I am thinking of taking a little trip to Italy in the spring. Rome is very pleasant at that time of year.'

'You are fortunate.' She leaned across and fondled him after the blatant manner of her profession. Then, coquettishly, 'Fortunate in more ways than one.'

'I think it could be arranged for you to accompany me to Rome. If you would like that.'

Carlotta launched into a quiet stream of Italian which sounded like a mixture of adoration and pleasure.

'You would want for nothing. New clothes. Everything.' He smiled at her across the pillow, deep and secretive. 'And a ruby necklace to wear at your pretty throat.'

'Real rubies?'

'Naturally.'

Her hand performed some exquisite tricks, things of which a girl of her tender years should have neither knowledge nor experience.

'Could I have my own lady's maid also?' she cooed in his ear.

Angus Crow always made a point of calling on his tame retired cracksman after dark. They never spoke of this arrangement, but it was a regular thing between them, as was the signal which the old man supplied. The curtains in his front parlour were drawn tight after sunset if he was alone (in summer the window was left closed). If someone was present, there would always be a strip of light showing between them.

Crow suspected that this was a signal used for others also, for Tom Bolton would invariably hobble through to the parlour whenever he arrived. They always sat and talked in the tiny back kitchen.

It was a relief for Crow to have an excuse to be away from King Street for the evening. Sylvia appeared to be losing her senses. The wretched servant, Lottie, was still in the house, constantly under his feet when he was there. To cap it all, Sylvia was planning all kinds of new diversions, dinner parties being her current obsession. Crow reflected, with a small happiness, that once friends had dined with them there was little likelihood of them doing so again. Not if Lottie continued to rule the kitchen.

It was with some sense of relief, then, that he now sat in old Bolton's back kitchen, a hot toddy in front of him on the red tasselled tablecloth, a warm fire burning in the stove, kettle spouting steam on the hob, and the lamp turned up. He reflected, as he had done on other occasions, that the china, displayed neatly on the small dresser, was of good quality; who, he wondered, had been its original owner?

Bolton, drawing quietly on his pipe, told the story of Ember's visits and their purposes with little adornment, and Crow allowed him to speak without interruption until the whole thing was out.

'So you let him take them?' he asked when it was over, his voice reflecting the constant disappointment he felt over the weaknesses of the criminal classes.

'I didn't have much option. You know what that lot can be like, Mr Crow. I know that I am old, and useless, and crippled, but we all cling to life. That lot work in the shadows. They crawl out of the sewers. You turn over stones and there they are.'

Crow grunted loudly. There was no way of telling whether this implied sympathy, understanding, or rebuke.

'I've done some bad things in me time, but I was never willingly involved in murder. I want nothing to do with being a victim now.'

'A German, you say?'

'He told me a German. A fellow who was wanted in his own country and had found this one crib to crack here. One screwing to set him up for a while.'

'Not for life?' Crow detected the cynicism in his own tone.

'That's the usual take, isn't it, Tom? A good one to set you up? Then you'll have done with it. Retire and lead a blameless life.'

'That's what a lot of them say, guv'nor. True enough, and I've said it meself before now.'

'A screwing or a cracking?'

'Lord love you, Mr Crow, there ain't much difference. You listen to too many tales. The lads who call themselves cracksmen and reckon they're better than those who are dubbed screwsmen. Haven't I taught you that? You get to a place thinking you can screw the door with a spider and find you can't, so you crack it with a jemmy. Any burglar worth his salt has done the lot: screwing, cracking, area diving, cutting out, star glazing, bending the bars. I remember when I was younger . . .' and he was off on one of his long reminiscences of which there were many, for Tom Bolton had started life as a chimney boy at the age of eight.

Crow heard him out before throwing the next question at him. 'Ember used to work for the Professor, didn't he? For Moriarty?'

It was incredible, Crow thought, how the name still produced a visible reaction from hardened criminals. The old thief's swollen hands clenched – an action which must have caused extreme pain – and his eyes twitched. The skin on his face went grey, like dry paper.

'I wouldn't know about that,' the aged voice had acquired a crock, as though the throat had become suddenly parched.

'He's been gone a long time, Tom. There's nothing to fear anymore.'

There was no sound but the crackle of the fire and the ticking of the clock.

'Look, Mr Crow,' as though he found breathing a labour. 'I've taught you things, but this is the first time I've blown on anyone. It's not in me nature. I only did this 'cos of me tools. I don't like to think of some foreigner using them.'

'It must be big though, Tom. For them to want your tools, I mean. You can't get quality like yours any more.'

'It's how he uses them as'll count.'

'A German,' murmured Crow, as though returning to the one sore point, trying hard to piece tangled ends together in

93

his brain. 'Was our Ember ever a cracksman?'

'I've known him since he was a lad. Small and wiry. He's done most things. He'd know how. But I wouldn't cross him. He held a certain position – you know. What you said.'

'The Professor.'

'I can't hear you.'

'Did you believe him? About the German?'

'He believed it.'

'So you lent him your tools. Simple as that.'

Bolton had omitted to mention the payment. It was a very large amount for the loan of a set of tools – even good ones like his. For a second, no more, it weighed on the old man's conscience.

'I didn't want me head bashed in, nor me gizzard slit. I don't fancy going at all, but when I do I'd rather it was in me own bed.'

It had to be something very big. Crow could not get Moriarty out of his head, for Ember was wholly the Professor's man. There was a German in London with Moriarty when all the foreigners met together in '94. Crow wondered about that. There would be something written down at the Yard. Still, there were a lot of Germans in England.

'I'll see if we can have a few words with Ember,' he said aloud.

'You won't say anything?'

'About you, Tom? Rest easy, old lad, you'll not be mentioned. We want Ember for more than borrowing a set of implements. Thank you for your help, anyhow. Now, do you lack for anything?'

'I manage. I always get through, even though it's a struggle some weeks.'

Crow laid four gold sovereigns on the red cloth.

'Have a wee treat, Tom. And look after yourself.'

'Lord bless you, Mr Crow. Take care of that Ember, he's a foxy one. Oh, and Mr Crow?'

At the door the detective turned. 'Yes?'

'Keep up wind of him. He reeks does Ember.'

'I'll bear it in mind.'

There were few people about at Scotland Yard, and nobody

at all in his part of the building. Crow turned the gas up and went through to Sergeant Tanner's room, opening the cabinet and looking through the folders. The one he wanted was not very thick. He carried it back to his desk and sat there in the silence turning the pages and trying to find inspiration in the neat entries. FOREIGN ELEMENTS AMONG KNOWN ASSOCIATES OF JAMES MORIARTY, the heading said.

It contained some twenty or thirty dossiers and among those of Germanic origin there was a fence by name of Muller who ran a pawnshop over Ludgate way; another called Israel Krebitz, a big fish named Solly Abrahams and a man known as Rutter. There were also Tanner's few notes on the Jacobs brothers.

By far the largest dossier was that of Wilhelm Schleifstein. Place of origin: Berlin. He was very well known there: robberies. banks, brothels, a finger in pies of every taste. He had certainly been identified as one of those with Moriarty in 1894. There was also a giant of a man who usually accompanied him – Franz Bucholtz, also well known and dangerous.

Tomorrow, he thought, I shall request permission of the Commissioner to telegraph Berlin and see if they know the whereabouts of Herr Schleifstein and his friend Bucholtz.

Sylvia was awake, sitting up in bed with a copy of Charlotte M. Yonge's *Lady Hester, and the Danvers Papers,* and a pound box of Cadbury's Special Vanilla Creams.

'Angus,' she began, putting down the book. 'Angus, I have a wonderful idea.'

'Good, hen. Good.'

His thoughts were still on Ember and the possiblity of a skilled German cracksman in their midst. He allowed Sylvia's prattling to go over his head, like water gurgling across rocks. He would like a word with Ember, so tomorrow he would have the little rat's face circulated to all divisions. Then he caught the Commissioner's name coming from his wife's pudgy lips.

'I'm sorry, hen. I did not catch that.'

'Angus, you should listen when I'm speaking to you. I said that I hoped you would not have any plans for the evening of the 21st.'

'The 21st? What day is that, my dear?'

'A Saturday.'

'Not unless I'm on a case.' Not unless Ember turns over this German and I am on a hue and cry. Or the German uses Bolton's tool-kit to crack open the Bank of England and the City Police want my help. Not unless . . . 'Why the 21st, dearest?'

'I have sent a note from us asking the Commissioner and his wife to dine here upon that night.'

Even Lottie, tucked away in her attic, heard the bellow of rage. 'You've what? You've asked . . . the Commissioner? My Commissioner . . . ?' Crow sank into a chair, his face a mask of stupefaction. 'Sylvia, you foolish woman. My God. You hazy lazy Daisy. An inspector does not presume to invite the Commissioner to dine. Particularly if he is going to serve up Lottie's skilly. Great merciful heavens, woman, he'll imagine that I am on the crawl.'

Angus Crow buried his face in his hands and thought that he might well be otherwise occupied on the night of the 21st. In a police cell awaiting trail for the murder of his wife, Sylvia.

'You'll stay here until it's time for you to go to the Edmonton house again. There's room for you in the attic – in Harry Allen's room. He'll not be needing it until the middle of December,' the Professor told Ember.

The lurkers were becoming more precise in their arrangements. Blind Fred had got a whisper, from an eye called Patchy Dean, that the coppers were putting about queries concerning Ember. He had sent a runner to find Ember and bring him the word: a young lad who sometimes did a spot of starving along Regent Street, up by the Quadrant. The lad, Saxby, caught up with the foxy lieutenant over in Bermondsey where he was looking at properties with the Jacobs brothers. Ember had queasy guts all the way back to Albert Square. Spear later confirmed that there were questions being asked and the esclops had orders to detain him.

'You haven't been chaunting where you shouldn't?' Moriarty asked of him.

'You know me, Professor. Not a word. Only to the Prooshan and his team, and then only what's good for 'em. Mind you, if they've let Wellborn out, there's no telling.'

'Wilhelm will keep Wellborn close. If he's properly hooked, he'll not cut off his nose to spite his face. What of Bolton where you borrowed the gear?'

'He knew nothing.'

'Except that you'd come on the touch for his instruments. He knew it was you.'

'Bolton wouldn't...'

'I trust not. Best have lamps on his drum all the same. By heaven, Lee Chow'll rip his wind if he's blown on you.' Moriarty paused, but Ember shook his head, refusing to believe that old Tom Bolton would whisper to the coppers. 'All is arranged, isn't it? Nothing forgotten?'

'I'll have to use one of the runners to tip the buck cabbie if I'm not allowed to go up there myself. I told the Prooshan that the cab'll be ready from three in the morning onwards.'

'That can be done. You've got a lurker listening to the workmen in the place?'

'The best. Spear's got the place watched from the shop across the road, and Bob the Nob is listening to the workman we got the word from originally.'

'You arranged any signs? If it's not clear?'

'Ben Tuffnell's still at Edmonton. If there's danger before we leave, he's to be singing drunk across from the house. *The Mower* he'll be singing.'

Moriarty nodded a dismissal, but as Ember reached the door, he issued one further command. 'Bathe yourself, Ember, if you are to stay here. I'll not have this house stinking of fartleberries and last summer's fish.'

Indeed, the Professor must have issued further orders, for Ember had hardly reached the room lately occupied by Harry Allen when Martha Pearson was up to tell him that his bath was drawn and Mrs Spear had laid out fresh towels, a bar of Sunlight soap and a scrubbing brush for him.

On the following morning a letter arrived from Paris for Professor Carl Nicol – the learned American gentleman living at Five Albert Square.

Dear Sir – *the letter read,*

We are settled in here very snug. While Pierre is still drinking like a funnel, he is doing at least four hours work each day. He tries to excuse himself constantly, and is often complaining about the light and it not being good enough, but I see to it that he gets on. It is a fair treat to watch him paint and I am certain that you will be more than satisfied with the result. The wood was marked as per your instructions.

I have also seen to it that he has not gone abroad unaccompanied. I have gone with him on all his visits to see the real thing and you can rest assured that everything else will be done exactly as you ordered.

I remain sir,
Your obedient servant,
H. Allen

LONDON:
Monday, 16 November–Monday, 23 November 1896

(The cracking of the Cornhill crib)

The Jacobs brothers had found just the place over in Bermondsey. A building that had been used as part storehouse, part offices for a small chain of grocery shops that had gone bankrupt a year before.

It had been on the market for some time, but nobody had snapped it up as the site was damp and unfit for expansion. It had never been much of a place for storing groceries either, for it backed onto a rubbish tip. However, it stood apart, some way from the nearest row of cottages; the locks and bars were all secure and there was a small yard and a stable at the back.

After some haggling, Bertram Jacobs paid over £200 of the Professor's money and the deeds were drawn up in double quick time. Lee Chow rounded up some of his yellow brethren and, in a matter of a few days, the place was scrubbed clean as a whistle; a few licks of paint were added here and there, while Harkness, the Professor's driver, took a couple of loads of cheap furniture over in the back of a hired cart.

During the week before Ember was due back at the Edmonton house, Spear saw to it that the black maria they had been constructing in a nearby stables, was taken over and put in the yard, and on the Saturday, the Professor himself paid the Bermondsey place a visit, to pronounce it good enough, providing those who had to stay there could put up with the stench from the nearby tanneries and leatherworkers' shops.

By this time Terremant had recruited more punishers,

there were facilities for cooking at Bermondsey, and provisions were laid in for a period.

The watch was still going on across the Cornhill from the jeweller's, and Spear had managed to get the police uniforms into the shop.

On the night of Monday, 16th, Ember, carrying the brief bag containing Bolton's well-swaddled tools, went to the *Angel* by hansom and walked the short distance to Schleifstein's house. He got a glimpse of Hoppy at the *Angel*; Sim the Scarecrow was still trading on his sores; Blind Fred and Ben Tuffnell were on the lurk. Apart from them, Ember was now on his own. As he hauled at the dirty brass bell-pull, he briefly thought of Bob the Nob over in the City, and of the invisible network of lurkers through which any danger signal had to come. He also thought of Moriarty's last words to him before he left Albert Square.

'If you get Schleifstein for me, Ember, you'll never want for hard cash again. If you fail, you will not be needing any.'

Franz opened the door. 'So, it is this week then?'

'Friday night,' said Ember as the door closed behind him.

It rained all day on Friday, 20 November. Not the foggy drizzle normal for London at that time of year, but a lashing torrent which hurled walls of water up the wider main streets, and flooded the narrow and more secret alleys of the metropolis. The runnels became small rushing streams and waterfalls sluiced off the rooftops, filling the gutters and creating a havoc of pools and local flooding where streets were uncobbled or badly made up.

Traffic slowed down and jammed in all the worst bottlenecks, while pedestrians fought their way through the streets, as though grappling with the bayonets of water.

By late afternoon the downpour eased a little, but by then most of those who had to be out and about in London were soaked through. Not so Bob the Nob.

Bob the Nob was better known by one of his many aliases, Robert Lamb, Robert Betterton and Robert Richards being but three, and Bob the Nob being the name under which he was known by family people. A slim, grey-haired, not quite distinguished-looking fellow of forty years or so, he was a frequenter of public houses and hostelries in all parts of the capital, yet never known as a 'local' in any of them. If he drank in Brixton, for instance, he would talk much of his business in Bethnal Green; or an evening spent in some Camden Town boozer would find him often referring to the little place he had in Woolwich.

His memory was accurate and he had a nose for a well-stocked crib. When drinking in City of London pubs he was usually known as a cheerful fellow who had a nice little grocery trade somewhere over Clapham way. In fact, the Nob lived in two rooms above a butcher's shop in Clare Market, from whence he would sally forth each day to pick up prime titbits of intelligence. He was smart, a dandy almost, and placid in temperament. On Friday, the 20th, he stayed in bed most of the day, listening to the rain washing the streets, drumming against his window and on the false front of the butcher's shop below.

He was the lurker who had first nosed the possibilities concerning Freeland & Son. Tonight his job was simple: to drink a few glasses in Dirty Dick's, the pub built over the old wine and spirit vaults in Bishopsgate. That was where the skilled workmen from Freeland's went after work on a Friday, and he had, in effect, promised to meet with a couple of them around eight. If anything was wrong, young Saxby would be waiting at a flash house in Whitechapel. What he did with any message passed on was no concern of Bob the Nob.

The saloon bar was busy when he arrived, mostly with office people lingering after the day's work was over. A large number did not have to come in on the Saturday, and some would make a night of it before returning to their wives with what was left of their wages.

By half-past eight none of the jeweller's craftsmen had appeared and the Nob began to sense the first twinges of concern. Nine o'clock and still no sign. It was nearly half-past the hour before they came trouping in, all four of them, tired and looking glum.

He greeted his particular cronies cheerfully and with some comment on the lateness of the hour. Old Freeland had kept them, they said, and they were none too happy about it. Work which had to be finished by Monday, for collection, was not yet done. They were not due to go in on the Saturday, but now that had been changed. Tomorrow would have to be a full working day.

For the sake of appearances, the Nob stayed on until just after ten, lingering by the door to pass a word or two with another aquaintance before going out into the night. The rain had started again. Not with the same force as earlier in the day, but enough to quickly soak the shoulders of his greatcoat and spray into his face, dripping from his eyebrows, forcing him to blink away the drops and run the side of his hands across the lids. Head down, he strode out towards Cornhill and Leadenhall Street, legs pumping automatically, hands thrust deep in greatcoat pockets, mind running on the simple chore of passing a message to Saxby for Ember. 'They'll be working tomorrow,' was all he had to say. Then home, perhaps with one of the molls who hung about near Clare Market. A night horizontalizing would do him good.

The Nob was crossing Aldgate when the hansom struck him.

It was a combination of bad weather and worse luck. Mainly the weather, for the rain was hard in the cabby's eyes and he glimpsed the figure in the dark patch of road a shade too late. He was able to rein his horse sharply to the right, a quick action which saved the Nob from being trampled under hoof, but not quick enough to stop the wheel catching him a nasty blow, sending him scudding and tumbling across the wet road where he lay, splayed out, unmoving: still as death.

They all wore their dark clothes with the tight jackets as Ember had directed. Sitting in the little dining-room of the Edmonton house, the five men went through their particular jobs for a last time – Evans, still looking surly; Franz; the neat German Peter, and his portly dishevelled companion whose name was Claus; and, of course, Ember who did most of the chatting.

Wellborn and the greasy-haired boy were somewhere in the house, and Schleifstein had gone to bed. The buck cabbie was due to pick them up in his growler at one o'clock and would bring them back later. Tomorrow, when they forced the safe, he would leave the cab ready for Evans to pick up for loading with the swag and the fast away from the site. All was set.

The nobbler, Evans, was to crow for them, and drive the cab on the following night; Peter and Claus were the labourers, doing the heavy work; Franz would act as go-between from Ember to Evans and vice versa.

'There's no need to be all of a rush,' Ember told them for the twentieth time in three days. 'That's the beauty of it: taking our time over two nights. Tonight we get the lie of the land, cut up into the shop; then tomorrow we crack it proper.'

There had not been a sound out of normal in the streets, and Ember felt rightly confident. No signals. All clear. Spear and Terremant would be watching from the shop across the road in Cornhill and it would not take more than a couple of hours to cut up through the floor. Probably less. Away from Edmonton at one. Back at five. All done in darkness.

He felt in his pocket for the brandy flask and took a swig. One last look at old Bolton's instruments, all packed and swaddled with cloth to baffle the noise. Chisels; four jemmies; American auger, short saw and blades, a set of bettys; spiders and doubled-enders; an outsider; a cutter and heads; rope, and the brass jack-in-the-box. On top, the dark lantern which would be their only light on the premises.*

*Burglar's tools. Some of these mentioned are self-explanatory – such as chisels and jemmies. Others are not. The American auger was a brace and bit; the betty was originally a type of jemmy shaped like the letter L, but by this time the name was applied to a much smaller instrument for picking locks. Spiders were wire pick-locks and double-enders were skeleton keys with wards at both ends – hence the name. The outsider was a pair of long-nosed, hollow-ended pincers used to grip and turn a key inserted in the other side of a lock. The cutter was, perhaps, the most difficult tool in a cracksman's arsenal and needed great skill in its correct use. It was a T-shaped instrument, the downward stroke of which was pointed and carried an adjustable bar at right angles, to which various cutting heads could be attached – for metal, wood or glass. When a head was in place the instrument was used, rather like a compass, to cut neat circular holes. By this time, however, modern safes were being attacked with the relatively new blowlamps or, in the case of older models, the tried and true jack-in-the-box, or screw jack, the operation of which is described later.

The buck cabbie had been paid in advance. It was always the way: honour among thieves did not often stretch to matters of cash. He had no idea where the robbery was to be. Nor did he wish to know. He would drop them in Bishopsgate and at half-past four in the morning would drive a set return route, first picking up Ember with his tools, then the others at intervals – two in Houndsditch and the other pair in the Minories. Then back, by the circuitous series of doubles, to Edmonton.

As they came down the steps to the cab, Ember thought he had a glimpse of Ben Tuffnell's white face in the darkness of the wall at the other side of the road. No signals. All safe. Just before they left the house he had hauled out his watch-chain and the old silver hunter showed one on the dot.

The Nob felt cold, wet and in pain. It was dark. There were voices. People were lifting him and the pain ran through his body in a great unspeakable wave. Next he was on some sort of cart. But that was only for a short time, for he lapsed into the darkness once more.

Then the pain came again, as though someone was crushing then wrenching at his shoulder. Time was unimportant and a lifespan could have passed, like a fevered dream, his mind dipping in and out of muzzied knowing and nightmare sleep. Then, lights and the smell of disinfectant, something holding down his right arm and shoulder. More light. Waking to strange surroundings and ... angels? White gliding angels.

'There, you are well,' said one of the angels bending over him. 'You are all right.'

'What ...?' His mouth was dry and he wanted to vomit.

'You have been in an accident,' said the angel. 'The police brought you here.'

At the mention of the police, Bob the Nob became fully awake. He was lying in a tiled white room, on a leather couch. The angels were women. Nurses.

'You are at St Bartholomew's Hospital,' said the nurse, her face close to his. 'Your shoulder has been broken but the surgeon has set it now. You'll live to argue with hansoms again.'

It all came back, and the Nob moved, trying to sit up, but

104

the pain stabbed down like a red-hot lance. As it subsided he asked, 'What's the time?'

'You must not worry about the time. They'll be taking you up to the ward in a moment.'

'What's the time? It's very important.'

'Very well. Just gone midnight. You've been unconscious for quite some time.'

He felt more shaky and the pain returned, in smaller stabs this time.

'I can't stay here,' he gasped. 'Can't afford it. Not a hospital.'

'Don't you worry. They'll talk to you about that in the morning. You really did have a rather nasty tumble.'

She was a sharp-faced woman, all starch. Starch all through, thought the Nob. Starch everywhere, I shouldn't wonder.

'Got to get a message,' he took a deep breath.

'To your wife?'

'Yes,' he grabbed at the idea.

'Well, I'll have to take your particulars before you go up and we'll see what can be done about your wife. The police will want details anyhow. I really don't know. You're the fourth accident case we've had in tonight, they'll have to do something about the traffic soon. Those cabbies all drive too fast and there are too many people on the roads. They're not built for it, you know.' She touched his head lightly as if feeling for fever. 'You just rest here. I'll be back in a few minutes.'

She was away, across the tiled floor, a whisper of starched authority.

The pain was very bad, but he managed to get to his feet, the room spinning and settling. Then another wave of nausea. The sopping wet greatcoat was lying on a chair, but he would not be able to get into it, his right arm and shoulder being strapped up as it was. No matter, thought the Nob. If I need other treatment, I'll spin them a yarn down at the Eastern Dispensary in the Chapel. Grabbing his coat with the left hand, gritting his teeth against the white pain which flashed through him with each step, the Nob shuffled towards the door. Outside there was a wide hallway and some glass doors.

A lot of bustle, for they seemed to be bringing two new cases in on stretchers. He caught a glimpse of his nurse giving a hand.

The way across to the exit was clear, so summoning all speed, the Nob lurched to the glass doors and was away. Outside, the rain still tippled down and seemed, for a moment, to clear his head. Then the nausea returned, and the pain making each step agony.

It was after one before he got down to the flash house in the Chapel. There were several vagrant wrecks there, and a couple of coves boasting of a blag they'd done up West. Saxby was asleep on a bench in the corner. The Nob gave him the message and he was off, looking white-faced and worried with dark circles under his eyes. It was a fair way to Edmonton.

The Nob watched him go, then, at last, he was sick and one of the coves propped him up in a corner and fed him brandy.

The rear entrance of Freeland & Son was reached through a narrow lane off Bishopsgate leading into a tiny yard. The back door was secure enough, protected by iron plates, but to the right of this some area steps descended to a cellar door which nobody bothered with.

The yard itself was littered with junk: old boxes, packing cases and such, as though it was the common dumping ground for the immediate area.

The beat man was well clear when they unloaded from the cab – Ember whispering instructions to the cabbie – and they were down the lane and into the yard within a couple of minutes, leaving Evans at the Bishopsgate end, for it was a perfect vantage point, dark and unlit. Ember reckoned they had about ten minutes to get in before the copper came down Bishopsgate again.

The dark lantern only gave a tiny circle of light, but enough for using a betty on the simple lock. There was always a way in, Ember mused as he worked at the tumblers. Some had safes with uncrackable doors but backs to them like thin tin. Some protected the main doors and forgot about the cellars below, or even the offices above. The lock gave way to his simple seduction, and Ember pushed the door open. It creaked slightly and there was a rusty groan from one of the

106

hinges. Inside, the place smelled of dust, damp and the neglect of ages.

He swung the little circle of light around the cellar, peering about him in the hope that his eyes would more quickly adjust to the darkness. Like the yard outside, the cellar was full of rubbish: a couple of large wooden packing cases, a pile of old boxes, a peeling display sign (*Gilding, Plating and Engraving on the Shortest Notice. Repairs Expeditiously Executed by Scientific Workmen*), part of an old window grille, made obsolescent by the iron shutters round the front of the shop.

'Stick by the door,' Ember whispered to Franz. 'Listen well.'

Then, in dumb show, he motioned Peter and Claus to close up with him as he moved into the cellar, the sovereign of light playing on the joists, beams and planking above.

The cellar was long and narrow, and there, some four paces inside, directly above their head, was the telltale square of heavy bolts which marked out the iron bed upon which the safe was set in the workshop. He signalled for the two Germans to drag one of the packing cases just forward of the square, then quietly, and with no undue haste, Ember opened the brief bag and located the American auger, screwing his largest bit in place.

He then passed the lantern to Peter, climbed onto the packing case and began to drill upwards through the wooden ceiling, turning his face to one side once the drill was in place to avoid the sawdust and splinters.

His object was to drill four sets of seven holes, each set forming a right angle, making the corners of a square in front of the bolted area, each set some three feet apart. Thus, if one joined up the angles, each of the sides would be roughly three feet in length. He had drilled two holes, close together, when they heard the double yap of a dog. Evans' first signal. Next time it would be a low whistle, then a night bird screech and so back to the dog.

Franz quietly closed the door, leaning heavily against it. Ember froze, pulling the auger away from the wood, Peter and Claus squatted, silent, covering the lantern. Outside, they knew Evans would have retreated into the yard to crouch behind the rubble.

They had deduced that five minutes would see them clear each time the copper passed: unless he decided to have a look around the yard, which he did about once each night. He did not come in this time around. Gently they relaxed and went back to work.

The wooden planks above were easy, the bit cutting through like a needle into a candle, roughening a shade when it got to the linoleum floor covering above. After three stops to let the beat man pass, Ember had completed the four sets of holes.

On the fourth stop, the copper came into the yard. They could hear his feet heavy on the cobbles as he marched up the lane. Then the flash of his bullseye lantern across the grimed cellar window. He tried the rear door and paused at the top of the area steps – Ember's heart thudding like a navvy's hammer. But he did not come down, and they soon began to breathe easy again as the footsteps receded.

'Evans is on his way back now,' hissed Franz, and Ember bent over the brief bag for his largest chisel to hack away the wood between the holes so that he finally had four small right-angled slits.

He then chose the best saw blade, screwed the butterfly nuts tight and handed it to the portly Claus. It was now up to the pair of Germans to do the heavy work of sawing through the wood, separating the angles, and so producing a square access hole into the workshop above.

It took an hour, with the pauses in work to let the beat man pass. Even so they only cut away three sides – Peter and Claus heaving on the planks and breaking them away from the fourth side so that they came down with a splintering crash fit to wake the dead. The noise was so great in the close confines of the cellar that Ember motioned them to stand still and listen, half expecting to hear the thud of the policeman's feet running back fast towards the shop.

With the tearing away of the boards, the brilliant gaslight from the shop above shafted down, completely illuminating the cellar. For the first time, Ember realized they would have to find some way of jamming the board back in place before leaving. If the beat man returned to the yard between now and their visit on the morrow, he would be immediately alerted by this unusual source of light from the cellar window.

'I'm going up for a peep,' Ember whispered, gesturing to Peter and Claus to give him a leg up through the hole.

They had worked it just right. The hole was directly in front of the metal bedding upon which the safe stood, gleaming in the middle of the workshop floor. One look told Ember that, in spite of its spruce appearance due to the coat of white paint, the safe was all of forty years old. He moved around, crouched by the hinge side of the door, and smiled. There was plenty of room to insert wedges between door and safe.

He straightened up and pulled out the hunter. It showed a quarter to four. They had plenty of time, and would be back in Edmonton before five, even with the chore of putting the floorboards back in place.

Ember looked around the workshop, neat and tidy with a long workbench against one wall; stools for the craftsmen and their tools set in wooden racks above the bench: four sets. In the outer part of the shop, the glass cases stood empty and gleaming in the light and, for a second, Ember wondered if he should go over to one of the slits in the window shutters and signal to Spear, who would undoubtedly be watching from the shop across the road.

His examination had taken longer than he imagined, for sudddenly there was Franz's urgent whisper from below. The beatman was on his way round once more.

'Stow the chant,' he hissed back, retreating from the safe, well out of line of view from the observation slits. He was breathing heavily and leaning against the workbench, conscious of the hollow tread of the copper's boots on the pavement outside, so close, mingled with the occasional night street noises.

Turning his head slightly, Ember glimpsed something white near his hand on the workbench. Directly in front of one of the stools, weighted down with a small piece of metal, was a paper. A florid flowing copperplate hand-writing below the letterhead of John Freeland & Son. The date neat at the top: Friday, 20 November 1896. Then, below –

Axton. Further to our conversation this evening, I find that I may be a trifle late getting in to open the safe in the morning. This is unavoidable, though irritating in view of the urgency of the work. You will, perhaps, use the time in order to assure the lads that they will be well recompensed for coming in to complete the work for Lady S and her Grace. The firm's reputation rests upon it. Yours etc. John Freeland.

A few seconds passed before Ember took in the full meaning of the note. He was conscious of the policeman's footsteps outside the windows of the outer shop, but his head was whirling with the ramifications. The workmen would be coming in within a few hours. Perhaps at half-past seven or eight o'clock . If they were to succeed with the robbery, the safe would have to be cracked now. Tonight. Crowding in upon this and linked with the ominous tread of the beat copper, was the knowledge that it would be impossible to crack the safe while the blue boy was on his rounds. Too much noise and no way of disguising the shattered door. That was part of the plan which he had so carefully kept from Schleifstein. The whole thing turned on the beatman being substituted by one of Terremant's punishers.

Even if they did manage it by some miracle, the inner core of Moriarty's intrigue would go for nothing: the black maria, the punishers disguised as coppers descending on them as they left, the raid on Schleifstein's house in Edmonton and the final dénouement, making it plain to Schleifstein that the Professor still ruled. All that would be lost. Worse, the Professor would blame him. He might even imagine that Ember had cross-bitten him and there would be only one conclusion to that.

The policeman's footsteps were dying away up the street and Ember knew that he now had to make the most important decision of his criminal life.

The lad, Saxby, got to Edmonton just after two o'clock and found Ben Tuffnell in his usual place, curled up in a doorway opposite Schleifstein's house. He was asleep with one eye open and looked startled when the boy shook him.

'They're not to go.'

'Who says?'

'The Nob had an accident. Got run over by a cab. But they're not to go.'

'They've bloody gone, young Saxby. A good hour ago they've gone.'

'What's to do then?'

'Did you see the Nob?'

'I saw him. Terrible mess. Got his arm bashed up.'

'What did he say? His actual words.'

Ben Tuffnell had hold of the boy by the coat and his eyes had a wild look.

'He said they mustn't go in tonight as the shop's being opened up tomorrow.'

'Gawd help us,' breathed Tuffnell. 'I don't know what to do, lad. Straight. I don't know.'

Spear would rather have been in bed with his Bridget instead of spending the night in the shop across the way from Freeland & Son in the Cornhill. Now, in the early hours, he found himself yearning for the warmth of his wife next to him, even though she had begun to fill out: the fruit of their coupling growing within her.

He granted that it was necessary to keep watch tonight, but tomorrow would see the real business. Looking around in the gloom, Spear had the feeling that Terremant and the punisher called Betteridge were as fatigued as himself.

All appeared to have run as smooth as silk. Earlier they had seen the cab turn into Bishopsgate, and since then nothing had intruded upon the routine of the night. The policeman marched the course of his beat, the traffic of the small hours remained light and normal, with the odd closed van and several stray hansoms still out plying until dawn.

Just after two, the rain had given up, and at half past the hour two young revelling gents, with a pair of likely girls, had proceeded merrily down the Cornmarket, their laughter echoing and dying away, evidence of youth having its fling even in the sober confines of the sacred square mile of the City of London.

A little before half-past four, the empty cab had come up slowly from the direction of the Royal Exchange and turned quietly into Bishopsgate. Though he could not see it from his watching point, Spear was certain that it would be slowing down and stopping near the lane which led to the back of Freeland's premises, where it would pick up Ember. It would then gather speed and clatter on to collect the two members of the gang who would by now have walked up to Houndsditch.

As he thought of it, something bothered him.

'We haven't had sight of the two that were to walk to the Minories,' he whispered to Terremant.

'Doubtless they've cut through the other way,' the big punisher replied.

Spear thought about it for a moment and realized that this was the only plausible explanation. Yet he did not feel happy about it, for it would mean that four men would, even for a short time, be heading in the same direction up Bishopsgate.

The constable appeared again, solemn and stately, no doubt thinking of his breakfast still an hour and a half away, yet going through the same motions he had performed since midnight: the guardian of law and order in the dog watch of an uneventful night.

'Time to sneak off, then,' Spear turned to the other men who were already gathering their possessions together, ready for departure.

Then Spear's head cocked at the sound of hooves and wheels. A cab coming up from Cheapside, reining in and drawing to a halt, as though depositing a passenger before pulling away again. As it passed, Spear had the feeling it was the same cab that Ember was using. Fragments of unease began to prick at his mind. The cab turned into Bishopsgate and, as it did so, a small figure flitted across the shop window. Spear knew the dark shadow and the manner of walking. Ember. A moment later a rapid low tapping at the shop door confirmed his observations.

'Something's up,' he called to Terremant who was already springing to the bolts.

Ember heard the policeman's footsteps fading down the street, leaving only the sound of one of the gas mantles popping away, burning through, in the main shop. He looked across at the safe, wondering how long it would take him to jack the door off; pulling out his watch as though to reassure himself of the time. Ten minutes to four. There was a little less than half an hour before they planned to disperse two to Houndsditch; five minutes later two to the Minories, leaving Ember alone, vulnerable with his brief bag of tools, waiting for the cab.

Ember made up his mind in double quick time, going down on his knees and calling through the hole to the cellar, for Franz to get up on the packing case.

'There's got to be a change of plan,' he said softly, so that the others would not hear. 'This damned place is to be open tomorrow, so I'll have to do the safe now.'

Franz muttered some oath in German, then, angrily, 'It won't do. The Boss will not be able to get rid of the glass till Sunday.'

'Well, he'll have to hang on to it. Pass my bag up and then warn Evans that we're not pulling out as agreed. I want you to watch the clock. I'll go out at half four, ride round the houses in the cab and give him instructions. You're to stay here.'

'Evans can give the instructions.' Franz was alert, suspicious even.

'I'm not letting him near the cab. It's my life . . .'

'He's been a good crow.'

'Being a crow is one thing. Working a plan is another matter. I'll be held responsible, not him. Sling the tools up here and let me get on. I'll be away at half four and back in ten minutes, but I'm going to open this tin before dawn so let's move.'

Franz did not look happy, nevertheless he shrugged and handed up the heavy bag. Ember stationed himself near the hinge side of the safe door, took out a thin flat jemmy together with the jack-in-the-box, and set to work. Inserting the jemmy in the crack between the door and the casing of the safe, he began to work it gently, removing all traces of paint, dust and grime just below the top hinge, opening the aperture to its widest natural extent. He then performed a similar operation below the bottom hinge. By the time this was finished, the constable was going round once more, and Ember had to slide out of sight, close to the wall, dragging the tools with him.

Once the all clear was given, he left the brief bag where it was, advancing on the safe again, armed only with a spanner cum lever key and the jack-in-the-box. The instrument was heavy, made in beautifully turned brass, the underside being circular, like an elongated drum, through which ran a strong screw, pointed at one end and cut square at the other to fit the spanner. This was normally used rather like a drill, the pointed end being inserted into a lock and then screwed home from the other end with the spanner, so that the lock was cracked open and the innards gouged out. An unsubtle though sure method of lock breaking.

However, it was the upper part of the tool which concerned Ember. This was a simple vice, but with jaws which ran upwards in two lips. When closed it was as though a pair of abnormally wide chisels were pressed together. This vice was worked by a solid screw on the side of the instrument, the end of the screw being a brass ball through which a hole just fitted the lever key end of the spanner.

Ember inserted the lips of the jack into the crack below the top hinge, sliding the lever key in place. Slowly he began to turn the key until the two lips started to press outwards on either side of the crack. Pulling heavily on the key, immense pressure was brought to bear on the door and main casing of the safe, literally jacking the two sections apart.*

Ember heaved, rested, and heaved again, putting all his force behind each pull on the lever key, then stopping to regather his breath and strength. On the sixth attempt he felt the door give slightly at the hinge. Then came the signal to stop work again. He quickly unwound the jack shut and retired to his corner until the copper once more moved out of range.

Time was pressing and he needed the policeman out of the way. He also had to make sure of the cabbie. Leaving the jack by the brief bag near the wall, Ember slid over to the hole and let himself gently down into the cellar. The time was now twenty minutes past four.

*The jack-in-the-box was capable of lifting three tons in weight. Any safe or door not built to withstand this pressure was bound to give way. (Noel Currer-Briggs: *Contemporary Observations on Security from the Chubb Collectanea 1818-1968.*) It will be noted that this was an old safe, dating before 1860.

'When I get back I shall need some brute force up there,' he said, panting, to Franz. 'Have you warned Evans?'

'It's all done; but, Ember, if you are pulling the cross, I'll see you in hell myself,' he threatened, his clipped accent flat and without any theatrical menace.

'Why should I cross you? We're all in this together with good shares when we bleed the boodle.'*

'See you don't cross me, Ember.'

Franz might prove difficult yet, and it flashed through Ember's mind that if the Professor was satisfied with the results of this night's work – if he did bring Schleifstein to heel – Franz would not be one to have at his back in the future.

He crept out of the cellar door, up the steps and across the yard, down to the end of the lane.

'No sign of the copper or the cab,' muttered Evans. 'What's the word?'

'You go back to the cellar and wait for me. I'll not be gone long. Just stay quiet.'

Evans was off, a silent shadow clinging to the wall. Ember positioned himself at the end of the lane, watching for the constable while his ears were pricked for the cab. It came, from the direction of Cornhill, some two minutes later, and, as it drew abreast of the lane, Ember sprang forward, grabbing for the door handle and calling up to the cabbie, 'Take me round to Old Broad Street and pull up – out of the way of any of the bluebellies.'

The cabbie whipped up his pair, passing the turn to Threadneedle Street, on up to the next left turn which took them across to Old Broad Street which ran parallel to Bishopsgate.

They pulled up just before the Excise Office, on the left hand side. Not a soul in sight, only shadows thrown by the gas

*A strange expression, but I have put it into Ember's mouth because it is mentioned three times in the Moriarty Journals. Presumably Moriarty heard it in America, so it would be known by Ember. It of course means 'share the loot'. Eric Partridge, in his invaluable *Dictionary of the Underworld*, cites its use in 1895 by J. W. Sullivan, *Tenement Tales of New York*. Flexner in his *Dictionary of American Slang* does not list this variant but notes that in 1893 the word boodle was already archaic.

standards onto the still wet streets. Above them the night had become pitch; the last hours before dawn.

'Can you give yourself a story for tonight?' asked Ember of the driver. 'There's been an alteration. I want you to leave the cab as though it was tomorrow.'

'In Helen's Place?'

'That's it.'

Saint Helen's Place had been fixed as the rendezvous for the following night, being on the opposite side of Bishopsgate and a fair way up from the robbery site. It was also a spot unlikely to cause suspicion.

The cabbie sucked at his teeth. 'If the price is right.'

'Another twenty guineas,' Ember blurted.

'That'll see me fair. When?'

'With the rest, as arranged. You know me.'

The driver nodded. 'I put it there now?'

'You take me up Cornhill and drop me on the right hand side. I'll show you where. Then you take her up to Helen's as fast as you can.'

'Jump up then guv'nor.'

Four minutes later Ember was tapping on the shop door opposite Freeland & Son.

'Best get hold of Blind Fred,' grunted Ben Tuffnell to young Saxby after much shaking of his head.

'Where?' asked the lad. He was feeling cold and not a little tired. He was also hungry. Too much liquor and not enough solids while waiting in the Chapel for the Nob.

'This time in the morning he'll be up near the Angel. I'd go myself, but – ' Tuffnell left the rest unsaid. It was not an excuse. His duty was to stay on watch at the German's house.

Saxby took an hour to find Blind Fred who was playing penny Nap in a sluicery which was no more than a cellar. The lad drew him to one side and whispered the urgency into his grubby, waxy ear. Fred looked uneasy once the message got fully home.

'Ben Tuffnell said I was to tell you,' Saxby made it sound apologetic. 'He said you'd know what to do.'

'Have to go to the fountainhead,' muttered Blind Fred. 'Nothing else for it. Have to go to Bert Jacobs. Can't get

Ember so he'll have to do. The girl's sleeping,' he bobbed his head towards the corner of the damp little cellar where a bundle of rags appeared to have been dumped in an unceremonious pile – Blind Fred's young daughter who guided him around the streets giving credence to his blind lie. 'You'll have to take me over to Notting Hill, lad.'

Saxby sighed, shivered and resigned himself to the chore of carting Blind Fred to wherever he wanted to go. Within five minutes they were out on the street again.

Ember blurted out the tale to Spear whose unease became more apparent by the second.

'What in tarnation's happened to the Nob? I'll rot the shirkster's bones if this is his making.'

'I have to get back before they catch my wind,' Ember was starting to sound plaintive. 'And I want that copper out of the way.'

'Never fear about the blue boy, we'll put him to sleep. I'm worried that you'll get clean away with the sparkling glass: and we'll not lay hands or eyes on any of you.'

Terremant was at Spear's side. 'We'll have to catch them in Edmonton, that's all,' he growled.

Spear nodded. 'Betteridge, get yourself in a blue suit, you'll be going on the beat, and pray that the copper's sergeant don't fancy an early morning stroll.' Then, to Ember, 'You get back to your job.'

As Ember closed the door behind him, he saw Betteridge climbing into one of the small pile of police uniforms that had been set ready for the following night.

Spear watched the grubby villain scamper across the road and disappear into Bishopsgate. He felt in his pocket, curling his fingers around the eel-skin – the short canvas sausage stuffed with sand, which he had taken to carrying. He exchanged a few brief words with Terremant, and grinned at Betteridge, who was now complete in his uniform with the broad-brimmed, combed helmet square on his head. Then he gave a come-on nod to Terremant and left the shop.

'Oh, constable, don't arrest me, I've a lakin and six nippers to support,' smiled Terremant as he followed Spear through the door.

Betteridge, unhappy in his disguise, waited, watching events from inside the doorway.

Spear and Terremant jog-trotted down to the narrow St Peter's Alley and waited out of sight, their eyes not leaving the corner of Bishopsgate. Within five minutes the police constable appeared and had hardly got around the corner when Terremant set off running towards him, shouting and waving, his voice shrill.

'Murder,' he yelled, 'Bloody murder, help.'

The constable, deflected from his normal round, began to run towards Terremant, and as the two met, the big punisher let fly a babble of information – 'Over there ... there ... in the alley ... it's a woman ... Oh my God it's horrible ... murder ...' And with these cries he almost pushed the hapless policeman into St Peter's Alley and into the arms of the waiting Spear.

Terremant knocked his helmet off and spun him around while Spear delivered the blow with his eel-skin, hard to the base of the skull. The copper folded up like a concertina, only uttering a short grunt as the wind went out of him.

Terremant doubled back to the shop, tipping the wink to Betteridge, who slid out into the street and began to pace the swooning constable's beat.

Back in St Peter's Alley, they dragged the copper up to the church railings, pulled his greatcoat down to his elbows, took off his boots and strapped his belt around his knees. Then, lifting him back, they pushed his wrists through the railings. Spear went into the churchyard as Terremant unlaced one of the boots. Using the laces, Spear secured the wrists. They then gagged him with his own socks.

'First time a copper tasted his own feet,' laughed Spear.

They returned to the alley entrance to stand guard, well acquainted with the dangers of the deception, particularly as Betteridge would have to pass uncomfortably close to the police station in Bishopsgate. The quicker Ember got on with matters the better. Once they were safe the uniforms would have to be got out of the shop and over to some other secure spot. Like as not to Bermondsey. In any case, they would have to be used smartly, and in daylight – a prospect which concerned Spear, for there was a great difference between carrying out a deception and nabbing a gang under cover of darkness, and doing the same thing in the full light of day. Particularly as it would mean a frontal charge on the house in Edmonton.

In the meantime, Betteridge walked the streets as a constable, Ember worked on the safe, and Spear together with Terremant, awaited results.

As soon as he got back to the cellar, Ember took the two Germans, Peter and Claus, up through the access hole into the shop. Evans returned to the look-out, and Franz stayed by the door.

They worked in strict rota, each of them exerting as much pressure on the jack's lever as was possible, then handing over to the next man. Within ten minutes the upper hinge was responding, starting to move and come away. Then Franz gave a low call, denoting that the beat man was again about to pace by. A minute later, the huge German's head appeared in the hole.

'Evans says he's working the other side of the road,' he called.

'Change is as good as a rest, so they say,' grinned Ember, thinking that Betteridge was using his loaf.

The upper hinge cracked some five minutes later. Claus was working the key when it happened, quite suddenly and with some noise, for it took the dirty unkempt rogue by surprise, causing him to fall forward, dislodging the lever key which rolled back to the wall and into the cellar with a clanging echo.

Franz retrieved it, and they began on the lower hinge, setting the jack into the crack just below the hinge itself. For half an hour it did not budge, and in that time they only stopped work once at Franz's command to Evans' signal.

In the few minutes which passed while they waited to carry on, Ember died a thousand deaths, his mind swarming with the worst possibilities – Betteridge discovered, something going wrong at Spear's end of the business. He could smell himself as he crouched near the wall – not his usual unwashed aroma, but the stench of fear rising from his pores and bowels, hating himself for this tangible evidence of cowardice. Then the moment was past, and they were back at the safe, working the jack until their muscles ached at full stretch and the breath became short with exertion.

Outside, the day was beginning to sneak its way through the overcast, the first traces of light above the rooftops. In the streets life was starting up, carts and vans beginning to roll and early workers stirring and moving on the pavements. In the houses lights blinked windows into being.

It was almost twenty minutes to six when the bottom hinge tore away.

Over by St Peter's Church, the policeman groaned and moved. Spear, at the top of the alley, whispered to Terremant that they could not risk waiting longer. The uniforms would have to be moved from the shop. They had to abandon things now or risk being seen near the copper.

'We'll send a lurker back once we're clear,' he murmured as they hurried up Cornhill. 'You'll have to get over to Bermondsey while I acquaint the Professor with what has become of matters.'

In the meantime, the Professor slept soundly and alone. He had been a mite on edge during the previous evening and decided to dispense with the services of either Sal or Carlotta. After all, if anything went amiss he did not want women cluttering his mind.

After dinner he sat by himself in the drawing-room, played a little Chopin and then took a bottle of brandy, a pack of playing cards, and his copy of Professor Hoffman's *Modern Magic* to his bedroom. He wanted to practise the six methods of changing one card for another, so he sat for a long time, before the tall mirror in his room, going through the sleights time and again. It calmed him powerfully, and finally when half of the brandy had gone, Moriarty undressed, climbed into bed and lapsed into a deep sleep, during which he dreamed of performing incredible tricks with a pack of cards made up of portraits – Schleifstein, Grisombre, Sanzionare, Segorbe, Crow and Holmes being the prominent pictures which sped, riffled, were palmed, made to appear and disappear at will in his dexterous hands. The clamour of the doorbell in the early hours did not penetrate his unconsciousness.

They were all there, the tiaras, earrings, necklaces, throwing glittering fire from their velvet-lined boxes and black velvet bags. Even in the gaslight, and with the early morning taste bitter in their mouths, the three men around the safe could not fail to sense the beauty of their haul.

Ember called to Franz, telling him to get Evans off to pick up the cab in St Helen's Place and get back. 'As if he's carrying the wind.'

Franz threw up the canvas bag they had brought for the loot and disappeared to find Evans. It was all speed now, and the Germans were as excited as boys let out from the schoolroom. Ember, who had been raised on the Professor's stern discipline as far as crackings were concerned, had to shut them up with threats. In spite of the need for haste, he took grave care in selecting the items from the safe and stowing them away in the bag, making positive that he had all the gems of real value before laying a finger on the trays of rings and watches which were Mr Freeland's stock. Last he jammed back the heavy door, leaning it against the safe, so that it might just pass muster to any real policeman squinting through the Judas slits in the shutters. Then, with a quick nod, he allowed the other two to clamber down into the cellar, before grabbing up the brief bag of tools and the canvas sack and making his final descent through the floor.

He was half-way down the lane to Bishopsgate when he heard the police whistles from up the street.

Betteridge had no option. He was plodding up Threadneedle Street, from the direction of the Royal Exchange, when he saw the sergeant bearing down on him from the Bishopsgate end. Bill Betteridge had much experience of the police, and not a little of the Houses of Correction. He was not of a mind to tussle with this burly sergeant, so he had no option: he turned on his heel and ran pell mell back from whence he came.

The sergeant, thinking some crime was being committed, or that Betteridge was in full chase of a villain, pulled on his whistle chain, blew three blasts and followed what he thought was his constable.

The shrill blasts from Threadneedle Street carried up

Bishopsgate to the ears of a pair of constables arriving at the station for the six o'clock shift. Being men of some character, they replied with answering blasts and started to run. At that very moment, Evans turned the four-wheeler out of St Helen's Place.

The police whistles sent a crazy streak of panic through Evans' head. Convinced the police were on top of him, he whipped up the horses and took the cab at speed, careering down the street. It was an action which set the pair of constables running at an even faster pace, both blowing their whistles and reaching for their truncheons.

Evans slewed the cab across the road, reining up the horses to bring it in close to the pavement hard by the alley leading to the back of Freeland & Son. He misjudged badly, going past and pulling up a good ten yards on, so that the four men crouched in the lane were forced to run in the open, down the pavement, scrabbling for the door and safety.

Ember was the last in, throwing the canvas bag in front of him as he leapt aboard, shouting to Evans, yelling at him to whip up the horses. Evans needed no bidding, being thoroughly rattled by this time, and they were away with such a jolt that Ember was almost toppled backwards into the road. As it was, his fingers were banged hard on the door causing him to release the brief bag, sending it flying into the roadway in the path of the two pursuing constables, one of whom hurled his truncheon after the departing vehicle.

Ember was shouting curses in the cramped interior of the cab. He knew that he should have used a canary – some woman to get the tools and the loot away in the opposite direction. Now they were marked in the cab. They would have to abandon it before long and make their separate ways back to Edmonton – with the canvas bag: and he would not be allowed to go alone, not with the loot. Franz would stick to him like they were frozen brothers.

They let the two Germans off near Finsbury Square, then left the cab in a side street off the City Road. Evans went off on his own with instructions to get to Edmonton using every back double he could find. Ember was right. Franz stayed with him as though they were manacled.

Bertram Jacobs personally woke the Professor shortly after six. Polly Pearson had been cleaning the grates – sometime between five and half past – when the bell had clanged from the tradesman's entrance down the area steps. Martha was in the kitchen seeing to the early morning chores, getting Bridget Spear's breakfast and stoking up the oven fire.

She was, not unnaturally, taken aback at the sight of the ragged Blind Fred and the little scrawny boy standing at the foot of the area steps. Taking them to be beggars, she was about to slam the door on them when Fred stuck his white stick into the jamb.

'Bert Jacobs, and be quick about it, girl, or I can promise you that you'll not hear the end of it from your master.'

An unpleasant smell emanated from the blind beggar's body. The reek of unwashed flesh; of grime and rancid fat in the hair and stale spirits on the breath. A smell which brought back stark memories to Martha Pearson, recalling the nights immediately prior to her salvation by Sal Hodges, when, with her sister, she spent nightmare hours in the lowest of common lodging houses.

Blind Fred struck a chord, however, and Bertram Jacobs was brought, dishevelled with sleep, to the kitchen. When the tale had been heard out, in the privacy of what had once been the butler's pantry, Jacobs ordered the lurker and Saxby to wait while he talked with the Professor.

At a quarter before seven, Moriarty met with both the Jacobs brothers. Lee Chow, Blind Fred and Saxby, in his study – the latter pair ill at ease amidst the somewhat paradoxical austere luxury of that room.

Moriarty spoke little, as though some white-hot burning anger consumed his most private thoughts. He questioned both Saxby and Blind Fred in some detail before dispatching the lad back to Cornhill to scout the lie of the land, and perhaps pick up rumour and fact on the ground.

At twenty-past seven Spear arrived, flushed and grimly disturbed. The robbery had taken place – fully, with his cooperation regarding the local beat policeman. Word was that the team had got clean away, though there had been unpleasant moments and a pursuit of some sort. Betteridge was missing. Apart from that all they could do was await events.

'I'll have none of it,' Moriarty was steady now, a hint of stubborn determination in his manner. 'If we await events, then we have lost this opportunity of laying Schleifstein and he'll be away to his midden in Berlin with the loot.'

His head oscillated slowly, that reptilian gesture of old which brought words of holy scripture unbidden into Spear's head – *And he laid hold on the dragon, that old serpent, which is the Devil, and Satan, and bound him a thousand years:* a vivid picture recalled from some unwilling Sunday School past.

'How long to get your punishers to Bermondsey?' Moriarty glowered at Spear.

'Terremant was seeking them out after he stowed the uniforms.'

'As quick as you can then. Get them together, dress them as you would have done for our original plot, then have them driven like Pegasus to Edmonton and beard the Prooshan poacher in his own lurk.'

'It's dangerous . . .'

'Of course it's dangerous, Spear. Do you think I pay you to sit at home and knit mittens? I part with chink for you to do my bidding. If there are any who don't like it they can fester at the Lump Hotel with my compliments.'

'The Helmets are City Police . . .'

'So the City Police will be thought to be poaching also. There's your answer. You'll have to fight the Metropolitans as well as the German gonophs. Great heavens, Spear, I've not seen you as cautious before.' Moriarty laughed, deep, throaty and uncompromising, turning to the Jacobs brothers. 'Spear will direct you,' the laugh was reflected by a smile which bore no hint of humour. 'Take the fools quick, with the sable maria outside the door and you'll be able to whip 'em over to Bermondsey with no questions asked.'

The Jacobs brothers both nodded assent.

'Go to it then,' Moriarty's hand raised imperiously to indicate the interview was finished. 'Tell Harkness I want my hansom here in one hour. I shall be coming over to see our friends when you've nibbed them. That's a pleasure I have been awaiting.'

Spear knew there was no arguing with him, for Moriarty

had put too much into the trap to see it sprung on nothing now. With solemn nods they withdrew, leaving the Professor alone with Lee Chow.

'You wish I come Bermondsey?' asked the Chinese.

'It might be as well.' A smile creeping slyly across the Professor's mouth. 'I will go as my more familiar self. Arm yourself, Lee Chow, and be ready for Harkness and the cab.'

He then went upstairs to his room in order to effect the disguise he had so often worn in the old days: donning the corset which helped make him rake-thin, the harness which held him in a permanent stoop, the boots with raised soles to give him extra height, and the incredibly natural bald pate wig which provided him with the domed forehead.

After dressing in the black clothes of a professional man, James Moriarty seated himself before his mirror, armed with the brushes, colours and other artificial aids in the craft of disguise. Then, with deft strokes, he turned himself into the living likeness of his long dead brother: the Professor of Mathematics whom the world regarded as the true James Moriarty, Professor of Evil, Napoleon of Crime.

By half-past nine, there were six punishers, not counting Terremant, gathered at the Bermondsey store house. Spear saw to it that they were all dressed as smartly as could be managed in the uniforms which were to have been worn for nabbing the raiders in Cornhill. In the first plan, the Jacobs brothers were to have gone, with Terremant, masquerading as plain clothes jacks, to take Schleifstein. Now they would all be involved.

Spear was far from happy when he looked at the helmets of those in police uniform, bearing as they did the dragon crest of the City force – a symbol which would instantly bring them under suspicion if they were seen carrying out a duty on the preserves of the Metropolitan Police Force. Spear was a sensible villain, and the last thing he wanted was an act of violence against even one member of the official police.

Bertram Jacobs was to take charge of the assault, for Spear was too well known to Schleifstein to show his face near the Edmonton house, and so tip the wink that the 'arrests' were not as they seemed.

'Treat Ember a bit brutal,' Spear counselled. 'Just for the effect. You'll not want a roughhouse in the back of the van on your way over. It might cause you to be more noticed than normal. You and William carrying barkers?'

Bertram nodded, lifting his jacket to reveal the long curved butt of the French Service double-action revolver which protruded from his belt.

'Only use it if it's to silence somebody you cannot take.'

'Don't worry. We know what we're about.'

'And you have the way of the place in your head?'

'Ember talked enough of it. They mostly live in the dining-room to the right of the hall. The guv'nor's room is first floor front. I'll take him myself.'

They were about to climb into the black Maria, which stood in the yard behind the buildings, when Betteridge arrived, flushed and tired, having discarded his police uniform at a girl shop in Gill Street near the West India docks. Spear quickly decided that Betteridge had done enough deception for one day and decreed that he should stay at Bermondsey to await the prisoners.

Ember was all in, nervous and jumpy as a bag of fleas. All the way back to Edmonton he had expected an arm to fall on him: the canvas bag being so conspicuous and Franz so certainly suspicious. Schleifstein, however, was overjoyed after the first irritation and dismay of hearing that the whole thing had been cracked in one night.

The German took the bag up to his bedroom while Wellborn and the greasy-haired boy fed them with bacon, bread and dripping, washed down by tea the colour of brown ale. It did much to revive Ember's spirits, though Franz continued to treat him with wary looks.

Peter and Claus got back, on foot, shortly after eight, announcing that there had been no bother. Evans, plainly frightened after his ordeal with the cab, arrived some fifteen minutes after that.

Slowly the tension of the night gave way to an atmosphere of boastful jesting, in which Ember found it difficult to join, knowing as he did, that there was likely to be an affray before the day was out.

A little after nine, Schleifstein sent for the boy, and a few minutes later Ember heard the lad come down and go out by the street door. Five minutes after, the German leader came into the dining-room and asked Ember to join him upstairs.

The canvas bag was laid out on the floor and the gems were on the bed, put down with care and order. Schleifstein's face showed good humour.

'You have kept your word, Mr Ember. It is as good a haul as I have ever seen. Once we get the stones out of the country no doubt word will go round that I put up for this night's work. I should imagine that will enhance my reputation among family people in London.'

'Greatly.'

'I do not wish for the stones to be here over long.' He could not take his eyes off the bed with its precious load. The most valuable counterpane in the history of crime. 'I would have preferred it if they had not been brought here until tomorrow morning, but what is done is done. The boy has gone to fetch one of the captains who will be transporting these pretty things.'

Ember's heart sank. It was possible that the Professor would miss the catch after all.

'They'll be safe enough here,' he said. 'You trust this man?'

Schleifstein's leathery face broke into a thin smile, which did not get as far as his eyes.

'His wife and children are in Berlin. He'll no more cross me than sail bows on into a reef.'

Downstairs the doorbell rang softly – a tinkling which seemed to echo in Ember's head like a dozen tiny musical boxes. The German's face showed only a passing interest.

'He'll be taking the larger pieces,' he continued. 'The tiaras and necklaces.'

Voices were raised below. Then a shout followed by the crash of a pistol shot.

Ben Tuffnell had watched the coming and goings at the Edmonton house, from his pitch across the road, and was wholly alert behind a mask of disinterest. The road was not over-crowded when the black maria drew up, just around the corner, and few people paid it any heed. Tuffnell saw the

Jacobs brothers and Terremant climb from the rear, muffled in greatcoats, and begin walking calmly towards the German's house. The other punishers, clad as police constables, stayed back by the van around the corner, and did not move forward until Bertram Jacobs mounted the steps and tugged gently at the dirty brass bell pull. The uniformed men walked in file, unhurried, nor did the fellow at the reins of the black Maria urge his horses on until he had a sign that the door was being opened.

Bertram Jacobs stood at the top of the steps, one hand inside his coat, resting on the butt of the revolver. His brother and Terremant were on either side, a little below him, on the steps.

The towering Franz opened up.

'We are police officers,' said Bert Jacobs, pushing forward.

Franz tried to slam the door in his face and dodge back into the hall, but both the Jacobs and Terremant had their weight forward and were in the hall as Franz staggered back, shouting in German that the police were there. The uniformed punishers were running now, doubling up the steps as Franz reached inside his jacket, heaved out a big revolver and fired once.

The bullet took one of the punishers – a stocky bruiser named Pug Parsons – in the chest, toppling him back down the steps, where he lay groaning, the blue uniform sodden with blood. There was screaming and shouts from the street behind them as Terremant leaped forward and brought his neddy – the small weighted cudgel he carried – hard down on Franz's wrist, and then, as the man turned, again to the side of his head.

Both the Jacobs boys were leaping up the stairs, while their uniformed colleagues smashed into the dining-room to collar those who were already trying to make an escape out of the front window.

Schleifstein was caught quite unawares, his face a mixture of shock and anger, eyes showing that he only dimly grasped at events as he half reached for the table drawer.

'We'll take you alive,' snapped Bertram Jacobs, showing the revolver – arm outstretched – as his brother grabbed Ember, turning him around and snapping handcuffs on his wrists, before shoving him unceremoniously against the wall.

Bertram was following suit with the German, who was now cursing alternately in his own language and English. It took less than a minute to dump the loot from the bed back into the canvas sack, William throwing a glance out of the window seeing a crowd gathering in the street as the uniformed men bundled the others into the back of the van.

Another minute saw them forcing Schleifstein and Ember down the narrow staircase and out, down the stone steps. At the bottom, one of the punishers was lifting Pug Parsons' head to see what could be done.

'He's dead,' the punishers grunted at Bertram as they negotiated their way past the body.

'Then leave him,' hissed Jacobs prodding at Schleifstein's back with the revolver barrel.

It had taken less than six minutes from start to finish, and, as the black maria clattered off, Terremant peered from the barred rear window – their prisoners all shut away in the little lockups which ran down each side of the van's interior. Through the crowd, he saw a pair of police constables running towards the commotion.

'Get a breeze on,' Terremant called softly. 'The bobbies are on their way.'

Just before Lee Chow and the Professor left for Bermondsey, Saxby arrived back at Albert Square with the news that there was a mighty hue and cry going on around Bishopsgate and Cornhill. The beat policeman had been found, bound and gagged at the railing of St Peter's Church; and on good evidence it appeared that the gang of robbers had left their tools behind. As the tools of a good cracksman were regarded as a 'signature', the police were confident that with these in their possession, they would not be long in apprehending the villains.

The Professor was silent on hearing the news. At last he turned to Lee Chow, as though about to say something of importance.

Lee Chow spoke before him. 'You wish to go St John's Wood, chop-chop?'

Again Moriarty weighed the matter before speaking. 'No.

You come with me to Bermondsey first. I do not like going abroad in the present climate without at least one of my Guard with me. When you have seen me safe there, you will go and settle matters in St John's Wood.'

It was a bumpy, cramped and uncomfortable ride in the police van out to Bermondsey. For one thing there were only six compartments for the prisoners, which meant keeping Ember out in the narrow passage with the punishers. There was little enough room anyway, and the vehicle swayed perilously, creaking with the unaccustomed weight.

Nobody challenged them, but it was with intense relief that they finally turned into the yard behind the store house and offices.

Six rooms and the large hallway had been made presentable. Tables and chairs were set in the hall, and meagre cots in the rooms, which had their windows securely barred. While these windows had been safe when the place was bought, the doors were only equipped with cheap locks, so during the previous week the Jacobs brothers had seen to it that strong mortice locks were added, together with iron plates and Judas' squints. The whole of this section of the building had been cleaned and whitewashed so that Schleifstein and his followers might well have been forgiven for thinking that they had been brought to some official centre.

They were all reasonably docile now, though anger was visible on each face, together with truculence in the case of Franz who had been told throughout the journey that he would be for Jack Ketch's apple tree – all of them being witness to his shooting the man on the steps at Edmonton.

Spear stayed hidden until the prisoners were all divided up, searched for the second time, and locked away. He took the news of Pug Parsons' death badly – not only because Parsons was an old comrade, but also for the fact that it had been necessary to leave his body in plain view at Edmonton. He agreed, however, that there had been no other course of action open to them.

A watch was set on the street, and Spear took charge of the canvas bag. Presently Harkness drove Moriarty's personal cab into the yard.

There was an audible intake of breath, from punishers and members of the Praetorian Guard alike, when the Professor entered the building, for this was the first time since arriving from America, that Moriarty had appeared in the guise of his famous brother.

It was one of the legends which James Moriarty had created – his ability to flit in and out of two personas. With his own particular sense of drama, he stood in the doorway for a moment, allowing his followers to take in the transformation to the full. The tall thin figure with stooped shoulders, the gaunt face, hollow eyes and thin lips: it was a truly masterly and complete disguise, and to be sure, Moriarty himself was well aware of this change each time he made it: for had he not disposed of his academic brother with his own hands in order to step neatly into his character, together with the aura of respect which surrounded it?

'Is all done?' he asked. Even his voice appeared to have altered slightly, becoming older and more in keeping with the body he occupied.

Spear stepped forward. 'They're all safe here. As is the booty.'

Moriarty nodded. 'No difficulties?'

Spear recounted the manner in which Parsons had died and the Professor sighed, taking the news, it appeared philosophically.

'Bring in the Berliner then,' he said at last.

The Jacobs brothers disappeared into the room where Schleifstein was lodged, and a second or two later brought the two great underworld leaders face to face.

The shock to Schleifstein's system was apparent from the moment the German set eyes on the Professor, his leathery skin suddenly drained and taking on the brittle yellow grain of old notepaper. His hands shook, and for a moment it looked as though he would be smitten with a seizure.

'What is this game?' he croaked out at last, reaching forward to lean on the table in order to remain standing.

'Good day, my dear Wilhelm,' the Professor spoke softly, his eyes never leaving Schleifstein's face for a second. 'Did you not expect me?' The voice rising a fraction. 'Did you really think I would allow you to put up a big screwing in my own garden? Would you have allowed me the same privilege in Berlin, even if I had asked pardon – which *you* did not?'

'You were . . .' Schleifstein's voice trailed away. He said something else but it was too indistinct to be heard by those present.

'Away? Abroad? In America? I was an absent tenant. Is that what you thought? When the cat's away? But I was forgetting, you and your cronies in France, Italy and Spain gave backword to all that we agreed, did you not?'

'My dear Professor,' the German appeared to have recovered a shade. 'You were under siege, your empire was being assaulted by the law.'

'So you decided that you would also assault it from within. Instead of standing together, you decided to divide. To drop me overboard like a bagful of rats. And you call yourself a leader; you think you cracked a fine crib, did you? Well, as you can see, you could not have sniffed near it but for me. How do you think it was really done? By one of my own, Wilhelm. How do you think the place was watched and the coppers taken care of, eh?'

'What do you want?'

'What do you think?'

'The loot.'

Moriarty's laugh was a howl of derision. 'The loot. No, sir, I have that already. What I want is the respect due to me. The acknowledgement that I am the natural leader of all our agencies here and on the continent. I wish to re-establish the alliance so that it may be run properly and not in this haphazard manner in which it founders at the moment – this come and do as you please confusion, which is worse than the chaos of established society.'

Schleifstein spread his hands. 'I will talk with the others, I will . . .'

'You'll talk to no person but me. The others will be dealt with in turn. There'll be no shirksters and they must all see for themselves that, in matters concerning family people, I am their master and the natural leader. Do you affirm that, Wilhelm Schleifstein?'

Schleifstein's face twisted in a contortion of anger. 'In

Berlin I would have you squashed like a beetle.'

'But we are in London, Wilhelm,' the Professor soothed. 'With you here at my mercy, I should not wonder I could gain power among your people in Berlin. Maybe I should do that.'

There was a long pause, Schleifstein's eyes shifting from side to side, like a beast trapped and looking for a clear way.

Moriarty laughed, a deep cackle. 'Wilhelm, you put up for an admirable screwing, only it was I who was really managing the affair – my people, my plan. If I spread the word...?' He allowed the sentence to hang, unfinished in the air.

All eyes were turned to the German.

'I could have been harder. I could still be utterly ruthless,' Moriarty did not smile. 'I merely ask for you to accept me as the natural leader. Come, I have proved it – and will do so to the others.'

The silence seemed endless, then Schleifstein shuddered, a long-drawn sigh, half anger and half capitulation. 'I know when I am bested,' he spoke low and tremulous. 'I have never given in easily, Moriarty, but you have me baulked – I believe that is the expression. I could go on fighting you, but where's the point?' In his attempt to remain dignified in defeat, the German succeeded only in looking even more of a beaten man. 'I always thought your grand design for the denizens of crime in Europe was sound enough. It was your failure at Sandringham and the rout of your family people that made me wonder.'

'You need wonder no more, then. I am back. Things will be as they were.'

'Then you have proved me a little your inferior. I will assist you in convincing the others.'

'I will convince them myself while you rot here a while. My aim, is as it always was. To control the underworld of Europe, and to that end I spin webs which are invisible to the naked eye. You are proof of that.'

Angus McCready Crow had gone through one of the most difficult days of his career, and he knew that the night would possibly be even worse: though in a different manner. To his lasting surprise, the Commissioner had accepted Sylvia's injudicious invitation to dine on the night of Saturday, 21

November, and in some ways, Crow had reasoned, this was an honour. He had been most firm with Sylvia, demanding, nay ordering, her to see to the preparation of the meal with her own hands. There had been some argument at first, Sylvia claiming that you did not keep a dog and bark yourself. Angus Crow retaliated, saying that you barked d---d loudly if the dog was an untrained bitch, and so finally won the skirmish.

But he had not bargained for what the day would bring. It began quietly enough, in his office at Scotland Yard, when Tanner came in with the news of a large and audacious jewel robbery in the City.

'Thousands of pounds, I understand. Their local beat man trussed like a chicken, and the safe door jacked off. Freeland & Son. The City boys will be running about like scalded cats. I'm glad we are not implicated.'

Crow pricked up his ears at the news of a robbery of some magnitude. Since hearing old Bolton's story, he had been on the *qui vive* for matters such as this. It could well be the one. He questioned Tanner closely, but all his sergeant could add was that someone had mentioned the villains leaving their tools behind.

Crow still regarded the telephone as a new-fangled invention of the devil – a strange attitude in one of such a radical persuasion – but on this occasion there was need to use it. He immediately got in touch with one of his few friends in the City Police – an inspector named John Clowes, a neat, bearded and reserved man, most shrewd in his dealings with the criminal fraternity.

Clowes, he soon discovered, was touchy over the question of the robbery, as well he might be, for his force had been made to look red-faced by the affair. However, he finally admitted to Crow that they had a set of burglary tools, dropped when the thieves fled from Bishopsgate.

'I wonder if you'd do me the honour of letting me have a wee look at them?' Crow asked. 'I have my reasons. I may well be able to identify them, and if I can do that I shall be able to name the rogue who last had his hands on the things.'

Grudgingly, Clowes said he would seek permission for his colleague to come over and examine the evidence.

One look told Crow that the brief bag, and various articles, were those which he had seen many times at old Tom Bolton's place in St John's Wood.

'You'll be looking for a fellow that's probably on your books,' he said dourly. 'He's certainly on ours. Nick Ember, a nasty little piece of work who used to be in the employ of one James Moriarty – of whom you have no doubt heard.'

'Ah-ha, the omnivorous Professor,' Clowes, seated behind his desk, placed the tips of the fingers of both hands together and appeared to be counting them off, separating each pair in turn and rejoining them. 'We all know of your involvement with the Professor, Angus. I know of Ember also, though I'm surprised he's turned cracksman. The tools are old and of extremely good quality.'

Crow indicated with a wink and a knowing look, that there was more to the tools than met the eye.

'I'll pass it on to the right quarter then, Angus.' Clowes rose and paced towards the door. 'You will doubtless inform us if you pull him first. We might like a word.'

'Anything to oblige,' beamed Crow. There was an unspoken rivalry between the two forces. 'In the meantime I'll make more enquiries concerning the tools. Good day, John, and my best wishes to your good lady.'

Crow felt unduly smug during the omnibus journey back to Scotland Yard. But there it ended, for there had been an affray in Edmonton and the Commissioner was shouting blue murder for him.

Tanner was already at the site when Crow got out to Edmonton, and the local police station people were milling around, taking statements and examining the ground.

As to the dead man, it was a puzzling business.

'I've been in touch with the City,' Tanner told him. 'They have no constable of that number, so it appears we have a dead policeman who was never a copper.'

Crow listened to the story as it unfolded – of a police raid, in plain view of passers-by; of one policeman being shot and of several men taken away in a police van. The number varied with the witnesses, for some said six or seven, others put the number as low as three, and in many cases as high as ten.

The neighbours were unhelpful. 'They kept themselves to themselves next door,' the lady of the adjoining house told

Crow. 'Mind you, I was glad of it. A rough crowd they seemed to be. Foreigners mostly.'

'What do you mean, mostly?'

'Well,' she was uncertain about it. 'I did hear them speaking English, but it was mainly a foreign lingo. German, I think my hubby said it was.'

Crow tramped through the house with Tanner at his heels. There were signs of a fight downstairs, while a table had been overturned in the first floor front bedroom. Crow made notes and returned to the Yard, worried, with several ideas, strands in the wind, which would not take formal shape. The Commissioner wanted to see him almost as soon as he was back in his office. Crow found him unsympathetic and bullying.

'People masquerading as police officers, Crow. It's the thin end of the wedge, even though they were in City plumage. You'll get to the bottom of it, or I'll have you back on the beat.'

It was an affront to Crow's pride, particularly as the man was dining with him this very evening. He blushed scarlet.

'What leads have you?' fired off the Commissioner. 'What clues?'

'Only one or two possible ideas. These things take a little time, sir, as you well know.'

'There'll be a public outcry. I've already told the newspapers that you are in command and I shouldn't be surprised if they are howling for your blood in the late editions. *The Times* will no doubt be carrying correspondence on the matter by Monday.'

'Well, sir, perhaps I'd best get on with my investigations.'

'Yes. Yes, of course, Crow. I don't mean to be hard on you, but there's going to be a row over this one.'

Crow, not unnaturally, took it out on Tanner, informing him that he must have all the statements taken at Edmonton in his possession by late afternoon. The Commissioner was demanding an early arrest. He then sat down to think out the logical explanation. There was obviously some link between this and the business in the City – unless it was a most unhappy coincidence: for he knew, from Clowes, that there appeared to have been a mythical policeman on the Cornhill-

Bishopsgate beat in the early hours.

If there was a connection, then it could easily be of great importance. Had not Tom Bolton told him that Ember had spoken of a German cracksman? After luncheon he would slip over to St John's Wood and have a word with Bolton. Perhaps the news that his tools had been used in the robbery would shock the old man into some unguarded statement.

There were four gentlemen of the Press waiting for Crow when he left the Yard for lunch. He parried their questions politely and told them, quite truthfully, that he was following one particular line of enquiry. It seemed to please them, and the detective pondered more on the business over a pint of ale and a pork pie in the select bar of a nearby hostelry.

It was one for Holmes, he decided. What would Watson have dubbed it? The Adventure of the Fraudulent Policeman? Crow finished his pie and left: first to send a note to Mr Holmes by Post Office messenger; then to take a hansom to St John's Wood where he alighted, as was his practice, a hundred yards or so from old Tom Bolton's dwelling.

It was now mid-afternoon and turning very cold, with the chimney smoke hanging like clouds over the rooftops. There was little breeze and Crow's head ached slightly as the chill bit around his nose and ears. Snow, he thought, snow in the air.

There was no reply to his double knock; no sound at all. He knocked again. Harder, the sound seeming to reverberate in the street. A woman with a small boy clinging to her hand walked past. On the other side of the road a wretched ragged urchin splashed along the wet gutter as though searching for treasure among the mud and leaves. A couple of hansoms clopped by. Still no sound from within the house.

Suddenly, Crow felt the hairs on his neck bristle and an appalling sense of foreboding swept over him. He left the front door, making his way around the side of the house to the rear, kitchen, entrance. He tried the door and it gave, immediately, to his push. All appeared cosy, as usual.

'Tom,' called Crow, but the silence appeared more intense than before. He crossed the room and opened the door to the front hall.

Old Tom Bolton lay on his back in the middle of the hall. One of his sticks was a few feet from the body, the other still clutched in his hand. The front of his shirt was soaking red with blood. Crow went down on one knee to examine the cadaver – he had no need for medical evidence to tell him that the man was dead, having, in his time, seen many a corpse. This one, however, was still warm, and the knife which had done the job remained protruding from Bolton's windpipe.

So it was that Angus Crow became implicated in a murder investigation on top of the shooting and strange affair in Edmonton. All in one day.

He was late, exasperated and tired when he got back to King Street where all was agitation for the impending dinner. Hardly had he set foot inside the door than Sylvia was chattering: telling him that he was late, that he would have to stir himself to be ready in time, that all was turmoil in the kitchen, that the butcher had sent the wrong cut of meat, that they had run short of best butter and Lottie had been sent for more, that they had only two bottles of claret left and would that be enough? Did he think her yellow crepon would be the right gown to wear, or would the blue silk be more in keeping with the evening?

Crow allowed this flow to go on unhindered for a few moments, he then raised his hand for silence.

'Sylvia,' he said with a firmness he could usually only muster when faced by those under his command, 'I have had to look upon two wretched creatures this day, both of whom have come to sudden and violent ends. I have no wish to look upon a third.'

The evening went off with few hitches. True, Crow was somewhat preoccupied with the business of the day and had one ear cocked for a knock at the front door – for he had asked Holmes to send a note direct to his home. But no message was forthcoming. The Commissioner unbent slightly, saying that he felt dining with the Crows was an excellent idea, as it gave him the opportunity to see how his officers lived. Sylvia bristled slightly when the Commissioner's lady referred to 63 King Street as 'your quaint little house'. But the fire merely smouldered.

The food, however, was of Sylvia's best – Julienne soup; slices of codfish in a Dutch sauce; saddle of mutton; apple tart – and when the ladies retired, leaving the gentlemen to their port, the Commissioner turned the conversation back to the events of the day.

Crow told him only facts – how the killing of old Tom Bolton was certainly connected with the jewel robbery in the city – keeping away from the suspicions which had become large and dark in his mind. Shortly after they joined the ladies, Lottie, who had managed to get through the evening without dropping anything, announced that Mr Tanner was at the door with a message for Crow.

The detective excused himself, half expecting a reply from Holmes. Instead, Tanner had been working overtime and now had a definite identification of the man found shot in Edmonton.

'Pug Parsons,' he announced blandly, as though this was a name rarely out of the newspapers. 'We've had him several times, sir. Some years ago he was quite a well-known Haymarket Hector – carried cash for some of Mrs Sal Hodges' girls.'

Crow's face lit up. 'So, by association, he had connections with friend Moriarty.'

'It would seem so. There is more if you would like to hear it. I am given to understand that Sal Hodges is very much in business again, with two new houses – at least she has been seen in two places that have recently opened.'

'So the money filched by Midas and Meunier may already be working in London.'

'Another point of great interest. The knife that killed old Bolton.'

'Yes.'

'Chinese origin, not sold in this country, but can be obtained in plentiful supplies in San Francisco.'

'Ember, Lee Chow and Spear,' Crow muttered to himself, certain sure now that there was a distinguishing pattern behind all that was happening.

'I'd give high odds that the German, Schleifstein, was at the house in Edmonton,' he said aloud. 'It makes sense. All of it. If Moriarty was rejected by his foreign friends, after the Sandringham business, he may well be on the rampage now, embroiled in some vast campaign of revenge. Let us presume, Tanner, that Schleifstein was involved – I cannot quite make sand nor moss of it all yet – then there are bound to be further intrigues which will include the other three – what are their names? – Sanzionare, the Frenchman Grisombre, and Segorbe. I wonder which one will be next?'

'If it is a pattern of revenge, sir, you can add another name.' Tanner swallowed hard, uncertain of his presumption.

'Who?' asked Crow sharply.

'Why, yourself, Mr Crow. You might well be on his list.'

Almost to the second that this conversation was taking place, James Moriarty was turning the pages in one of the leather-bound books of his coded journals.

He sat, propped up with pillows, in his bed, the book open on his lap. Sal Hodges was at the dressing table; completing her toilet.

The Professor turned to the back of the book – to the coded notes he kept of those six persons upon whom he planned to wreak subtle retribution. Taking up his fountain pen, Moriarty drew a thin line diagonally across the pages which had been devoted to Wilhelm Schleifstein.

He closed the journal and looked up, his face twisted into a wicked smile. Sal Hodges wrestled with her stays.

'Sal,' said the Professor. 'In a few weeks I shall be spending a little time in Paris. You will not be too put out if I do not invite you to accompany me?'

LONDON AND PARIS:
Saturday, 28 November 1896–
Monday, 8 March 1897

(The robbery of art)

The last Saturday in November was a busy day for the shop-keepers of Oxford Street and its environs. Not only did they have to keep their customers happy on that day, but also see to it that their stock was well ordered to cover the next few weeks. It was always the case as they neared Christmas. 'The shopping seems to begin earlier each year,' they would say to one another. Not that they complained, but, out of respect for the great Christian celebration, some of them put on wry faces and voiced their wonder at such a festival becoming more and more an excuse for gluttony and drunkeness, not to mention the plain extravagance which preceded it.

Even in Orchard Street, Charles Bignall, the chemist, made certain that he was well set up with good supplies of all those extra little things which were much in demand in the weeks just before the Christian feast of the winter solstice.

He had been busy looking over his orders – Blaud's very superior Antibilious Pills, Blue & Black Draught, Liver Pills, Cascara Sagrada – when the lady came into his shop for a small purchase: a simple two-ounce bottle of Wyeth's Beef Juice.

She was an attractive woman, a regular customer, and it was not until she left that Bignall realized he had another customer; the Chinaman who dressed so well, almost like a businessman and not at all like some of the ruffians of his race whom one sometimes saw in the West End.

'I haven't a great deal of time,' Bignall said curtly.

'Then you will have to make time, Mr Bignall.' The

141

Chinaman's eyes were hard, glittering like glass. 'You still supply the gentleman from Baker Street?' he asked.

'You know that I do. And the others you send to me.'

'Good, Mr Bignall. You will be rewarded. We are very pleased with you. You pay your money on time, and I doubt if you are unhappy with the profit you make from our transactions.'

'There'll be other customers in a moment. Please state your business.'

'Just small warning. Just so you are ready.'

'Well?'

'Some time,' the Chinese appeared to choose his words with care. 'Some time. Maybe soon, maybe in few weeks or few months, we give you instructions.'

'Yes?'

'Instructions to cease providing our mutual friend from Baker Street.'

Bignall showed his unease in the small tic under his left eye. 'But it is his medicine. He could become very ill if...'

'If his medicine is denied him, he will become extremely nervous. He become depressed. Bad temper. He sweat a lot. He become very pleased to do things we ask, in return for medicine.'

The revulsion showed patently on Bignall's face.

'Not worry, Mr Bignall. You get paid good money. You do as told, otherwise...' The Chinese went through a graphic piece of mime which indicated an unpleasant and final solution to all of Charles Bignall's cares on this earth. 'Not worry, Mr Bignall,' he repeated. 'It been done before. It been done that gentleman before. He very clever man, but all man have price. His price white powder. So, when you get message, you do as told.'

Bignall nodded his acquiescence – an unwilling, but inevitable gesture of his whole body. Moriarty had made another move in the deadly game.

Ember was brought from Bermondsey to Albert Square by night – the same night that they summoned Bob the Nob to the house, his arm still painful and in a sling.

Both men stayed for thirty-six hours, spending much of

their time with Moriarty in his study, before leaving for the continent, to the shores of Lake Annecy. Their departure killed two birds with one stone, for Moriarty was aware of the desirability of getting both men out of the country and at the same time using them in a manner which would serve his ultimate ends. From this time on, the woman, Irene Adler, would be watched at close hand, her daily round charted with care, noted in detail and reported to the Professor every three or four days.

Much to Sal Hodges' disgust, the Italian girl, Carlotta, was now installed at Albert Square and, while Sal was more often than not the Professor's companion in the bed chamber, she was also required to instruct the 'Latin Tigress' – as Moriarty called her – in matters of etiquette, deportment and fashion.

As for other business, nothing of any value had been uncovered regarding the policeman, Crow, whose life, it seemed, had been one of conscientious blamelessness with no hint of bribery or corruption in his career with the Police Force.

Polly Pearson still pined for Harry Allen, Bridget Spear daily grew in size as her child swelled within her. Spear saw to the daily running of the rejuvenated empire of crime, reporting regularly to the Professor, who, with immense flair, was able to direct his Chief of Staff – for that is what Spear had now become – with unerring judgement. Schleifstein and his band were kept, in reasonable comfort, incommunicado at Bermondsey. In his spare late evening hours, Moriarty rehearsed the sleights and tricks culled from Professor Hoffman's *Modern Magic*; and for an hour each night, before retiring, he sat at his dressing-table with his disguise materials perfecting a new image which he would use before many months were out.

In the second week of December, Harry Allen came back to Albert Square.

Harry Allen had never been a natural nor willing school-master. The pampered son of a minor rural squire, his own schooling had been, like so many others, brutal; while the short time he had spent at Oxford University was notable only for excessive debauchery and wasted time.

143

He was, in effect, a somewhat charming wastrel, and when his father had died leaving little but his own and his son's debts, Harry had found himself, for the first time, thrown back upon his own meagre resources. A powerfully-built young man with a penchant for the ladies, drink and gambling, in that order, he had quickly found a place for himself as usher at a small private school in Buckinghamshire. There, in spite of his better nature, he had practised the same brutality on his charges which he had himself suffered only a few years previously.

His downfall had come when he discovered that his small stipend could not keep pace with the cost of his natural pleasures. Like many before him, Harry Allen took to petty thieving from his pupils, and when this did not net him as much as he required, he resorted to simple extortion – a relatively easy abuse of his position.

The headmaster and owner of the school was an aging and kindly cleric, interested in his charges, but squeamish over matters of discipline. For a long time he turned a blind eye to his usher's way of life, but, as with all things, the day of reckoning had to be faced eventually. Retribution for Harry Allen came with the sudden and unexpected arrival of three sets of parents, concerned about the amounts of money for which their offspring were constantly pleading. The truth would out, and at least two of the parents were inclined to place the errant usher before the local magistrates without delay.

Allen fled to a life of petty villainy, far below his natural talents, in the capital, and he had been at the fake, gonophing and on the demand for almost three years – including the year spent in the Model – when Spear found him and brought him to the Professor.

Now, Harry Allen had returned from Paris, looking smart and spry, carrying a large valise and with his demeanour showing clearly that he had done Moriarty's bidding – and done it well.

Martha Pearson took the news down to the kitchen, and on hearing it, her sister, Polly, was thrown into such a flustration that Bridget Spear had to threaten her with dire punishments if she did not keep her mind on her work.

'If I could only go up and see him for a moment,' wailed the infatuated Polly. 'I'd get on with the vegetables then like nobody's business.'

'He'll be down presently,' she was told. 'It is the master's orders that he is to be kept apart in the study. He has been busy in Paris and has much to recount.'

There was, indeed, much that Harry Allen had to recount to Moriarty, but when the two met, behind the locked study door with William Jacobs standing guard outside, the Professor had but one thought on his mind.

'You have it?' he asked as soon as the door was closed behind him.

'Naturally, sir, and I do not think you will be disappointed.'

So saying, Allen opened up the valise, and rummaging to the bottom through a pile of soiled linen, drew out the poplar wood panel, some thirty inches long by twenty wide. He turned the piece of wood to face Moriarty.

The Professor gasped. It was far better than he had ever, even in the wildest moments of optimism, dreamed. Facing him was the *Gioconda*, the *Mona Lisa*, enigmatically smiling from the panel, faded, cracked, badly varnished, yet still haunting: the lady with her soft amused brown eyes, looking out from a background of rocky crags and lakes which seemed to accentuate the human beauty. A calm serenity in opposition to the rugged landscape.

For a moment, Moriarty dared not even touch the painting. Labrosse had not boasted in vain. Not only had he taken on the genius of Leonardo in its creation, but also, as if by some miracle, the work had aged almost four hundred years in a matter of weeks.

'An amazing piece of deception,' whispered Moriarty, still in awe.

'Quite incredible,' answered Allen. 'See, even the craquelure is reproduced exactly.'

Moriarty nodded, close to the painting, examining the network tracery of cracks which gave credence to its age.

'Everything else is in order?'

'Under the work in the right hand bottom corner,' Harry Allen pointed. 'Scrape the paint from there and it will be clearly revealed.'

'And Labrosse?'

'Will bother you no more.'

'Tell me about that, Harry. You used nobody else?'

'Just as you commanded. I did it all myself. He was very difficult towards the end of the work; slowed down and wanted to spend more and more time drinking and with the girls. I had to be quite firm with him.' He smiled as though reflecting on amusing memories. 'Anyhow, it was finished last week and he said it would have to be left for one week before you could see it. I fell in with that, and three days ago suggested that we should make a real night of it. He expressed a desire to go down to the *Moulin Rouge*. The swells like to go there for the dancing and to rub shoulders with family people – there is an element of danger about it which seems to draw them in: that and the *cancan*. Merciful heavens, Professor, that dance, and the girls. It has to be seen to be believed. I thought that I would...'

'Tell me of the lechery later, Allen. I have seen it all. I presume my old friend, La Goulou, is well? But it is Labrosse I am really interested in.'

Allen was visibly perspiring. 'Well, we went to the good old *Moulin Rouge* and had a right evening. Everyone was there, even the little stunted painter Lautrec. I watched my drinking, but Labrosse was well away. It was like giving him a farewell party. I half carried him back to the studio where I shot him – neatly enough, through the back of the head as he slept. Then I bundled him up in the bedclothes, popped him in the trunk and travelled back with him.' He laid a luggage ticket onto the desk. 'He awaits collection at Victoria Station now. It would be best to have him picked up as soon as possible – before he becomes too ripe.'

'I will see to it at once. William Jacobs will go down with another of the men. You have more details for me though?'

Allen drew another paper out of his pocket.

'The painting, as you already know, hangs in the Salon Carré at the Louvre. I have stood and looked at it for long periods during the last weeks, and here are the intimate matters regarding its hanging. Each occasion I visited the Louvre I found there were always times when the Salon was empty – for once as long as half an hour. I was able to examine it at leisure. The clasps used in the framing are simple and I judge that it could be taken from the frame and replaced with this one,' a nod towards the replica *Mona Lisa*, 'in a matter of five or six minutes.'

Moriarty studied the drawing which showed how the painting was held in place at the rear of the frame by small clasps – some fourteen of them. He glanced up at Allen, thinking that this was the kind of man he had much use for – highly intelligent, yet as cold and ruthless as some predatory animal, for he had shown not the slightest regret, or emotion, in dispatching Pierre Labrosse. He would be a good partner to Lee Chow.

Moriarty unlocked the top drawer of his desk and drew out a small wallet of cash, some two hundred pounds, which he passed across the desk.

'A bonus for a task well completed,' he said, lips curved in what passed for a friendly smile. 'Now, Harry, you had best get below stairs. I understand that one of the hugsome wenches down there is of a mind to have you at the grindstone 'ere long.'

Allen had the decency to blush.

Moriarty growled a half-approving note. 'Take care, young Harry, I do not mind her having a hot pudding for supper, as long as no marrow is left in her belly.'

As soon as Harry Allen had left the room and Moriarty had taken a last look at the remarkable forgery, he summoned William Jacobs, gave him the luggage ticket and instructed him to go, with one of the other men, to collect the trunk from Victoria and from thence take it by closed van to Romney Marsh where they were to dispose of it in such a manner that Labrosse's corpse would never see light of day again.

Later that evening, he sat in the drawing-room – Sal being with Carlotta teaching her the rudiments of polite manners – and toyed with a pack of cards, practising how to palm cards one at a time from the top of the pack. He was really becoming quite proficient in these arts and found that an hour or so with the cards helped greatly to concentrate his mind. His instincts now told him that the plot against Grisombre in Paris had all the makings of success. Only two things could go wrong. If, for instance, the authorities should happen to finally decide that the Mona Lisa should be cleaned, there would be an obvious danger. The other problem concerned Grisombre himself. Moriarty wondered if the little Frenchman could possibly find another artist with the ability to make such a splendidly accurate copy of the painting.

Sitting there, in the firelight, with the oil lamps turned down, the Professor flicked the queen of hearts into his palm, then shuffled the pack so that it showed on the bottom: then with a quick pass he changed it for the queen of spades. The small sleight amused him. Changing one lady for another was part of the plot, and to do it without ever being discovered – he chuckled at the thought, the shadows on the walls seeming to dance to the eldritch music of his laughter.

Tomorrow, thought Moriarty, I shall go out and purchase some photographic equipment. Possibly at the Stereoscopic Company in Regent Street, for they gave free lessons in photography and were also By Appointment to Her Majesty. That would complete stage two in the plan against Jean Grisombre.

It was not until 1 December that Crow heard from Holmes: a telegram at noon asking him to come to Baker Street at four.

'I am sorry you have had to wait so long for my response to your note,' Holmes apologized almost before Crow had settled himself by the blazing fire in the great detective's rooms. 'On the day your message arrived, I was not available. It is always the case – long periods of inactivity followed by bursts of interesting work. Watson and I were out of London on that Saturday. In Sussex, on the trail of a vampire,' he laughed. 'A nasty young vampire at that.'

Crow rehearsed the facts concerning the Cornhill robbery and the strange business at Edmonton, without giving Holmes the benefit of his own conclusions. Lastly he told of the Bolton murder.

'You can be sure Moriarty is behind all this,' Holmes got to his feet and began pacing the room in an agitated fashion. 'I detect that wicked man's hand in so many things of late. Is it not true that there has been a rise in criminal matters in the last weeks?'

Crow had to admit that things did seem to be turning out

that way: thefts in the street, burglaries and shop-lifting were all on the increase, while there appeared to be more forgeries than ever passing through the hands of tradesmen and bankers alike.

'He is back without doubt,' Holmes continued to pace. 'And I have little doubt that our old German friend, Wilhelm Schleifstein was involved. Have you any conclusions of your own?'

Crow ventured his theory that the Professor was engaged in a series of intrigues and vendettas.

'I could not have put it better myself,' Holmes nodded. 'Mark my words, we shall hear of other strange happenings. Be on your guard, Crow, for you could also be a candidate for Moriarty's malevolence.'

'You also, Holmes, particularly if he has wind that we are working in harness.'

Holmes was immediately alert. 'You have told no one?'

'Not a living soul.'

'Good. I have been most careful to keep our association in the shadows. Great heavens, even the good Watson still imagines Moriarty dead.'

'Be that as it may. It does seem to me that the Professor has eyes in the very wallpaper of our chambers.'

Holmes thought for a moment. 'His intelligence is good. But I also have my ways. And, Crow, I am determined to bring him to book, through your own good offices.'

As Christmas grew nearer, so the minions of Moriarty's criminal family began to pay their respects, offering gifts as well as the normal tribute which they were paying once more for his protection and patronage.

Bertram Jacobs, who during Ember's absence was in control of the lurkers, brought the most valuable gift – intangible but of great importance to the Professor: news that Crow was still frustrated with his wife, restless and ill at ease in the house at King Street. Moriarty, concerned about ways in which he could deal with the Scottish policeman, knew that this, and this alone, might be the only weak spot in the man's forbidding armour. He immediately sent for Sal Hodges, who found him in his study tinkering with the photographic equipment he had purchased.

Sal Hodges was out of sorts, though not because of the dark Carlotta. There were other matters on her mind which she was not yet ready to reveal to Moriarty.

'Merciful heavens, James,' she exclaimed on discovering him hunched behind the tripod camera stand, his head enveloped in a black cloth. 'You are positively a man of hobbies these days. If it is not the card tricks, it's the piano. Now this.'

'Ah, my dear, but this is a means to an end. As far as photography is concerned, the click of the shutter is the springing of the trap. But I wish to discuss women, Sal, or rather a woman.'

'The Tigress has scratched you?' Sal's eyebrow shot up, her elegant mouth twisted in a sarcastic smirk.

'It has nothing to do with the Tigress, and I pray you to remember that she, like this camera, is but a means. Bait.'

'Well, mind you are not snared too heavily by her honey trap. Did you keep her happy last night?'

'And if I did?'

'My womanly intuition tells me you keep her content each time I am absent.'

Moriarty laughed. 'Well, let your womanly intuition work on another problem. The girl we have at Crow's home.'

'Lottie?'

'If that is her name.'

'It is. I saw to that one on Bertram Jacobs' instructions before you returned to England.'

'I want her removed and something of a different mettle put in to replace her.'

'Carlotta would be good. Can I use her?'

'Carlotta is a shade obvious.' Moriarty had the grace to smile. 'No, I want someone a little more subtle. A girl that will stir Crow's blood.'

'I see your way, James, but it might misfire. Big Sylvia is not a fool even though she is foolish.'

'Big Sylvia, as you choose to call her, is, I am given to understand, much taken up with improving her station in life. Present her with a *fait accompli* – a well-mannered, subservient girl who will show Crow a pretty ankle. He is tired of his wife's posturing. Just see to it, Sal. Choose the right one and have Lottie out and her in before Christmas. It is a risk, I know, but it has been managed before. I'd like as many pounds as pretty servants have brought their masters to bed and provided many a happy year's comfort under the mistress's nose.'

Sal laughed. 'Indeed, James, it's an old trick and can be happy intrigue. I fear poor Lottie's mother will be taken suddenly ill, and her cousin sent for as a replacement. I believe I can find just the girl for the job. A butterfly who has mastered the art of innocence so that it would bring a saint on like an old ram.'

As a policeman, Angus McCready Crow prided himself on his sensitivity to atmosphere. This sixth sense worked most strongly four days before Christmas when he returned to King Street. He was in low spirits that evening, for Ember could not be found, and Lee Chow – whose description was at every police station in the metropolitan area – seemed to have disappeared from the face of the earth. Neither was there scent nor sniff of Schleifstein and his companions, though Crow now had descriptive proof that it was indeed the German who had been living at the Edmonton house. More, known villains had now returned to that old stubborn silence whenever the name of James Moriarty was mentioned.

'They have gone blind, deaf and dumb,' said Tanner, after a foray amongst criminals who were normally wont to sell their own fathers for a bottle of spirits.

'Like the three wise monkeys,' Crow commented sadly, knowing all too well that it could mean but one thing. The Professor had reclaimed his hold on the lawless of London.

The moment he opened the door of 63 King Street the subtle atmosphere hit him like a pugilist's fist in the belly. There was a new tranquillity, coupled with more tangible and delicate aromas filtering up from the kitchen.

Sylvia, however, still appeared spiky. Hardly had he entered the parlour when she began. 'A fine how-de-do we've had here today.'

Crow said nothing, a tactic which, in the past weeks, he had found best to adopt when faced by Sylvia's unqualified statements.

'With all the preparations for Christmas,' she sighed. 'With the comings and goings, the arrangements and plans. Too bad. Too bad . . .' She left the sentence unfinished, as though her husband could define its meaning by some mode of mind reading.

Crow brightened. Perhaps, he thought, Sylvia's two uncles and their attendant wives would not be coming to spend the holiday after all – a possibility which would lighten Crow's life not inconsiderably. The uncles and their wives being unutterable social mountaineers of great diligence.

'A telegram,' said Sylvia, cryptically.

'Ah.'

'For Lottie, would you believe?'

'The postal services are open to all, my dear.'

'No notice. Nothing. She must pack her bags and go this very afternoon. Her mother, it seems. People are so inconsiderate, being ill at this time of the year.'

Crow's face broke into a grin of Cheshire cat dimensions. 'You mean that Lottie has left us? Gone?'

'I said to her, what am I to do? I said.'

'And?'

'And the madam had it all in hand. There was no option. A cousin recently arrived in London, it seems. From a very good little family, but fallen upon bad days and willing to take any form of employment. She arrived within the hour, so there we are. Lottie out. Harriet in.'

Crow groaned. Lottie had been bad enough. A cousin fallen upon hard times might prove even worse.

'It is all the extra work,' moaned Sylvia, as though the small King Street house was some kind of a mansion. 'Teaching her the ropes, so to speak.'

At that moment, a tap on the door heralded the arrival of the newly installed Harriet – pert, dark, pretty, with rounded hips and a smile, even in the teeth of Sylvia Crow's glower – announcing that dinner was served.

At first, Angus Crow was inclined to think that his wife had cooked the meal, it was so good. But upon enquiry, between the grouse pie (a favourite not often provided at King Street) and the excellent lemon pudding, it turned out that the entire dinner was of Harriet's making. Things, he considered, were looking up.

She was certainly brighter than the dour Lottie, and much more pleasant on the eye; particularly when later in the evening the girl came in to bank up the parlour fire – showing a great deal of ankle, and not a little calf in the process.

Harriet, the detective thought, would be a pleasure to have in King Street. He pondered upon the double meaning of that notion, much surprised to find the old Adam rising within him, rejuvenated, as it were, by a dazzling smile, a manner of walking, and the arch way in which the girl asked if there was anything else she could do for him.

Christmas came and went at the house in Albert Square with a genuine sense of celebration. For Martha and Polly Pearson it was a time to be well remembered, for their master appeared to take the good cheer of the season most seriously: allowing everybody to join in as though they were one big family.

On Christmas Eve they all gathered in the drawing room, around a tree which had been delivered two days previously, and hung about with garlands and baubles by Mrs Hodges and Miss Carlotta. There was sherry wine to drink, and the Professor himself handed out small gifts to all. A locket for Polly and a gold brooch for Martha.

On Christmas Day they were kept busy by Bridget Spear, preparing the banquet which was partaken by all but themselves and Harry Allen, who volunteered to keep them company and share their portion below stairs.

Late in the afternoon, however, they were instructed to serve tea, with the big iced cake, in the drawing room, and hardly had they taken the trays and stands up, than they were told to stay and take part in the celebrations – which included some roistering songs around the piano, games, which gave Polly and Harry Allen even more opportunity to intertwine in dark corners of the house, and a display of incredible card tricks performed by the Professor. A strange topsy-turvy Christmas indeed, and puzzling to the girls, who were most conscious of the barriers which society decreed should be maintained between servants and master.

The day ended with Martha, head reeling from too much wine, lying alone in the attic bedroom – Polly having found the necessary courage to finally cross the borderline of womanhood, snug tight in Harry Allen's bed.

Two days later, the Professor left for a short excursion to Paris.

Neither of the girls saw him go, for he left in the early hours, being driven to Dover by Harkness, seen off only by the faithful Albert Spear.

Yet if either Polly or Martha had caught sight of the figure leaving the house on that morning, it is doubtful whether they would have recognized him. Instead of the familiar, and sometimes forbidding person, they would have observed a gangling man of middle age, with straggling fine grey hair, thinning, and so unruly that the least breath of wind whipped it into a wild sparse thatch. His nose was slightly hooked, and the eyes stammered of vagueness. Nor were this man's clothes as immaculate as those in which the Professor was usually to be seen. They fitted, yet did not fit: the trousers being a shade long, and the arms of his jacket and greatcoat a trifle short. He carried a portmanteau, and had a large oblong photographic box slung, with a strap, about his shoulders. Indeed it was James Moriarty, but now he carried in his wallet papers which presented him as Joseph Moberly – artist and photographer extraordinary.

Moriarty enjoyed travelling: particularly when in some disguise, for nothing pleased him so much as to know that he was hoodwinking those around him. It was his general rule that a good disguise helped one to blend, unnoticed, into one's surroundings. As Joseph Moberly, however, he took on a different line of attack. Moberly was the epitome of the vague, highly-strung, artist with an interest in every human being who came his way. A loud, high-pitched voice and braying laugh signalled his arrival wherever he moved, and a strange, almost birdlike series of mannerisms – including an odd clicking of the tongue and lips – betrayed, perhaps, a lack of confidence.

He spoke to everyone who even looked at him, telling them – whether they cared or not – that he was making his first visit to Paris where he planned to photograph some of the great

154

paintings in the Louvre Museum. He might also, he claimed, take some photographs of the streets of that great city and he proposed to exhibit the lot next summer in a gallery off Bond Street.

Passengers on the afternoon packet from Dover, and later, on the train to Paris, were heartily sick of him long before they steamed into the Gate du Nord. Smiling inwardly, for the day had been a game – a diversion to pass the journey – Moriarty took a cab to a quiet, unassuming *pension* near the Place de L'Opéra where he dined well and spent a restful night. The next day could well be crucial.

He breakfasted leisurely on the following morning, constantly engaging the harassed waiter in execrable French, before taking himself, at about half-past ten, to the Louvre – lugging the large photographic case with him.

Up to this point, all the intrigue and plotting against those whom he had sworn to bring under domination, or be revenged against, had been directed by Moriarty but carried out by his trusted minions. At last, he the greatest criminal intelligence of his time, was to carry out a lawless act on his own. As the cab drew nearer to the Rue de Rivoli, Moriarty felt the old stirring in the blood, that sense of half-fear and half-expectation which sends a quiver through both mind and body on the verge of a great criminal adventure. The crime of the century they would have called this. It was a pity, he thought that he could not allow it to be publicly recognized. That was, perhaps, part of the brilliance, the incisive genius of the project. That he ruled the great criminal family of London was common knowledge; that he was able to evade capture by the police of a dozen countries might be envied by other members of the underworld's hierarchy, or cause great embarrassment to the forces of law and order; but this, the theft of one of the world's great masterpieces, had to go unsung. After this had been accomplished, what he had in store for Grisombre would be one of his crowning glories. Sadly, that also had to remain in the shadows, from whence it might only become hearsay in the folk lore of crime.

It was a bright, if chill, day as Moriarty made his way across the Place du Carroussel to the great building with its long arms of annexes stretching out as though to embrace the visitor. He went first to the administrative offices where it took half an hour to make the application for permission to take photographs in the Grand Gallery and the Salon Carré. Then there was another half hour's wait before the permit was issued.

Certainly if Moriarty was desirous of drawing attention to himself as Joseph Moberly, his actions did not fail him. There was little doubt in the minds of the concierge and the many museum attendants, that the strange English photographer was a great eccentric. As the dishevelled figure entered the main vestibule and showed his pass to the attendant on duty, people turned to stare, while others covered their mouths to hide smiles at his appalling accent and even worse grammar.

But the French have always appreciated those who live a life of mad nonconformity. The attendants took to him, and, in the days that followed, referred to him, with affectionate smiles, as Monsieur Plique-Plaque – from his habit of clicking his tongue and lips as he worked at his photography in the Grand Gallery on the first floor of the museum.

He would start work relatively early each day, finishing before three in the afternoon, because of the light. For the first two days, Moriarty confined himself to making photographs of paintings in the Grand Gallery – that six hundred yards of walls packed tightly with paintings, running between the Salon Carré and the Salle Van Dyck overlooking the Quai du Louvre. He would have preferred to work straight away in the Salon Carré, where the *Mona Lisa* was hung in pride of place, but, to his frustration, two official photographers were already installed in there, doing commissions for the Director.

He would pass the time of day with this pair of artists who would come into the Grand Gallery from time to time, stopping to see if they could learn anything new from the Englishman's technique.

Within himself, the Professor was becoming more and more irritated. He had hoped to get the business dealt with quickly, but the two official photographers put an end to that, and he was forced to improvise, going through the motions: taking pictures of Vanucci's *St. Sebastian*, Titian's *Man with a Glove* and two Leonardos – *St John the Baptist* and *Bacchus*.

He was further concerned, on the third morning, when a student came into the Grand Gallery and set up his easel to start on a copy of Andrea del Sarto's *Holy Family*.

On the fourth day the two official photographers were not there, though the tyro artist still worked at his copy. The eccentric Englishman commented on the absence of his friends to one of the passing attendants, making his occasional round of the Grand Gallery. They had finished up here, he was told, and were now working in the Salon du Tibre downstairs.

Moberly nodded enthusiastically, using the whole of his body, telling the attendant that he would now be able to take some photographs in the Salon Carré, remarking that he would have to go down and see his colleagues later, as he also might be leaving after today. With that he began to fold up his tripod camera stand, pack his equipment into the large oblong case, and make his way back to the Salon Carré.

There were several people in the long gallery, two watching the student, still laboriously sketching out part of his canvas in preparation for his copy of the *Holy Family*, the others strolling and stopping, almost at randon, in front of paintings which took their fancy among the vast patchwork of canvases which littered the walls. One group – mother, father (pince-nez firm on his nose), and consumptive-looking daughter – stood in front of the large Murillo generally called *The Angels' Kitchen*. Moriarty glanced at their faces which were fixed with that look folk have when they are conscious that exposure to great art will do them some spiritual good.

Cretins, thought the Professor as he passed by. Art is only good for two things – its financial value or the deep secret knowledge that you own something unique which nobody else can have in a million years. Great art could equal great power, particularly if you used it in the way he was, at this moment, planning.

He passed through the archway into the Salon Carré and began to set up his camera in front of the *Mona Lisa*, his eyes taking in all the angles from which he could be viewed. There were three entrances to the small Salon: the one from the Grand Gallery, through which he had just passed; another directly opposite, into the Gallery d'Apollon which housed what was left of the Crown Jewels of France,* and so called because of the Delacroix panel in the ceiling, depicting Apollo slaying the Python; the third entrance was through the door to the small room which housed *The Virgin and the Donors* by Hans Memling, and the Luini frescos.

Moriarty reflected that he could only actually be seen from relatively small areas of the Grand Gallery and the Gallery d'Apollon, though it was still possible for visitors, or attendants, to enter quietly from the fresco room without his knowledge. When the moment came, he would have to work quickly and with great stealth.

He stayed, adjusting his camera, peering through the lens and viewing the painting for the best part of ten minutes. In that time only two visitors came through the Salon, hardly pausing, on their way into the Grand Gallery. It was a most admirable time. His ears were adjusted to every sound, cough, footfall, shuffle or unexpected noise. He so concentrated on his hearing that he could detect even the smallest vibration. At last, he bent down and opened the oblong photographic box at his feet, hardly looking at it, his eyes intent on scanning the dangerous entrances and exits.

Feeling with the tips of his fingers, Moriarty found the hidden catch on the right hand long side of the box. He pressed down and the side fell away, revealing a recess in which the Labrosse copy lay cushioned with velvet, fitting exactly but for one small area which contained a pair of long-

*We know from the Moriarty Journals (the whole story is in *The Return of Moriarty*) that the Professor was thwarted, in 1890-91, in an attempt to steal the Crown Jewels of England from the Tower of London. The French Crown Jewels were another matter and consisted of the Crown of Charlemagne (supposedly the genuine stones in a modern setting) which was used at the coronation of Napoleon; the Crown of Louis XV (possibly set with false stones); a diamond-encrusted sword belonging to Napoleon I; a watch encased in diamonds given to Louis XIV by the Bey of Algiers; and the splendid Regent diamond – if not the largest diamond in the world, probably the purest. From some notes in the *Moriarty Journals*, it would appear that the Professor toyed with the idea of making these Crown Jewels his own property in the late 1880s, but he records at one point that 'The Regent is the only piece worth taking'.

nosed pliers, similar to a cracksman's 'outsider'.

Grasping the pliers firmly, his senses straining to the limit, Moriarty began to cross the small area which separated his camera from the space of wall containing the painting. He was about to grasp the lower ledge of the frame when the muffled sound of voices reached him from far away at the other end of the adjoining d'Apollon Gallery.

Three strides and he was back at the box, sliding the pliers into their place and closing the partitioned side before resuming his position behind the camera.

The voices were raised and coming closer: a steady monologue punctuated by grunts from a second party; the tapping of a stick, and the sound of at least four pairs of feet.

The Professor ducked his head under the black cloth behind his camera just as the quartet entered the Salon.

'I know that my eyes have almost gone, Monsieur le Directeur,' one voice rattled on. 'But even in this foggy autumn of my sight, I can see the truth.'

Moriarty raised his head, prepared to give the intruders the full Moberly treatment. An imposing picture met his gaze. The central figure wore thick-lensed glasses and walked precisely, with a cane tapping in front of him. At his side the grey-bearded figure of the Louvre's Director bent in deference. Behind them two menials hovered.

'I know that I am a worry to you, Directeur,' continued the short-sighted one. 'But, like other artists, I am only concerned that essential truth and beauty may be preserved.'

'I realize that,' the Director smiled indulgently. 'Just as I realize you have a great number of weighty and influential artists on your side. I have to deal with the mules, though, Degas.'*

'Mules, dolts, fools, who would not be able to distinguish

*There is little point in cataloguing the talents of Edgar Degas the artist, for they are well known to all. At this time he was sixty years of age and his eyesight, weakened during army service in the Franco-Prussian war, was daily growing worse. He was also, by now, concentrating on sculpture, which he called 'a blind man's art'. He held very strong views about Leonardo's *Gioconda* and, together, with many other artists, campaigned vociferously against any attempt being made to clean it.

oils from watercolours. All they want are pretty pictures hanging on their walls. Pictures which look clean and freshly varnished.'

'We seem to be interrupting one of our photographers,' interjected the Director.

One of the menials coughed, the other shuffled towards Moriarty as though to guard the two great men.

'It is all right, Monsieur le Directeur,' Moriarty fawned and bowed.

'An Englishman,' Degas beamed. 'You have to come to Paris in order to see priceless works now, eh?'

'I have the privilege to be taking photographs, sir, of some of the finest paintings in the world.' Moriarty drew in his breath, about to launch into a Moberly speech.

'I trust his photography is better than his French,' rattled the short-sighted Degas. Then, more slowly, for the Englishman's benefit, 'And you are photographing *La Joconde?* You are, perhaps, an expert on this painting?'

'I know its priceless worth. Just as I know how honoured I am to be speaking to such an artist as yourself, Monsieur Degas.' Inwardly, he scoffed: a dauber, a painter of dancers, blurred ballerinas and women completing their toilet.

Degas laughed. 'I am making an irritation. A small storm. The idiots here at the Louvre would have *La Joconde* cleaned. What do you think of that, Englishman?'

'I have read the arguments, sir,' he threw a sidelong glance at the Director who was unwilling to become involved. 'In my own humble opinion, you and your colleagues are correct in fighting such a decision. Clean the *Mona Lisa* and you risk doing it great damage. Clean it and you risk more than damage, you risk a transformation.'

'You see,' cried Degas, thumping his cane on the floor. 'Even English photographers understand. Clean it and it would become unrecognizable. Look at her, Directeur. I cannot see her as plainly as I would like, but I can feel. To clean and revarnish *La Joconde* would be like stripping the most fascinating woman on earth. You can still desire a woman whom you have seen stripped to the flesh, but the sense of mystery always departs with the flutter of the last garment. So it would be with *La Joconde*. The fascination would be consigned to history. You might just as well burn her as clean her.'

'Bravo,' Moberly's high-pitched bray echoed through the Salon, and the Director, sensing an embarrassing speech by this unknown visitor, took hold of Degas' arm.

'We must let our English friend continue with his work. You have made your point, and you can make it again to the Committee this afternoon.'

The great artist allowed himself to be turned slowly back towards the d'Apollon.

'I am almost blind, photographer,' he called back. 'But not as stone blind as the cretins who look after the heritage of mankind.'

Moriarty breathed a sigh, standing stock still behind the camera, his eyes fixed on Leonardo's small masterpiece. So, they were still thinking of cleaning her. It was a risk he had to take.

The family which had been so impressed with *The Angels' Kitchen*, were now coming back through the Salon, and one other visitor had entered, together with an attendant. He looked as though he was going to settle down and examine each painting in minute detail.

'You saw the great man then?' asked the attendant.

Moriarty nodded. 'An honour, a considerable honour.'

'He makes things warm for the Director and the Committee,' chuckled the attendant. 'Me? I do not know if they should clean her or not. I only work here. I know nothing of art,' and he shrugged, heading for the Gallery d'Apollon.

Five minutes later the coast was again clear. To his surprise, Moriarty found himself sweating heavily. He held up his hands and noticed that they trembled slightly. Surely his nerve was not failing him? He glanced around, hearing once more stretched to the limit as he reached for the camera box and again released the hidden partition. There was a dry smell in his nostrils, and in the archway between the Salon and the Gallery d'Apollon he was conscious of dustmotes drifting downwards in the light. Far away, someone dropped something with a loud clatter. He was at the picture now, hands on the frame, lifting it from the wall hooks, heart thumping in his ears, perhaps distorting the sounds elsewhere in the museum. The frame was heavy, much heavier than he expected, but it came away from the wall easily enough.

Moriarty lowered it to the floor, leaning it against the wall, turning it as he did so, exposing the back, where the fourteen clasps held the original painting in place. He stopped working for a split second, hearing something unusual in the air, only to realize that it was his own breathing. Then, the pliers down onto the clasps, swinging each of them outwards, towards the frame, one at a time until Leonardo's poplar panel was free. Grasping the top of the frame, the Professor tipped it forward from the wall, his other hand behind the picture, allowing it to drop from the frame.

To hold it was almost a sexual experience. He had to will himself to move quickly, taking the three strides back to the camera box; holding the real Mona Lisa with one hand while he lifted the Labrosse version from its recess; sliding the Leonardo into the secret hiding place: a perfect fit.

Now he found himself counting as he moved back to the frame, positioning the copy's bottom edge onto its ledge. For a second, Moriarty felt an obstruction in his throat as the copy did not seem to fit snugly. Then a slight juggling and it dropped into place. The pliers again on the clasps, and the exertion of lifting the whole thing back into place on the hooks.

As he returned the pliers back to their niche in the camera box there was the scrape of a footstep from the fresco room. He slammed the false side closed, went down on one knee and began to rummage in the box. An attendant had come in behind him. He wondered how long the man had been there? How long had he taken to complete the exchange? The dustmotes still drifted in the air and the background noises were still distant.

'Charlot tells me you are not coming back tomorrow,' said the attendant.

Moriarty let his breath out slowly, controlling it, fighting the pounding in his ears.

'No, no,' he replied – Moberly's bray of laughter. 'I have completed my work here.'

It remained only for him to spend a little more time in the Salon Carré, not rushing his departure, before walking from the Louvre with the black camera box over his shoulder. Nobody seeing the gangling figure, lopsided with the weight of his equipment, crabbing his way across the Place du Carroussel, could ever have imagined that he carried with him one of Leonardo da Vinci's great legacies.

Two days later, Moberly was gone from France – in fact from the face of the earth – and Moriarty returned to the house in Albert Square in order to put the treasure in a safe hiding place. It was a strange sensation for him to sit in the study and look upon the original painting, knowing that it was now his. Yet there was also a sense of anticlimax. Only he was now certain about the location of the *Gioconda, La Joconde*, the *Mona Lisa* – whatever they wished to call it. He also knew that nobody but himself would set eyes on it until the final settlement with Jean Grisombre, who had betrayed him so badly. To set that part of the plot in motion, however, he had to return to Paris – and quickly. This time he went as yet another character from his repertoire of disguise – an American gentleman of great and undisputed wealth.*

The American was not loud or flash in any sense. He wore his riches with the ease of one born to them, without the aggressive and brash manner of so many who came to Europe

*The theft of the Mona Lisa. In the light of the theft revealed in this chronicle, and the further events documented in the next few pages, it is interesting to note the following:

On Monday, 21 August, 1911 – some fifteen years after James Moriarty removed Leonardo's work from the Louvre – the *Mona Lisa* was found to be missing. It was not traced for two years. Finally, in the second half of 1913, Vincenzo Perugia, an Italian house-painter, was arrested for trying to sell the picture in Florence.

During the 'missing' period, two theories were voiced by various factions of the French Press. (1) It had been stolen by a French newspaper in an attempt to prove an *earlier* assertion on that newspaper's part, that the painting had already been stolen. (2) The theft had been engineered by an American collector who would have an exact copy made and, in time, would return the copy to the Louvre, keeping the original for his own private collection. We now know that in many ways both theories were correct – though late in their exposition.

from the American continent these days, having made their money quickly in gold or railroads, and who splashed, bullied and ordered as though their new-found opulence was the key to life – as, unhappily, it so often was.

He appeared to be a portly man in his late forties, pudgy of cheek, florid of countenance, dark-haired and soft-voiced. It was one of Moriarty's most simple transformations, accomplished with skilfully-made padding under his clothes and in his cheeks, a cosmetic preparation to increase his colour, and dye for his hair. To this he added horn-rimmed spectacles, his own not inconsiderable talent for assumed vocal illusions, and papers, including letters of credit, which showed that he was Jarvis Morningdale from Boston, Mass. With him travelled a secretary whom he referred to as Harry. They were both booked into a suite at the *Crillon*.

The reputation of Paris as the city of pleasure grew directly out of the Montmartre area of the early nineties, and it was to the streets and lanes around Pigalle that the visitors and tourists came, intent on seeing the scandalous sights which had been the whispered talk of the western world since the end of the 1880s. On his first night in Paris, Jarvis Morningdale, from Boston, headed directly into Montmartre, seeking, not so much sin, as one person whom he knew would almost certainly be where sin blossomed most prolifically.

It was a cold and raw winter in 1897, yet the cabarets and cafés were still packed to the doors. By eleven o'clock, the American sat at a table near the dance floor of the *Moulin Rouge*, watching the girls perform the *cancan* with athletic enthusiasm; twirling, flashing their skirts high, whirling in the *port d'armes* and jarring with wild whoops in the *grand écart*.

Jarvis Morningdale, sipping champagne, his face more flushed than usual, turned to his secretary and spoke low.

'My dear Harry, you really should have been here a few years back,' he smiled. 'This is all for show. In those days it was for sex. These girls have clean underclothes even, and I have yet to glimpse a naked thigh. When Zidler ran this place, the women were women – La Goulue, Jane Avril, Cri-Cri, Rayon d'Or, La Sauterelle and Nini Patte-en-l'air. You could see their womanhood drip from them with their sweat, and smell it clean across this room.'*

'I still find this puts me on highly,' replied Harry Allen, not taking his eyes from the row of white-frilled bottoms which were being presented to the audience as the brassy orchestra came to a ragged finale.

They joined in the applause as heartily as the rest of the throng, and Moriarty nudged his companion.

'Here comes one of the genuine ones now,' he whispered, nodding his head towards a slim, dark, gypsy-looking girl who slid and hipped her way between the tables as though looking for someone. Moriarty's eyes followed the girl, as though willing her to look in his direction. 'I know this one

---

Zidler and the Moulin Rouge. Zidler, the impresario, has been rightly called 'one of the architects of Montmartre's fame'. As early as the 1870s the centre of the more vulgar, exciting, night-life of Paris was to be found around the Clichy and Pigalle areas of Lower Montmartre. This was the swarming territory through which a large section of the Parisian underworld passed: a place of thieves, fences, pimps, prostitutes, tricksters, gypsies, singers, dancers, and rogues. It was most notable for its wine shops, café-concerts and cabarets, and was also the womb of that dance which is so popularly evocative of Paris in the so-called 'Naughty Nineties' – the *cancan,* which began life as *le chahut,* a wild improvised version of the quadrille, in which modesty was thrown to the wind. Its popularity began to spread from places like the *Elysée-Montmartre,* but came to full commercial maturity when Zidler converted a former dance hall, the *Reine Blanche* in Pigalle, into the famous *Moulin Rouge.* Toulouse-Lautrec, in his paintings and posters, has made it, and those associated with it – in particular the extraordinary sensual La Goulue, and Jane Avril – familiar to all. To the *Moulin Rouge,* and other night haunts of the area, came fashionable Paris, not to mention the fashionable world (La Goulue, at the height of her fame, is reported to have taunted the Prince of Wales with the words, 'Hey, Wales. It's you who's paying for the champagne.'). By this time, however, Zidler had sold out the *Moulin Rouge* – in 1894 – and, though still a popular attraction, its fortunes were diminishing. La Goulue left in 1895 and, by the time Moriarty went there in search of Grisombre, Jane Avril was working at the more popular *Folies Bergère.*

165

from other times,' he murmured to Allen, 'though I presume she will not recognize me in my current persona.'

The girl paused, looking straight at Moriarty, who nodded. She smiled, a flash in her dark eyes, and then progressed in a blatantly sensual long stride towards his table. She was even dressed in a fashion which had bohemian overtones, a loose skirt which did not reach the ground, and a tight blouse showing that she wore little underneath.

'You wish to buy me a drink, Monsieur?' The voice raw, as though she spoke the language with a foreign accent.

The American nodded and replied in fluent French, 'Sit down. Champagne?'

'Is there any other drink?'

A waiter was at the table before Moriarty even lifted his hand.

The girl appraised them both almost with contempt.

'You wish . . .?' she began.

'What I wish is no concern of yours,' the soft voice hinted possible danger. 'You are Suzanne, yes?'

Her nostrils flared. 'I have not seen you here before. How do you know me?'

'I make that my business. It should not worry you. Like you, I am here to do business.'

'Yes?'

'Whatever your price I'll double it and you can take my friend here off to your place.'

Suzanne looked at Harry Allen as though she was examining a horse for stud. 'And what else?'

'I have come a long way with a proposition for a friend of yours – never mind how I know, but he is famous even in America. How can I reach Grisombre?'

'Is that all? Grisombre you will find easily. Off the Rue Veron there is a cabaret – just a small one, like all the others up there. It's called *La Maison Vide*. Grisombre is usually there at this time, in fact I think the place belongs to him, as do so many in Montmartre.' Without showing any more interest she turned to Harry Allen. 'You have a good friend to buy you a present like me.'

The American, Morningdale, gave a quiet laugh, almost slipping back into his real self, for his head moved to and fro

166

in that familiar reptilian manner.

'Go ahead, Harry. I will not tell your little skivvy at Albert Square. They tell me that Suzanne the Gypsy is worth every sou you spend.' He chuckled at his pun and tossed a small jingle of coins on the table, threw back his champagne and prepared to leave.

'You will manage on your own?' Harry Allen shot a covert, concerned glance at his master.

'Harry, I have managed on my own in more dangerous and corrupting places than Montmartre. Enjoy yourself and I will see you at the hotel in the morning.'

Outside in the Place Blanche it was bitterly cold. Across the road a group of cabbies stamped their feet, warming their hands around the braziers of a pair of chestnut sellers. A streetwalker detached herself from a small huddle of ladies of the night on the corner, seeking the Professor as an easy mark.

'Hallo, *chéri*,' she began brightly. 'I can show you the time of your life.' Her little nose was blue with cold and her teeth chattered.

For a moment, Moriarty allowed the role of Jarvis Morningdale to slip.

'Touch me, harlot, and I'll have your heart,' he mouthed.

The girl spat, directly at him, and Moriarty reached out, taking a bunch of her cheap coat in his fist, pulling her close and speaking a quiet fast French – in the argot of the alleys and back streets.

'*Ferme ton bec, ma petite marmite, ou je casse ton aileron.*'*

He flung her back so that she staggered and fell into the gutter, Moriarty's manner rather than his words crushing her into silence. By the time she had picked herself up, he was already in a cab, ordering the driver to take him up to the Rue Veron.

La Maison Vide had a small frontage – a door with a cut-out oriental design in the porch, and a window decorated from

---

*Literally, 'Shut your beak, little cooking pot, or I'll break your wing'. The French criminal argot, according to M. Joly, 'transforms living forms into things, assimilates man to animals'. Thus: the mouth *un bec*, the arm *un aileron*. Moriarty's most insulting remark was to call the girl a *marmite* – one who supports a pimp.

inside with a candle in a red glass shade and several small posters advertising performers who were either appearing at the place currently, or had made past appearances there.

A heavy-jowled man took a small tip from Moriarty when he applied for admission, passing him on to a bowing waiter in stained and rumpled evening clothes. The interior was no different from most of the cabarets of its kind: rough tables jammed together, separated from the dance floor by a wooden rail. At the far end a band was crushed into one corner next to a small stage. The place was crowded, and obviously popular, and Moriarty had to blink once or twice to accustom his eyes to the heavy pall of cigar and cigarette smoke. The waiter, with uncanny accuracy, led him in a complicated threading dance through the tables to a place just vacated by a man and woman. The chair was still warm from the woman's rump and the glass that was set before the Professor could well have been the one which she had just used, the dregs tossed out onto the floor. He did not have to order, for the waiter produced a bottle of champagne as though from mid-air, uncorked it and poured a glass, before there was any chance of demanding other refreshment. The champagne was flat.

Now that he was seated, there was still no time to look around. The band blared a chord, the drummer rattling a short roll, his instrument sounding like a biscuit tin, and the curtains of the little stage divided revealing a small divan. To another crash from the drum, a plump, coquettish girl appeared from behind the drapes, winking and ogling the patrons who, by their shouts and whistles, showed that they were agreeably predisposed to her performance.

The girl, who was fully clothed, minced downstage in an exaggerated Alexandra limp. Paused. Winked, then suddenly reacted as though stung or bitten somewhere near her right breast. The audience, many of whom had obviously seen it all before, howled with mirth. The girl was, without doubt, being caused much inconvenience by a flea. As matters progressed, so she scratched more, and then was forced to divest herself of her gown in order to trap the naughty little insect. As the gown came off so the imaginary flea changed its position, and so on, all necessitating the removal of various undergarments, until she was revealed, coyly, with very few clothes at all.*

The final divestment was as inevitable as night follows day, and the performance ended to delighted applause. The band struck up again, and the Professor began to glance around.

Jean Grisombre sat at a large table set near the dance floor, dispensing hospitality to a pair of hard-looking coves who might just have been bankers. Grisombre was a short, lithe man who looked and moved like a dancer, though his peeked face held none of the necessary charms of that profession. His movements were compact, but he rarely smiled with his whole face, only his mouth moved in an almost simulated reflex. He sat opposite the two businessmen, flanked by his omnipresent bodyguards, who both had about them the look of the apache – slim and deadly with dark faces and constantly moving eyes.

After ten minutes or so, the pair of serious businessmen rose. Grisombre shook hands with each of them in solemn farewell. Some form of compact had been sealed over the wine. Moriarty wondered who had, perhaps, been betrayed, or who was to be robbed, swindled or worse. One of the bodyguards accompanied the guests to the door while Grisombre spoke quietly, as if giving orders, to the other.

As he watched the lips moving, the Professor could almost hear Grisombre's voice, in his head, on the last occasion of their meeting. 'I am sorry,' he said. 'It is the decision of us all. If one of *us* has failed and been put into a compromising situation by the police, you would doubtless have done the same. You have failed us as a leader, Professor, and I have to ask you to leave Paris and quit France with as little delay as possible. There is no more to be said, except that I can no longer assure you of my protection here.'

Well, thought Moriarty, you will soon be sniffing at my bait and pleading for my leadership again, my little grey one. He

*Such performances – like the famous *Le Coucher d'Yvette* – were commonplace in the cabarets of Montmartre. One of the most famous artistes was Angèle Hérard who disrobed while miming a flea hunt. But it is unlikely to have been Mme. Hérard whom Moriarty saw at *La Maison Vide*, for she performed almost exclusively at the *Casino de Paris*.

lifted his hand to attract the nearest waiter, who came hurrying over, harassed, but bowing unctuously.

'Another bottle, monsieur?'

'I wish to speak with Monsieur Grisombre.'

The man's attitude changed, the smile vanishing, suspicion lancing his eyes.

'Who shall I say . . .?'

'My name would mean nothing to him. Be good enough to give him this.'

Moriarty's hand dived into his coat pocket, bringing out the letter which he had personally dictated to Wilhelm Schleisfstein. *M. Jean Grisombre. By Hand,* it said on the envelope. Inside, the message was simple. *Dear Jean,* it read. *This is to introduce you to an American friend, Jarvis Morningdale. He is extremely wealthy and has a proposal which, I believe, is your right to receive rather than mine. Be certain that whatever financial figure he quotes you will be paid. He does not joke about money. Your obedient friend, Willy.*

Grisombre tore open the envelope almost before the waiter presented it, casting a quick look in Moriarty's direction. He scanned the contents slowly, as though it was a Latin text which he found difficult to construe, and then raised his head. This time he eyed the Professor with more interest. Moriarty raised his glass. Grisombre said something to the bodyguard, and nodded, beckoning the Professor to his table.

'You are Jarvis Morningdale?' he asked in French.

'I am. Herr Schleifstein commended you to me.'

'You have a good accent for an American.'

'That is hardly surprising. My mother came from New Orleans. French is my second language.'

'Good.'

Grisombre motioned him to be seated. One of the bodyguards poured a glass of champagne. This time it was not flat.

'I have the feeling that we have met before.' Grisombre was looking at him hard, but Moriarty met the Frenchman's gaze without a flinch, confident in his disguise.

'I think not,' said the Professor. 'My visits to Paris have, until now, been rare.'

Grisombre still held him with a steady stare.

'Willy Schleifstein says that I can probably be of help to you.'

Moriarty allowed himself a smile. 'I do not know, but I would like to think you can.'

'Tell me then.'

The girls were whooping onto the floor, lining up for the *cancan*. It was probably going on like this in half the cabarets in Paris, thought Moriarty. Aloud, he said, 'What I have to say can only be told in private.'

Grisombre indicated his bodyguards. 'Whatever your business it can be discussed in front of them.'

Moriarty shrugged. 'I'm sorry. This is too large a scheme. A great deal of money is involved.'

Grisombre appeared to be thinking, and if Moriarty had the right measure of the man, money would be uppermost in his cogitations.

'All right,' the Frenchman finally nodded. 'There is a room we can use here. Upstairs.'

Then a whispered word to the bodyguard who had now returned from seeing the previous guests from the premises. The man bowed his head and left, oblivious to the wild cavortings of the dancing girls.

'You like the ladies, Monsieur Morningdale?' Grisombre smiled – bleak as ever.

'In moderation, M. Grisombre. I find this dance a trifle too flamboyant for my tastes.'

'You are from America. Perhaps I can arrange a meeting with a girl whom I know you would like – a mulatto who has lived here in Paris for most of her young life. She is very discreet, and – how can I put it? – Eager?'

A woman was the last entanglement Moriarty required: particularly in this disguise which, in the bedchamber, would be seen through with little difficulty.

'I think not. You see I am after a lady of exceptional breeding.'

'If you wish to be so choosey.' He shrugged.

'Her name,' Moriarty said slowly, 'is Madonna Lisa, wife of Zanobi del Gioconda.'

Grisombre's eyebrows twitched. 'So. I believe you are right. We should talk in private.'

The normal use of the room to which they were taken, upstairs, was not difficult to define. A large brass bedstead took up much of the space; there was also an ornate dressing table and many mirrors, including one on the ceiling. Grisombre and Jarvis Morningdale sat opposite one another on a pair of walnut armchairs with beautifully carved cabriole legs, the seats, arms and backs richly upholstered in red and gold brocade. They were good reproductions yet, like the girls who Moriarty presumed used the room, not quite the real thing.

The bodyguards left a bottle of brandy and two glasses, but Moriarty would have wagered heavily that the two men were within easy call outside the door. He would have done the same.

'Tell me more about the Madonna Lisa,' said Grisombre, feigning amusement. The corners of his mouth turned up but his eyes remained dead – the eyes of sheep in jelly.

'There is little to tell. I am merely putting an abstract question to you, Monsieur Grisombre. If you wished to obtain some treasure without the owners knowing it had gone, what would you do?'

'I understand that the usual method is to take it, leaving some form of copy in its place. I am told this has been done many times before – often by people who should know better. It is done with jewellery, I believe. But you speak of a painting. A work of great value and age.'

'The painting hangs in the Louvre Museum. In the Salon Carré. I will be open with you, I had thought of carrying out this scheme by myself. I have enquired into it, but, alas, it needs experience in certain arts – robbery, for instance. Tell me, would it be difficult to steal such a painting?'

Grisombre gave a short laugh. 'The theft would be easy. As I recall it is not a large picture, and the Louvre has no idea of how to protect its treasures. Why should they? Who would be so foolish as to steal such works? They cannot be sold.'

'If the theft could be concealed, that picture could be sold to me.'

Grisombre remained silent for a full minute. 'And how much would you be prepared to pay for such a thing? What is its worth, Monsieur Morningdale?'

172

'They say that it is priceless, but everything on earth can be given a calculated price. I had a relative once – he is gone now – who was no mean mathematician. He calculated a price for me. It was some years ago, mind you. We are told that Francis I bought the painting from Leonardo for 4,000 golden florins.'

'I know the story,' Grisombre leaned forward as though scenting money.

'Well, if you take that as an original investment made in the early 1500s, and calculate at three per cent compound interest, today that investment would be worth something like nine hundred million dollars. Eleven million pounds sterling.'

'In francs?' asked the Frenchman.

'I am not interested in francs. Only dollars or pounds sterling, and, to be honest with you, sir, I do not put a great deal of faith in the currency of nations.'

Grisombre raised his eyebrows quizzically. 'So?'

'Can you not read the signs in the wind? It is the same in America as it is in Europe. On the one hand there is great wealth, power. On the other, great poverty, unrest. Between the two there is incredible progress. Inventions which stagger the mind. But the poverty and the wealth must eventually clash. It is inevitable. The seeds of revolt and chaos are all around us, my dear sir – the bombs, the anarchists, the workers organizing themselves. They will eventually inherit the earth, but they forget the corrupting influence of power. It may happen in five years, or ten. It may not happen for seventy or eighty years – not in our lifetime. But when the corruption is complete, the world will return to a feudal system. It will be like the dark ages, and between now and that time only the strong will survive. I believe we must store up against the time with things of lasting value. The really priceless things, such as this piece of wood covered with paint by an artist of the sixteenth century. For that, now, I will pay a reasonble price in the currency which will eventually be worthless.'

'How much?' Simple. The question for which Moriarty had been waiting.

'I am a wealthy man, monsieur. Six million pounds

sterling. But on one condition.'

'Yes.'

'That the theft goes undiscovered.'

'That a reproduction is exchanged for the true painting?'

'Quite so. You know someone who could provide you with a work which would pass even close inspection?'

'There are possibly only three men of such talent.'

'I have enquired also. Their names?'

'Oh no, Monsieur Morningdale. I give you names and, maybe, you save yourself a great deal of money.'

Moriarty's head began to oscillate to and fro. He had to use considerable will power to control the nervous action.

'Very well,' he took a gulp of brandy. 'A man here in Paris called Pierre Labrosse; an Englishman, Reginald Leftly; and an artist who lives in Holland and calls himself Van Eyken, though that is not his real name.'

Grisombre's voice dropped almost to a whisper. 'I am impressed, Monsieur Morningdale. You must be very serious about this.'

'I wish to own that painting: the *Mona Lisa*, the *Madonna Lisa*, *La Joconde*, the *Gioconda*. The lady with the smile who sits waiting in the Salon Carré. Of course I am serious, and I will tell you more. Labrosse is no good. He drinks too much and I understand he has now left Paris. The so-called Hollander is old and unreliable – though he would probably produce the best imitation. Reginald Leftly is the only possible candidate. Just as you are the only man with nerve and resources to exchange the paintings.'

The Frenchman moved his head to signify agreement. It was like a fish opening his mouth, sliding fast through the water to hit the bait and the hook.

Moriarty had to play him gently now. 'I will pay five thousand pounds, now, to cover your expenses. After that, you will have to move with haste. I shall be in London for one week – the 8th to 13th March. At the Grosvenor Hotel. If you are willing to undertake this commission you will send me a telegraph on any of those days. It will read, *The lady is willing to see you*. You will sign it *Georges* and it will signify that you have exchanged the paintings. I will wait at the Grosvenor Hotel, every evening, between eight and nine, until the 13th following receipt of that telegraph. You will bring the painting to me there. In return I will pay the remaining millions.'

'It is a great deal of money,' Grisombre's voice was guttural, throaty, almost as though the thought of such riches was too much.

Jarvis Morningdale smiled and spread his hands in almost an act of humility. 'I have a great deal of money,' he said.

Within twenty-four hours, Jean Grisombre had called upon the American at the *Crillon* and taken away the five thousand pounds sterling. Within forty-eight hours, Jarvis Morningdale and his secretary were out of France and James Moriarty had returned to Albert Square. Eight weeks would pass before Morningdale was resurrected. Eight weeks of bitter winter weather, snow and ice turning gradually to the first hint of spring.

By the end of January, Angus McCready Crow was set on a firm course of action regarding the tracking and detection of James Moriarty.

His thinking on the matter had been direct. A week or so after Christmas, Crow realized that there was little point in hoping for some constable, or detective, to come up with the apprehension of Ember or Lee Chow, or even any of the other named associates of the Professor.

As he was now logically certain that Moriarty was engaged in a series of vendettas, and as one of the victims, Schleifstein, appeared to be missing, the answer lay in going out and keeping some kind of watch on the others.

Holmes, it seemed, had people on the continent who would inform him of anything unusual concerning Grisombre, Sanzionare or Segorbe. But the detective made it plain that too much reliance should not be placed on these spies. Crow, therefore, had to make some move himself. He began by writing to his old friend Chanson of the Police Judiciaire indicating that any current intelligence on Jean Grisombre – contacts, strangers, sudden moves, unusual occurrences – would be greatly appreciated. At the same time, Crow wrote similar letters to officers in Rome and Madrid. These were men he had never met – Captain Meldozzi of the *Carabinieri* and Captain Tomaro of the *Guardia Civil* – but were both known to be highly thought of in their own forces. Both sent careful replies, acknowledging Crow's letters, assuring him in almost poetic phrases that they would assist in any way possible, but adding nothing of substance regarding Sanzionare or Segorbe. Chanson alone provided intelligence, though it was little. Grisombre, he said, had been keeping to himself and his own kind, but one trivial detail had been noted at the beginning of the year. It concerned a visit which the French gang leader had made to the *Hôtel Crillon*, 10 Place de la Concorde, on the night of 4 January.

A detective from the 1st District (which covered the 1st and 8th Arrondissements – the *Crillon* being situated in the 8th) was at the hotel on the night in question, making an enquiry concerning some trifling complaint, when he recognized Grisombre in the foyer. The notion of Grisombre at the *Crillon* put the officer on his guard. He immediately asked about jewellery lodged in the hotel safe, and questioned the concierge on duty regarding Grisombre's presence. From these enquiries the detective elicited that Jean Grisombre had been calling on an American guest – Mr Jarvis Morningdale. A description of Morningdale was also attached with a note stating that he had arrived in France from Dover on 3 January, travelled directly to Paris, leaving via the same port two days later.

Chanson could not resist a sly dig at the end of his letter, saying that he hoped these dates of entry and exit would be useful, for the British police would have no track of the American's movements, allowing, as they did, visitors to roam their country at will.

The French detective knew that Crow had long been an advocate of the *carte d'identité* system (and the German *Meldewesen*) for keeping a check on visitors and subjects alike.* Crow was irritated by this inference, and decided that it was time for him to send another memo to the

---

*The various continental systems – which kept a careful track of all personal movement – were most strongly resisted by both the British police and Government as an infringement of individual freedom.

Commissioner on this matter – even if it would be to no avail.

But Angus Crow had other things on his mind. The number of crimes which he was investigating had undoubtedly risen since Christmas, and this increase of work was not helped by the domestic situation at 63 King Street. It was not easy for him to be resigned to the many soirées and dinner parties which Sylvia was arranging, not to mention those to which they were invited. Time and again Crow returned to King Street, late and tired from investigations which took him into the iniquitous areas of the capital, or even further afield, to find Sylvia in a mood of high and touchy temper. Guests were due to arrive any minute, or they had only half an hour to be at some function – usually at the residences of people with whom Crow had little in common. But nothing would stop Sylvia, who was determined to rise in society, and Crow was quite unable to impress upon her obsessed mind that she was only mixing with people who had similar pretentions as herself – a mid-strata of middle-class folk cast adrift in their own revolving limbo.

This eternal round and comic task of dinners and musical evenings was also playing havoc with the pleasures of the bedchamber, and Crow was not slow to discover that the unbridled passions, which had been theirs before marriage, now became dulled and, at times, non-existent.

Fobbed off from what Sylvia referred to as his 'conjugals' – with headaches, fatigue or simply plain bad temper – Crow's frustration rose. He was a fit man, in his prime, who had always been used to the pleasures of the flesh. Now, it seemed, they were to be denied him. He fretted, brooded and, more and more, took note of the hard-working and most attractive Harriet, whose bright smile and constant happy mood made a deep impression upon the detective.

So it fell out that on a night in early February, after a dinner party of intense boredom, Sylvia, complaining of a headache and the onset of a cold, departed to bed with unusual haste, leaving Crow alone sipping a nightcap in the parlour.

A tap on the door, some fifteen minutes after Sylvia's exit, announced the arrival of Harriet, smiling and asking if anything more was required.

'Is the mistress between the sheets, Harriet?' asked Crow,

the dark unthinkable already forming in his mind.

'Indeed she is, sir. And with the lamps all out. I think her cold is much worse tonight. She had me prepare her warm milk and aspirin before she retired.'

'Well then,' Crow swallowed. 'Harriet, would you care to take a glass of brandy with me?'

'Me, sir? My, I do not know. What would...? Well, if that's what you wish, sir.' She came towards the settee upon which Angus Crow sprawled.

'It is what I wish, Harriet. Get yourself a glass, then come and sit by me.' He could only presume that it was an excess of claret at dinner which now made him bold.

'Yes, sir,' she replied in a small voice.

He stood up as she approached, glass in hand. In fact his timing was bad – or impeccable, whichever way you wish to look at it, for the two suffered a mild collision. Crow felt the soft yielding of Harriet's bosom against his chest.

'Oh my, sir,' she gasped, putting up a hand to his shoulder in order to steady herself. 'Oh goodness, what would madam think?'

Crow could hardly believe it was himself who said, 'The blazes with what madam thinks,' and, wrapping his arms about the girl, he clasped her to him.

'Sir?' Still the small voice, breathless and bird-like: questioning his forward action, yet not resisting. Rather pushing against him, the hand holding the glass feeling backwards seeking a resting place.

'Harriet, did you know that you were deucedly attractive?' Crow's voice now breathless.

Harriet's hand found the edge of the occasional table, upon which she set down the glass.

'There have been men who have told me so, sir. But then you are flatterers all.' As she spoke, Crow felt her push even closer, the very junction of her thighs hard against him.

He bent to their mutual will. Their lips met, and it was as though each was parched and would never be done slaking a thirst which burned their mouths, so hot was the onrush of lip upon lip, tongue upon tongue.

Angus Crow was hardly aware that it was Harriet who pulled him down onto the sofa, nor that she unbuttoned her own blouse, presenting her bust to him, uncorseted.

'What pretty wee bubbies,' gasped Crow. 'Wee modest crimson-tipped flowers.'

'Oh, Mr Crow. Poetry,' she gasped, thrusting upwards to his swooping mouth and pulling at her long black skirt; assisting him in the raising of it.

'Angus,' moaned Crow between sips at her orbs.

'Sir?'

'Angus.' Sup. 'When we are like this ye must call me Angus, lassie.' Always in moments of drama and tension, Crow lapsed into his more obvious Scots accent. 'Oh,' he moaned again, his hand touching the leg of her drawers. And, 'Oh, what a fine garden hedge. Harriet, my dear.'

'Dig it deep, sir ... Angus. Dig deep.'

At the moment of their interlocking, Crow had a sudden vision. It was as though Mr Sherlock Holmes was standing at his shoulder, shaking his head and clicking his tongue as a sign of disapproval.

On the morning following, Angus Crow was beset by a great sense of guilt. So much so that he found it difficult to look either Sylvia or Harriet in the eye. This did not, however, stop him that night from seeking out the servant in the kitchen, when Sylvia had retired, and ploughing her briskly and with the passion of a much younger man, across the table.

In Albert Square many things of importance took place between the onset of the New Year and the beginning of March, the most singular of which was Sal Hodges' revelation to the Professor that she was with child. Since before Christmas she had pondered long on discovering the right moment to break the news, and had made up her mind that it had to be done with on his return from Paris.

Moriarty was, happily, in a good frame of mind on that first evening back, knowing that he had done all things well in France. A goose was ordered for dinner, and Bridget hounded the Pearson girls in the kitchen to make certain the meal was a fitting banquet.

A little before six, Sal brusquely ordered Carlotta up to her room, and set out to beard Moriarty in the drawing-room where he was partaking of a glass of sherry.

'There is no easy way to say what I have to tell,' she began, glancing almost shyly at him as he stood, smiling, in front of a cheery fire freshly made up with logs.

'Why, Sal, you've never been bashful with me. Out with it.'

She came over to him, placing a hand on his sleeve.

'James, you will hardly believe this, but you are to be a father.'

For a second, she thought he would fly at her with rage.

'Foolish little minx,' Moriarty roared. 'She was to take care. It's her Latin blood, Sal, damn me if it ain't. It's the breeding in the hot climate, even if she's never been near Italy. They germinate more rapid. Blast the woman, now all my plans for Sanzionare in Rome are gone up on a balloon.'

She let the small storm run out, controlling her own patience and temper as only a woman of strong character is able.

'No, James, you mistake my meaning. It is not the Tigress that you have ridden to a pudding. It is me.'

His stunned expression lasted all of three seconds.

'Now, there's a relief, Sal,' he laughed. 'If it had been Carlotta the pitch would have been queered, for she's making well that one. She will be ready by the spring, yes?'

'Yes, James, she will be ready and trained as you wish. But I am to suckle your child.'

'Yes, yes, Sal. You said. Do you expect marriage then? You'll not get that from me.'

'No, James, just a little understanding and the promise that you'll own to the child.'

'If it's a boy he'll be my pride, Sal. No boy will be better looked after, I can promise you that. It will be Harrow School and Cambridge University for him and that's a fact. Then, when he's had a good education, my family people can give him a grounding in our trades.' His face became wreathed in a huge smile, the like of which Sal Hodges had never yet seen on him. 'He will be my heir, Sal. Think of it, heir to the criminal Empire of Europe.' He lifted her off the floor and spun her around like some young sentimental gadabout. 'This, Sal, is the founding of a dynasty and it makes me happy. My, the place will be crawling with infants what with Bridget and yourself. Let us hope that Harry Allen is being

180

more careful with young Polly.'

'What if it's a girl, James?'

'Nonsense. I forbid it. See to it that it's a boy, Sal, or I'll disown the pair of you. When did I perform this prodigious feat?'

'By my calendar it would seem it happened on our first night here in London.'

'No better time. Nurture him well, Sal,' he placed his hand gently on her stomach. 'You hold within you my hope for a future.'

Sal knew better than to argue, or bring the Professor to a more realistic frame of mind. If it was a girl, then that hurdle would have to be jumped when the time came. James Moriarty was too deep within his plots and plans for revenge to listen to other arguments; and if the possibility of a son gave him more power of concentration, than she would be satisfied. Accepting the situation, Sally Hodges took herself down to the kitchen, breaking the news to Bridget Spear who was of great comfort.

Bert Spear, himself, was proving to be an exceptional Chief of Staff, and Moriarty had very little need to concern himself with family affairs. Tribute came in regularly and at a growing pace. The jewellery from the Cornhill robbery was now – all but one piece – in the hands of fences in Holland and Germany, the rewards trickling back to swell the coffers. Spear also, with the assistance of the Jacobs brothers, was well able to handle matters of discipline and decisions concerning robberies and raids which individual villains wished them to put up.

Each week, Moriarty would be driven over to Bermondsey by Harkness to see Schleifstein. The German was being sensible and accepting his defeat, not only in a philosophical vein, but also in a manner which made room for future planning. Moriarty, he accepted, had proved himself the natural leader and he now pledged himself, and those who followed him, to the furtherance of the Professor's grand design.

Moriarty, however, refused to show any sign of weakness, insisting that Schleifstein and his lieutenants should stay close at the Bermondsey place. He did – as a concession –

allow certain telegraphs to be sent to Berlin so that the German could keep his people controlled. Each week they would talk, and Moriarty promised him the company of Jean Grisombre ere long, explaining exactly what he was doing in order to bring the French leader back into the fold.

'It is clever, Professor,' Schleifstein guffawed when the whole plot was revealed to him. 'His face. I would like to see that when you break the news. But what have you up your sleeve for our Italian friend?'

'For Luigi – or Gee-Gee as they call him? I have a plot to catch him on each of his Achilles heels at the same moment. All men have their weaknesses, Willy. All men. It just so happens that Sanzionare has more than most.'

'So?'

'His avarice is more finely honed than that of many of us. Like Grisombre he loves beautiful jewels. He also loves women upon which to hang them. Most of all his woman, Adela Asconta. A jealous lady. Sanzionare is, like many of his race, a man of superstition. The Latin church has exploited the natural characterisitics of the Italians and the Spanish. Would you believe that Gee-Gee Sanzionare, a criminal of ruthless mould, still performs his duties to Mother Church with the assumed piety of an innocent? The escape clauses in his religion are written with that subtlety usually reserved only for the clever sharks at law. By using all these elements, I will bring him back into the grand European family of crime. A lure is what I have for Sanzionare.'

'You say we all have weaknesses, Professor?' Schleifstein adopted a bland look of innocence – a favourite expression which had so often trapped his own victims.

Moriarty's head oscillated slightly. 'You do not catch me with questions, Willy. To conquer in our precarious trade is to be aware of one's weaknesses; one's besetting sins. I know mine and so guard against them.'

On his way back to Albert Square, Moriarty reflected on his current weakness – this all-embracing, surging desire to dominate the European criminal leaders, and see Crow and Holmes brought low and in disgrace. The desires swamped him, sometimes so completely that he reached for excesses as a drowning man reached for driftwood. To know that was not

182

always enough.

As well as the tribute, and the lion's share of robberies, small and large, the other trading commodity came regularly into Albert Square: intelligence, culled almost from the very cobbles of the streets, the woodwork of the four ale bars, the rancid dribbling of the gutter. That great network of lurkers, which had been at its zenith before Moriarty's last enforced exile, was once more arranged and recruited so that news came on quiet whispers, first to Bert Spear and then to the Professor himself. Late in January, for instance, there was word that Grisombre had spent two days in London, returning to France with a particular companion – the short, bushy-bearded, eccentric painter of portraits, Reginald Leftly. With that news, Moriarty's heart sang, for it meant the plot was hatching as sure as eggs under a good hen. It was ever thus. One had but to make suggestions, set people in juxtaposition, and human nature with its frailty, desires, lusts and quirks, would do the rest.

In early February, Sal Hodges came with more news which set the Professor into a mood of evil glee.

'Our fair lady at the Crow household has reported,' she told him, almost nonchalantly as they were divesting for the bed.

'Indeed,' he paused, one hand to his waistcoat buttons.

'The news could not be better.' Sal began to chuckle. 'The man is incensed with love for her. She says that he can hardly keep his hands from her bodice even when his wife his near.'

'A prisoner of lust,' the Professor joined in the laughter. 'A man in that condition has no conscience. So many have come toppling because of a pair of bright eyes, a smooth bust and the sweet breath of carnal desire.'

Sal, coyly unbuttoning her gown, looked at him from under half-closed lids. 'Have you no conscience, James? I would like to think so. Come, before I am too swollen with your pup, show me that sweet breath.'

Amidst all the comings and goings, the Professor found time for quiet, snatched hours spent with his cards. He also disciplined himself – probably more than at any other time in his life – to work upon his disguises. Some were easy – particularly the transformation, which he could now effect in a matter of minutes, which turned him into the living image of his gaunt, bald and hollow-eyed, ascetic academic brother. Yet, each evening he worked steadily at what was to be his greatest impersonation. In front of the mirror, behind the locked doors of his bedchamber, Moriarty plied his arts, altering his body and physiognomy to that of a man well known in all walks of life, recognizable by rich and poor alike, and famed throughout the world. By the end of February he had achieved an amazing likeness.

On 7 March, a day earlier than he had led Jean Grisombre to understand, the American, Jarvis Morningdale, together with his secretary, arrived with much baggage at the Grosvenor Hotel. No messages awaited him, though on that first night as a guest, he received at least three callers.

On the following day, 8 March, a telegraph arrived from Paris. It was handed in to Mr Morningdale's suite of rooms at ten o'clock in the morning, just as the American was taking his breakfast. The message read – *The lady is willing to see you.* It was signed, *Georges.* Half an hour after the telegraph arrived, Morningdale's secretary left the hotel. If anyone had been following they would have seen him hail a cab on the corner of Victoria Street and Buckingham Palace Road, then set off in the direction of Notting Hill. Eventually the secretary arrived at Albert Square where he let himself into number five. He stayed in the house some two hours, leaving to rejoin his employer at the Grosvenor. This time he carried a long flat case.

In the meantime, Jarvis Morningdale had been down to the main foyer of the hotel. He was, he told the clerk on the desk, expecting an art dealer from Paris. He was possibly going to buy some paintings and would like the hotel to arrange for a pair of easels to be sent up to his suite.

The easels were taken to the rooms during the afternoon, Morningdale himself supervising their erection at opposite ends of the drawing-room.

During the late afternoon, the manager of the Grosvenor Hotel, up in his inner sanctum, glanced through his current guest list. The name Jarvis Morningdale caught his eye. It was a name which he had seen recently; not simply when Mr Morningdale's secretary had booked the accommodation. He had seen the name on some piece of official correspondence.

The manager worried about that name for the rest of the afternoon.

At a little after five o'clock, three men enquired for Mr Morningdale at the reception desk. The clerk asked if Mr Morningdale was expecting them and they assured him that he was.

'Oh, you must be the gentlemen from Paris,' said the clerk with a greasy smile.

The largest of the men – a somewhat menacing figure with a jagged scar running down one cheek and dissecting the corner of his mouth – returned the smile.

'No,' he said. 'We are from the Donrum Detective Agency. Mr Morningdale is expecting to look at some rather valuable paintings in this hotel sometime this week. We have been hired to make certain the works of art come to no harm. It is in your interest as well as his.'

The clerk agreed that it certainly was, and had a page show Albert Spear and the Jacobs brothers up to the suite which Jarvis Morningdale occupied.

As he was preparing to go down for dinner, the manager of the Grosvenor Hotel suddenly recalled where he had seen the name Jarvis Morningdale. He hurried to his office, unlocked his desk and began to flip through the correspondence files. A few minutes later he had the letter in his hand. It was an official piece of paper with the crest of the Metropolitan Police at the top, and the printed letterhead of the Police Offices at New Scotland Yard.

This letter, he read, *is going to all good hotels in the metropolis. It is not concerned with a specific crime, nor even a specific criminal. We are, however, most anxious to speak with an American gentleman, a Mr Jarvis Morningdale. If, therefore, Mr Morningdale reserves accommodation at your hotel, or presents himself with the object of being a guest, we ask that you quickly contact Inspector Angus McCready Crow of the Criminal Investigation Department at New Scotland Yard personally. In doing this you may well save Mr Morningdale and yourselves a great deal of trouble.* The letter was signed by Inspector Crow himself, was dated early in February, and how the manager had come to let it slip his mind he would never know. He immediately telephoned the Police Offices, only to be told that Inspector Crow had already left and would not be back until the morning. The manager presumed that it would be all right if he left it until then, though he half suspected that he should have asked for the Inspector's private address. It would have been to no avail, however, if he had done so. Sylvia Crow was on her own at King Street on that particular evening. Her husband, she was certain, was on duty until quite late and it was Harriet's evening off.

The Grosvenor Hotel abutted directly onto the side of Victoria Station with its main entrance in busy Victoria Street which abounded with traffic, from cabs and drays to the many green or yellow omnibuses which plied constantly to and from the station from morn till midnight.

As an hotel, the Grosvenor was probably the most extensive of those managed in association with the railway companies, and, as such, took pride in its standard of service and cuisine.

On the night of 8 March 1897, the Grosvenor was watched almost from every angle. Well-dressed lurkers of both sexes took turns in patrolling the Buckingham Palace Road, over which the largest part of the hotel looked, while a small group of men in disguises, running from beggar to railway porter and traveller, guarded the hotel entrance and the various approaches to it from the railway station. Moriarty had chosen the venue on the assumption that Grisombre would wish to hand over the painting as soon as possible after landing in England, and Victoria Station was the main terminus for the London, Chatham and Dover Railway. Grisombre had but to step off the train and proceed straight to the hotel in order to unload the treasure, in return for the vast fortune offered by Jarvis Morningdale.

Moriarty was also shrewd in suggesting that he would be available at the hotel from eight o'clock on each of the prescribed evenings, for one of the coast trains connecting with the Cross-Channel packet arrived each night at Victoria a little before eight.

The Professor also considered that Grisombre, hungry for the reward, would leave little time before his arrival. In fact he expected him on the first night. He was correct in that assumption, and when the Dover train drew in, it was one of the lurkers, wearing the uniform of a porter, who first approached Grisombre and his pair of bodyguards, placing their four portmanteaux onto his trolley and responding, with a pulling of his forelock, to the instructions to take them to the Grosvenor Hotel. None of the Frenchmen even noticed their porter nod briefly to a pair of boys idly watching the train come in, nor did they see one of the boys speed off up the platform and wave a signal to a group of three men and another boy – this time in the uniform of the Post Office – lounging at the end of the platform. A few seconds later, this same uniformed boy was handing in a yellow telegraph envelope at the reception desk of the Grosvenor. The telegraph was passed on to a page who took it speedily to the third floor, where Jarvis Morningdale's suite was located.

The envelope was in Moriarty's hands before the trio from France had even arrived at the desk of the foyer.

'He's here already, then.' The Professor held the envelope aloft so that it could be seen by all – Harry Allen, Spear and the Jacob brothers. They were gathered together in the drawing-room, one door of which led directly to the corridor, two others to the bedrooms occupied, respectively, by Allen and Moriarty. 'They will be a while yet, but it is best to be prepared. Harry, bring the lady out.'

Harry Allen went straight to the Professor's room where the true Mona Lisa lay on the bed, covered by a black cloth. Also on the bed, laid out as if ready for some party, were the clothes which Moriarty used when donning the disguise of his late academic brother – the striped trousers, white shirt and collar, the long black coat, and the harness. On the floor stood the boots with built-up soles, while the remainder of the disguise – the cosmetics and that extraordinary bald pate wig – were on the dressing-table.

There were other things on the dressing-table. The Professor's favourite weapon, the Borchardt automatic pistol which Schleifstein had given him three years before, when they had all met in London to make the alliance. Beside the pistol stood a bottle of Winsor & Newton's turpentine, a flat-bladed palette-knife, and a dry rag.

Harry Allen took the painting, cradling it in his hands,

hardly allowing his fingers to touch the work, and carried it through to the drawing-room where Moriarty himself assisted in setting it up on the easel nearest his bedroom door. Allen then went to fetch the black cloth which they draped over the Leonardo, assuring that it hung down well at the back in order that no chance touch would dislodge it.

'They will, doubtless, be washing and settling themselves in their rooms,' Moriarty addressed the assembled quartet. 'I'll not be caught napping, though. To your places. We'll wait it out ready for them.'

The four men gave their assent, Bertram Jacobs and Albert Spear going off into Harry Allen's bedroom while William Jacobs, with a sly smirk, left the room through the main door.

Outside, he paused, listening for the sound of any rustle or tread on the thick carpeting. Some fifteen yards up the long corridor there was a broom cupboard. William Jacobs headed straight for this hiding hole, slipped inside and pulled the door almost close upon him.

They had some forty minutes to wait before Grisombre and his pair of rampsmen came up to the third floor, one of the thugs carrying a flat brief bag. They had enquired in the foyer for Mr Morningdale and, on hearing the French accents, the clerk had informed them that they were expected. After going through the necessary formalities of booking in, Grisombre had ordained that they should get rid of the painting as quickly as possible. He had no wish to stay in London longer than could be helped and, though they had rooms in the Grosvenor, it was his avowed intention to catch the night train to Dover, and so be in Paris again, a richer man, by the morning.

Harry Allen answered the tap on the door and Morningdale rose to meet his guests.

'Come in, gentlemen, I had a feeling that you would not keep me loitering.'

The door was closed behind the visitors, hands were clasped, glasses of brandy handed around, smiles everywhere. Outside in the corridor William Jacobs came out of the broom cupboard and took up his station in front of the door to Morningdale's suite.

'So you have it,' Morningdale's gaze seemed not to shift

from the brief bag clutched tightly in the French bodyguard's paw.

'I have it,' Grisombre made a small gesture towards the bag. 'There is no hue and cry, it can be yours, Monsieur Morningdale, if you have the money.'

Morningdale gave an impatient click of the tongue. 'The money, the money, that is no problem. It is here, of course. But let me see it. Let me look at what you have brought.'

Grisombre hesitated. 'Monsieur, this transaction has been performed on trust, I . . .'

'Trust backed up with five thousand pounds. You can hardly call that mere trust. The picture.'

His snap, he knew, came perilously close to the normal voice and manner of his real self. But it passed unnoticed. After another slight hesitation, Grisombre nodded to the man with the bag which was now set down on the floor, the key produced and the painting, wrapped in velvet, drawn out. Harry Allen came forward to take the piece of wood, ready to set it on the vacant easel near his own bedroom door.

'Hold.' Morningdale stepped into the circle before the painting was even unswaddled. 'I'll look at the back before you set it up. I'm not an expert for nothing, Monsieur Grisombre. There are certain identifying marks.'

Grisombre's face went dark, anger brewing like thunder on his brow. 'You are suggesting that I would cross you?'

'Shush-shush,' Morningdale made placating motions. 'There is no need to become waxy with me, Grisombre. A simple precaution. There are marks on the right hand side of the panel; and other things: specific cracks, certain smudges on the back of the right hand; abrasions around the mouth; marks on the index finger of the right hand, and, of course, that network of cracks across the entire picture. It sounds like a medical report, yes? There, you see, on the back of the right hand of the panel.' The painting was now unwrapped and the marks plain to see. 'Just place it on the easel, Harry.'

Harry Allen took the wooden panel from the bodyguard and began to place it on the easel. As though noticing it for the first time, Grisombre gestured towards the other easel.

'And what is that?'

'A mere daub,' Morningdale raised his eyebrows. 'A dealer

is trying to pass it off as an unknown Rembrandt. I will show you later. Ah,' he stood back to admire the *Mona Lisa* now in place. 'Is she not beautiful? The mystery. The knowing yet unknowing. The timelessness. A tangible link with true genius.'

It was, without doubt, the copy which Labrosse had done for him, and Moriarty wondered what the Leftly reproduction was like. He hoped that it was of a similar standard. Inwardly he smiled, for whatever it was like, the Louvre would never allow it to be known that it was not the original – even if they discovered it. He went close to the painting, as though examining it in minute detail.

'Who did the copy?' he asked, almost as though he spoke to himself.

'As you suggested. Reginald Leftly.' Grisombre was at his elbow.

'It is good?'

'They are like peas in a pod.'

'And Leftly will not carouse and spill out the truth in some garden shop or gin house?'

'Mr Leftly,' said Grisombre softly, 'will remain silent as the grave.'

Morningdale nodded. 'Why should you share your commission, eh?'

'What about the money?'

'In a moment. How was the... er... the exchange effected?'

'As I told you, it was easy. By some mischance there was a small accident to one of the windows. A glazier had to go and put it right – in the Salon Carré. After the museum was closed. The man worked there.'

'I see.'

'Very sad, as it turned out, Monsieur Morningdale, very sad. The next day he was killed. An accident on his way to work. A runaway horse. Very sad. Now, what about the money?'

'You have done an excellent job,' Morningdale looked him straight in the eyes. This proposition had cost three lives. 'Excellent. Yes, it is time for you to be repaid, Monsieur Grisombre. If you gentlemen will just wait for a few moments. My secretary will provide you with another glass. Sit down, my friends.' He turned and walked slowly into his bedroom.

It took a few seconds over six minutes. When he returned it was as Professor James Moriarty, the one-time Mathematician, author of the *Treatise on the Binomial Theorem* and *The Dynamics of an Asteroid*. The three Frenchmen were ranged easily on the couch between the pair of easels and Harry Allen stood by Moriarty's door. As the Professor entered, so Harry Allen's hand came out of his jacket holding a pistol. The door to the other bedroom opened, Spear and Bertram Jacobs coming fast into the room, the barrels of their revolvers pointing steadily at the French trio, while, at the same moment, the main door opened disclosing William Jacobs similarly armed.

Grisombre and his companions moved slightly, their hands reaching for hidden weapons, then freezing in mid-air as the potential danger of the situation became apparent.

'How nice to see you again, Jean.' Moriarty's voice was almost a whisper, his head performing the familiar reptilian oscillation. 'Mr Jarvis Morningdale sends his compliments, but he is unable to help any further.'

Grisombre appeared to have lost his voice. The pair of bodyguards glowered, and Bert Spear stepped forward to relieve them of the weapons they carried.

'I really have to congratulate you, Monsieur Grisombre,' Moriarty spoke in his Jarvis Morningdale accent. 'It is time for you to be repaid.'

'I knew there was something. I knew that I had seen you before.' Grisombre's croak came from the back of his throat. 'That first night in *La Maison Vide.*'

'What a pity you did not identify me then, Jean. But, calm yourself, my friend. I am not a vindictive man. I know your value to my grand strategy. You remember that? Our united plan for Europe? The alliance with me at its head. No harm will come to you. I merely wished to show you who is superior.'

Grisombre made a disgusted noise. 'I stole *La Joconde* for you, did I not? Without a hint to the authorities.'

Moriarty gave a heavy mock sigh. 'I am afraid that is where

191

you are wrong, my friend. It is on that point alone that I rest my case. Harry,' his head inclined towards the bedroom door.

Harry Allen stepped back into the bedroom, reappearing almost immediately with the bottle of turpentine, the palette-knife and rag.

Moriarty, who had been clasping the Borchardt automatic, transferred the weapon to his waistband and took the items from Allen.

'Just watch, Jean. Watch and learn.'

He walked over to the painting which the Frenchmen had brought with them, and proceeded to saturate the cloth with turpentine. Handing the bottle back to Allen, Moriarty began to rub hard at the lower right hand corner of the *Mona Lisa*. One of the French bodyguards stifled a cry. Grisombre responded with a sharp oath. 'Moriarty. The Leonardo, you'll destroy . . .' But a jab in the ribs from Spear's revolver stopped him from going further.

'You think I do not know what I am doing?'

The Professor had taken the bottle again to add more turpentine to the cloth. The paint was starting to soften under his pressure, and now he assisted it with short hard strokes of the palette-knife. Quite quickly the dark area below the *Mona Lisa's* left arm was being stripped away.

'There.'

Moriarty stood back. Beneath the paint they could all plainly see a word cut into the poplar panel. MORIARTY.

Grisombre stared transfixed, shifting his gaze to the Professor for a second before it was drawn back to the carved name under the great painting which he personally had arranged to be stolen from the Louvre.

'It can't . . .' he began.

Moriarty, with great showmanship, turned and pointed dramatically at the despoiled picture.

'That is the painting you brought from France, Grisombre. The painting that was hanging in the Salon Carré. The one which you replaced with a copy. You see, my friend, I had already taken care of the lady, long before I commissioned you to steal her.' Two steps and he was beside the easel covered with the black cloth. 'You stole a worthless piece of wood and oil, Grisombre. The true Leonardo is already here.'

With a flourish, he whipped back the cloth to reveal Leonardo da Vinci's masterpiece.

Grisombre's face was a grey mixture of wonder and fear.

'I will admit that my charade has been a little dramatic,' Moriarty chuckled. 'But I think it well demonstrates my powers and proves my point. Surely, you will agree that it is I who should lead any alliance of our people in the continent of Europe.'

Slowly, Grisombre rose, walking like a man recovering from a grave illness, moving first to the real *Mona Lisa* and then to the one he had brought from Paris. The two bodyguards remained seated, covered by the revolvers. William Jacobs had come closer also, standing next to Grisombre.

'What will you do now?' asked the Frenchman.

'You betrayed me, my friend. With the others, you ousted me from leadership of a society which has a potential for plunder unknown since the days of Attila the Hun. What do you think I shall do?'

'I'll not stand and let you kill me like a dog,' shouted Grisombre, reaching up with his right hand, grasping the easel which held the fake *Mona Lisa* and, in one motion, whirling it round him, spinning in a full circle, scattering and skittling Moriarty's men who were taken off-balance by the sudden move, speed and enormous force with which the Frenchman swung the wooden frame. At the full circle of his turn, Grisombre let go of the easel, shouted to his bodyguards, and lunged for the door, dragging it open as Moriarty shouted –

'Grisombre, you fool, stop. I am not here to harm you. Grisombre.'

But he was gone, running helter-skelter down the corridor.

One of the bodyguards tried to follow, but William Jacobs, recovering quickly from the blow which had sent him to the floor, barred his way, the revolver cocked and pointed an inch from the man's head.

'Bertram. William,' snapped the Professor. 'Get after him. No shooting. As little violence as you need. Bring him back. If not here, then to Bermondsey.'

He had the Borchardt out, levelling it at the pair of

Frenchmen, as the Jacobs brothers, tucking their revolvers away, went tearing from the room in pursuit.

Spear went over to the door and kicked it closed, while Harry Allen began to clean up. The cases were repacked with haste, all traces removed from the rooms, the pictures stowed away, while Moriarty returned to his Morningdale disguise.

Within twenty minutes they had collected the luggage from the Frenchmen's rooms, and Spear, with Harry Allen in attendance, had left the hotel with Grisombre's bodyguards. A little later, Moriarty went down and paid all the bills. By this time Harkness had been summoned to drive the Professor away, leaving no trace except for the invisible presence of the lurkers around the hotel. They were still there when the police arrived.

Grisombre reached the bottom of the staircase and slowed his pace to a walk: patting his hair, smoothing his clothes in order to saunter through the foyer without attracting attention. He could, perhaps, reach some kind of cover in the large railway station. Possibly hide until the next Dover train was due to leave, then board it at the last moment. In the forefront of his mind, logic told him not to trust Moriarty. If he was in the Professor's place he would have no mercy on one who had betrayed him in an hour of need. Why should the Professor be any different?

As he reached the hotel doors, he glanced back to see the two burly figures running down the staircase. They were not bothering with niceties, not slowing down or trying to create an impression of normality. They came across the foyer towards him like hounds bearing down on a fox.

With panic jangling through him, Grisombre pushed through the doors and into the cool evening air outside. Uncertain, he ran across the forecourt which separated the hotel and station from Victoria Street, then, throwing all caution aside, plunged in among the traffic to reach the far pavement.

The street was a babbling, noisy bright river of human confusion. On the pavements people moved about their business, some sauntering, enjoying the hubbub, others with set faces, moving quickly towards late appointments, dinners spoiling, assignations which would not wait and might change the course of personal histories, trains to be caught, messages to be delivered, hours to be taken up in an outward show of activity, wives watching clocks, employers to be satisfied, consciences to be appeased. There were chattering pairs, soulful strolling lovers, silent married couples, pleading beggars, rogues and cheats, drunks and temperance men, shouting newsboys and bedazzled visitors.

In the road itself, the traffic passed slowly under the bright illumination of the gas standards: the winking lamps of the hansoms, the fully lit parade of omnibuses, each painted in its particular vivid colour – the open top decks giving passengers vantage views – moving advertisements glaring out their messages in whites and reds, greens and yellows – *Sanitas Disinfectant – non-poisonous and fragrant; Tomato Soup 57 Heinz varieties Baked Beans*, the long modesty boards under the top guard rails pleading for you to use *Okley's Knife Polish, Fry's Cocoa, Pears' Soap*.

Grisombre tried to hail a passing hansom, but the driver shouted back – 'Goin' for me supper, guv'nor' – so he turned, intending to weave back through the crowded pavements and, perhaps, retreat up some side street. He glimpsed the station and hotel, now far away across the road, and knew that Moriarty's men were somewhere amidst the traffic between.

He was about to move when one of the green *Favourite* omnibuses slowed, its horses coming dangerously near to the curb. The curving open steps up to the top deck seemed to issue an invitation as bold as its modesty board advertisement for *Ogden's 'Guinea Gold' Cigarettes*. As he leaped up onto the step, the conductor shouted, 'Where to, mate?' and Grisombre could only stammer, 'Wherever you're going.'

'All the way, mate? Right you are. Hornsey Rise, a tanner.'

Grisombre had no real idea of English money, and little enough of it in his pocket, so he pressed a florin into the man's hand, grabbing some change and his ticket as he pulled himself up the stairs, hardly heeding the conductor's, 'Watch your step. Hold tight.'

On the top deck the bus appeared to be swaying, and he was forced to clutch at the backs of the seats as he made his way up the narrow aisle, towards the front where a double, on the right, was empty. As he made the short, and seemingly precarious, journey, he could hear a commotion below him, on the platform: the sound of one particular voice drifting up. Moriarty's men were undoubtedly on the vehicle.

They would wait below. That was all they had to do: stand on the platform with the conductor, or take seats inside. Eventually Grisombre had to come down, and when he did, they would be there to greet him.

The omnibus was moving a little faster now, the driver edging his horses out into the main stream of traffic so that they were almost brushing wheels with the hansoms, carts, drays and buses moving in the opposite direction, back towards the station. Two buses passed, not more than a couple of feet from him, the drivers, below, shouting greetings or jeers to one another.

Grisombre looked forward. Coming towards them was another bus, a yellow *Camden* with the top deck half full, the occupants muffled and buttoned against the chill of the night air, chatting and pointing, laughing, one couple oblivious to everything except each other.

The buses were drawing almost level now. He could not hesitate for long. The seats at the rear were empty, and as they came abreast, Grisombre stood up, grasped the guard rail and vaulted full over the foot or so between the vehicles, landing half across the *Camden's* top rail, his feet on one of the seats, conscious of a shriek from a woman passenger near him, and a growl of protest from her companion.

Sliding into the seat, he glanced back. One of his pursuers had seen him and was leaping from the *Favourite's* platform, running hard, dodging and ducking through the jumble of traffic towards the bus upon which he had landed.

'Come on then, I'll have none of them larks on my bus.' The conductor was poking his head up from the stairs, only a few feet away. 'Orf, my lad, you should know better at your age. You'll do yourself a mischief. We had a lad last week nearly killed himself playing this hare and hounds lark. It's getting a craze. Come on orf before I call a copper.'

Moriarty's man was behind the conductor, on the stairs, saying something to him. The conductor registered surprise, then deference, and began to move down so that the big fellow could come up the steps.

Grisombre looked around wildly. Another green – the *Haverstock-Hill* – omnibus was almost alongside, the top deck empty, but the gap between the buses wide, almost three feet.

The man on the stairs was coming up. Grisombre turned towards the gap separating the two buses moving in opposite directions. He could see the other's modesty board commending the efficacy of *Grape Nuts*. He grabbed the guard rail, placing one foot on it to give himself the necessary spring, and launched himself in the direction of the other bus.

He knew it was no good as he jumped, for the two buses seemed to separate, swinging away from each other as he leaped, grabbing forward with clawing hands.

His fingers clutched momentarily at the rail of the *Haverstock-Hill*, then slipped. He scrabbled at the advertisement – the N of *Nuts* against his nose and eyes for a fraction before he fell between the shafts of a hansom driving up between the buses. There were shouts, a clatter, other noises. Then darkness.

Crow got back to King Street a shade before eleven o'clock to find Sylvia, her face set in a hard line not unlike the visages of the gargoyles they had noted on the Cathedral of Notre Dame in Paris, during their honeymoon.

'Angus, they have been here for you. From Scotland Yard.' Her inflections were much as you would expect from a gargoyle.

'Really, my dear,' Crow's mind spinning, stretching for the right answers to the questions as yet unasked.

'They said that you were not on duty tonight. Can you explain this?'

'No,' Crow said firmly. 'There are some things concerned with the job that I do not have to explain. I certainly would not weary you with a recital of all the odd things a detective is called upon to do in order to earn his wages.'

'Really.' That she did not altogether believe him was patently obvious.

'And what did they want from the Police Office, my dear?'

'They asked that you should go as directly as possible to the Grosvenor Hotel – something about a Mr Morningdale.'

Crow was already reaching for his hat which he had set down but a second ago. 'Jarvis Morningdale?'

'It would appear so.'

'At last.' One hand on the street door.

'He was there, earlier, it seems. Also there has been some kind of affray in Victoria Street nearby. In any case, your presence is required with some urgency.'

'Do not wait up for me, Sylvia. This may take some time.'

On the corner, he bumped into Harriet returning from her evening out. Crow raised his hat to the girl, his heart bouncing and stomach turning over at her smile, which was as warm as the one she had given him but an hour earlier when they had parted.

Crow's step was light as he almost danced along the sparkling pavement, turning this way and that in search of a hansom to take him to the Grosvenor. The world, it seemed to him, smiled broadly. In Harriet, Crow fancied he had at last found the answer to all his secret thoughts and hidden longings. Why, she was a mere slip of a girl, yet she made him feel like a young lad again, a dizzy young lad all sentiment and roses. The soot of the city, even, smelled to him like the rich heather of his youth. Her touch sent him into frenzies, and to have her near, in his arms, plunging in mutual congress, was as near heaven as he felt he would ever come.

At the Grosvenor, his spirits sank. Morningdale had been there, but was gone. A party of Frenchmen had also been there. They had gone as well. There were garbled and insubstantial tales from the staff concerning one of the Frenchmen leaving in haste followed by two consulting detectives from the Donrum Agency.

There was also a story from one of the beat constables. A ridiculous business – some foreigner being chased among the traffic, leaping from omnibus top to omnibus top and finally falling, between the shafts of a hansom, and being picked up in a stunned condition.

'His two friends said they would take him to the hospital, sir,' the constable told him. 'It was all something and nothing really, and I had my time cut out directing the traffic. He'd had a mite too much to drink, I believe. Don't think he was hurt bad, but I said as how I would call up at the Western

Dispensary as soon as I could.'

Crow would have put a hundred sovereigns on there being no trace of the injured foreign gentleman, or his friends, at the Western Dispensary. Nor any other hospital. He sat down, in the manager's office of the Grosvenor, and attempted to piece together what he could concerning Mr Jarvis Morningdale's visit to the hotel, the presence of the fictional employees of the, equally fictional, Donrum Detective Agency, and the trio of French visitors. He was quite convinced, an hour or so later, that he had once again missed James Moriarty. A black despair settled over Angus McCready Crow on his way back to King Street. It was a despair which, he knew, could only be dispersed by the tender ministrations of Harriet.

Grisombre knew that he was alive by the aching in his head, the pain across his arm and the voices coming from the blurred shapes around him. He seemed to recall that he had been driven uncomfortably in some kind of cab. He also had a vivid picture of the side of the omnibus, the frightened snort of horses, and that terrible sensation of falling.

His sight cleared and he began to struggle. James Moriarty was leaning over him, and there were others in the background. Among them Wilhelm Schleifstein.

'You are safe, Grisombre,' Moriarty cooed. 'It was foolish of you to run. Nobody wishes you harm.'

He struggled again, but had to sink back onto the pillow out of weakness.

'It is true what the Professor says, Jean,' Schleifstein came closer. 'You have a broken arm, some bruises, and no doubt your pride is hurt. I know that mine was when the Professor led me such a merry dance, but what he says is true. He merely wishes to prove himself in the ascendancy. We have talked much and I am convinced. The continental alliance between us should stand, with James Moriarty at its head.'

'Do not bother yourself with it now.' Moriarty even sounded concerned. 'You are safe, and will be kept so for a time, but my people will treat you like your own. Sleep and I will return tomorrow.'

Grisombre nodded and closed his eyes, slipping into a deep healing sleep during which he dreamed of the top decks of a hundred omnibuses moving steadily down a well-lit street. All the passengers were women, their eyes and faces reflecting a mocking smile. The women were all identical and he could name each one. The Madonnae Lisas.

Moriarty took out the leather-bound journal, turning to the rear pages which contained the coded notes on the six men at whom his total reserves were directed. Taking his pen he drew a thin diagonal line through the pages that dealt with Grisombre.

LONDON AND ROME:
Tuesday, 9 March – Monday, 19 April 1897

(A fall from grace and a Roman interlude)

'The timing is of great importance,' said Moriarty. 'But, Spear will attend to that side of the matter. What I really need to know, dear Sal, is whether or not you feel our Italian Tigress is ready.'

'She's as ready as makes no odds.' Sal Hodges sounded a trifle put out, as though diffident to the Professor's questioning. She turned to view her half-clad body in the long mirror which graced the wall of the bedroom. 'These new French drawers, James, do they titillate your fancy?'

'Fripperies, Sal, icing to a cake that is already good enough at any time.'

'As good a mixture as Carlotta?'

'More spicy. Tell me about Carlotta's readiness.'

'I have done so. She's as ready as she will ever be.' She came over to where the Professor lay. 'Your questions tell me that you are about to take the journey to Rome, James.'

Silently he nodded. 'Easter is the only time that it can all be brought together with any certainty.'

'The girl is well-schooled. Just mind that you do not teach her other things while she is with you.'

'Am I not to be her father?'

'Then I've no doubt it will be an incestuous business.'

'She is but bait, Sal, and, talking of bait, it is time to take other steps. You say that Crow is well hooked?'

'Harriet tells me that he says he cannot live without her.'

'Excellent. It sounds as though he is well into the madness which takes men at his time of life.'

'What do you plan?'

'When a man takes to a habit and circumstances suddenly deny it to him, Sal, the man often plunges to his own destruction. I have seen it happen again and again. Crow has sown his own seeds. He must now reap the harvest. Get word to Harriet. She must now leave, with stealth, without word, without explanation. Here today. Tomorrow gone. We will need do no more, for human nature will arrange matters for us.'

'And you are off to Italy?'

'With two disguises, the ruby necklace that looked so pretty on Lady Scobie's throat – the Scobie Inheritance, I believe they called it – and our pretty young Miss Carlotta.'

Harriet's unexpected departure struck Crow all of a heap. She had been there, her usual smiling and pretty self in the morning when he left for New Scotland Yard. She even gave their special secret signal which was a token of the beautiful, if illicit, experience they shared. When he returned that evening, tired and concerned regarding the interview he had been called to by the Commissioner, she was gone.

Sylvia did not stop talking. 'Just a note on the kitchen table, Angus. A plain note. *I am leaving*, signed *H. Barnes*. No explanation. Nothing. I am leaving. H. Barnes – I did not even know she had another name. Servants just do not know their place any more...' And so on in the same vein until Crow's head seemed about to burst.

There was no note for him. No message. Not a hint. After dinner – a scratch affair put together at short notice by Sylvia – he sat in the parlour, with his wife still prattling on and on, and sank into such gloom that he could have wept.

At bedtime it was worse than ever, for his mind began to play tricks, turning him to great fantasies of what might have happened to her. She was, in truth, the one constant factor that stayed in Crow's head, almost to the banishment of all else. So, when the Commissioner sent for him on the following afternoon – for the second time in two days – the detective found himself hard pressed to give any reasonable account of the day's activities.

The Commissioner was not pleased. 'There are three

robberies on which you appear to have made no progress,' he chided, irritable and peppery as a curry. 'Not to mention that disgraceful business in Edmonton, and the murder of old Tom Bolton. Now there is this Morningdale matter.'

'Morningdale,' repeated Crow as though hearing the name for the first time.

'My dear man, I need explanations, not repetitions. Your mind seems to have been elsewhere these past few weeks. If I had not seen your private arrangements with my own eyes, I would take it that you had a spot of domestic turmoil. Or worse, that you had become involved with some woman.' He made the last word sound like some dreadful serpent.

Crow bit his tongue and swallowed hard.

'Now, the Morningdale thing. You, and you alone, Crow, apparently circulated that name, and a description, to the best hotels in London, asking that you should be informed if the fellow turned up as a guest. Yesterday you told me that it had something to do with the erstwhile Professor Moriarty. Yet you have given no details.'

'I . . .' began Crow.

'Even your sergeant did not know who Morningdale was, nor what was required of him. The result was that when an hotel manager reported his presence, there's none to take action, and you are not to be found. This is no way to run a detective force, Inspector, let alone a police force. Now tell me about Morningdale.'

Crow told him, in a somewhat garbled form, of his correspondence with Chanson, and his suspicions regarding the strange goings on in and around the Grosvenor. He was quite aware that he had not told the tale well.

'It is all mere supposition, Crow,' barked the Commissioner. 'You do not even make it rhyme. You are looking for a man called Morningdale because a former associate of Moriarty's is seen talking to him in Paris. He turns up at the Grosvenor. So do some fakesters posing as detectives; so, indeed, do three Frenchmen. The manager tries to find you and fails. You leave no message as to where you can be found. There is some kind of fracas at the hotel. Two of the so-called detectives chase one of the Frenchmen out of the hotel. Morningdale leaves – paying all the bills in a proper manner.

The manager again tries to find you. An officer is even sent to your house, and your good lady wife does not know that you are off duty. When you finally arrive at the Grosvenor, the birds have flown. You offer no explanation as to what you imagine they were about, nor even evidence that the law has been flouted – except for a bit of horseplay involving public transport: a misdemeanour at the most. That kind of thing comes before the courts every day, or is dealt with by the constable on the spot. Or perhaps you are not conversant with the dangerous game of hare and hounds which the young rips play across the tops of omnibuses? Perhaps, Inspector Crow, a term of duty back in uniform, dealing with everyday problems, would make you more familiar with the difficulties of this force.'

It was a direct threat, and Crow knew it. What the Commissioner was saying, in effect, was do your job properly or you'll be back at some divisional police station up to your ears in paperwork and routine – with a generous loss in status to boot. A fate worse than death to the ambitious Crow.

Even with this knowledge, he could not pull himself out of the dreadful lethargy, loneliness and sleepless desire which now possessed him. Every waking thought turned on Harriet. Where was she? Why had she left? Had he caused some calamity? In the weeks that followed, Crow's work began to run downhill at an alarming rate. His mind could not seem to grasp at the most simple pieces of evidence; decisions became more and more difficult to make; he was vague in giving orders; on two occasions he followed wrong trails and once made an arrest so unjustified that the man had to be released with grovelling apologies from all involved. The most galling problem was that he had nobody in whom to confide. In the week before Easter it became apparent, even to Crow in his state of mind, that the axe would fall at any moment. The Commissioner would be upon him like the proverbial ton of bricks. Yet he still yearned for Harriet; mooned over her like a lovesick boy; pined for her; could not sleep for her.

In a final act of desperation, Crow sent a message to Holmes for an interview, under the private conditions which they had maintained since the spring of '94.

'My dear fellow,' Holmes greeted him in good humour.

'You look unwell, Crow. If I was not so set in keeping you and Watson apart, I'd get the good doctor to take a look at you. What's amiss, man? Are you off your feed or what?'

'More than that, Mr Holmes,' replied the unhappy police officer. 'I fear that I am in great trouble and have none but myself to blame for it.'

'You have come to make a clean breast of it to me, then,' said Holmes, seating himself in his favourite chair and igniting his pipe. 'An indiscretion, perhaps?'

Crow poured out his sorry tale, leaving nothing hidden, and even including the embarrassing details of his intrigue with the comely Harriet.

Holmes listened gravely, and when all was finished, he pulled hard on his pipe.

'The story you have told me is as old as time, Crow. Women, I have found on the whole, come between man and his natural flow of clear thought. I have personally eschewed their company like the plague, though I understand the problems. Indeed, there was one woman who might just...' His voice trailed off as though his heart had momentarily taken control of the incisive brain. 'If you can remain a bachelor, taking pleasure without becoming emotionally troubled, all well and good. It would seem that you managed to do this for a long while. Until Mrs Crow, eh?'

Crow nodded sadly.

'As for your marriage, you are old enough to know that the art of a good marriage is not so much in the loving as in the controlling. There is an old Arabian proverb which says that the discontented woman asks for toasted snow. It strikes me that Mrs Crow, begging your pardon, is just such a woman. You have to decide. Do you provide the toasted snow for her, or do you remain master in your own home? You have done neither. You have sought refuge with a woman below your station – and one who has given you up on a whim.'

'It is difficult with Sylvia,' Crow tried lamely.

'I am quite disappointed in you, Inspector Crow, for you have committed one of the most deadly sins. You have allowed your emotions to affect your work, and that could be the end of you.'

'I think the Commissioner will send for me any day.'

'You must address yourself to your work and put the wretched Harriet from your mind.'

'It is not that easy.'

'Then to blazes with you, sir. It should be. What of our pact against Moriarty? Come, tell me more of this business with Morningdale and Grisombre – for I have no doubt that you are right in your deductions there. Morningdale equals Moriarty.'

Crow spoke for some five minutes concerning his theories on Professor Moriarty and the revenge he was seeking against those whom he imagined where his enemies.

'You see,' said Holmes gleefully. 'You are really quite capable of logical thought, even in the midst of your darkness. There has been no sign of the German since the business at Edmonton, and I doubt we'll hear much more of the Frenchman now. Both at the bottom of the river if I know Moriarty's diabolical methods.' He suddenly stopped in mid-flow. 'Describe this Harriet creature to me again. In her mid-twenties you said?'

Angus Crow described the object of his affections in great detail, though with a certain amount of dramatic license as is often the case with those afflicted by Cupid's dart.

'I see you are riddled with this damnable disease,' remarked Holmes. 'But be a good fellow and make a long arm for that large volume there. You say her surname is Barnes? It rings a bell that may well blot out your misery.'

Crow passed over the large index volume in which Holmes kept references on every subject and person who proved an interest to him.

'Barnes . . .' Holmes turned the pages. 'Baker . . . Baldwin . . Balfour – bad business that, Crow, fourteen years penal servitude,* Banks, Isabella – a shade before my time but

---

*Balfour. Holmes is referring here to Jabez Spencer Balfour, the English businessman who, in 1895, had to face an extradition order from Argentina and trial in London for fraud, concerning his huge Balfour Group of companies. He served a term of fourteen years penal servitude during which he wrote the famous *My Prison Life* – possibly the best-written of all books of prison reminiscences.

interesting, like all murderous doctors.* Ah, here we are, I thought as much. Barnes, Henry: born Camberwell 1850. Common thief. 1889 vagrant though with some resources. See Parker. One daughter, Harriet, brought up in common lodging houses. 1894 prostitute working from house owned by Mrs Sally Hodges. Is that not a load off your mind, Crow?'

'I don't . . .?'

'Indeed? Parker, as we both know, ran Moriarty's network of spies for a long time. Barnes worked for him, and if you have no idea who Sally Hodges is, then you have no right to your present occupation. The Professor is on to you, Angus Crow, and you have been enticed like a rabbit into a gin. Moriarty is diabolically clever. I've seen him at this game time and again. He catches people by the hip, traps them by the weakest chink in their fabric. Miss Harriet was meant to lead you into this, and through it Moriarty has all but consumed your mind.' He had risen and was pacing the floor in an agitated manner. 'A pity I cannot use Watson in this. We have to give you a breathing space, so that you can recover your senses and be saved from the wrath that is to come. I would suggest a good doctor who will order you to rest for a week or two. In that time we might well lay that devilish man by the heels. I'll warrant there's evil work afoot in Italy or Spain now.' He ceased his pacing and faced Crow. 'I know of a good man in Harley Street. Will you go to him?'

'I will do anything to put myself straight. And bring Moriarty down.'

Crow's fury, at having been duped by a woman in the Professor's employ, showed in his face and the tense way in which he held his body.

'Dr Moore Agar will put you right,' Holmes smiled grimly. 'Though he probably despairs of me. He recently prescribed a

---

*Isabella Banks (or Bankes). Bigamous wife of Dr Thomas Smethurst. Smethurst was found guilty of murdering her by poison in 1859, but after sentence a prominent medical authority, Sir Benjamin Brodie, was directed to look into the case for the Home Office. As a result, Smethurst was reprieved and served one year's imprisonment for bigamy. Holmes' remark clearly shows what he thought of the case.

rest cure which was somewhat interrupted. You must remind me to tell you of the Cornish Horror sometime.'*

'Then I shall go to your Dr Agar.'

Luigi Sanzionare, the most dangerous man in Italy, was a person of habit when it came to matters of religion. He went to Mass twice in the year – at Easter and on his saint's day – and made his confession each Holy Saturday, at the same confessional box in Il Gesù, the Jesuit church in Rome.

No matter what other plans were pending, what robberies to be arranged, what orders to be given to the many criminal men and women who looked to him as a leader, Luigi Sanzionare did his best to make Eastertide a holy time, therefore insuring his soul against hell and damnation.

His mistress, Adela Asconta, who had little in the way of religious faith, did not care for the manner in which Luigi would leave her at their villa in Ostia on each Good Friday, and not return until after the High Mass in the Basilica di Pietro within the walls of the Vatican, on Easter Day. She could quite well have stayed in their large house on the Via Banchi Vecchi, but Adela Asconta could not abide the city at this time of the year: there were so many foreigners, and the place became unbearably crowded. She understood that this was good for her lover's trade: for visitors were easy marks,

*There is no specific dating, regarding this conversation, in Inspector Crow's notes. However, it must have taken place sometime after 20 March. Holmes was certainly in Cornwall between 16 and 20 March; and probably for some time before those dates, which cover the period of *The Adventure of the Devil's Foot*, and are exactly recorded by Dr Watson. The real interest here, in view of following events, is, however, Holmes' mention of Dr Moore Agar who was the cause of the great detective being in Cornwall at all. Watson records that Holmes' 'iron constitution showed symptoms of giving way in the face of constant hard work of a most exacting kind, *aggravated, perhaps, by occasional indiscretions of his own*'. Moore Agar prescribed a complete rest. There can be little doubt of the indiscretions, and the fact that they were connected with the drug being supplied to Holmes via Mr Charles Bignall of Orchard Street. Of this, more later.

particularly for the pick-pockets and hotel thieves who had their own feast days with pilgrims to the Eternal City.

However, each Holy Week was the same. Adela Asconta would fret at Ostia, worrying, not for Luigi Sanzionare's immortal soul, but for her possible betrayal. Luigi had a way with the ladies and Signorina Asconta was capable of extreme jealousy. This year it was all worse than ever because of the telegram from England.

The telegram had arrived on Holy Thursday, as Luigi was preparing to make the journey into the city. WE NEED YOU HERE URGENTLY. GREAT PROFIT ASSURED. ROOM RESERVED FOR YOU ALONE AT LANGHAM HOTEL. WILLY AND JEAN.

'Willy Schleifstein and Jean Grisombre,' Luigi explained to her.

'I know who they are. You think me as much a buffoon as yourself?' For all her beauty and charm, Adela Asconta had a rocket temper, and the pudgy Luigi Sanzionare was complete master of his world, except when it came to women. In particular, he was slave to his mistress. 'You will go to them, Gee-Gee?' She continued to spit fire. 'It is they who should be coming to you.'

'They would not send for me unless there was some great profit, *cara mia*. The best kind of profit which buys you the things you like best.'

'And which you also like. You will go alone?'

'It would seem so. My heart will not be still until I return to you, Adela. You know that.'

'I know nothing. There are women in London also. Alone, Luigi? Is that really safe?'

She would at least prefer one of his close men – either Benno or Giuseppe – to be with him. Either would report any indiscretions to her.

'Benno can come as far as Paris. After that I go alone.'

'And you'll give up your precious Easter in Rome?'

'Never. I leave on Monday. You think I would miss our Easter Sunday afternoon together?'

'Yes, if it meant more power, more money.'

'I shall go on Monday. There is a poste restante address here.' He tapped the form. 'I will telegraph them today.'

Having betrayed her anger at the thought of being

separated from her protector, Adela now tried a wheedling approach.

'You bring something nice back for me. Something really special.'

'The gift of a lifetime.'

In truth, Luigi Sanzionare had already begun to look forward to a respite from the toils of crime in Rome. The city was an ugly place at the moment. The politics of last year still sent reverberations through the streets. They lived in a time of turmoil in Italy, and the defeat of the army at Adowa in the previous March, had caused the government to fall. Now, a year later, the wounded and prisoners were just returning, bringing their own personal humility with them, reminding people of the instability.

Sanzionare recalled that meeting with the great Professor Moriarty on the last time he had travelled to London. Moriarty had said they should sue for chaos, for in a state of chaos their own particular trades would prosper. He wondered now if Il Professore had been right. There was not much prosperity to be scavenged from a defeated army. But then, Moriarty had been proved useless. A failure. Yes, it would be good to get out of Italy for a while. The spring would soon turn to summer, and Adela was never at her best in the heat – so demanding.

He travelled in to the city, with Benno, swarthy, hawk-eyed, always somewhere near in case enemies – and there were many, particularly from among the Sicilians – decided that it was time for a change in the power structure.

On Good Friday, Sanzionare addressed himself to his religion, visibly moved at the rituals of the day – the unveiling of the cross, the veneration and the solemn chanting as the altar was stripped bare and washed, like the washing of the body of Christ after the crucifixion. He prayed for the souls of his parents, and friends who had died in his service. He also prayed for his own soul and reflected upon the evil which ran riot in this vale of tears.

After the liturgy of the day, Sanzionare returned to his house on the Via Banchi Vecchi and received various visitors – two men who were to be trusted with starting a fire in a well-known shop on the Via Veneto. The increase of prices was affecting everybody. The owner of this establishment was refusing to pay more for the honour of being insured by Sanzionare's people.

'Just a small fire,' he told the pair of *piromani*. 'So that they will understand.'

He saw a young man who was to arrange for a café proprietor to be badly beaten.

'Not until after *Pasqua*, counselled Sanzionare. 'And I do not want him dead, you understand?'

'*Si, Padre mio.*' He was a handsome lad with strong muscles and shoulders like a statue. 'There will be no killing.'

Sanzionare smiled and waved him away. He was pleased, as he did not like robbing people of their lives – only when it was unavoidable. For a moment he thought of the confession he would have to make tomorrow. He would confess to theft which would cover a multitude of sins, from robbery to murder – for murder was in reality the theft of life: a mortal sin which would be washed away by the grace of God invested in his priestly servant, and the sincere act of contrition which Sanzionare would make with his penance.

Benno came into the high airy room with a small tray containing a silver coffee pot and cups.

'Many more?' Sanzionare asked wearily.

'Two only. *Carabinieri*. Capitano Regalizzo from the Ludovisis and Capitano Meldozzi.'

Sanzionare sighed. 'We know what Regalizzo requires – a little more olive oil, eh?' He rubbed his right thumb in a circular motion across his fingers. 'But the other, do we know him?'

Benno shook his head.

'Let me see Regalizzo. Tell Meldozzi we shall not keep him long.'

Regalizzo was a dandy and his uniform probably cost him the best part of a whole month's salary. He was polite, solicitous concerning Signorina Asconta, and talked of how depressing it was with the prisoners from the Ethiopian campaign now on the streets; and how terrible the prices were. He was sorry, but there were two houses – 'You know the ones, I think' – which were causing him much trouble. He thought that he might have to close them down.

Sanzionare nodded, opened his desk drawer and paid over the money, as they both knew he would even before the conversation began. The police officer left, all smiles, bows and good wishes.

Sanzionare lit a cigar and sat back to await the other policeman. He was in plain clothes and they had not met before.

'You are a friend of Capitano Regalizzo perhaps?' asked Sanzionare once they were seated.

'I know him,' said Arnaldo Meldozzi. 'In fact, I know him quite well, but I am not here to talk about his problems, but yours, Signore.'

Sanzionare shrugged, lifting his right hand, palm upwards, in a gesture of giving. 'I did not know I had problems.'

'They are not serious. At least they can be easily, shall we say, rendered harmless.'

'Tell me about my problems.'

'The police in London have been asking about you.'

It was a sudden unnerving blow which Sanzionare felt go through him like a physical pain. 'In London?'

'Yes. I have had this letter. Are you familiar with this Inspector Crow?' He passed the document across the desk.

Sanzionare devoured it, his eyes racing over the page.

'What do you make of this, Capitano?' he asked, rubbing the back of one hand with the other. His palms were wet.

'I make nothing of anything, Signore. I merely feel that you should know when the police forces of other countries are showing an interest in such a renowned citizen as yourself.'

'Tell me,' he paused, inspecting his manicured nails as if looking for some defect. 'Tell me, have you replied to this extraordinary request?'

The policeman smiled. He was young and perhaps, Sanzionare reasoned, ambitious. 'I have acknowledged its receipt. No more.'

'And what do you propose to do? He asks for news of any unusual visitors or incidents concerning myself.'

'I know of nothing to report.' The eyes slid up, briefly holding Sanzionare's then away again. 'I know of nothing to report. As yet.'

'Capitano,' he began, as though broaching a difficult

subject. 'What do you require most in life at this moment?'

Capitano Meldozzi nodded. 'I was hoping that you might ask me that. I have a wife and three children, *Eccellenza*. It is a calamity that befalls most men, I know. My wages are not good. I was wondering, perhaps, if you could put me in the way of some extra form of employment.'

'It can be arranged,' Sanzionare said wearily, thinking to himself that here was another mouth to feed, or another five mouths to feed and, perhaps, one of the girls giving up her time for nothing once a week. It was ever thus for a peaceful life.

The news concerned him, though. London police asking about him was not a good sign, particularly as he was about to travel to England. Was it wise? He pondered long. Schleifstein and Grisombre would come to him if he called. It would be better not to mention the incident to Adela. He would have to go.

Through Holy Saturday the city seemed to be waiting, poised on the brink of the great Christian festival, bursting with the desire to ring out its bells and join in the cry of 'Christus Surrexit. Hallelluja'. The day was clear and warm, pleasant, without the terrible overpowering heat which would eventually descend. Luigi Sanzionare prepared for his yearly confession, and then left the house. He had one or two small matters to attend to before making his way to Il Gesù. The tickets to be bought for the journey. A few small purchases to make.

He first saw her at the Spanish Steps around mid-morning. Tall, dark, enchanting in a lemon-coloured gown and broad hat, a sunshade furled and carried with elegance. As he approached, he could almost swear that she stopped talking to her companion and turned her dark eyes upon him. She had that same smouldering quality which Adela had possessed when he had first set eyes on her – a look, not quite of promise, but of possibility. It was a very special sensation that came with the look, and it sent a cold trickle down the back of Sanzionare's neck. The girl, who could not have been much more than twenty-five years old, was with a man almost twice her age, maybe more – in his late fifties or early sixties, Sanzionare considered – a tall, stooping person with short

213

dark hair, gold pince-nez and elaborate manners, most solicitous towards the girl: even fatherly. In some ways the man reminded Sanzionare of the English criminal, Moriarty, but the resemblance was only superficial.

He saw them again at lunchtime. Sitting only a few tables away from him in the trattoria he liked to use off the Cavour, near the Castel San Angelo. She appeared diffident towards the man with her, talking little and picking at her food. Sanzionare was now convinced that her companion was a relative rather than a lover. On several occasions, when his eyes were drawn to her, he found the girl was already looking across the room at him. Each time, she lowered her eyes in a demure manner, and each time the same cold sweat broke out on Sanzionare's neck. As the meal progressed, so the cold turned to a glow, and then heat – a flush spreading downwards.

He looked up again, and the girl was gazing back with what might have been adoration in her eyes. He smiled, inclining his head slightly. For a moment she appeared confused, then she too smiled, lips parted and the look even more obvious than before. It was the sort of visual flattery which Sanzionare enjoyed, a hint that he still had the magnetic power from which his great confidence flowed.

The girl's companion said something, leaning forward over the table, and she answered, fussing with her napkin and smiling in a set fashion, like a bad painting. Shortly afterwards they left the restaurant, but, at the door, the girl paused and threw a quick backward glance in Sanzionare's direction.

An hour later, Luigi Sanzionare, full of piety, entered the sumptuous Baroque church of Il Gesù – mother church of the Society of Jesus – to keep his yearly tryst with God's pardon.

It was cool inside, a hint of smoke from many flickering candles, grouped around nests of prickets set before statues and altars, of which there were many. Whispers, coughs, shuffles and footsteps echoed around the walls, as though intruding on the pent-up prayers of the faithful, stored in the pillars and stones for over three centuries.

Sanzionare breathed in, the scent of lingering incense and drifting smoke pungent in his nostrils – the odour of sanctity.

Crossing himself with holy water from the stoop by the door, he genuflected towards the High Altar and joined the kneeling group of penitents near the confessional box on the right hand side of the nave.

Sanzionare was not to know that Father Marc Negratti SJ, who should have been hearing confessions from this box, and whose name was in fact displayed outside, had met with an unfortunate minor accident. His superiors did not even know of it. Nor did they know the priest who sat quietly dispensing counsel and absolution at this station.

The priest was soft-voiced and thorough. One could not have known that he was waiting to hear one voice and one only from the penitent's side of the fine wire grille. He listened to the repetitious lists of sins with a slight smile playing around the corners of his mouth, though when any sin of great enormity came whispering into his ear, the priest's head moved very slightly from side to side.

On his lap, where nobody could see, the priest held a pack of playing cards. Without looking down he was silently performing a series of sleights and card changes with great expertise.

'Bless me, Father, for I have sinned.' Sanzionare pressed his lips close to the grille.

Moriarty smiled inwardly, this was the supreme irony which he had plotted. Moriarty, the most advanced criminal mind in Europe, listening to the devout confession of Italy's most notorious villain. More, giving him absolution and sowing the seeds of the man's decline so that he could raise him again.

Sanzionare had neglected God, failed to pray regularly, lost his temper, used blasphemous and obscene language, cheated, stolen, committed fornication and coveted his neighbour's goods, not to mention his neighbour's wife, after whom he had lusted.

When the list was finished and the penitent had made an act of contrition and begged for forgiveness, Moriarty began to speak quietly.

'You realize, my son, that your greatest sin is that of neglecting God?'

'Yes, Father.'

'But I need to know more of your venial sins.'

Sanzionare frowned. Jesuits sometimes probed. This was not his usual priest.

'You say that you have stolen. What have you stolen?'

'Other people's possessions, Father.'

'In particular?'

'Money, and things.'

'Yes. And fornication. How many times have you committed fornication since last Easter?'

This was impossible. 'I cannot say, Father.'

'Two or three times? Or many times?'

'Many times, Father.'

'The flesh is weak then. You are not married?'

'No, Father.'

'You do not indulge in unnatural practices?'

'No, Father,' almost shocked.

'The fornication must stop, my son. You should be married. With the strength of the Sacrament of marriage around you, the flesh would be easier to control. Marriage is the answer. You must think seriously about this, for continued fornication will only take you into the flames of eternal damnation. You understand?'

'Yes, Father.'

He was worried. This priest was taking him nearer to the brink. Marriage? He could never marry Adela. If he married her she would never leave him in peace. She might even intrude into business matters. Eternal damnation though, that was a price indeed.

'Very well. Is there anything else you have to tell me?'

It was not such a good confession. He had misled the priest over the question of stealing. Would that also negate the absolution? No. He had confessed. He knew what he meant and so would God and the Holy Virgin.

'For your penance you will say three Paters and three Aves.' Moriarty raised his hand in blessing. 'Ego te absolvo in nomine Patris, et Filii et Spiritus Sancti.' It was the ultimate blasphemy of the Professor's career.

Outside, in the fresh spring sunshine, Sanzionare felt in need of a drink. No, he must take care. He must not put himself in the way of sin before making his communion in the morning. He would walk for a while. Perhaps go to the Borghese Gardens. They had looked beautiful that morning. It would be pleasant there. Benno was behind him, watching, eyes peeled.

Then he saw her again. Just a fleeting glimpse of the lemon-coloured dress and the hat. It is like some kind of paperchase, he thought.

Much troubled by the priest and his advice, Sanzionare walked, turning matters over in his mind. True, he supposed that it was natural for a man like himself to be married, but his appetites had always been so varied. He was as good as married anyway. Adela was always behaving like a wife. She nagged as much as a wife. The girl in the lemon dress. Now what a wife she would make. What a wife indeed. Perhaps, once Easter was over and he was on his way to some new venture in London he would be able to think properly. That was it, he needed to be away from the cloying atmosphere of Rome.

Towards six o'clock, Sanzionare turned into the Via Veneto. A small drink before going back to the house for the evening. Just one to lay the dryness in his throat.

She was sitting at a pavement table at one of the larger cafés, with her male companion, watching the passing parade and taking sips from a tall glass. She saw him at almost the same moment as he caught sight of her. Sanzionare beat back the instincts which flooded into his body and mind, but he could not control the urge to make some sort of advance. The café was crowded, white-aproned waiters almost running between the tables to keep pace with orders, swinging their loaded trays of coffee and drinks high above their heads, performing feats of balancing which would not have been out of place in the circus.

On the pavement people thronged in an almost ritual walking: women, young and old, arm in arm, with each other or their husbands, couples dourly chaperoned, pilgrims from other parts of Europe and as far away as America, young boys eyeing pairs of girls: a happy, self-conscious bustle, full of chatter and colour.

The table at which the girl sat had one spare metal chair drawn up to it, tilted forward with the back angled against the

217

table. It was not in the best of taste, but Sanzionare was determined. He approached the table, glancing back for a second to ensure that Benno was not far away.

'Pray excuse me,' he bowed over the couple. 'There is little room, would it be an imposition if I joined you?'

The man looked up. 'Not at all. We shall be leaving in a moment.'

'Thank you, you are most kind,' steady and not gushing. Then, turning to catch a passing waiter, he ordered a Vermouth Torino. 'You will not join me?' To the couple.

'Thank you. No.' The tall man did not smile and the girl shook her head, her eyes telling Sanzionare that she wished she could say yes.

'Allow me to introduce myself,' Sanzionare thrust forward. 'Luigi Sanzionare, of this city.'

'My name is Smythe – with a *y*.' The girl's companion spoke Italian with the slow, short-accented speech of an Englishman. 'My daughter, Carlotta.'

'You are not Italian?' Graceful, flattering surprise.

'My mother was Italian.' The girl's accent was pure Neapolitan. 'But,' she smiled, 'this is my first visit to her country.'

'Ah. It is beautiful, no?'

'Very. I would like to live here, but my father says we must return to England because of his work.'

Sanzionare turned to Smythe. 'Your wife is not with you in Rome?'

'My wife, sir, died a year ago.'

'Oh, excuse me. I could not know. Then this is a pilgrimage?'

'I wished to show Carlotta her mother's native land. We have been spending a few days in Rome before returning to London.'

'To London. Ah, a fine city, I know it well,' lied Sanzionare. 'You are staying for Easter though?'

'Just until it is over,' Carlotta was imperceptibly moving closer to him. 'I am most sad to be leaving.'

'A pity. I would have liked to show you the great sights. Nobody can show off Rome as well as the Roman born.'

'We have seen all the great sights.' Carlotta's father was

decidedly prickly.

Sanzionare remained unperturbed. 'Perhaps you would do me the honour of dining with me?'

'That would be . . .' Carlotta began.

'Out of the question,' snapped Smythe. 'We have much to do this evening. Kind of you to ask, but impossible.'

'But surely, Father . . .'

'Out of the question. Carlotta, we must leave. Dinner awaits at the hotel.'

'I am sorry. My manners are lacking,' oozed Sanzionare, rising. 'I did not mean to intrude.'

Smythe was paying the bill, examining the ticket as though the waiter was out to defraud him.

'I hope that we may meet again, Signorina,' Sanzionare bowed over Carlotta's hand.

'I would like that very much.' Her eyes were almost pleading, as though she was in great need of help. Fantastic thoughts formed pictures in Sanzionare's head. A lady in distress. He saw himself as a knight of old, riding to the rescue. 'Very much,' Carlotta repeated. 'But I feel it is not likely.'

Smythe bowed stiffly, took his daughter's arm, and they were gone, swallowed by the stream of strollers.

Sanzionare fleetingly caught sight of one of his best pick-pockets, weaving through the crowd, making for Smythe. He looked around for Benno, signalling frantically until the man closed with him. He gave quick instructions for Benno to head off the pickpocket.

'He is not to touch that Englishman. I will have his hands crushed if he does.'

Benno nodded and was away into the drifting crowd.

It was one of those strange meetings in life, Sanzionare reflected. A moment which, if the circumstances had been different, might have blossomed into a new way of living, a way with some certainty of eternal salvation. It was obviously not to be, so he would go on ruling the underworld of this part of Italy, presumably with Adela as his consort. Maybe, while he was in London he might see the beautiful Carlotta again? No, this period of separation from Adela and Rome would be best used making up his mind about his future state. If need be, he might even marry his mistress. A passionate affair with a woman like Carlotta – for it would be most passionate – might be the end of him, at least it would be overtaxing.

On Easter Sunday morning he attended Mass early and then went to the High Mass at St Peter's, mingling with the crowds outside to receive the Papal Blessing before returning to Ostia and the tearful Adela, now greatly emotional over his impending journey.

Moriarty, divested of his disguise as the Englishman, Smythe, sat at the writing desk in his room at the Albergo Grande Palace, composing a letter. Carlotta, who was bored and had come in from her own adjoining room, lounged on the bed, sucking fat red grapes.

Signorina, Moriarty wrote in a hand well disguised from his own, *I must warn you that your protector, Luigi Sanzionare, has departed today by train for Paris in company with a much younger woman than yourself. She is Miss Carlotta Smythe, half English and half Neapolitan. I fear they may be planning to marry secretly in London which is their final destination. I am a well-wisher.*

Smiling to himself, the Professor read through the note twice before folding it and sealing it within an envelope. He then addressed the epistle to Signorina Adela Asconta at Sanzionare's house at Ostia. He would hand it to the porter tomorrow before taking the train to Paris. With luck it would prove to be a mild bombshell to the Asconta female – a propellant, even.

He rose and walked to the mirror set above the heavy chest of drawers which stood between the two shaded windows, looking at his face from numerous angles. In the past year or so he had been so many different people with different mannerisms, speech, language and age. Madis; Meunier; the American Professor, Carl Nicol, of Five Albert Square; the photographer, Moberly; the stout American, Morningdale; the Jesuit priest, and the widower, Smythe. Each part fitted like a glove, but there would be one more left to play once they returned to London. The role of a lifetime. He shrugged with a kind of mock modesty. For a little longer he would be Smythe.

'Do I get to keep the rubies?' asked Carlotta from the bed.

Moriarty crossed to her, gazing at the girl with that strange mesmeristic look he so often affected.

'No, my darling daughter. Not that one anyway. Perhaps I will find some other trinket for you.'

'That'll be nice,' she snuggled her head into the pillow and giggled. 'Are we to be about incest again, Papa?'

Holmes had been as good as his word. Dr Moore Agar, of Harley Street, gave Crow a thorough examination and pronounced that he should take at least a month's leave of absence – preferably at a watering place. He could do some light duties but would not recommend full-time work with the Force. He would write to the Commissioner that very night explaining the situation, saying that when Crow was ready to return, he could guarantee him one hundred per cent fit and completely his old self.

Crow mentally girded himself for the fray with Sylvia.

'Do you provide the toasted snow for her?' Holmes had asked him. 'Or do you remain master in your own home?'

The way was quite clear, his mind steadfast, for had not his pride taken a severe tumble over the machinating Harriet? He had yet to get over the fact that not only had he harboured one of Moriarty's people in his house, but also been driven half out of his wits by her. That alone would not be easy to forgive. The leave of absence would provide two opportunities: to set his house in order, and make another determined effort, with the assistance of Sherlock Holmes, to take Moriarty by the coat and bring him to justice.

Sylvia was bemoaning the scarcity of good servants when Crow got back to King Street.

'I have interviewed a dozen today alone,' she said petulantly from her seat near the fire. 'It is impossible. There are two that might be of use. I do not know.'

'Then I do,' said Crow firmly planting his back to the fireplace.

'Angus, would you move from there, you will keep the warmth from me,' barked Sylvia.

'I will not move, from here or anywhere else, and if we are to talk of warmth being kept from people, then consider, madam, what warmth you have kept from me.'

'Angus.'

'Yes, Sylvia. We were perfectly happy when I was here as your lodger, and you cooked, cleaned and were warm as toast to me. Now that we're wed, it's been all razzle-dazzle, rag-sauce, airs and graces, by your leave, yes ma'am, no ma'am, and three bags full of it, ma'am. I for one am tired of this way.'

Sylvia Crow opened her mouth in protest.

'Be silent, wife,' Crow bawled like some drill sergeant.

'I will not be spoken to like this in my house,' Sylvia flounced.

'In *our* house, Mrs Crow. *Our* house. For what is yours is mine, and what is mine is yours. Moreover, I am master now. Why, Sylvia, it has so got me down that this very afternoon I have been to a physician in Harley Street.'

'Harley Street?' The wind dropping from her sails.

'Aye, ma'am, Harley Street. He tells me that I must rest a while and that if you go on denying me the pleasures of a decent and ordered household, then you may well be the death of me.'

'But I have given you a decent household, Angus,' concern in her voice now.

'You have given me airs and graces. Servants who burn the meat and water the cabbage. You have given me headaches, and dinner parties, and behaviour like some Grand Duchess. I'll have no more of it, Sylvia. No more. I'm away to me bed now, and would like one of your tasty meals on a tray. Served by yourself. After which you can come up and serve me as a wife should.'

So saying, Angus Crow, not knowing if he was the victor or no, stumped out of the parlour and up the stairs to the bedroom, leaving a red-faced, fish-mouthed Sylvia staring blankly at the closed door.

Sanzionare had a first-class sleeping compartment on the Rome–Paris Express. Benno was in the next coach, and, as the engine picked up speed past the outer suburbs of the city, the Italian gang-lord relaxed. He would doze a little before luncheon in the well-appointed restaurant car. Perhaps he would take a few more glasses of wine than usual, for the afternoon could be spent in sleep. Then, as was the custom, he would dress for dinner. Perhaps there would be some lonely woman on board. He might as well use what time he had away from Adela to good advantage.

He went to the restaurant car at noon to find a pleasant, and not altogether subdued, atmosphere. The waiters were smart, the food exceptional. The first part of the journey would go well.

He had, of course, no way of knowing that, in the carriage next to his, there were two sleeping compartments reserved in the names of Joshua and Carlotta Smythe.

This pair had boarded the train early in Rome and, since departure, had not set even a nose outside Joshua Smythe's compartment. Nor did they intend so to do until the evening, for Moriarty maintained that the most forceful impact could be accomplished if they made a spectacular appearance at dinner. It was then that Carlotta could best show off the Scobie Inheritance and – if Moriarty was any judge of human nature – Luigi Sanzionare would be drawn deeper into the web that was prepared for him.

As the train drew them away from the Eternal City, Moriarty sent for the restaurant car conductor and made certain arrangements for the evening. The rest of the day he spent in good humour, as well he might, for of all his schemes this one contained an element of farce which would have delighted the greatest exponents of that theatrical art. Carlotta dozed and lethargically leaved through copies of the papers and magazines which Moriarty had provided against boredom.

Much later that night, they would arrive in Milan to be coupled to the French train which ran between that city and Paris. The dinner menu was, therefore, utterly Italian, as though giving a last taste of the country before plunging passengers into the extravagances of French cuisine. In the dining car, preparations for the dinner were approached with the solemnity of a religious feast, the lamps lit early, tables crisp with fresh linen, and cutlery polished, gleaming in the reflected light – the whole far removed from the more modest surroundings of second-class passengers and the downright spartan conditions of third-class.

The gong was sounded a little before seven o'clock along the first-class corridors, and Sanzionare, dressed impeccably, hair groomed with scented oil and the dampness of his cheeks laid with a dusting of cosmetic powder, took his place in the dining car within minutes of the call to dinner.

When the Smythes arrived, he was at a fateful moment of decision, uncertain whether to choose the antipasto, or one of the four available soups, or, perhaps the Melone alla Roma, to precede the Anguilla in Tiella ai Piselli and the Pollo in Padella con Peperoni. Deep in thought, he sensed, rather than actually observed, their entrance.

When Sanzionare did look up, he saw that it was as though some unseen authority had called a halt to all activity. Waiters about to take orders were frozen like waxworks; ladies silenced in mid-flow of genteel conversation; gentlemen about to make a choice of wines lost all interest in the fruit of the grape; glasses half-raised to lips remained poised in mid-air. There was an illusion of great stillness, the normal babble dying to a hush that even precluded a whisper, and a sense that the carriage had even stopped rolling.

Carlotta Smythe stood framed in the doorway, her father slightly behind her. The dress she wore was a simple white gown of exquisite taste, showing off her colouring and the dark sweep of her hair to contrasted perfection. It was modest enough, but somehow the simple style managed to convey a brand of allure enough to take the very breath from every male within sight.

She was stunning by any standard, but, to set off the picture, Carlotta's throat was encircled by a necklace of rubies and emeralds linked with silver chains, in all three circlets sweeping down in an upturned triangle to a point from which hung a ruby pendant of a deep and blazing colour. It was as though the girl's throat was on fire, the light flashing from the stones like small tongues of red and green flame.

She held herself as if she knew there was a fortune around her neck: the pair – the woman and the jewels – making a combined object of total desire.

Sanzionare, like every other man in the carriage, was riveted, not knowing which he coveted most in that second of first clapping eyes on her – the woman or the necklace. The whole encapsulated everything he had ever wanted – wealth, elegance, the beauty of treasure, and the sensual promise of the girl's body sheathed in white silk. This would be worth the risking of life and liberty, honour, power and even sanity.

The effect and impact of the Smythes' arrival seemed to last for an age. In reality only a few seconds passed – hung still in eternity – before the car and its occupants returned to their normal functions.

The conductor was in front of the pair, bowing as if to royalty, apologizing, it seemed, for the fact that there was no available table at which the couple could dine alone. He kept turning back to cast his eyes over the groups of diners as though expecting that by some miracle space would suddenly be made. Then, joy upon joy for Sanzionare – who still stared like a man transfixed – the minion was leading them down the car towards his table.

He bowed low over Sanzionare with half of his body so that the greater part of it could be still turned towards the Smythes – an act of almost acrobatic unctuousness.

'A million pardons,' whispered the conductor. 'There is no room for this lady and gentleman. Would you possibly do them the honour of allowing them to share your table?' All this very low.

Sanzionare rose and bowed, smiling and nodding, 'It would be an honour to be allowed to share my table with you, Mr Smythe and Miss Smythe.' As he pronounced the latter name, he dropped his head even lower in obeisance. 'Please, please share with me.'

'Why, Father,' Carlotta wide-eyed and obviously pleased to see him, 'it is Signor Sanzionare whom we met on Saturday. You remember?'

'Yes. Yes, I remember.' Smythe made it perfectly clear that he would rather not have recalled their meeting. To the conductor he said, 'Is there no other table?'

'None, milord. Not one.' A puzzled expression clouding his smile.

'Then we have no choice,' Smythe shrugged, looking unpleasantly at Sanzionare who was, by this time, rubbing his hands and using much will power to stop himself from actually jumping with pleasure.

'Come, Father,' Carlotta had already slid into a seat opposite Sanzionare. 'You shall have to thank Signor Sanzionare for his kindness. This is the second time you have shown generosity towards us, sir. Father, please do not be churlish.'

With an open display of ill grace, Smythe took his seat. 'It is unfortunate. But if we have to share your table, Signore, then I must thank you.'

'Please,' gushed the Italian. 'Please, it is truly my honour. The other night I asked you to dine with me and you were not able. Fate has taken a hand. This meeting was obviously preordained. I am a great believer in fate.'

'Oh, indeed, so am I,' said Carlotta with a dazzling smile. 'What fun it is to find a friend on such a tedious journey.'

'I do not wish to be rude,' her father cut in pompously. 'Signore, please do not take this amiss, but I am not in favour of my daughter mixing over-much with persons of your race. I am sorry, but that is how it is. Forgive my bluntness.'

'But, sir, you told me yourself that her mother was a Neapolitan born. I do not understand.'

Carlotta leaned forward, her breasts touching the table, sending blood to Sanzionare's head.

'What my father says is true.' She took on a tone of deep regret. 'My mother's family treated her badly after she married and went to live in England. My father, unhappily, takes it out on your entire country and race. Why, I had to lay siege for years before he would allow this small visit.'

Smythe cleared his throat noisily. 'I shall be glad when we get back to England and good honest food.' He looked with great disdain at the menu.

His daughter began to shush him, for he was talking loudly.

'The food here reminds him much of Mama, I fear,' she confided. 'He becomes upset very easily.'

'And my stomach becomes upset with all the oil they pour upon their victuals,' grunted Smythe.

'I too can speak my mind, sir,' Sanzionare was a little irritated by this arrogant Englishman's behaviour towards his daughter. 'I do not much care for English food. They put over much water on theirs. Yet when I am a visitor I do not complain at the customs of the country. Might I advise you to be discreet in your choice of food. A little plain melon and perhaps some cold meats.'

'Your cold meats are too full of garlic and over rancid with fat to my taste.'

'Then some pasta.'

'Starch. Filling without the flavour.' He dropped the menu to the table with an irritated pshaw. 'Not a decent thing. Not even a good broth or Brown Windsor, or a well-cooked roast. And we are forced to share. This would not have happened on the Great Western.'

So the meal progressed uneasily, with Carlotta sparkling like the necklace at her throat, and her father growling and full of miseries throughout. Indeed, it became so difficult that Sanzionare stopped addressing Smythe by the time they had reached the main course, giving his entire attention to the daughter who seemed to have only eyes for him.

At the dessert, Smythe suddenly leaned over, gruffly asking the Italian what he did for a living, the question itself put in a tone so offensive that Sanzionare was quite taken aback.

'I hold a position of great power in Rome, if you must really know, sir,' he replied.

'Politics?' asked Smythe warily. 'I do not hold much with politicos. It would seem they always want a hand in your pocket or your affairs.'

Sanzionare wished that he could tell the man that in his business he had his hand in the politicos' pockets as well as those of the common man.

'I deal in valuables, Mr Smythe.'

'Money? You're in finance, are you?' Moriarty smiled secretly. Sanzionare was not the buffoon he looked.

'Money, yes, and other things also. Precious stones and metals, objects of fine art, antiques.'

'Precious stones like those around my daughter's neck, for instance?'

'It is indeed a most beautiful necklace.'

'Beautiful?' roared Smythe so that all in the carriage could hear. 'Beautiful? Great Caesar, man, if you were a real expert you would say more than that. It is worth a king's ransom. A fortune. You deal in precious stones, eh? Precious coals more

227

like. I doubt you can tell glass from garnet.'

Sanzionare felt his gorge rise. In Rome he could have had this evil-tempered Englishman dealt with in a matter of minutes.

'If it is so valuable, sir,' his voice cold, 'then you had better look to it. To travel with such valuables on display is dangerous. In any country.'

Smythe coloured crimson. 'Do you threaten me, sir?'

Several people at nearby tables could hear the conversation even above the train's rattle, and were looking on with shocked interest.

'I merely offer advice. It would be a pity to lose such a bauble.' People who really knew Sanzionare would have quivered with fear at his tone.

'Bauble indeed? You hear the man, Carlotta. Bauble?' The Englishman pushed back his chair. 'I have had enough of this. It's bad enough to be forced to eat at the same table with a greasy fellow like yourself. I'll not stay here to be threatened.' He wagged a finger an inch from the Italian's nose. 'And I've seen how you've been eyeing my daughter. You're all the same, with your Latin blood. You think a rich girl is easy meat, I'll be bound. A rich English girl, anyway.'

'Sir,' Sanzionare rose, furious, but Carlotta put out a restraining hand.

'Forgive my father, Signor Sanzionare,' she smiled, embarrassed by the stir they were causing. 'It is a great strain for him to return to Italy. It has many bad memories, and is also a constant reminder of my mother, whom he loved dearly. Please forgive him.'

'He should take care,' the Italian's voice trembled. 'With someone of a less understanding nature, he could be in serious trouble.'

'Carlotta,' Smythe was a few paces away now. 'Come, I'll not leave you alone here.'

She bent forward, her voice dropping to a whisper. 'My compartment is number four, car D. Come to me after midnight, so that I may make some reparation for this terrible scene.' And she was gone, following her father with cheeks blushed pink with shame.

Sanzionare dropped back into his chair. The Smythe man

was unhinged, surely. There was no cause for a scene like this. The English are so reserved as a rule, he thought. Then he turned his mind to the girl. Splendid, enchanting, a prize. But what a price to pay, to be saddled with the father as well. No, thought Sanzionare, it is better to stick with the devil you know. At least Adela Asconta did not have apoplectic relatives. To marry, or even court, the winsome Carlotta would be like facing judge, jury and the public executioner. Sanzionare was a brave man where villainy was concerned, but he yearned for domestic peace. Nevertheless she had offered some form of compensation. He ordered a glass of brandy and thought of the private delights which Carlotta could provide in the secrecy of her sleeping compartment. As he sipped the brandy, Luigi Sanzionare savoured the idea of one nocturnal adventure.

He would like to teach Smythe a lesson. Would the prize of Carlotta's body be enough? A train had such restrictions. Perhaps when they reached London he could persuade Schleifstein and Grisombre to put up for a spectacular robbery. Why, he might even return to Adela with the necklace. That was business, and the flame of interest, the hot flush of lust that he felt for Carlotta, was almost dowsed by the idea of a burglary in London to line his own coffers and repay Smythe for his insults.

He waited in his own compartment until after midnight before making a move. Benno had come along to see that all was well soon after Sanzionare had left the dining car.

'You wish for me to deal with the Englishman?' Benno asked.

'Fool, the scene was in public, and over nothing.'

'He insulted you. I've seen you have men disposed of for lesser things.'

'If he comes to harm here on the train, they would lose no time looking for me. *Calma*, Benno. I do not wish to draw attention to myself. I will have plans for him.'

'For his daughter also?' grinned Benno.

But Sanzionare would not rise. There was no point in letting underlings like Benno know too much of one's private desires. In Italy's secret world there was enough intrigue and competition. Chinks in armour had been used as fulcrums to

229

topple men from positions of power before now.

There was nobody in the corridor as Sanzionare slipped from his compartment and made his way along the unsteady floor to the next coach. The lighting was dim, but he found compartment number four without difficulty.

She was waiting for him, much as he had imagined, clad only, as far as he could see, in a most flimsy peignoir and little else.

'I am so glad you have come.' Her voice was husky, even breathless. A good sign, Sanzionare judged.

'How could I refuse such an invitation?' He laid a hand on her arm.

'My father was unforgiveably rude. You were exceptionally patient. I only wish that all men were so with him. There have been times during this present visit that I have genuinely feared for his safety. Please, please do sit down.' She gestured towards the seat which had been pulled down and made ready as a bed.

'My dear Carlotta,' he struggled for the right words. 'What can I do to help? To soothe your troubled breast?' His hand hovered gently over the area adjacent to that part of her body. 'Your father treats you in a most presumptuous fashion. I would not speak to my dog as he orders you.'

She pulled away slightly. 'You have a dog, Signor Sanzionare? How lovely, I've always wanted a dog.'

'A figure of speech, dear lady. I wish to help you.'

He lowered himself onto the bed, one hand still around Carlotta's arm, gently attempting to pull her down also.

She resisted. 'I need no help, Signore. No help at all. I merely wish to thank you privately for being so understanding.'

Sanzionare nodded. 'I know, *cara mia*. I know what it is for a woman like yourself, starved of the company of a real man. Dominated by a sick father. He is a brute.'

She took a step back. 'Oh no, sir. Far from it. I admit that he is still dazed with grief from my mother's death, but that will pass.'

Outside in the corridor, Moriarty, his ear to the door, smiled, nodded, and began to make his progress towards Sanzionare's compartment. Carlotta would have the Italian there for a while yet.

There was nobody in the corridor, no sign of life as the train rolled on through the night. In the darkness outside the windows, the Professor occasionally glimpsed a light from some house or cottage where they were keeping late hours.

He had not been called upon to act much over dinner, he reflected. Italy was not his favourite part of the world and he really was not over fond of the food. True, Rome was a beautiful city with its fountains, narrow streets and avenues which basked in the shade of cypresses. But nothing, he considered, could really compare to his own London. Only the amusement of ensnaring Sanzionare compensated for those particular deprivations which he was forced to endure.

Moriarty reached Sanzionare's compartment. Still nobody could be seen in the dim and noisy corridor. Softly he turned the handle, put his shoulder to the door and stepped inside.

'When I first set eyes on you in Rome, I felt that we were kindred spirits,' charmed Sanzionare.

'That is good to know.' Carlotta stood at the far end of the bed. Sanzionare edged up towards her, his palms damp, breath short in his throat. 'It is good to know,' she repeated, 'that one has a friend.'

'I can be more than a friend, Carlotta. Much more.'

'Do keep your voice down,' a finger to her lips. 'I would not want my father to find you here. I am not in the habit, you realize, of entertaining men under these conditions.'

'Believe me, I do understand.' He had edged right up to the end of the bed now, half rising as though to pin her against the window. 'There is nothing to be afraid of. Nor is there any reason for you to feel guilty. These urges are often stronger than our wills. Come to me, Carlotta.' His arms opened wide.

Her body pressed against the dark window. 'Signor Sanzionare . . .?'

'Luigi, *bambina*, Luigi. There is no need to be coy with me.'

'I am not being coy.' Carlotta's voice was raised to a shrillness that had not been present before. 'I do believe that you mistake my intentions. Oh . . .' Her mouth suddenly formed itself into a wide circle, her eyes opening as though she realized his purpose for the first time.

Sanzionare lunged forward, one hand, for a fleeting second, connecting with the soft restraint of her breast, but she twisted sideways, leaving him clutching air, his knees buckling to the floor as she backed quickly towards the door, letting out a short high scream.

'You thought I had invited you here to . . .' screeched on a rising scale.

'Shush, Carlotta, shush. Your father will hear . . . *cara*.'

'Perhaps he *should* hear. You thought . . .'

'What else should a man think?'

'But you are old.' Her mouth turned down as though she had drunk sour milk. 'I imagined you did all simply out of kindness and generosity towards two travellers in a foreign land. My father is right about Italian men, they only seek one thing. They wish only to take their pleasure. Have their wicked way . . .' She was hysterical now, tears forming in her eyes: the performance in which the Professor had coached her with the help of Sal Hodges.

Sanzionare made soothing noises. She had said he was old and that had cut through to his very heart. The innocent. She was rebuffing him. Him, Luigi Sanzionare whom women fought over in the dark places of the Eternal City. Yet his common sense held him back from revenge. It would be a tragedy if scandal was to run riot on this train. His loins ached with the need for her.

He scrabbled to his feet. 'A million pardons, Signorina. I mistook your meaning.'

'Please go.' She appeared to have hold of herself, panting and leaning against the door.

'I cannot.'

'Touch me and I'll scream for help. Go.'

'Carlotta, I cannot go. Please.'

'Oh my God, am I to be raped?' It was like something from grand opera.

'I cannot go,' he almost shouted. 'You bar the way.'

'Oh!' She stepped to one side, tears running down her cheeks, as Sanzionare's fat hand reached out for the door.

'I am sorry. Forgive me. Please forgive.' Feeling utterly ridiculous, and not a little frustrated, he lurched into the corridor.

Carlotta leaned back, the tears still streaming and her shoulders heaving. But now it was not with terror or hysteria. Her whole body shook with mirth at the picture of the most dangerous man in Italy retreating, in terror, from a situation which he could not handle. Moriarty would be pleased with her. It had all gone exactly as he had said.

The humiliation of the matter seared Sanzionare not only in his sense of pride, but also right through to the very roots of family honour. If the circumstances had been different, he brooded, then the bitch would have had him, screams or no. His background, the values by which he had grown and lived, all taught him that this half-Italian girl should pay some form of penalty – and the father also. True, his father had only been a baker, but he still recalled the time, when he was but seven years old, when the butcher's daughter had turned down his elder brother. That had sparked such a feud that their area of the city was not done with it even now.

Mixed with the humiliation, however, there was the nagging horror of Carlotta's words – 'But you are old.' Many women found him increasingly attractive; why, even Adela – a jewel of a woman – was constantly jealous of him. Could this be the beginning of the end? Luigi Sanzionare's virility and charm beginning to wither like an old plant, drooping and dying?

He lay in the darkness of his sleeping compartment, his head bedevilled with both the frustration and despair which came from Carlotta's rejection. He tossed and turned, was conscious of every movement of the train; could have counted the number of wooden sleepers over which they passed; each change in speed; every shrill whistle from the steam locomotive. When they reached Milan, he thought that, in the stillness, perhaps rest would come, but there was so much banging and bumping as the coaches were shunted this way and that, to couple them to the French train, that it was impossible.

Red-eyed, he faced Benno in the first light of day, instructing him to see that all meals were brought to his compartment. He had no wish to run face to face with either

Carlotta or her father during the remainder of this journey.

At the villa in Ostia, Adela's maid brought her breakfast late in bed, and with it the morning papers and the one letter.

Sanzionare's mistress propped herself up with pillows and prepared for a day of being cosseted in her lover's absence. She sipped her coffee, looked hard at the envelope, as if trying to define the handwriting, before slitting it open with the silver paper-knife.

A few moments later she was screaming, in language laced with the more colourful expressions of the city's slums, for Giuseppe to come up, for her maid to start packing, and for horses to be brought around. Within the hour nobody in earshot of the villa could have doubted that Adela Asconta was about to set forth on a journey to London.

Spear was waiting at Albert Square when Carlotta and the Professor returned, in high humour.

'Success?' he asked, once closeted alone with his leader.

'Magnificent. I'll need to see Sal as soon as she blesses us with her presence. Our little Italian Tigress should be performing in the theatre. We have our Roman friend trussed up like a Christmas goose – though he does not know it yet.'

'And there's good news here, also,' chuckled Spear.

'Yes?'

'Crow.'

The Professor looked up sharply, all else draining from his mind.

'He has been given leave of absence from his employ,' said Spear with great emphasis.

'So.' The smile swept over Moriarty's face once more, his head oscillating slowly. 'So we have him. They are careful, these policemen. Do you notice how rarely they allow a scandal to become public knowledge? Leave of absence indeed, he's handed in his knife and fork to the Metropolitans or I'll never climb pillicock hill again.' He seated himself behind his desk, a picture of confidence. 'It's good news, indeed, Spear, knowing that the meddling Crow has been nailed. Now, is all else arranged?'

'The lurkers are watching the railway stations for the lady,

234

Professor. News will be here within minutes of her arrival.'

'Good. There'll be no time to be lost once she's in London. You'll have Harry Allen at the ready also. He knows his part?'

'Trained like you said and good enough to be in one of Mr Ibsen's plays.'

'And the note?'

'Is delivered and waiting for the Italian as you directed.'

'And the Langham is watched?'

'Night and day.'

'Good. Now that all is ready, Spear, you can tell me what else has been happening during my visit to Rome. How the remainder of my family of villains fares, what cribs have been cracked and what pockets emptied.'

Later, when Spear had rehearsed the many affairs which were the daily business of the Professor's reunited empire, Moriarty took down his journal, turning to the page of notes he kept on Angus McCready Crow. As had now become his custom, he drew a diagonal line over the pages, so closing it as an account settled. For a moment he browsed through the pages containing intelligence on Luigi Sanzionare, his pen hovering, but not yet making the final lines. That pleasure would come soon enough.

Mr Sherlock Holmes of Baker Street sent for Crow after a week.

'You are feeling recovered, my good Crow?' he enquired brightly, rubbing his hands.

'I still feel much of a ninny regarding what has passed,' retorted Crow. 'To be made such a fool by the damnable Moriarty does not keep me in the best of humour.'

'And your domestic affairs appear to be mending themselves.'

'How can you know that, Mr Holmes?' Crow looked alarmed.

'By simple observation. You have the new pin look of a man who is now being well cared for. I'll wager you have put your foot down.'

'Aye, I have that.'

'Good. Good.' Holmes was busily filling his great pipe from the tobacco jar. 'I doubt that I will have any objections from you regarding the poisonous qualities of nicotine,' he smiled.

'Indeed no. I have great regard for the soothing properties of tobacco.' Crow took his own pipe from his pocket and followed the great detective's example.

'Capital.' Holmes applied a light and began to puff large clouds of smoke, a contented look passing over his face. 'There's no better fellow in the world than Watson, but he does have the facility of reminding me, all too often, of my weaknesses. Though I dare say he's right in doing so.'

'I look forward to meeting Dr Watson,' ventured Crow.

'No, no.' Holmes shook his head. 'That will never do. There are some things I do not wish. Let him remain in ignorance regarding our occasional meetings and the particular purpose of our endeavours. It would never do to let Watson know that Moriarty lives.'

'Where is he now, then?'

'If I only knew.' Holmes appeared lost in thought for a moment. 'Ah, you mean Watson, do you not?'

'Indeed.'

'For a moment I thought you referred to the Professor. No. I have sent Watson down to Cornwall again. Doubtless I shall have to repair thence before long, or I'll not hear the end of it. I believe that I told you Moore Agar had ordered me to rest.'

'Then should you not be doing so?'

Holmes nodded. 'I have pleaded a little time under the pretext of ordering some books, and making a few notes at the British Museum. A harmless ruse, but Watson knows I am interested in the Cornish language and that I intend to publish a paper on it in due course. It will serve to direct his attention elsewhere. Now, Crow, are you fit for a journey?'

'A journey? But to where?'

'To Paris. Where else, my dear fellow? We know Moriarty is back at his old game. By reason alone we are both convinced that he had a hand in the Cornhill business, and old Bolton's murder. We know also that his sights were set at your head, Crow, and you almost went under. Yet the only definite thing we have is the French criminal Grisombre's meeting with Morningdale.'

'True.'

'You are agreed with me that Morningdale and Moriarty are one and the same?'

'I am convinced.'

'We have a description of Morningdale, yet nobody has seen fit to make any deeper enquiries concerning the man. He cannot have stayed in his rooms at the *Hôtel Crillon* during the whole of his visit to Paris. Others must have seen him, even spoken to him. We must speak to them, Crow.'

The simple, yet divine logic caught Crow's imagination. Of course, Holmes was right. Paris held the only possible clues at this point in time.

The Langham Hotel, in Langham Place – which also contained the famous Nash church of All Souls – was a magnificent Gothic structure, covering over an acre of ground, containing more than six hundred rooms and with facilities for dining two thousand persons. It was chiefly noted as a great resort for travelling Americans, though the staff were well accustomed to entertaining foreigners of every description, so Luigi Sanzionare did not feel out of place on arrival.

He had been worried lest something should have gone amiss with his colleagues' schemes, as there was nobody to meet him at the station. He had, after all, telegraphed his intentions well ahead.

However, these fears were soon set at rest in the great foyer of the hotel as he signed the visitors' book, for there was a note, written on the Langham's stationery, signed by Grisombre on behalf of both himself and Schleifstein, telling Sanzionare to make himself comfortable, to rest well after the arduous journey, and not to worry himself over anything. They would, the note said, be calling upon him in the very near future, when all things were arranged.

Sanzionare wondered if they would leave enough time for him to make enquiries regarding the residence of Mr Joshua Smythe and his daughter. The insulting behaviour of both the Smythes having truly got under the Italian's skin, as he had brooded on the business during the entire journey. He had been careful, though, to keep out of their way. So careful that he had not even caught a glimpse of them in Paris, where he had stayed overnight in order to avoid travelling on to the coast and crossing to England in the same steamer.

As he settled himself into the luxurious rooms which had been reserved for him, Sanzionare decided that it would be best to leave the Smythes well alone, at least until he had the backing of his French and German friends.

Dismissing the valet, who politely enquired whether or not he should unpack the Italian's portmanteau and small travelling bag, Sanzionare set about getting himself in order. He could never stand strangers rooting about among his clothing and linen. Benno and Giuseppe, sometimes even Adela, managed these things in Rome. Here he would see to it himself.

In the bedroom he unlocked the portmanteau and started to remove his shirts, collars, and other clothing. He had placed the shirts neatly in a drawer of the dressing-table and just returned to remove a pair of newly tailored trousers, when he felt something hard and unfamiliar lower down in among the clothes. He pushed his hand deep among the various items until his fingers touched the object. A puzzled look came into his eyes and, scowling, he withdrew his hand.

He was clutching a small tissue paper packet. Unwrapping the paper, he almost threw the object from him, for there in his hand were the three silver-linked strands of rubies and emeralds, with the magnificent pendant ruby hanging from them. Carlotta's necklace which he had so coveted on that disastrous first night of the journey.

Sanzionare caught sight of himself in the long mirror across the bedroom, hardly recognizing what he saw – a stoutish, middle-aged man, white faced as though shocked, with trembling fingers clutching at the elaborate necklace.

He looked from the mirror to the necklace and back again. A dream? Hardly. The precious stones in his hand were real enough. He had been close to it during dinner on the train, and had handled too many jewels in his time to be wrong. But how? Why? He had the keys to his baggage during the entire journey. Benno? It was the most likely solution. Benno, against all instructions, might have stolen the necklace before they reached Paris. He could quite easily possess the spare luggage keys, and he certainly had the opportunity to slip the jewels into the port-manteau. A plot? Or merely an act of unthinking vengeance on behalf of his master? Well, Benno was on his way back to Rome now.

Sanzionare slumped on the bed, hands still clutching the necklace loose in his lap. This was a dangerous piece of goods to keep. Yet far too valuable to let go.

He began to think logically. The Smythes could not have missed the piece before Paris. If they had discovered their loss since, he would most certainly have been stopped in France, before taking the boat to England. Or if they had found it gone since, he would have been questioned on arrival at the port, or in London.

Had he mentioned this hotel when talking to the Smythes? He thought not. Twenty-four hours. He would give it one day. Maybe a few hours more. If Grisombre and Schleifstein did not come to the hotel by then, he would be off – with the necklace. The long journey would then have been at least worthwhile. Yes, he could not risk staying longer.

Sanzionare, fingers still trembling, completed his unpacking and looked around for a safe hiding place for the jewels. Long ago he had learned that often the most obvious place was the safest. His travelling bag was fitted with all the usual appurtenances, including five glass jars and bottles with sterling silver dome tops. The largest of these he kept filled with eau de cologne, and it was, at the moment, half empty. Unlocking the bag, Sanzionare took out the jar, unscrewed the lid and, holding the necklace by its clasp, dropped it into the liquid.

The lurkers had both Charing Cross and Victoria railway stations well watched, and a team of good young boys placed at intervals from both stations to act as runners right back almost to Albert Square itself. They were, as usual, in many and varied disguises, each carefully instructed.

The Langham Hotel was also the target for a dozen pairs of eyes. Harkness, with the Professor's own private vehicle, stayed at the ready and Terremant, the big punisher, was playing a new role – that of a hansom driver, moving between the two railway termini and the Langham Hotel in a very special cab which, strangely, avoided picking up any fares.

Adela Asconta arrived, with her retinue of maid and the swarthy Giuseppe, exactly as Moriarty had predicted – some twenty-four hours after Sanzionare made his appearance.

She was tired and travel-stained, sharp-tempered with the porters who carried her luggage out to the hansom, driven by Terremant who helped her inside, together with her maid. Giuseppe was instructed to follow in a second cab.

The chain of boys, stationed at street corners and in doorways, began to do their work, and, within a short space of time, a raggedy runner arrived at the door down the area steps of Number Five Albert Square.

Moriarty – in the guise of his academic brother – had been waiting and ready since an early hour, and Sal Hodges had got Carlotta out of bed some three hours before her normal rising time. Harry Allen was in the hall, dressed respectably, his suit covered with a Chesterfield waterproof coat, a brown bowler in his hands. Harkness had the cab at the door, and Moriarty spoke a few last words to Harry Allen and Carlotta before this pair left, en route for the Langham. Harkness would deposit them there and return for the Professor so that the last act in the snaring of Sanzionare could be played out with perfect timing.

Adela Asconta had not reserved rooms at the Langham, but the hotel had plenty of space to spare and she was greeted affably by the staff, allotted a suite on the second floor, with accommodation next door for her maid and a small room for the manservant – as she so described Giuseppe.

She remained calm, if a little tetchy, during the formalities of booking in, and it was only as she was leaving, to follow the page and the two porters towards the great staircase, that she paused to ask after, 'A kinsman who I believe is staying in this hotel. A Signor Luigi Sanzionare.' She was told that Signor Sanzionare had registered on the previous day and that his room number was 227 – on the same floor as herself.

Arriving at her room, Adela Asconta paused only to fling down the claret-coloured travelling cape she wore, before marching with great purpose towards room 227.

Sanzionare had decided that if Grisombre and Schleifstein had not arrived, or sent word by ten o'clock, he would leave, catch the first boat train available, and head back to Rome. It

240

was common sense. He had breakfasted alone in his room, scanning every column of *The Times* for any report regarding Carlotta Smythe's necklace. Nothing. Yet he felt uneasy, as though some predestined doom was crashing towards him with the inevitable force of an avalanche.

He sipped his coffee, and at a quarter to ten made up his mind that he would be leaving that very morning. At five minutes to ten there was a tap on the door. The Frenchman or the German?

Adela Asconta stood in the corridor, one small foot tapping an impatient tattoo, her cheeks flushed with anger pent up during the journey, building within her like a head of steam in a boiler.

'Where is she?' She pushed Sanzionare out of the way and stalked into the room, her head turning from side to side, fists clenched aggressively. 'I'll kill her. And you also.'

'Adela! You're in London. What?' stammered Sanzionare.

'You're in London, you're in London,' mimicked Adela. 'Of course I am in London,' she rattled it out in fast Italian. 'And where would you expect me to be? Sitting quietly in Ostia while you betray me?'

'Betray you, *cara*, I would never betray you, not even in my thoughts. Not for a second.'

'Where is the whore?'

'There are no whores. Who ...'

'That woman. That Carlotta.'

It struck Sanzionare then that he was deeply in trouble.

'Carlotta?' he echoed hollowly.

'Carlotta,' shouted Adela. 'I know, Luigi. I know about Carlotta.'

'You know what? There is nothing to know.'

A jumble of possibilities raked through his head – that Benno had betrayed him, filling her with some fabrication; or that Carlotta, discovering the theft of her necklace, had been in touch with police in Rome. So bemused was he that he did not even realize this last was impossible.

'Nothing to know? You deny then that you travelled to London with Carlotta Smythe?'

'Of course I deny it.'

'She was on the train. The Cook's man in Rome had her

booking.'

'Yes, there was a Carlotta Smythe on the train. Travelling with her father. They dined with me on the first night. I have not set eyes on them since, let alone journeyed with them.'

'She is not with you?'

'Certainly not. I have you, what would I want with this Carlotta? You take me for a fool, Adela?'

'I take you for a man. You are telling me the truth?'

'On my mother's grave.'

'I don't trust you. Nor your mother either.'

'Calm yourself, Adela. What is this? Why have you followed me?'

She stood, shoulders drooping, her perfect chest rising and falling rapidly, the red spots on her cheeks more crimson than before.

'A letter,' she said in a voice more uncertain than any of her statements so far.

'A letter?'

'Here.' She had the paper in her sleeve, in preparation.

Sanzionare quickly scanned the document, looking hard at the date. Terrible possibilities started to surge through his already fuddled mind. The letter had been written at least on the morning of his departure. The author had known the Smythes would be on the train. Carlotta had goaded him on, he had been certain of that at the time. Then the necklace suddenly appearing in his portmanteau. A trap? It could be nothing but a trap. Who, and why, eluded him for the moment.

'Adela,' he willed his voice to speak calmly. 'I cannot explain all now, but we have been duped, the pair of us. For what purpose I cannot tell, but I know we must be out of here very fast.' People, he thought quickly, had to rise uncommonly early to get the best of Luigi Sanzionare. He would still show them. Even to getting away intact with the necklace.

He dashed for the bedroom, fingers fumbling with his key chain to open the travelling bag and tear out the glass jar.

Later he recalled stuffing money into one pocket as he tipped the contents of the jar into the wash basin, in which he had so recently performed his morning ablutions. He recovered the glittering trophy from the scummed cold water, wiped it off on a hand towel, and was emerging into the drawing-room of his suite to face Adela with some triumph, when the main door burst open.

'That is the man, Inspector,' Carlotta screamed, an accusing finger pointing at him. Behind her was a solid young man with a brown bowler hat crammed onto his head.

'That's the man who tried to rape me, and who stole my jewels. Look, he has them there.' Carlotta went on screaming.

The young man closed the door carefully behind him and approached Sanzionare.

'I should come quietly, sir, if I were you. Now, just you hand over the necklace to me.'

'Luigi! Who are these people?' Adela, the crimson now replaced by chalk white.

'I am Inspector Allen, ma'am, if you speak English.'

'I speak.'

'Good. This lady is Miss Carlotta Smythe.'

'*Sanguisuga*!' hissed Adela. 'Bloodsucker!'

'I am from the official detective force of the Metropolitan Police,' continued Allen.

'*Vecchia strega*,' spat back Carlotta. 'Old witch.'

'I can explain,' offered Sanzionare lamely, looking at the necklace and then away again as if to pretend it was not there. 'Miss Smythe claims, sir ...'

'He forced his way into my sleeping compartment, attempted to rape me. Later I found that my ruby and emerald necklace was missing. He has it now, in his hand.'

There was an intake of breath from Adela: the sound of a wild beast about to spring. Sanzionare opened his fingers allowing the necklace to fall to the carpet, lifting his arms to protect his head.

'*Monstro informe*!' Adela launched herself towards him.

'What's all this then?' 'Inspector' Allen reached forward to separate the struggling pair. 'Luigi Sanzionare,' he continued, bravely holding on. 'I am taking you into custody for the theft of this ruby and emerald necklace, and I must tell you that anything you say may be taken down and used in evidence.'

'*Scandalo*!' wept Sanzionare, knowing that this was the springing of the trap. Adela whimpered, occasionally forcing obscene abuse from her lips.

Then, suddenly everything went quiet. Sanzionare saw Adela Asconta look fixedly towards the door. Allen's grip relaxed slightly.

Luigi Sanzionare lifted his head. Inside the door stood the tall, thin and gaunt figure of Professor James Moriarty.

'Luigi. How good it is to see you again.' Moriarty's head moved slowly to and fro.

Carlotta was smirking, stifling a laugh.

'Be silent, girl,' snapped the Professor. 'You think this is now a laughing matter.'

'What...?' Sanzionare felt his legs turning to the consistency of well-boiled spaghetti, and there was a thumping in his head. The room spun once before his eyes, then settled uneasily. He blinked, staring at Moriarty, fearing the onslaught of death at any moment. Dimly, he perceived the full extent of his undoing. 'Moriarty,' he breathed.

'The same.' The Professor's mouth was set in a grim line.

'This is all your doing.'

'You grow astute in your dotage, Sanzionare.'

'They told me you were finished. Done for after the business at Sandringham.'

'Then you were foolish to believe them, my friend.'

The Italian looked around him, as though not fully in his right senses. 'But why? Why this?'

'Is your brain so full of vanity that you cannot see why?' Moriarty took a step towards the hapless Italian villain. 'It is to teach you an object lesson, Luigi. To show you several things. To inform you in the best possible way that I am master of crime in Europe; that at any time I can reach out and have you flicked from the earth like a piece of dung.' His voice was low, like the soughing of wind in trees.

Sanzionare shivered. 'Then...?'

'Yes, I have fitted you, as they say. If this had been real, and not the charade I planned, you would be on your way to judgement at this moment.'

'Charade?' The Italian croaked weakly, casting about him, his eyes full of dread.

Moriarty allowed himself a thin smile.

'You deal in precious stones, eh?' he said, using Smythe's

voice. 'Precious coals more like. I doubt you can tell glass from garnet.'

'You were Smythe.' Sanzionare's voice was dead, flat and without music.

'Of course I was Smythe.' The Professor turned to Adela. 'Signorina Asconta, you must forgive Luigi. He stood little chance against Carlotta here. I think she could have lured even St Peter himself.'

Adela Asconta made a discontented spitting noise.

'The inspector? He is ...?' gulped Sanzionare.

'My man. Just as you are all, in truth, my men and women. I only wish to prove to you, Luigi, that at any time, and in any place, I can control you, bend you, break you, remove your own paltry power. I have shown this already to Grisombre and Schleifstein. They have seen their errors and now stand by me. You have only to say the word.'

Sanzionare whispered an oath.

'The old alliance,' Moriarty's voice rose. 'I am determined that the old alliance be reformed. Together, with myself once more at the helm, we can dominate the denizens of crime throughout Europe. It is your choice. You can still have Italy. But on your own, I somehow do not think you would last long.'

Later, after they had given Sanzionare brandy and soothed Adela, the Italian asked, 'But what if I had fought? What if I had tried to make good an escape?'

'Unlikely,' smiled the Professor. 'I believe in so bemusing my victims that they even lose sight of reality. However, in that unhappy event, I would have used certain strong methods. Come here to the window.'

They stood together, looking down on Langham Place while Moriarty pointed out Terremant and his hansom.

'He would have seen to it that you did not get far. If I had considered it necessary, you would have been killed.'

A few hours later, when Sanzionare had been taken over to Bermondsey to be reunited with his old partners in crime, Moriarty sat down and went through the ritual of closing the account in the back of his journal. Only two more. Segorbe and Holmes. The other three would be an object lesson to Segorbe. It would be a direct approach, and if that failed, then

Segorbe would have to be an object lesson to the other three.

He called for Spear and dictated the simple telegraph addressed to the quiet Spaniard in Madrid. It read – WE MUST SPEAK WITH YOU URGENTLY IN LONDON. PLEASE INFORM US OF TIME AND PLACE OF ARRIVAL. It was signed by Grisombre, Schleifstein and Sanzionare. The return address was given as Poste Restante, Charing Cross Post Office, London.

LONDON, ANNECY AND PARIS:
Tuesday, 20 April–Monday, 3 May 1897

(The Spanish lesson)

'One has to admit that Paris is a singularly attractive city,' remarked Sherlock Holmes as they drove, in bright sunlight, from the Gare du Nord.

'I have always thought so,' said Crow.

'The problem is,' continued Holmes, 'that too much beauty, coupled with the fact that it is renowned as the great city of pleasure, makes it a breeding ground for idleness. And idleness, Crow, as I have observed in my own case, leads one to the devil's work. See there,' he pointed down one of the many side streets, 'the poisoner Lachette had his home just four minutes' walk from that corner. It is not generally known that I had a hand in his final capture. A question of a most toxic Japanese fish being inserted into the bouillabaisse.'

Crow attempted to bring the conversation back to matters in hand.

'You really believe that we will find some relevant clue to Moriarty's whereabouts by enquiries here?'

'No doubt at all,' Holmes appeared listlessly diffident, as though Moriarty was the last person that interested him. 'That *pension* we have just passed,' he turned to point back at the little corner building. 'I remember that well enough. It is there that Ricoletti, the one who used his club foot to such diabolical purpose, stayed for a short time en route for England, after his escape from Italy. I believe his abominable wife went on ahead of him. But that was in my youth, Crow.'

Holmes had insisted that they sample the luxuries of the *Crillon* for this visit. 'If we are to question the staff without arousing too much interest, our best disguise will be as guests,' he had told Crow, who felt the extravagance truly a little above his means.

Once they were installed, however, in the somewhat palatial apartments which Holmes had reserved for them, Crow found himself quite enjoying the visit. The only cloud on the horizon was the thought of Sylvia left to her own devices back in King Street. On the last occasion that he had left her alone, the wild goddess of social betterment had entered into her heart. He now prayed fervently that the lessons he had tried to teach her since becoming resolute of purpose would not go unheeded. Crow dreaded yet another tussle with his wife.

The Scottish detective bathed and dressed at his leisure, emerging to discover that Holmes had already been about their business. A curt note was attached to the mirror of the dressing-table. *I have jogged the servants' memories*, it read. *Please join me for dinner as soon as you feel purified enough to expose yourself to the wickedness of the city.*

Crow hurried downstairs to find Holmes sitting comfortably among the elegant diners in the large restaurant.

'Ah, Crow,' he made an expansive gesture. 'Do sit down and try some of this excellent duck, it is positively the best I have ever tasted.'

During the meal Crow attempted to draw the great detective, but he remained resolutely silent on the question of Morningdale and his enquiries so far; chattering away knowledgeably about Paris, and, in particular, French cuisine and the good wines of the country.

It was not until they reached coffee that he finally spoke of their venture.

'Friend Morningdale is well remembered here. Apparently he was what they call a good tipper, and to begin with it is clear to me that his sole purpose was some form of meeting with Grisombre, the famous French criminal leader.'

'We were pretty certain of that already,' said Crow, somewhat disappointed.

'Indeed we were, but the talk I have had with the porter, and some of his staff, has made it positive beyond doubt that Morningdale was Moriarty. For one thing, this Morningdale claimed to hail from Boston, Massachusetts. By some judicious questioning I am led to believe that his accent was that of a man who has lived extensively in California. I am something of an expert on American dialects as you may know. Some years ago I published a short monograph on the subject of the natural vowel sounds among people born and bred in the various states.'

'And your case rests on this alone?'

'Oh no, there are other reasons which I will not bore you with at present. But, Crow, we must be about our business. It appears that Morningdale spent some time, together with his secretary, roistering in the Montmartre area. A sleazy part of the city at the best of times, but that is where we should be looking.'

So Crow and Holmes spent that first evening together combing the bars and cafés of Montmartre. To no avail, for however subtly Holmes phrased his questions, he was met with blank stares or shakings of the head.

Three days passed before they even touched upon anyone who remembered the American and his English secretary, and Crow judged that Holmes was becoming increasingly depressed, a nervous irritability replacing the more jovial manner of his arrival in the capital.

They had almost given up, on the third night, having covered a dozen or so of the dubious haunts of pleasure, when Holmes suggested that they visit the *Moulin Rouge*.

'I am not anxious to view the heathen spectacle of women displaying themselves in that wild orgy again tonight, Crow,' he remarked somewhat sourly. 'But I fear we will have to put up with it once more for the sake of criminal science.'

At the *Moulin Rouge* they encountered a waiter who thought that he recalled the American and his companion, but could not be absolutely certain.

'I'll warrant that a large tip would loose his tongue,' said Holmes. 'But I'll only stoop to the method of bribery as a last resort.'

At a little before one in the morning the two detectives left the establishment, and, as they awaited a cab in the Place Blanche, they were approached by one of the girls who, inevitably, plied their wanton trade on the streets of that area.

Crow was about to turn the girl away – as he had done many

times since their nightly peregrinations – when Holmes stayed his hand.

'You may well be able to assist us, dear lady,' Holmes addressed the girl with unaccustomed charm. 'We are making enquiries regarding an American friend of whom we have lost sight. We are aware that he was certainly enjoying himself in these night haunts of your city early in the year. I wonder if you set eyes on him. If not you, then your friends.'

'There are many American gentlemen who pass this way, Monsieur,' the girl replied. 'I have not got time to discuss them in the streets. I am here to make money.'

'You will not lose by it,' declared Holmes pulling some silver from his pocket. 'Let me describe this particular man to you.'

The girl grabbed hungrily at the coins, listening intently as Holmes drew a concise word picture of the stout, red-faced Morningdale.

'*Salaud,*' the girl mouthed. 'I recall that one. He threw me into the gutter. Almost broke my arm.'

'Tell me about it,' Holmes fastened her with his eyes, which, Crow observed, were not as clear as usual.

The girl told of the night that she had approached the American, and of his threats.

'He was a strange one,' she said. 'He could speak our language well – the argot if you know what I mean.'

Holmes nodded.

The girl gestured in the direction of the *Moulin Rouge*. 'He had been in there, talking to Suzanne the Gypsy. One of the waiters is a good friend, he told me that they talked together for some time.' She gave a bitter laugh. 'She went off with his friend.'

'Who? This Suzanne?'

'That's right.'

'And where shall we find her?'

'Anywhere.' She spread her arms wide. 'Suzanne is a law to herself. I have not seen her for two, maybe three, weeks.'

'First thing in the morning we must begin our search for Suzanne the Gypsy,' Holmes counselled when they were back at the *Crillon*. 'The trail grows warm, Crow. She spoke to the man, and I should imagine that she is the kind of woman whose tongue will be set running with a small financial reward. As you have seen, it is now time for bribery.'

But on the next morning, Crow was disturbed to find Holmes in a dispirited mood. He did not rise at his usual hour and appeared to be in great turmoil, sweating profusely and in a kind of agony which racked his body at frequent intervals.

'I fear that I shall have to return to London,' the great detective said weakly. 'This is what I dread, and it is the reason for Moore Agar advising rest in congenial surroundings. I fear there is now only one place where I can obtain the medicine which will arrest this state; and that is in London. Crow, you will have to continue without me, find this Suzanne and speak with her. You still have time before you are due back at Scotland Yard. I shall catch the next train to Calais.'

It was with a heavy heart that Crow saw the detective onto the train, before returning, alone, to the quest.

During the weeks that had passed since Moriarty had acquired the buildings at Bermondsey, much had been done in the way of refurbishing. Even since Schleifstein had become their first guest in this hideout, groups of family men – mainly cracksmen and sneak thieves who posed as builders, decorators and painters – had moved in to enlarge the premises, and make them more comfortable and safe from any person who might take an interest from the wider, and more law-abiding, world outside.

Pleasant alternative quarters had been furnished for Moriarty himself, and the main members of his Praetorian Guard, not to mention a large dormitory for transient family people; rooms for storing goods, lock-ups and, in fact, many of the amenities which they had so relied upon a few years before in the converted warehouse hard by the docks near Limehouse.

Bridget Spear, with only a few weeks to go before her confinement, had been moved into one of Sal Hodges' properties, together with a midwife to see that all went well. Sal Hodges, herself now like 'a galleon in full sail,' as she described it, would use the same room and midwife when her time came.

Martha Pearson, who had well proved herself about the Albert Square house, had now taken over Bridget Spear's duties – with the help of a skivvy brought in by Bert Spear – while little Polly, still constantly in raptures over the handsome Harry Allen, was, on the Professor's orders, instructed on all necessary matters and appointed as housekeeper and cook at the Bermondsey lair – Allen himself having also moved there.

Carlotta had disappeared from Moriarty's immediate circle once Sanzionare had been brought in, leaving to earn exceptional money at Sal Hodges' second house, where she was appointed madam.

During the last week in April, word was received from Segorbe, in far off Spain, that he would be arriving in London on 2 May, and would be pleased to meet Grisombre, Schleifstein and Sanzionare at their own convenience. He had rooms reserved for him at a small hotel off Upper George Street, not far from the site of Old Tyburn where so many a villain had met his end.

It fell out that, on the afternoon of Tuesday, 27 April, Moriarty called together a conclave at Bermondsey. The three reconverted continental leaders were there, together with the few attendants they had retained. Of Moriarty's people, Spear, Lee Chow, the Jacobs brothers, Terremant and Harry Allen joined the group.

The Professor spoke for some time on the plans he already envisaged for the new alliance, and went on to speak of Segorbe's visit.

'I do not intend to waste my time with him,' he said, darkly. 'We all know of his power in Madrid, and what he can offer us by way of contribution. I consider it best if we do not bring him down here to Bermondsey immediately, so I would suggest we meet with him at a place I have already appointed – a flash house at the corner of South Wharf Road and Praed Street, up near the Great Western Railway Terminus at Paddington. We can speak fairly with him. You gentlemen,' he indicated the three continentals, 'can bear me out. I think there is little doubt in your minds as to whether I am a fit person to lead this union or not. Any dissension which may still linger in his mind, because of past happenings, will soon be dispelled. I see no difficulties.'

Later, alone with Spear, Lee Chow and Terremant, he made further plans.

'It is best to be safe,' he looked gravely at Terremant. 'You still have the device we held in reserve for Sanzionare?'

'All in working order, Professor.'

'Good. You will bring the Spaniard to our meeting, and take him away. If it is necessary...'

'All will be done.' Terremant grinned. 'It will not be a case of merely singeing this king of Spain's beard.'

'And you, Lee Chow,' the Professor turned to the small Chinaman. 'We have kept you secure and close since the unfortunate death of old Bolton. Now you must be abroad again. I am within sight of my goal. Once more the broad spectrum of European crime is about to come under my overall leadership. We can only move forward from now on. But I am determined, before we proceed, to settle with Holmes once and for all.'

'You want me to...?' began Spear.

Moriarty's face shrank into a pained expression. 'Spear, have you not learned from me in the past weeks? Have I not taught you how much better it is to move with cunning? To bring men down through their own weaknesses rather than with the pistol, knife or bludgeon? Certainly it can only be accomplished in the cruder manner with the more rough and ready of our rank and file, or with enemies who can understand only the methods of violence. For Holmes I have a better kind of death. Social ostracism, a complete loss of face. Lee Chow will understand. You have a particular leaning towards these methods in your native land, have you not?'

Lee Chow grinned his evil yellow smile and bobbed his head up and down like a Buddha.

'It is time, Lee Chow. Go and remove that which Holmes most needs. It is quite like old times. You remember when we did it before the Reichenbach fiasco?'

Spear laughed. 'I think I follow you now, sir.'

'A small turn of the screw.' Moriarty did not smile. 'It is also time to bring in our old friends Ember, and the lurker known as Bob the Nob. They'll bring one of Mr Meddling

Holmes' friends with them. And with her in London, I think I can lead a dance in the West End that will ruin the reputation of that, so-called, great detective.'

Within the hour a telegraph had been dispatched to Ember who was still watching the lady known as Irene Adler, in Annecy. The telegraph read – BRING THE EAGLE HOME.

Lee Chow entered Charles Bignall's chemist's shop just as it was closing in the same evening. He noted with satisfaction the sudden look of mingled fear and concern which spread, like a stain, across the man's face.

The Chinese stood back, holding the door for a departing lady customer who smiled in haughty thanks.

'Another dose of opium? Or perhaps laudanum to keep her happy?' asked Lee Chow as he closed the door and slid the bolts in place.

'What do you want?' Bignall did not disguise his revulsion for the Chinese.

'You thought you get rid of me? You thought you not see me again, Mr Bignall?'

'Your friends are bad enough without having you here. I've done everything as instructed.'

'Oh, I quite aware of that, Mr Bignall.' He still pronounced it as two separate words. 'You would have known pretty damn quick if that had not been so. I come in person with the special message. You remember? The one we spoke about last time we meet?'

'I remember.'

'Good. That ver' good, Mr Bignall. So you do it now. Our mutual frien' Mr Sherlock Holmes, to whom you supply cocaine. When he come nex' time, you tell him it no more possible.'

'Have you people no mercy? Cannot I let him have even a few grains? Why, the man will suffer agonies.'

'Not even speck. No cocaine for Mr Holmes. I know if you disobey, and his dear frien', the Dr Watson, has closed all his other sources of supply. Yes, poor Sherlock Holmes will be in pretty pickle. If he not, Mr Bignall, then I promise that you will be hung by thumbs and flayed alive. That no idle threat. I mean what I say. I done it to others.'

'You swine,' mouthed the chemist. 'You utter swine.'

Lee Chow grimaced and made a small grunting noise. 'See to it, Mr Bignall. See to it.'

Esteban Segorbe usually travelled alone. His control over the darker populace of his sunny area of the continent was so complete, so total, that he had little to fear from any man. Soberly dressed, short and almost nondescript in appearance, Segorbe was always one to be reckoned with. He was the least well-known of Moriarty's former allies, except for the fact that the man was ruthless and single-minded when set upon a venture. The Professor also had plenty of evidence that the Spaniard earned himself a truly vast sum of money each year from the many criminal activities in which he was concerned.

Watched as ever, by the unseen lurkers, Segorbe arrived at his small unprepossessing hotel soon after eight on the evening of Sunday, 2 May, just as the many families who lived in the vicinity of Upper George Street were returning from Evening Prayer.

Half an hour later, a note was delivered, via the hall porter, telling him that the three other continental criminals would see him at two o'clock on the following afternoon, and that a hansom cab would call for him, a quarter of an hour before the appointed time, to take him to the rendezvous.

Segorbe nodded and told the man there would be no reply. Since 1894, and Moriarty's rout from the alliance, Segorbe had done small, but lucrative, pieces of business with all three of the men he was here to meet. He had no reason to think that his presence this time would end in any other way but financial gain. He retired early, but did not turn out the lamp before completing a summary of the day's cost in the small accounts book he always kept by him. Esteban Segorbe was a man full of avarice. He hoped that the visit would soon start to show a profit.

At a quarter of an hour before two o'clock on the following afternoon, Segorbe was ready and waiting for the cab, which arrived promptly with Terremant in the cabby's little perched seat at the rear.

Terremant climbed down and, treating the Spanish visitor with great deference, assisted him into the cab before returning to his seat and whipping up the horse in the direction of the Edgware Road.

South Wharf Road ran – as it still does – diagonally between Praed Street and the Great Western Terminus at Paddington, and was so called because it backed directly onto the Paddington basin of the Grand Junction Canal. Its houses were drab, full, for the most part, with loaders, bargees, and men from the railway company. It was not a street in which one lived permanently, but rather through which one passed; the flash house which the Professor had marked down as a meeting place being a favourite haunt of small fences, dragsmen, who stole from carriages and cabs, and those who preyed upon the canal cargoes, not to mention the dippers who worked the crowds at the railway station.

On the previous afternoon, the owner of this seedy limbo – one Davey Tester – had received a visit from Bert Spear. Money changed hands, and, at midday on the Monday, the owner had passed the word that he was closing shop for the rest of the day.

At one o'clock, four of Terremant's punishers arrived, to make certain that no villain remained within the confines of this small five-roomed hostelry. Unseen outside, the lurkers gathered, placing themselves at vantage points in doorways and other nearby buildings, for the house in question was set in a perfect position, with a clear view down both South Wharf Road and Praed Street, as far as the railway station.

A little before a quarter to two, a pair of coaches came up from the Edgware Road, four punishers leaping onto the pavement before the horses had drawn to a halt, to see the way was clear. Only when they were certain that all was well did they allow the passengers to alight and move quickly into the building.

At the Tyburn end of the Edgware Road, Harkness slowly edged the Professor's private hansom forward through the tightly-packed traffic. Ahead of him he could see Terremant turning his cab from Upper George Street across the flow of cabs and omnibuses, and into the stream moving up towards Paddington. Moriarty spotted it as well, from the back of the cab, and nodded contentedly. Segorbe would be won over within the hour.

Promptly at two o'clock, Terremant's cab drew up in front of the house at the top of South Wharf Road, and Segorbe was ushered inside. The punishers guarded the doors. Five minutes later, Harkness brought the Professor's cab to a halt and Terremant, who was waiting by his horse, hurried forward to assist the Professor.

Inside, in the small narrow room which served as a parlour, the four continentals greeted one another with the kind of reserve that criminals the world over use when meeting afresh after a long absence.

They were just taking their places, around a rough wooden table, when the Professor came quietly into the room. Segorbe's back was to the door and he turned in quick surprise at Moriarty's greeting.

'Good cheer, Esteban. I am glad you could come.'

The Spaniard's hand flashed towards his belt as he turned, the Toledo steel dagger half out by the time Schleifstein clamped his wrist.

'There is no need for that, Esteban,' smiled Moriarty. 'We are all good friends here. Just like it was in '94 when we first formed the alliance.'

'You resigned from the alliance,' Esteban Segorbe said with a slight intake of breath, his eyes showing a tiny gleam of disquiet.

'No, I was forced to resign. I now wish things to return to their status quo.'

Segorbe looked around, searching the faces of the other leaders.

'He failed. We agreed that failure in a leader could not be overlooked.'

'You chose no new leader, my friend.' Moriarty's smile remained fixed. There was little warmth in it.

'We met,' Segorbe was equally cool. 'We met and discussed the entire project. Our decision was unanimous.'

'There was no decision.' The Professor's lip curled in anger. 'All that happened was that you occasionally did one another a service. You allowed the situation here in London – one of the great criminal capitals of the world – to fall into pieces. It was a free territory. I do not know about you, Segorbe, but at least Grisombre and Schleifstein poached on my London preserves. My offer now is simple. That we return to our former alliance, with me at the head. I have proved myself. Ask them.'

'He made ninnies of us all. It's true enough.' Grisombre spoke without anger or emotion.

Schleifstein sighed, 'There is no answer to the Professor, Esteban. He trapped each of us at our own game, and he has put the most dangerous detective in the Metropolitan Police Force out of action. Discredited.'

'Together we can prosper as never before,' Sanzionare nodded.

Segorbe was not convinced.

'You remember our former schemes?' Moriarty came over to the table, taking his seat at the head. 'I counselled you all that we could work together for chaos in Europe. Through chaos our aims would be more easily obtained. And do not forget my other warning. The police forces of the world are daily becoming more efficient. We can best combat this in the alliance.'

Segorbe did not speak for a full minute. 'Gentlemen, I have my own society in Spain. The police do not bother me over much and all my people make a good living. They are content. It is true that there has been some profit in working together, but I do not altogether trust your motives, Professor Moriarty. I am not certain that the criminal population of Europe united under your overall leadership is necessarily a good thing. In the long term it means a common sharing, a common market place if you like. Countries go through varying periods of prosperity and poverty. My feeling is – on due reflection – that the more impoverished a country is, the more it might have to give away in the common cause.' He made a gesture of some eloquence with both hands. 'It could be that the more wealthy countries would simply become increasingly wealthy on the plunder of their poor relations. The poor relations might even go to the wall.'

Moriarty shrugged, 'My feelings are that the wealthy ones should assist those who are not so well provided for.'

'I know my people,' said Segorbe firmly. 'When we met to form the alliance in '94, I felt that it was worth while. I am not so certain now, particularly if we return to a leadership which has already been found wanting.'

'I will brook no refusal in this matter,' snapped Moriarty angrily.

'I cannot see how you can force me. Or my people.' Segorbe looked, and sounded, complacent.

For an hour they pleaded, cajoled, flattered and persuaded, but the Spaniard would not budge.

'Perhaps,' he conceded towards the end, 'if I think it over, talk with my own people, for a month or so, I could return and we might speak of this again.'

'I think not, Esteban. There is much to do. Time has already been wasted and lost. I am anxious to proceed with my grand design for the European underworld.'

'Then I must reluctantly refuse to be part of it.'

It was obviously final.

Moriarty rose to his feet. 'We are all sorry. However, if you have made up your mind, and we cannot move you, then that is how it must end. Allow me to see you to the door. The cab will take you back to your hotel.'

Segorbe made his farewells and the Professor shepherded him from the room. There was not over much activity in the street outside. Terremant stood by the hansom, and as Segorbe shook hands with the Professor, turning towards the vehicle, the big punisher looked meaningfully at Moriarty.

The Professor gave him one downward nod accompanied by a steady look which spoke of hideous retribution.

Terremant nodded in return, assisted the Spaniard into the cab and walked unhurried to the rear. Before climbing onto the driver's seat, the punisher bent under the framework and felt for a hook which hung in readiness by the axle. He found it immediately and slipped it around one of the spokes of the wheel nearest to the curb. Then, mounting into his seat, Terremant gently eased the horse into Praed Street, having set a simple, yet ingenious, timing device in motion.

The hook, now fast around the spoke, was attached to a length of strong sheep's gut fishing line, which ran free through several other hooks under the cab. The other end of this line disappeared into a sizeable wooden box positioned directly below the passenger seat.

Inside the box were two deadly objects: the first, an old

flintlock pistol mechanism, cut away at butt and barrel, screwed down firmly in an upright position with the trigger downwards; the second, and most deadly, item was a tightly-packed bundle of dynamite.

Moriarty himself had designed this method, not trusting the cumbersome weight of electric batteries so often used in the manufacture of explosive devices. The technique was simple and almost foolproof. The end of the fishing line was tied strongly to the trigger of the flintlock mechanism which was cocked and primed. As the cab's wheels turned, so the line was pulled in until at last it jerked on the trigger. The hammer then dropped forward, striking a spark and igniting a quantity of powder which would flare strongly for some seconds. A length of fast-burning fuse ran from a percussion cap set in the dynamite, its end resting among the powder on the flintlock mechanism, tied securely in place with strong twine. Once the powder was ignited, so the fuse would start to burn.

Terremant knew, from previous experiments, that he had a little over three minutes after urging the horse forward. He did not like the thought of having to activate the device in a normally busy thoroughfare, but Moriarty had been adamant that, if its use became inevitable, the bomb would have to be fired in the vicinity of the other leaders. 'Harsh lessons must be seen in order to be believed,' he had told the punisher.

Though the traffic was sparse in Praed Street, Terremant did his best to direct the horse along the most open way. There were still a few quite innocent people on the pavements, and, as they gathered speed going down towards the railway terminus, he saw to his dismay that a group of nurses, presumably bound for duty at St Mary's Hospital, were gathered on the pavement, about to cross the road. A large, two-horsed cart was pulling up ahead of him, forcing him to slow. He reckoned he had only a minute, now, to leap clear.

Terremant hauled on the right rein, at the same moment flicking his whip over the horse's flanks to drive it forward around the cart. He heard one of the nurses, crossing in front of the cart, cry out in anger, but by this time he was guiding the vehicle into an open pathway between the traffic.

Letting the reins go, Terremant, swivelled in his seat and then leaped for the pavement. The horse feeling that it now had its head, began to canter fast. There were shouts of dismay from alarmed people, one man even throwing himself forward to grasp the dangling reins, but to no avail.

Terremant rolled over, picked himself up and ran, pell mell, down nearby Cambridge Street.

The cab bumped on for another block, and was adjacent to the railway terminus when it exploded.

A sheet of scarlet flame enveloped the entire vehicle, and at the same moment came the roar of the explosion. Fragments flew in all directions – a piece of metal shattering through a nearby greengrocer's display of fruit, lumps of wood curving into the air, or being projected with great force, slamming between pedestrians and traffic alike.

There were screams and the desperate whinny of the horse. One wheel was to be seen still bowling along the road, and, as the smoke and fragments died, so the horse was visible, snorting forward in a panic-stricken gallop still pulling the blazing shafts which were all that was left of the hansom.

Men of metal leaped to grab at the still flowing reins, but the terrified animal swerved out of reach, narrowly missing another hansom, the driver of which was having the greatest difficulty in restraining his beast which was rearing up in the shafts.

The noise, shrieks and shouts were as horrible as a sound picture of hell itself, as the wretched animal careered onwards, the flaming shafts dragging on the ground with a loud scraping noise.

On the other side of the station, a small boy had somehow wandered into the road and now stood as though rooted to the spot in terror. He could not have been more than two years of age, and the poor mite whimpered as the horse galloped towards him, the child's nurse, as terror-struck as her charge, immobile on the pavement.

It was at this point that a constable, on normal beat duty, saved the day, running with all his force and launching himself at the reins. His hands grasped at the leather, from which he swung with all his weight, turning the horse from its natural path, missing the frightened child by a hair's breadth, and gradually slowing the animal to a trot, and then a walk as he was dragged some fifty yards down the street, the metal studs on his boots striking sparks from the road.

In the room so recently vacated by Segorbe, they heard the mighty explosion and stood, stock still, white-faced with alarm.

All but Moriarty.

'*Gott im Himmel*,' from Schleifstein.

Sanzionare crossed himself.

'The Irish Dynamiters again?'* queried a visibly shaken Grisombre.

*Terrorist bombings, spread over a long period, were quite frequent during the last three decades of the 19th century. The bombing of Clerkenwell Prison, in 1867, is but one example of bombs both large and small. An attempt to blow up the Mansion House, in March 1881, almost succeeded. Two years later the Local Government Office, Charles Street, Whitehall, was the target: this time the bomb exploded. In the same year there were at least two more explosions – in an Underground tunnel between Charing Cross and Westminster, and a more serious explosion on 30 October, strangely at the Praed Street Underground station, seriously injuring 62 people. Bomb scares during the late eighties seem to have been as rife as those recently experienced in contemporary London; and in February, 1884, an explosion wrecked a cloakroom at Victoria (Underground) station. On 30 May, in the same year, part of Scotland Yard's Detective Department was damaged, and a nearby public house demolished. It is possible that two bombs were used here, the public house being the second target. Following what must now seem to us an almost traditional pattern, the terror tactics were changed, and the Junior Carlton Club and Sir Watkyn Williams Wynn's neighbouring house were damaged. On the same day – 30 May – a more serious tragedy was averted when sixteen sticks of dynamite were defused at the base of Nelson's Column. Other targets in that same year, happily discovered before detonation, were London Bridge, the Houses of Parliament, Westminster Hall and the Tower of London. In 1893 a postal worker was killed by a parcel bomb and a year later another similar device exploded in New Cross Post Office. A quick summary would not, of course, be complete without reference to the unfortunate anarchist Martial Bourdin who died when the explosives he was carrying were detonated

'I think not,' Moriarty spoke quietly. 'I fear that little bang was of my making, gentlemen. You may now mourn the passing of Esteban Segorbe who has gone by way of hansom cab to Kensal Green.'*

'You had him . . .?' Grisombre.

'If there is one thing this society now needs,' the Professor still did not raise his voice, 'it is discipline. Mark well, my fine coves and be prepared to use the same extreme measures if there is no other way. Tell me Jean, in my position, what would you have done by way of revenge against the lot of you?'

Grisombre shuffled his feet. 'I suppose I would have sought you out and dealt with each in turn just as you, Monsieur le Professeur, have dealt with Segorbe.'

'Quite so. Gee-Gee?'

Sanzionare nodded gravely. 'The same. You have been merciful to us, Professore. I would have been ruthless.'

'Wilhelm?'

'I too would have slaughtered all, in anger and for the need of revenge, Herr Professor.'

'So, lest you should think I was weak-willed, you can see what would have happened to all, or any of you, had you not seen the obvious sense of reuniting under my leadership. I suggest, gentlemen, that we now leave this house with some haste. You will all be required to return to your native cities ere long, and there is much to discuss regarding ways and means.'

That evening, the Professor sat opposite Sal Hodges before the fire in the drawing-room at Albert Square.

'You look as though you've supped cream today,' Sal smiled.

'Capital. Capital,' Moriarty mused almost to himself, gazing into the flames, trying to spot faces and shapes among the coals.

Sal moved uncomfortably in her chair, her legs stretched out onto a leather footstool.

prematurely in Greenwich Park on 15 February 1894. This last incident was, of course, used as a basis for Mr Joseph Conrad's novel *The Secret Agent*.

*Moriarty is referring, of course, to Kensal Green Cemetery.

'I shall be glad when it is all over,' she sighed, patting her swollen belly.

'I also. Yes.' But Moriarty was not thinking of the impending arrival of their child, his mind far away among other matters.

Sensing his distraction, Sal Hodges frowned slightly, small crows' feet etching around her eyes. She pouted, smiled, and then returned to totting up the week's accounts from her two houses. Moriarty's coffers would make a tidy profit from them this week. The girls had been hard at it. Day and night. Momentarily Sal was distracted by the noise of cards being shuffled.

The pack of cards in the Professor's hands was constantly moving as he shuffled, passed, cut with one hand, changed suits and colours, palmed packets from both top and bottom. Yet his mind drifted far away from the fifty-two pasteboards. For a moment he imagined that he could glimpse Segorbe's face, racked with pain at his moment of extremity, in the fire.

Earlier that evening, he had taken his pen diagonally over the pages of notes on the Spaniard. Another account closed and only one set of notes left. Revenge, he considered, was sweet as a nut. He grimaced into the flames. Revenge and its accomplishment had a satisfying sensation to it. Schleifstein, tricked with that enormous robbery; Grisombre caught after stealing what he thought was the *Mona Lisa*; the despicable nosey Scot, Crow, put out to grass, trapped into adultery and, from thence, into a kind of madness; and Sanzionare, also lured by lust, but this time with a fair tincture of greed to boot. Segorbe, dead. Now only Holmes was left, and the screws were already on him. After Holmes, Moriarty would begin again. He could feel the power already. Not one sizeable robbery in Europe without his support, nor a single fraud, burglary or decent forgery. His control would reach everywhere: lying on the pickpocket's fingers, the whore's legs, the cracksman's hand and the demander's menaces.

It would all come, just as it had done already in London. But now for Sherlock Holmes. The fire flared and spurted a small shower of glowing fragments against the soot of the chimney-back, like red stars in a black void. James Moriarty's head began to move in the reptilian oscillation as he reflected

264

on the downfall of Holmes.

Four days earlier, two men had made their way through the quaint cobbled streets of the old quarter of Annecy. There was pleasant peace here, beside the calm lake with its backdrop of the Savoy mountains. The pair walked, as though at leisure, towards the *Pension Dulong*, situated right on the lake side, at the far corner of the town where the road moves on towards the village of Menthon-St-Bernard.

The two men did not appear to be in any hurry as they came close to the pink house, with its neat shutters, the wide balconies empty of guests – the season was yet to begin for Annecy.

In fact, they had timed their walk most carefully, in order to arrive at the *pension* a little before five o'clock: the time at which they knew the woman would be preparing for her late afternoon promenade.

'It will be best to take her then,' Bob the Nob had suggested to Ember after they had received the Professor's telegraph. Ember agreed, but then he was prepared to agree to anything, so out of sorts was he with this quiet watching game they had been playing in the unfamiliar French town.

After the intense and active life these two villains had been leading in London, it was indeed tame to act as secret nursemaids to a woman who led a routine, if not dull, life centred around the small *pension*.

Yet being Moriarty's men, and knowing that much may hang on their activities, Ember and the Nob had meticulously followed their instructions, reporting back to the Professor with regularity, and never letting a day pass without being certain of the woman's movements.

This did not stop them grumbling over the boredom, and speculating on how the woman would receive the contents of the envelope they now carried, and which Moriarty had entrusted to their care until the time was ripe.

Inside the main door of the *Pension Dulong*, Ember and the Nob encountered what at first sight looked like the long entrance hall of an ordinary private residence. But, as their eyes became accustomed to the less glaring light – for the spring sun had not yet sunk below the mountain tops outside

– they perceived a small hatch set in the wall, in front of which a brass spring bell was placed on a ledge, and a neatly written card invited visitors to ring for service.

The Nob brought the fleshy base of his thumb down upon the bell push, sending a loud tinging tone echoing through the empty hall.

A few moments later the hatch was thrust back to reveal a grey-haired man of rosy complexion, with the shrewd eyes of one who has been in business on his own account for a considerable time.

'You speak English?' asked the Nob with a smile.

'You require rooms?' The proprietor – for that was undoubtedly who he was – replied.

'No, sir, we wish to see one of your guests. A permanent guest. A Mrs Irene Norton.'

'I will see if she is in. Wait. Who shall I announce?'

'Friends from England. Our names would mean nothing to her.'

The proprietor gave a short somewhat curt nod, and slammed the hatch close. Some three minutes later he reappeared.

'Madam Norton is about to go out, but she will spare you a few moments. You are to wait in the parlour.' He indicated a door on the far side of the hall.

The Nob thanked him, and the two men crossed to the door. It was a large airy room strewn, almost haphazardly, with armchairs and occasional tables upon which books and magazines had been placed for the convenience of guests – who, at that moment, were notable for their absence.

Ember sank into one of the armchairs while the Nob walked over to the large window and gazed out at the glassy waters of the lake.

A few moments passed before the door opened to reveal a woman dressed for the street: a cream skirt and blouse showing beneath an open cloak of similar hue. A matching bonnet graced her head, under which dark tresses were clearly visible.

Ember gauged her to be in her mid-thirties, but still handsome with a pair of eyes that might well tantalize any red-blooded male.

266

'You wish to see me?' She looked with some hesitation at the men, taking in each of them with a long stare, as though memorizing their features.

'If you are Mrs Irene Norton,' the Nob replied with a gracious gesture.

'I am.' The voice sweet and melodious, yet a hint of alarm in her eyes.

'Mrs Irene Norton whose maiden name was Irene Adler?'

'That was my name before marriage, yes.'

Both the Nob and Ember caught the slight American inflection in her voice.

'Who are you, and what do you require with me?' the lady asked.

'We come as emissaries.' The Nob crossed to stand in front of her. 'There is a gentleman who has been seeking you for some considerable time.'

'Well, he has found me. Whoever he is.'

'I think this will explain, Ma'am.'

The Nob drew out the envelope entrusted to them by Moriarty, placing it in the woman's hands, in the manner of a summons server.

She turned it over, seeing that the seal was intact, looking almost reluctant about opening it.

'How did anyone find me?' Her voice dropping to a whisper. 'It has been put about that I am dead.'

'Read the letter,' said Ember.

Her eyebrows lifted for a second before she plied her dainty fingers to the envelope, slitting it open and drawing out the heavy sheet of paper.

Both men could glimpse the letterhead which signified that the paper had come from 221B Baker Street, London.

'Sherlock Holmes,' Irene Adler grasped. 'After all these years he has sought me out?' She raised her head to look at the Nob. 'He asks me to return to London with you.'

'That is so. We are instructed to give you our utmost attention, and guard you with our lives.'

But she was reading through the letter a second time, her lips moving silently.

Dear Lady – the script ran – *I can only trust that you remember me from the business in which we both figured some years ago, and in which, I cannot deny, you bested me. Some time ago it came to my notice that your husband, Mr Godfrey Norton, had been killed in an avalanche near Chamonix, and that you were also feared dead. It was, therefore, with great joy that I stumbled upon the fact that you still live, even in the somewhat reduced circumstances in which I have now found you.*

It may not have escaped your notice, from the public jottings of my friend and companion, Dr John Watson, that I have, from our first meeting, held you in the greatest regard. I only wish to help, dear, dear lady, and offer what assistance I can. If it is not too forward of me, I ask you to accompany the two gentlemen whom I have sent with this letter. They will bring you back to London where I have prepared a small villa for your use in Maida Vale. I ask nothing more than to be of service to you, and see that you are looked after in the manner to which you were formerly accustomed.

Your dearest friend, who has nothing but admiration for you – Sherlock Holmes.

'Is this true?' she asked in bewilderment, 'or can it be some trick?'

'There is no trick, Ma'am. We have money and the facilities for travelling back to London.'

'I am overwhelmed. Since my husband's death, which left me in a state both of despair and pecuniary disadvantage, I have not wished to face the world again. But Sherlock Holmes of all people . . .'

'You will come?' the Nob asked in a kindly tone.

'Well, it certainly gives me new heart. I am approaching a time of life when a woman feels . . .'

'You cannot me much over thirty years.' Ember bowed with considerable gallantry.

'You flatter me, sir. Yet I must admit that Mr Holmes' letter has set me aflutter like a young girl again.'

'You will come?' repeated the Nob.

'Yes.' Her face lit up in the most pleasing of smiles. 'Yes, of course I will come. What woman would not for Mr Sherlock Holmes?'

LONDON AND PARIS:
Tuesday, 4 May - Friday, 14 May 1897

(Vice-versa)

'Allow me to regale you with a tale which may already be familiar to some of you.' Moriarty faced those who were most privy to his thoughts.

They sat in the largest chamber of the Bermondsey buildings: Ember, Lee Chow, Bert Spear, Harry Allen, the Jacobs brothers and the Professor himself.

'After the tale,' continued Moriarty, 'I shall show you a small miracle. You will recall that, soon after my return to London – following our American episode – I asked for intelligence concerning a woman, by the name of Irene Adler. Well, as Ember will tell you, Miss Adler is now in London; suitably set up in a pleasant little villa in that most respectable suburb of Maida Vale.'

Ember nodded, his foxy face reflecting the complacency of one who is party to a great leader's innermost schemes.

Moriarty's voice took on that well-known mesmeristic lilt. 'Now, Irene Adler is a lady with a past, if you follow my meaning. At one time she was a most fashionable contralto. Concerts everywhere. She even appeared at La Scala, and was for some time prima donna of the Imperial Opera of Warsaw. She was also an adventuress.' He gave a short laugh. 'Indeed, it would not have taken much to push her into our camp. She would have made an admirable family woman.'

He paused for effect. 'Let me tell you here and now that I have the greatest respect for this lady. For she shares one great dignity with myself. Some eight or nine years ago she got the better of Mr Sherlock Holmes. Indeed, Mr Holmes, who is noted for his somewhat reserved attitude to the fair sex, also holds her in high esteem. At the time of this clash, Miss Adler married. A love match it seems, the gentleman being a solicitor, by the name of Godfrey Norton.* They were married in some haste and left the country almost immediately, living in Switzerland and France for the three or four years of their marriage. Then tragedy befell the lovebirds. While out walking on the lower slopes of Mont Blanc, the pair were overtaken by an avalanche, Mr Norton losing his life and his wife hovering near death for several months. She was, however, spared. Yet so distressed was she that a story went about which claimed that she too had perished.'

He allowed the facts to sink home. 'Unhappily, Mr Norton died leaving very little provision for his widow, while she, in despair, was reluctant to face the world again. She has been living, these last years, in great and frugal simplicity: her singing voice gone, and her spirit almost broken.'

Moriarty beamed at his audience. 'You will be pleased to hear, gentlemen, that all this has been changed; by that paragon of virtue, the dedicated and coldly analytical Sherlock Holmes.'

Ember smiled knowledgeably, the others looked puzzled.

'If you will bear with me,' Moriarty continued happily. 'I would like to introduce you to a visitor who has done us the honour of agreeing to come to our simple retreat. I shall go and fetch him, though it will take twenty or thirty minutes. You would do well to charge your glasses. Be patient.' Bowing like an actor, the Professor retired, heading for the quarters which he now often used in the refurbished building.

The members of the Praetorian Guard talked among

---

*The full account of Holmes' battle of wits with Irene Adler, together with the curious circumstances of her marriage to Godfrey Norton, can, of course, be found in Dr Watson's excellent résumé entitled *A Scandal in Bohemia*. The reader will recall that in this piece, Watson comments: 'To Sherlock Holmes she is always THE WOMAN ... In his eyes she eclipses and predominates the whole of her sex. It was not that he felt any emotion akin to love for Irene Adler. All emotions, and that one particularly, were abhorrent to his cold, precise, but admirably balanced mind.'

themselves, replenished their glasses, and probed Ember for more details of the Professor's devious story. But the foxy man would not be drawn.

Some five and twenty minutes later, they were called to silence by the Professor's voice behind the door.

'Gentlemen,' he said loudly. 'I have the honour to present to you, Mr Sherlock Holmes of Baker Street.' The door opened and Holmes stepped into the room.

All but one of the assembled villains looked aghast, for it was in truth James Moriarty's deadly enemy: the tall lean figure, the sharp piercing eyes, alert and shining above the hawk-like nose and prominent square jaw. The delicate hands moved in a precise gesture as Holmes took in the scene.

'Well, gentlemen, we meet face to face. I see you have been enjoying the pleasures of your native food, Lee Chow. And, you, Spear – if that is your real name – did you enjoy your walk by the river this morning? As for our good friends the Jacobs brothers, it would appear they have recently been playing billiards.'

Bertram Jacobs took a pace forward, as though about to perpetrate an act of aggression, when Holmes' voice changed.

'No, Bertram, you are safe,' said James Moriarty.

Sherlock Holmes' head oscillated slightly, and the laugh which broke from his lips was the laugh of their leader, the Professor. 'Is this not my greatest triumph in disguise?' he said proudly.

Irene Adler was enchanted by the house in Maida Vale. In truth it was a small place, but neat, tidy and cosy, furnished with consummate taste, and containing everything for which a woman could wish, including the services of an excellent young maid-servant, by name of Harriet.

On her arrival there was another letter from Mr Holmes, couched in the most affectionate of terms. Flowers were set fresh in the vases and a small carriage was at her disposal, day or night.

At the end of his note, Holmes had written – *I am much entangled in a matter of some importance at the moment, but will call upon you as soon as it is humanly possible.*

It was, however, three days before the great detective put in an appearance at the villa.

He arrived in the late afternoon while Irene Adler was changing, prior to taking a drive in her newly acquired carriage. Harriet, all agog, came with the news that he was waiting for her in the parlour.

She came down to greet her benefactor some fifteen minutes later, dressed in a simple grey afternoon gown, her face radiant and looking nowhere near her nine and thirty years.

'Mr Holmes, I know not how to thank you. I am overcome with your kindness. Would it be presumptuous of me to offer a kiss?'

'Dear lady,' his tall frame towered above her, the firm features composing themselves into a smile of intense pleasure as he took her in his arms. 'I have waited long for this moment. I am only happy that you have seen fit to take advantage of my offer.'

She hugged him close. 'Mr Holmes, I can still hardly believe it, your reputation is that you would go a hundred miles rather than be found in any position of compromise with a mere woman.'

'True.' He gave her an affectionate squeeze. 'True, I have been presented as such, but you so softened my heart all those years ago when we met – under most dubious circumstances – that I have longed to be of assistance to you. I have never understood why, if you were alive and in such difficult financial straits, you did not return to your chosen profession in the theatre.'

She sighed, took his arm and led him to the couch which stood near to the window, seating herself and patting the velvet to indicate that he should take his place beside her.

'My voice is gone, Mr Holmes. The shock of that terrible avalanche, and the death of my husband, of Godfrey.' Her eyes filled up and she was forced to turn her face away.

'I am so sad for you, Irene,' he said, his hand reaching out to pat hers in comfort. 'I know what such a loss must have meant. I am a cold fish in some ways, but I can imagine the void and ache which such a bereavement leaves behind. If I can help to dull the pain, you have but to ask.'

'I must first thank you for all you have done already. For all this.' Her hand swept in a circle round the room. 'And for the clothes and, and everything. Have you really forgiven me for that last business?'

He discerned a small twinkle replacing the tears in her brimming eyes.

'I have never had anything but admiration. There is nothing to forgive.'

'But what can I give you in return for your kindness, Mr Holmes? I feel I have so little to offer.'

'If I could offer you marriage, I would do so at once.' He moved closer. 'But, as you know, I am a bachelor confirmed. However,' his tongue slid across his lips, as though to moisten them. 'However, what can a woman offer to a man who has been so starved of feminine affection?'

Irene Adler's face was lifted to him as she twined her arms around his neck and pulled him down towards her.

'Oh, Mr Holmes,' she murmured.

'Later,' he whispered in her ear, 'we can, perhaps, have a champagne supper at The Monico.'

'Lovely, dear Sherlock,' she replied softly, eyes closed and mouth parted. 'Lovely.'

Crow was running out of time, and he knew it. In the days which had gone by since Holmes' sudden and ailing departure from Paris, he had searched the length and breadth of the Montmartre quarter for the girl known as Suzanne the Gypsy. There appeared to be plenty who knew her, yet none who had set eyes on her for some time.

There were but two days left before he was due back on duty at Scotland Yard, when the wire arrived from Holmes. It contained only four words – TRY FOLIES BERGÈRE TONIGHT. Mystified by this sudden, and yet such certain direction, Crow spent the day in some agitation, dined with less composure than usual, and set out for the Folies Bergère in high hopes.

He had already visited the place on several occasions during his quest, so was quite acclimatized to the noise and the superior quality of the performances – not to mention the young women who paraded themselves along the promenade. After an hour or so of putting hasty questions to harassed waiters, Crow steeled himself to take a turn along the promenade where he had already suffered some indignities at the hands of the night ladies who offered themselves there.

Success came quickly. A girl, dressed in the height of fashion, but with too much paint and powder for Crow's taste, seized on him almost as soon as he showed himself.

'Were not you asking for Suzanne the other night?' she queried breathlessly, one eye on Crow, the other cocked for any passing trade which she might miss. 'Suzanne the Gypsy?'

'Indeed I was. Have you news?'

'You're in luck. She's here. She only returned to Paris today.'

Crow cast around him, trying to identify the girl among the throng.

'Over here,' cried the prostitute who had grabbed him. 'Here,' dragging him by the sleeve and at the same time calling out, 'Suzanne, I have a friend for you, if you have not become too fine a lady among your actress friends.'

Crow suddenly found himself face to face with the jet-haired beauty whose features undeniably showed that her veins contained gypsy blood. The girl looked him up and down, her mouth red, inviting and open in a wide smile.

'You wish to buy me a drink?' she asked in coquettish style.

'I have been searching all Paris for you, if you are known as Suzanne the Gypsy,' gasped Crow.

She laughed. 'That's me, only I have not brought my tambourine with me tonight. We'll have to play other tunes.'

'I merely wish to speak with you,' Crow answered primly. 'It is a matter of some importance.'

'Time is money, chéri.'

'You will be paid.'

'Good, then lead me to the champagne.'

Crow took her along, found a fresh table, ordered the wine and then gave her all his attention.

'I have been searching for you,' he started.

'I have been out of Paris,' she giggled, shaking her elegant shoulders. 'Monsieur Meliés has been taking moving pictures of me. You have seen the cinematograph?'

'Yes. No. Well, I've heard of these things.'

'I have been acting for Monsieur Meliés. In a cinematograph film he has been taking at his country house at Montreuil.'

'Fascinating. But ...'

'Indeed it is fascinating. He wanted several girls to act at being gypsies. I am the real thing. He said so himself. You wish to hear more of how he takes the photographs?'

'No, I wish to hear of something else.'

'What?'

'Suzanne, please cast your mind back to just after Christmas.'

'Zut,' she raised her hands. 'That is hard. Sometimes I cannot remember what happened yesterday. Christmas is a long time ago.'

'You were at the *Moulin Rouge*.'

'I am often at the *Moulin Rouge*. I would rather talk about Monsieur Meliés, he is coming here tonight. A whole party is coming tonight, you could meet him.' She stopped suddenly, staring at him. 'I don't know your name.'

'My name is Crow.'

'Good,' she bubbled, 'I shall call you *le Corbeau*. See?' Suzanne made flapping motions with her hands, and a cawing noise from the back of her throat.

Crow considered that in all probability she had taken more than enough to drink. 'On the night I am talking about,' he said firmly, 'you met an American. A stout American, who, I think, was asking where he could find a gentleman called Jean Grisombre?'

Suzanne seemed to sober up with remarkable rapidity. 'You want to know about Grisombre?'

'No. Do you remember the American?'

'I don't know. I might. It depends. Why do you wish to know?'

'He is a friend of mine. I'm trying to find him. His name was Morningdale. There was some kind of a fracas outside the *Moulin Rouge* when he left. Something to do with a girl. A street girl.'

'Yes, I know about that. I remember him. He was not pleasant. But his friend, Harry, he was good to me.' She shrugged. 'The American paid.'

275

'And they were looking for Grisombre?'

'Yes.'

'Did you help them?'

'I sent them up to *La Maison Vide*. Jean Grisombre is there most nights. Was there most nights. I went up tonight, he is travelling somewhere, so you'll be out of luck if you want to see him.'

'But the American would have seen him that night?'

'If he went there, yes. No doubt at all.'

'This American and his friend, where had they come from?'

'London. I think it was London.' Her brow creased as though she was making a great effort to remember. 'Yes. He said something to Harry about where they lived. It seemed strange.'

'Try to think.'

'Another glass of champagne.'

Crow poured, not taking his eyes from her. Around them the place was alive with music, laughter, dancing and the thick, crowded, hurly-burly of people determined to enjoy themselves whatever the cost.

'How much are you paying me?'

'Enough.'

'You wish to sleep with me also?'

'No.'

'You do not find me attractive?'

Crow sighed. 'My dear young woman, I find you most attractive, but I have made a small vow to myself.'

'Vows are made to be broken.'

'What did he say?'

'Money.'

Crow tossed a small pile of gold coins onto the table where they disappeared like lumps of fat in a hot pan.

She gave him a quick smile and stood up.

'Can you not remember? Or is this some fraud?' He asked with alarm.

'I remember,' she smiled again. 'He said ... When he gave me the money to be with Harry, he said, "I will not tell your little skivvy at Albert Square. They tell me, Suzanne the Gypsy is worth every sou you spend". And I am, Monsieur le

Corbeau, worth *every* sou.'

'Albert Square? You're sure of that?'

'I'm worth every sou.' She gave a little mocking laugh and disappeared into the crowd.

At that moment the band struck up and the wild whoops of the cancan girls filled the salon, drowning everything else. The detective considered that he should go and find the other little fancy lady and tip her for leading him to Suzanne. Then home as fast as steam would carry him.

Crow got back to London late on the following evening, tired, but feeling that he at least had a scrap of intelligence for Holmes. It was, however, too late to call on the great detective that night. In any case Sylvia greeted him like she had when they were courting. So much so, in fact, that Crow wondered whether she was planning some new act of folly. It was a nervousness which would soon pass, for Sylvia Crow had learned her lesson, and was determined to be a dutiful wife.

The detective, enjoying the comforts of his own home, and bed, soon decided that he would visit Baker Street as quickly as possible after reporting in to Scotland Yard on the morrow.

He was up betimes, and in his office before eight-thirty. Yet not soon enough to escape the powers that be. A note on his desk told him that he was to see the Commissioner at nine o'clock sharp.

Tanner came in as he was about to leave.

'You look fit, sir. Quite recovered?' he asked jauntily.

'Never felt better.' Crow remarked to himself that this was indeed true. The thrill of the chase had infused his blood, cutting out all thoughts of Harriet's treachery.

'Better than Mr Holmes, then.' Tanner almost leered.

'Why do you mention Mr Holmes?' he asked sharply.

'You've met him, have you not, sir?'

'Two or three times, yes. But what is wrong?'

'You've not heard then?'

'Not a word.'

'The great Mr Holmes is making a fool of himself with a woman. It's become a proper scandal. Half London's talking of it.'

'I don't believe ...'

'It's true enough, sir. A former singer they say. Name of

Irene Adler. Goes everywhere with her.'

Crow hurried off to the Commissioner's office, anxious to have done with his interview.

'Well, you look fit enough,' said the Commissioner tersely. 'You think you are completely better?'

'Ready for anything, sir.'

'You'll need to be. It's your last chance, mind. I had a word with Moore Agar, and he assured me that you would be as good as new. I trust that he is right, for he has another patient who does not do so well, I hear.'

'Oh?' Crow forced himself to look as blank as he could muster.

'Don't let it go any further, mind.' The Commissioner leaned forward in a confidential manner. 'It's Sherlock Holmes. You remember what a firm self-disciplinarian he always was? Wouldn't go near a woman?'

'Indeed.'

'I've seen it happen before at his age, mind you. Finds a filly and loses all sense of proportion.'

'Mr Holmes?' Crow was genuinely disturbed now. Tanner could have been exaggerating, but not the old man.

'Taken up with a woman who's no better than she should be.'

'I can hardly credit it.'

'Seen it with me own eyes. Out every night at The Monico, The Cri or The Troc. Canoodling in public as well. Disgustin' display. Fella in my club told me he'd seen the pair of them half tipsy at the Ambassadeurs, and I gather he won't even speak to his brother Mycroft. Damn shame, but it often happens. When men like that kick over the traces...' The sentence trailed off and Crow quickly changed the conversation to the duties which the Commissioner required of him.

The interview lasted a full hour and contained some disturbing news concerning an explosion in Praed Street, and an unidentified body – the only casualty in this unpleasant affair. However, no sooner had Crow been dismissed than he hurried out of the building, hailed a hansom and was off at a spanking pace towards Baker Street, dread in his heart at what he would find.

'Thank heaven it's you, sir,' Mrs Hudson cried with relief

when she opened the door to Crow's agitated knock. 'He's left word that you are the only one he will see. I have even thought of telegraphing Dr Watson, but he has forbidden it.'

'What on earth's the matter, Mrs Hudson?'

'He's been that ill, sir. I've never seen him like it before. I thought he was close to death, but he would not have a doctor near. And the stories they are telling about him. All lies. But he will not listen nor say a word.'

Crow bounded up the stairs towards Holmes' chambers, from whence came the high and mournful sound of a violin. Not even waiting to knock, Crow burst into the room.

Holmes sat in his favourite chair, clad in a robe, eyes closed and his violin to his chin. Crow was aghast at the great man's appearance. His body, always lean, now appeared wasted, his cheeks gaunt and haggard, the eyes sunken. From the way he was holding the bow to his violin, Crow also deduced that his hand was not as steady as it had been.

'Great Scot, Holmes, what is wrong with you?' he all but shouted.

Holmes opened his eyes, stopped playing, and leaned back in his chair.

'Crow, it's good to see you. Did you get my wire? What news?'

'I have some, but what of you?'

'Don't worry, my good fellow. I've beaten it now. I am almost recovered.'

As he said the words his body became racked by a great shaking so that he was not able to speak for a few moments. Crow saw that huge beads of perspiration were running from his brow.

'This is a malady of my own making, I fear, Crow,' Holmes said weakly. 'But, truly, I am almost better. A little of Mrs Hudson's chicken broth and I'll be good as new.'

'But, Holmes, what is it?'

'A long story, and one of folly, I fear. But, your news first. We'll have him yet. You've heard what he is doing to me in the restaurants and hotels?'

'You mean the stories of you and Irene Adler?'

'Quite so.'

'I've heard. They're scandalous and you must refute them

at once.'

'Not until I am recovered, or you have done the trick for me. It will be a seven-day wonder, you'll see. But what news?'

'I found the girl.'

'Yes, I thought you would. When I read in the newspaper, during one of my more lucid moments, that Monsieur Meliés had been using gypsy girls for one of his moving pictures at Montreuil, and was holding a party at the Folies Bergère, I was convinced you would find our elusive Suzanne there.'

'They most certainly found Grisombre – at least Morningdale did. And she says they mentioned a place in London. Albert Square.'

The old light came into the great detective's eyes. 'Hand down my revised Fry's *London* and we'll see.' He pointed to the bookshelf. 'My hands are unsteady. Ah, here we are – there appears to be one Albert Square, up near Notting Hill. It would seem James Moriarty has found himself more respectable lodgings than his last bolt hole. I feel better already. I think I will try some of Mrs Hudson's broth now, would you be good enough to ask her, Crow?'

He was still very weak and listless, but once the broth was inside him, Holmes' remarkable powers of recovery were certainly apparent.

'Can I trust you, Crow?' he asked.

'With your life, you can count on it.'

'Good, I pray none of this business will get back to Watson. He is a dear man and I do not wish to offend him in any way. He can also be injudicious in what he puts into print. I should never have allowed him to make those remarks, flattering though they are, concerning Irene Adler.'

'I can understand that.'

'But let me tell you a moral tale, Crow, concerning myself.'

'You have my entire attention.'

'I have always driven myself hard, Crow. I think you know that. I dislike inactivity, get bored easily, and I cannot abide the restrictions my body sometimes places on me. So, very early in my studies I resorted to medical means in order to increase my ability; to stimulate my mental processes and to allow me to work with little rest. The medical means is – I should say was – cocaine. I saw no harm in it, indeed used it only as others have used it. You are aware that, on the continent, there have been many experiments in the use of cocaine to make troops more efficient in the field? Yet it was not long before I discovered its somewhat serious side effects, the same side effects which are now well known to the medical profession.' He smiled, almost benevolently, as if to suggest that his researches were far in advance of known medical science.

'By the time I knew the dangers, it was too late. My body craved for the wretched stuff, and I had become what one might call addicted. It is, you must be aware, only in the last year or so that leaders of medical science have begun to press for restrictions on the use of certain substances, so there has never been any difficulty in obtaining the foul powder. But old Watson was quick to spot the problem. He pleaded with me time and again, Crow, using all the arguments. I knew he was right, but the drug had such a hold on me that I found it impossible even to contemplate giving it up. However, my mental discipline finally overcame, and I agreed that Watson, with the help of Moore Agar, should wean me off the cocaine. That is one of the reasons I do not wish him to hear of this. Poor fellow, I duped him.' He gave a short, tired laugh.

'Watson and Moore Agar between them closed off all my sources of supply. No chemist in London would give me even a grain of the drug – not even Curtis and Company down the road, or John Taylor at the corner of George Street. They had me well buttoned, I can tell you. Or so they thought.'

He now seemed to settle happily into his narrative. 'You see, the addict is sometimes a most cunning person. Believe me, I know to my cost. At first, Watson and our companion from Harley Street began to slacken off the doses quite easily, and I put up with the occasional discomfort. Then I became – I am not ashamed to admit to it – frightened. So I made sure that there was always a source of supply if I needed to supplement the doses which our medicos were doling out. I found a man in Orchard Street who supplied me regularly, overriding the doctors.'

Crow gave the great detective a look which was meant to convey a complete understanding of his dilemma.

Holmes stared gravely at his feet, shook his head, and then

went on. 'I feel most badly about it all. They really thought they had me cured. The dosage dropped to a minute amount, but, unbeknown to them, I was still using cocaine. Until Paris, that is.'

'Your illness there?'

'Quite so. I found myself without the drug and in the grip of the most terrifying symptoms. Withdrawal can be most painful and agonizing.'

'You were in need of it?'

'Very much so.'

'Then why did you not purchase it freely in France?'

'There are some restrictions, but I suppose I could have done. The brain plays funny tricks. I could only think of getting back to London and my man in Orchard Street.'

'But ...'

'But he would not supply me. Yes, you may well look like that, I too detect the diabolical hand of James Moriarty in this also. I was a physical and mental wreck, but somewhere at the back of my mind, Crow, the will was showing through. I returned here, and in one of my few lucid moments, made up my mind to quit myself of the drug for all time, no matter what. I cannot ever tell you what it was like...'

'I can see for myself, Holmes.'

'Perhaps. It is like wrestling with the very devil himself, and all his fires. However, I am home now, through the darkness and free of it forever.'

'Yet in the time you have been in agony, Moriarty has done you a grave public disservice.'

'Indeed he has, and one for which he will pay heavily.'

'But how will you convince those who are already spreading scandal?'

'A word or two in the right quarter, a wink here and there will do the trick. My brother Mycroft is already half crazed with anxiety, but I have sent him a telegram telling him to remain calm, and that it will soon be over. Another day or so of food and rest and I will be ready for action once more. It is not for nothing, my dear fellow, that I have what is termed an iron constitution.'

'I could take the villain tonight, while he is with his woman.' Crow's face was red with anger.

'What, and spoil me of confronting him myself? No, Crow.'

'I too have made a vow to bring him down, and you have already told me that you have no wish to be publicly involved.'

'You will get all the credit, never fear.' The old clarity was in his eye now as he gave the inspector a grim smile. 'I have a plan which will hoist him with his own petard, Crow. I have lost weight, yes?'

'You have, Holmes.'

'And my face has become gaunt? Eyes sunken?'

'Yes.'

'Good, those features will make it easier than ever for me to take on the guise I have in mind.'

'How can I help?'

'First I want to know how he lives in Albert Square – if that is indeed where he is hiding himself. I would do it myself, but...'

'Conserve your strength, I'll see to it.'

'I need all details. Who is in the house with him. How well he has disguised himself as me. What his movements are.'

'I'm your man.'

'I knew I could count on you, Crow. Stout fellow.'

The brilliance of his portrayal of Holmes, Moriarty considered, was not in the small details. It was the overall picture – the height, the slight remoulding of the face with actor's putty, the voice and mannerisms. Faced with the detective's brother Mycroft, for instance, he would not have lasted five minutes. Yet, to Irene Adler he was Holmes complete, for she merely worked from memory.

It was the same with all those who had seen him in public places with the Adler woman. They expected Holmes; and that was who they saw. He eased his feet into the built-up shoes – the same shoes which he used when in the guise of his dead brother – and set himself comfortably at the dressing-table, beginning to mould the hawk-like nose.

The Professor had decreed that, during this period of charade, the Albert Square house was to be empty but for himself, Martha Pearson and the young skivvy. The others were at Bermondsey, going about the family business. Bridget Spear was lying in at Sal Hodges' best house, for it was said she would have the child early. Sal herself was also there. The remainder collected, stole, defrauded and pillaged. The reborn family grew stronger each day.

As he applied gum to his own eyebrows, in order to overlay them with hair to achieve a verisimilitude of Holmes' own brows, he vaguely heard the bell ringing downstairs. Only in emergency were any of the others to come to the house. It was probably some tradesman.

It was, in fact, Bert Spear.

'Crow,' said the lieutenant after Moriarty had admitted him to the bedroom.

'What of Crow?' He ran a red sable brush, dipped in a flesh-coloured preparation, down the join between nose putty and flesh.

'His leave of absence is over.'

The brush remained posed in mid-air for a second, the only sign that Moriarty was in any way alarmed.

'You mean he has not been permanently dismissed the force?' The voice something of a cross between his own and that of Holmes.

'It would seem not. He was back on duty at Scotland Yard this morning. Reinstated.'

Moriarty let go a quiet foul oath, for this meant abject failure for one of his schemes. 'Is he being watched?'

'As soon as we knew of it, I informed Ember. He's seeing to the lurkers now. They'll be in position within an hour or so.'

Moriarty swore once more, a troubled obscenity. Then, as though regaining confidence, 'Worry not, Spear. We'll have the nosey jack yet. Bridget is near her time, I hear.' Changing the conversation, swerving it onto another path until he could think clearly regarding the problems which Crow's re-emergence presented.

'Any time. Sal's there, and the midwife.'

'And the gay ladies doing their business on the other floors.' The Professor gave a chuckle.

'Aye, it all goes on there. It's a fine house.'

Silence for a few moments between the two men as Moriarty smoothed out the putty around his jaw. Then Spear spoke once more.

'You think one of us should come back here? Or be near you as you go about this game?'

The Professor did not give it much thought. 'No, I shall be safe. Tonight and tomorrow night on the tiles with the Adler woman should be enough to blacken Mr Sherlock's name for good. The last few days have been both amusing and interesting, Spear. I've had much enjoyment out of it all. Like a Christmas game.'

Spear left shortly after, and an hour later Harkness arrived with the cab. Moriarty, in the character of Sherlock Holmes, left the house and flitted down the steps, the cab whisking him from Albert Square out to Maida Vale and the ever-willing Irene Adler.

As they turned from the square into the main thoroughfare, neither Harkness, nor Moriarty – still wrapped in thought – caught sight of the shadow pressed hard in a doorway.

As the cab turned away, so the shadow detached itself from cover. Crow stepped out plainly into the light, moving purposefully after the disappearing cab.

Another hansom, empty, was making slow progress up the street. The detective raised his hand to hail it.

'I am a police officer,' he said to the sullen cabby. 'Follow that cab, but keep back and do exactly as I tell you.'

The cabby, much impressed, touched his hat and urged his horse forward.

Crow returned to Baker Street on the following morning with the distinct impression that he was now being followed. He had been pretty certain of it from the moment he left King Street on his way to the Yard, and the thought concerned him.

He found Holmes sitting up, still gaunt and haggard, but with the old light in his eyes, and much more his normal self.

'Tell me all,' said the great detective. 'Every detail.'

Crow settled himself before the fire and began his history of the previous night's events, conscious that Holmes' eyes did not leave his face for one moment during the telling.

'To start with, there is no doubt that the Professor is keeping some evil ménage at number five Albert Square,' he began. 'I went first to the Notting Hill Police Station and used my influence. I have talked to the beat coppers – they are always the ones who know most about houses, and their occupants, in their area.'

'And?' Holmes snapped, irritated and anxious to hear the facts.

'And he has been at number five since last September. Living as an American Professor. Name of Carl Nicol. A right evil crew he's had with him.'

'All the old faces, eh?'

'The Chinese we have been seeking, the ferrety Ember, Spear . . .'

'All his Praetorian Guard.'

'Yes, and some women.'

'Hum!'

'But, this you will find interesting, they are all gone now. For the past week or so he has been there alone, but for two female servants.'

'You saw him, Crow?'

'It would be more exact, Holmes, to say that I saw you.'

'Ah.'

'It was an amazing likeness.'

'I have never underestimated James Moriarty. Not for a moment did I think his performance would be anything but professional. You followed him?'

'To a little villa in Maida Vale where he has the Adler woman.'

'You saw her?' asked Holmes with marked interest.

'Indeed I did. Moriarty was in the house some two hours, after which they both came out and drove to The Trocadero.'

'Ah, the good old Troc,' mused Holmes.

Crow was happy to note that he really did seem to be his former self.

'Where they dined, very much in full view and making a public spectacle of themselves. Hand holding and blowing kisses across the table, secret jests and loud laughter. It was embarrassing, Holmes, for if I did not know better, I would have sworn it was you.'

'Then back to Maida Vale, I presume?'

'Indeed yes. Moriarty did not return to Albert Square until

the small hours. At around four in the morning. I fear that my Sylvia, who is mighty loving now, suspects me of some new dalliance.'

'Tell her to cease worrying. By tomorrow it will be over. How are you with locks, Crow?'

'In what way, Holmes?'

'At cracking them, of course. Never mind, I have my own kit of tools here. It will present no difficulty.'

'You mean to...?'

'We are forced to indulge in a spot of housebreaking, Inspector. Have you any objections?'

'Not if we can nail the Professor.'

'Capital. Now, did you know that you were followed this morning?'

'I thought as much.'

'Yes, and they have a fellow watching this house. A rogue who poses as a blind beggar. Fred, I believe they call him. The men on to you are a pair called Scarecrow Sim and Ben Tuffnell. We shall have to put them off the scent tonight, but allow me to worry over that. I have some street urchins handy here who can outwit even the cleverest of the Professor's lurkers. Just go about your business, Crow, and leave that to me. I shall want you here at nine, or before. It will be a long wait at Albert Square, but I think worth our while.'

Crow nodded. 'I'll be here.'

'Good man. And, Crow, bring your revolver.'

Bridget Spear was delivered of a fine eight-pound boy at six o'clock on the evening of Friday, 14 May.* Spear, an overjoyed and proud father, broke all rules and, for the second night running, presented himself at Albert Square.

Moriarty, again at his dressing-table, greeted him with less than joyful enthusiasm.

'I am glad to hear about Bridget,' he said coldly. 'However,

*For those who have read the first chronicle, and who care about these things: at the time of receiving the Moriarty Journals from Albert Spear's grandson, I was given to understand that his father was born in the year 1895 and I have so tabled it in the preface to *The Return of Moriarty*. From the Journals it would seem otherwise.

I would be happier if you kept your distance, Spear, until this lark is done. I shall see the Adler woman this last time, tonight. After that Lee Chow has his orders. It will not be such an arduous or late night, tonight, for I shall tell her I have pressing business.'

'You'll know what it means to be a father yourself, soon enough.' Spear stared sullenly at the carpet. 'Have you had the word about Crow?'

'A boy came in earlier. He's been commiserating with Holmes, which makes me uneasy. But the Baker Street detective is so discredited that it'll do no good.'

'I trust you're right.'

'He'll be out of the swim for a long time I'll warrant, and we can get on with our business in peace. I'll be down at the Bermondsey place to see to our capers first thing tomorrow. Now, Spear, go back to your Bridget and take her my good wishes. I'll be godfather to the boy, never fear.'

'There'll be another marriage before long also. Young Allen and the Mary Ann – Polly – they can scarce be prized apart with a jemmy.'

'I'll bless that and play the uncle too,' laughed the Professor.

Harkness arrived at the appointed hour, and Spear left at the same time as Moriarty. The lamps were dowsed one by one, and, around ten o'clock, Martha and the little skivvy made their way to their beds, leaving but one oil lamp lit in the hall against their master's return.

Crow's eyes almost popped out of his head. He had presented himself at Baker Street, promptly at nine, as Holmes suggested, and made his way up to the detective's chambers to find them empty.

He called softly for Holmes, but, receiving no reply, he settled himself by the fire, which was well made up in the hearth, and took out his old American revolver in order to make certain it was in good condition.

The rattle of a hansom, pulling up outside, drew the policeman to the window. There were few people about, though he could swear that he glimpsed shadows across the road, and the fleeting figure of a man moving between the doorways up the street.

Below, a hansom was stopped, and its fare descending onto the pavement. A tall figure, gaunt and with a stoop. Crow caught his breath as the light from the gas standard passed over the man's face. He had seen him twice before, and knew his description as well as the back of his own hand. Below the hat there was, he could be certain, a high domed forehead. The eyes would be sunken. The man in the street below was Moriarty, the Professor – the guise in which that Napoleon of Crime often showed himself to his corrupt army.

Crow fingered his revolver, standing back from the window and watching, heart in mouth. The tall figure crossed the road, making for the doorway in which Crow had seen the lurking shadow.

The Professor paused for a few moments, as though speaking to someone in hiding, his head moving to and fro, as if in earnest conversation. Then he turned, glanced up towards Crow so that the light struck his face fully. It was certainly he, now pacing back across the road towards the door of 221B.

Crow heard the door slam downstairs, and footsteps coming towards Holmes' chambers. In a flash he was before the door, revolver up and ready for the man who would enter.

The door swung open, and Moriarty walked into the room.

'Hold, sir,' barked Crow, 'or I'll have your life this time.'

'My dear Crow, pray try to be less aggressive,' said Sherlock Holmes from the face that undoubtedly belonged to his enemy.

It was then that Crow's eyes appeared to be popping from his head. His jaw dropped and the revolver weighed heavy in his hand.

'Holmes?' he stammered.

'In person,' said Holmes, removing the tall hat to reveal, as Crow had suspected, the high-domed forehead.

'But you are Moriarty to the life,' his eyes searched the face and figure of the man who stood before him.

'I should hope so,' chuckled Holmes. 'Two can play the game, Crow. If Moriarty is posing as me, then I do not see why I should not pose as him. The confrontation will be neat, don't you think?'

'Merciful heavens, it's masterful, Holmes.'

'Elementary, Crow. The simple arts of any good actor, though I must confess that I am a shade better than most of those who tread the green these days. But quick, man, to the window. I believe I've set the cat among the pigeons down there.'

They crossed to the casement, Crow blurting out questions which came tumbling one after the other into his head.

'I saw you in the street. What were you up to?'

'The lurking watchers. I had words with blind Fred who, naturally, took me to be his leader. A simple device. I merely told him that in a few moments three boys would be leaving this house – after I had entered. Friend Fred, and the other two, Scarecrow Sim and Tuffnell, are to follow them, one man each. I think the lads will lead them a merry dance around the city. Look, there they go now.'

It was just as he said. Three raggedy urchins had come out onto the pavement below, and were setting off in different directions, at a steady trot. As they watched, figures glided from hiding places to give chase.

'There,' Holmes rubbed his hands, 'that has settled their hash for the night. We can make our way to Albert Square without fear of the Professor's men being on our tails.'

At Holmes' instructions, Mrs Hudson had set a selection of cold meats and some beer on a tray, and the two men ate heartily before leaving. During this cold collation, Crow continually cast glances at his companion, hardly believing that he was indeed Holmes, so convincing was the disguise.

They left a little after midnight, taking a cab to Notting Hill and going the remainder of the journey on foot, arriving at Albert Square near fifteen minutes to one.

'The area steps, I think,' Holmes whispered as they passed along the square, keeping close to the wall. 'I fancy the servants will be well asleep by now, but I beg you to remain as silent as you can.'

Before the door at the bottom of the area steps, Holmes paused, producing some instrument from his pocket and, inserting it in the lock, had the hinges swinging back in a trice.

'Just stand still a moment,' he whispered once they were inside. 'Let your eyes adjust to the darkness.'

The kitchen in which they stood, smelled of crisp pastry and the scent of roast meat.

'The Professor does himself well,' muttered Holmes. 'That's best beef or I'm a Dutchman.'

Slowly, Crow began to distinguish the shapes of objects around him.

'The stairs are over there,' Holmes pointed a long finger. 'You noticed the lamp outside. It burns in the hall. We have enough time to examine the contents of Moriarty's study, I think – though I doubt we'll find anything worth while. I've examined his papers before now, some years ago.'

They made their way up the stairs and into the main body of the house, their progress made easier by the lamp placed on a table near the entrance lobby.

It was after one now. 'Two or three hours, I think,' Holmes grunted. 'That should give us time enough. The wait should not be tedious.'

As he spoke they heard a hansom come into the square and pull up before the house. Voices from outside – at least one unmistakable in its timbre.

'He's grown tired of playing my role with the woman,' whispered Holmes. 'Only just in time it seems. Quick, up the stairs, we'll beard him on the first landing as he comes up.'

Crow felt as though he had two left feet, Holmes was so nimble and quiet, moving up the broad staircase like a cat, and they had only just reached the landing when the front door opened below them, and Moriarty's footsteps were plain in the hall.

Crow hardly dared breathe as they hugged the wall on the darkened landing, watching the stairs and listening to the sounds coming from below.

Moriarty was humming to himself, some catchy tune which all the errand boys were whistling, *Girlie Girlie*, or some such rubbish. They could hear his coat go down on the hall stand, and saw with their own eyes the change in the light as he picked up the lamp and began making his way, heavy footed, up the stairs.

Crow tensed, his hand curling around the revolver butt, drawing it out slowly. Holmes laid a finger to his lips.

Moriarty was passing the turn in the stairs now, the lamp

held high and the light falling on his face: the face of Sherlock Holmes.

As his feet reached the landing, Holmes took a pace forward.

'Mr Sherlock Holmes, I presume,' he said, in a voice as soft and menacing as Crow had ever heard.

Moriarty almost lost his balance and fell backwards, grabbing at the bannister rail to steady himself, raising the lamp even higher. Crow came forward, revolver levelled. Never had he seen such a bizarre sight: Holmes and Moriarty facing one another on this landing, each in the guise of the other.

'Rot you, Holmes,' snarled the Professor. 'I should have taken care of you at Reichenbach instead of playing games.'

'I dare say,' Holmes countered politely. 'You know my friend here, Mr Crow? He almost had you at Sandringham, I believe. Well, Moriarty, this is certainly the end. We'll have you on Jack Ketch's gibbet within a month or so. Now kindly move into your drawing-room so that the Inspector here can cuff you – after we have rubbed all that paint and putty from your face. I must compliment you on that. A good likeness.'

Moriarty had no option but to pass before the two men, at pistol point, into the spacious drawing-room. They followed, and Holmes crossed to the fireplace which still contained the ashes and embers of its daily blaze.

Moriarty stood in the centre of the room, his lips moving with obscene and despicable oaths.

'Cuff up the blackguard, then, Crow,' Holmes said brightly. 'Then we can be on our way.'

The policeman moved forward, his hand going to his back pocket to grasp the handcuffs which he had in readiness.

'If you would hold the revolver, Holmes, and you, sir,' to Moriarty, 'place down that lamp on the piano there.'

He turned slightly to hand the pistol to Holmes, and in that one second off guard all was lost.

'I'll place the lamp for you,' screamed Moriarty, and suiting action to the word, hurled the brass-embossed burner with full force against the wall, only a foot from Holmes' head.

'Shoot, man, shoot,' yelled Holmes, diving forward as the

burner crashed, spilling oil and flame over the carpet.

Crow's hand came up and his revolver jerked, the shot passing only an inch or so wide of Moriarty who was at the door.

'After him.'

The door slammed, and they heard the blood-chilling click of the key turning in the lock. Behind them, the room was already filling with flame as the spilled oil caught.

'The door, Crow. Break the door.'

From outside came the mocking, haunting laugh and the sound of Moriarty's feet on the stairs.

'For heaven's sake, the door, man,' cried Holmes, 'or we'll be roasted alive.'

Crow, cursing himself for a fool, put his shoulder hard to the door, feeling the bruising pain as it connected. The wood did not even budge, the solid oak and strong lock not giving an inch to Crow's weight.

Moriarty leaned against the landing wall, breathing heavily, the laughter dying on his lips and the sound of the fire growing louder each moment.

He tore at his face, pulling off pieces of putty and hair to rid himself of his enemy's visage. The putty on Holmes' physiognomy would be bubbling soon enough. He gulped at the air, thick with smoke dribbling out from under the door.

The shock was still in his head and stomach – the fright of seeing his other self on the landing, framed in the dim light. He had thought, for a second, that it was his brother's spectre come to haunt him at last.

The thumping on the door was becoming more intense. Rats, he thought, caught fast in the devouring flames. He turned for the stairs, and then remembered Martha. Did a servant girl matter? There was another noise now, from far away the shout of 'Fire! Fire!' If they were saved, Martha knew something of Bermondsey, and could lead the jacks to him.

The Professor turned and leaped for the upward stair, running three steps at a time to the topmost landing and the attics.

There was no ceremony in his dragging the two girls from

their beds, shouting loud for them not to be concerned as to their appearance, but to grab at their robes and follow him to safety. Stunned with sleep and fright, Martha, and the child skivvy, blundered down following him. As they reached the bottom landing they could hear the flames' roar and the crash of glass from the drawing-room.

'Hurry,' Moriarty shouted.

In the hall they heard the babble from the street, and the sound of horses' hooves, the rattle of wheels and the clang of the bell: the brigade was arriving to deal with the inferno which must now be raging above them.

Moriarty wrenched open the front door and hurried into the street, the two girls at his heels. People were clustered around the steps, two policemen pushing back the small knot of men and women. Doors had been flung open, and the other occupants of Albert Square, in motley disarray, stood at their doors, or in the street, as the two fire engines pulled up, horses snorting and helmeted men leaping for the pumps.

There was a small cheer as the Professor came down, shepherding the servants: cries of, 'He's saved them.' 'Well done, sir,' and offers of blankets and shelter.

But Moriarty would have none of it. He shook comforting hands from his shoulders, dragged arms from around Martha and the child, replacing them with his own hands as he hurried them from the vicinity of the house.

As they reached the centre of the square he heard someone shouting, 'Jump into this tarpaulin and you'll be all right.' He did not look back.

The heat in the room was becoming unbearable, the smoke already starting to clog at their lungs. Still neither Crow nor Holmes could make any impact on the door.

'It's no good, Crow,' shouted Holmes. 'Stand back. Your pistol.' He had retrieved the revolver from where it had fallen in the middle of the room, aiming it straight at the lock.

Crow waited for the explosion, but it did not come.

'The hammer,' Holmes yelled. 'The hammer is jammed. The window, it's our only chance, man.'

Crow turned, searching for the right implement, then, picking up the piano stool, he hurled it with all possible force at the window nearest the piano. It crashed through, taking glass and part of the frame with it.

Holmes was by the open casement in a moment, one of the fire irons in his hand, smashing remaining glass and debris from the surround.

Below, they could hear the surge of the crowd and the sound of the engines reaching the square. Crow moved to his side, feeling the flames charring at the back of his coat, singeing the short hair on his neck. Glancing at Holmes, he saw that the detective had ripped off the bald pate Moriarty wig and clawed the make-up from his face. Below there was a drop of some twenty feet into the milling throng, through which the brass-helmeted firemen were running the hoses and manning the pumps.

In the centre of the square, arms wrapped around two young women, away from the pressing crowd, Crow saw a familiar figure hurrying towards the square's entrance.

'Get that man,' he shouted with all the strength he could summon from his aching lungs. 'Catch him!'

The back of his throat was seared by the acrid smoke, and he leaned forward, retching and coughing, impotent as the Professor hurried from sight.

Then, from below, came the firemen's call to jump – six of them holding a black tarpaulin firmly by rope bindings to receive Crow and Holmes.

'You first,' gasped Holmes. 'Jump, man.' And Crow pulled himself to the sill and leaped.

Among the dirt, flying debris and smoke pall in the square, he faced Holmes a few minutes later. The crowd had been pushed back, as the firemen bravely fought to save the whole square from total destruction.

'I am sorry, Holmes,' Crow looked at the detective's blackened and sooty face. 'We so nearly had him.'

'Our time will come, Crow.' Holmes put out a hand and rested it on the Scot's shoulder. 'It was as much my fault as yours, but do not despair. I have a feeling we shall be hearing from Moriarty again.' He frowned, uneasy for a moment. 'Crow, you will doubtless have to do something official regarding *the* woman in Maida Vale.'

Crow nodded, the cough coming back to his throat, his

lungs feeling as though they would burst.

'Deal kindly with her, Crow.'

Across the city, in Bermondsey, James Moriarty ran a hand over the leather binding of his current journal. It must have been a premonition, he felt, which led him to bring the books over to this lair on his last journey. He smiled. A pity he had not brought the Jean-Baptiste Greuze and the *Mona Lisa* also.

Looking down at the book, he thought sadly that there would be no crossing out of the notes on Holmes. However, it might well have been worse, he considered. At least his family people were safe, and he once more had control of the French, German and Italian underworlds. Tomorrow they would continue, and there was a time coming when he would again meet face to face with Angus McCready Crow. And Sherlock Holmes.

He crossed to the small window, dreaming of his labyrinthine intrigues, and looked out to where the dawn began to glow across the sooty grimy roofs and spires. Out there, at this very moment, men and women would be already about his business; proud to be in his service; content to abide by his methods and be members of the Professor's family.

ENVOI

The register of Marriages and Baptisms of the, now defunct, church of St Edmund The King, Bermondsey, shows three items of great interest which took place on Saturday, 14 August 1897.

A marriage between Harold William Allen and Polly Pearson.

The baptism of William Albert Spear.

The baptism of Arthur James Moriarty.

Fresh blood for the Professor's family.

APPENDIX
The Moriarty Journals and the Chronicles of Dr John H. Watson

These few notes, appended to this manuscript, will be of interest mainly to dedicated scholars of the life and work of Mr Sherlock Holmes and his chronicler, Dr John H. Watson. They are included here because of the, mercifully, few dissenting voices which were heard amidst the generous praise after publication of the first of these present volumes – *The Return of Moriarty*.

Some of those who have doubted the authenticity of the documents from which I have worked approached the subject with that charitable amusement of scholars who are aware that the subject is debatable. However, I was both shocked and surprised to find that one or two gentlemen simply dismissed aspects of the narrative with illogical and unscientific arguments like – 'Rubbish, this could never have happened!' or, even more unlettered, 'Junk!' So displaying a marked lack of attention to the theories and practice of Mr Holmes himself.

Four items were seized upon by these happy few:

1. The old chestnut concerning the possibility of there having been three brothers Moriarty – each named James.

2. A strange, and illogical, revulsion to the fact that Professor Moriarty appeared to be a nineteenth-century 'Godfather' with great knowledge of the underworld, and its language.

3. The events at the Reichenbach Falls.

4. A comment reported to have been made years after the Reichenbach incident in which Holmes speaks of 'The late Professor Moriarty ... (and) ... the living Colonel Sebastian Moran.'

Apart from the indisputable facts concerning real crimes, I have worked solely from the so-called *Moriarty Journals* and the private papers of Angus McCready Crow. I have personally not sought to impose my own conclusions upon Moriarty's text – yet two people, at least, have suggested that I have invented the incredible story of what, according to the Professor, happened at the Reichenbach Falls, and the other matters. This, I must dispute categorically.

But let us take the items in turn.

First, the question of the three Moriarty brothers, each named James. The evidence seems to me to be perfectly straightforward. References are made to Professor Moriarty, Mr Moriarty, the Professor and Professor James Moriarty in five of the cases written up by Watson (*The Valley of Fear, His Last Bow, The Missing Three-Quarter, The Final Problem* and *The Empty House*); Colonel James Moriarty is referred to in *The Final Problem*; and a third brother, reported to be a station-master in the West country, is spoken of in *The Valley of Fear*.

Holmesians have, to my mind, always made heavy weather over the possibility of all three bearing the same Christian name – James. *The Moriarty Journals* certainly solve the problem. I should imagine that James is a family name, possibly the middle name; and, in the journals, Moriarty makes it quite plain that the three brothers regarded this as an idiosyncrasy and spoke of each other as James, Jamie and Jim. In the journals, Moriarty claims that he is really the youngest brother, a criminal from an early age, who, incensed with jealousy at his eldest brother James' academic success, finally *framed* and murdered him, becoming a master of disguise and impersonating James Moriarty the Eldest in order to have his underworld minions stand more in awe of him. This claim does seem to me to have a certain validity, though for once Mr Holmes appears to have been taken in by the subterfuge.

Secondly, the question of Professor Moriarty the nineteenth-century 'Godfather', leader of a vast criminal army: a man with great knowledge of crime, the underworld, its methods and language. This seems even more obvious. In *The Final Problem*, Holmes speaks of the Professor as '. . . [the] deep organizing power which forever stands in the

way of the law.' He mentions Moriarty's involvement in
'...cases of the most varying sorts – forgery cases, robberies,
murders...' More, he describes him as '...the Napoleon of
Crime... the organizer of half that is evil and nearly all that is
undetected in this great city... a genius, a philosopher, an
abstract thinker. He has a brain of the first order. He sits
motionless, like a spider in the centre of its web, but that web
has a thousand radiations, and he knows well every quiver of
each of them. He does little himself. He only plans...' (If we
are to believe the *Moriarty Journals* this was not quite
accurate, though planning was his main preoccupation)
'...his agents are numerous and splendidly organized...'
And so on in the same manner. Is there not something
incredibly familiar about this description? One has only to
marry it to the criminal language of the time – including the
fact (see Glossary) that the English underworld spoke of itself
as The Family – and we have all the elements of present-day
organized crime. Can one really believe that the organizing
genius of this underworld would not have spoken to his
minions in their own language, nor known the darkest
methods?

Thirdly, the incident at the Reichenbach Falls, where the
Moriarty Journals claim that there was no struggle, no death,
simply an agreement between Moriarty and Holmes. I am
essentially a reporter and not a commentator. As a reporter I
have set down the facts, as written in the journals. If called
upon to comment, I would join with those who declare that
this story is rubbish. Then why does the Professor maintain
that it is the truth?

If the journals are indeed the diaries of James Moriarty,
Napoleon of Crime, then he certainly lived on after
Reichenbach. Holmes is insistent to Watson that the evil
genius died. Note that he was not so insistent to Inspector
(later Superintendent) Crow. I personally suspect something
more sinister, and I certainly do not believe that Holmes gave
in to an agreement without some battle of wills. Moriarty, in
writing his own diary, would, being the man he is, wish to put
himself in the best possible light (he is always at his most
arrogant when claiming victory). Something strange certainly
occurred at the Reichenbach Falls and the evidence contained

in this current volume may well suggest what it was – it certainly throws more light on the matter, without making direct mention of it. By the time we have deciphered the whole journal, and I have combed Crow's papers, we may have something approximating the real truth. However, in the unlikely event of the *Moriarty Journals* being forgeries, I would still submit, with my publishers, that they have an inherent interest – bringing, as I trust they do, some spark of thrill and vicarious excitement into our drab and worried lives.

Lastly, there is the question of Sherlock Holmes' comment, set down in *The Adventure of the Illustrious Client*, which took place some ten or eleven years after the Reichenbach incident. Readers of the previous chronicles will recall that Moriarty describes in some detail how Colonel Sebastian Moran met his fate, yet in *The Illustrious Client*, Holmes says 'If your man is more dangerous than the late Professor Moriarty, or the living Colonel Sebastian Moran, then he is indeed worth meeting.'

Regarding this, one can only point to the fact that Watson describes Holmes as prefacing this remark with a smile. So we can now, perhaps, judge the depths of irony in that smile, and appreciate Holmes' jest in investing life in one who he knew was dead, and . . . possibly death in one who he knew was living. I have no way of knowing, for the remains of the journals have yet to be deciphered.

GLOSSARY

area-diving	A method of theft which necessitates sneaking down area steps and stealing from the lower rooms of houses.
blag	To snatch; usually a blag is a theft, often smash and grab, but applied to any theft in a public place.
broadsman	Card sharper.
buck cabbie	A dishonest cab driver.
cash-carrier	Ponce, or whore's minder.
Chapel, The	Whitechapel.
chink	Money.
cracksman	A housebreaker; burglar; safebreaker.
crib	A house, room, shop, brothel, etc., often used by the criminal fraternity to denote a place or building to be burgled.
crimping shop	Barbary coast boarding house, mainly associated with the practice of forcibly impressing, or shanghaiing, sailors.
crow	A look-out (particularly for a burglar).

demander	One who demands money with menaces.
dipper	Pickpocket.
esclop	Policeman. Backslang, though the *c* is never pronounced and the *e* often omitted.
Family, The	The criminal underworld. (Viz. *Tait's Magazine*, April 1841. 'The Family... The generic name for thieves, pickpockets, gamblers, housebreakers, *et hoc genus omne*'.)
gonoph	Minor thief.
growler	A four-wheeled cab.
Haymarket Hector	Prostitute's bully, or 'minder': applied to those who worked in the neighbourhood of the Haymarket and Leicester Square.
lakin	Wife.
lamps	Eyes.
London particular	A thick London fog or 'pea-souper'.
Lump Hotel	The Workhouse.
lurker	Strictly speaking, a professional beggar. Here it is used to denote beggars and confidence men in Moriarty's employ as spies, watchers and purveyors of intelligence.
macer	A cheat.
magsman	An inferior cheat.

mark	Victim – usually intended victim of prostitute or confidence trickster.
mobsman	Swindler, pickpocket working with a gang or mob.
mug-hunter	A street robber or footpad. Hence contemporary *mugging*.
mumper	Beggar or, more possibly by this time, a scrounger.
nobbler	One who nobbles, i.e. criminal used for the express purpose of inflicting grievous bodily harm.
palmer	Shop-lifter.
pigeon	Victim.
punisher	Superior *nobbler*, employed to inflict severe beating.
rampsman, ramper	A tearaway, a hoodlum.
ream	Superior; good.
roller	A thief who steals from drunks, or a prostitute who steals from her clients.
screwing	Burglary, usually by using false or skeleton keys.
shivering Jemmy	One who practises the art of begging while partially clothed.
slap-bang shop	A night cellar frequented by thieves and where no credit is given.

snoozer	A thief who specializes in robbing hotel guests while they sleep.
star-glazing	Cutting out a pane of glass to gain access to a door or window catch.
starving	Device used by beggars, or lurkers; posing as one in need of food.
tooler	Superior pickpocket.

STAR BOOKS BESTSELLERS

THRILLERS

SHATTERED	*John Farris*	£1.50* ☐
BLOODSPORT	*Henry Denker*	£1.75* ☐
THE AIRLINE PIRATES	*John Gardner*	£1.25 ☐
THE INFILTRATOR	*Michael Hughes*	£1.60 ☐
IKON	*Graham Masterton*	£2.50* ☐
TERROR OF THE TRIADS	*Sean O'Callaghan*	£1.50 ☐
HUNTED	*Jeremy Scott*	£1.50 ☐
DIRTY HARRY	*Philip Rock*	£1.25* ☐
MAGNUM FORCE	*Mel Valley*	£1.50* ☐

WAR

BLAZE OF GLORY	*Michael Carreck*	£1.80 ☐
CONVOY OF STEEL	*Wolf Kruger*	£1.80 ☐
BLOOD AND HONOUR	*Wolf Kruger*	£1.80 ☐
PANZER GRENADIERS	*Heinrich Conrad Muller*	£1.95* ☐
THE RAID	*Julian Romanes*	£1.80* ☐
GUNSHIPS: NEEDLEPOINT	*Jack Hamilton Teed*	£1.95 ☐
THE SKY IS BURNING	*D. Mark Carter*	£1.60 ☐
TASK FORCE BATTALION	*Tom Lambert*	£1.60 ☐

STAR Books are obtainable from many booksellers and newsagents. If you have any difficulty tick the titles you want and fill in the form below.

Name _____

Address _____

_____

Send to: Star Books Cash Sales, P.O. Box 11, Falmouth, Cornwall. TR10 9EN.

Please send a cheque or postal order to the value of the cover price plus: UK: 45p for the first book, 20p for the second book and 14p for each additional book ordered to the maximum charge of £1.63.

BFPO and EIRE: 45p for the first book, 20p for the second book, 14p per copy for the next 7 books, thereafter 8p per book.

OVERSEAS: 75p for the first book and 21p per copy for each additional book.

While every effort is made to keep prices low, it is sometimes necessary to increase prices at short notice. Star Books reserve the right to show new retail prices on covers which may differ from those advertised in the text or elsewhere.

*NOT FOR SALE IN CANADA

STAR BOOKS BESTSELLERS

CHILLERS

CHAINSAW TERROR	*Nick Blake*	£1.80	☐
SLUGS	*Shawn Hutson*	£1.60	☐
SPAWN	*Shawn Hutson*	£1.80	☐
CARNOSAUR	*Harry Adam Knight*	£1.95	☐
SLIMER	*Harry Adam Knight*	£1.95	☐
BLOWFLY	*David Lowman*	£1.95	☐
THE PARIAH	*Graham Masterton*	£1.95*	☐
THE PLAGUE	*Graham Masterton*	£1.80*	☐
THE MANITOU	*Graham Masterton*	£1.50*	☐
SATAN'S LOVE CHILD	*Brian McNaughton*	£1.35*	☐
SATAN'S SEDUCTRESS	*Brian McNaughton*	£1.25*	☐

STAR Books are obtainable from many booksellers and newsagents. If you have any difficulty tick the titles you want and fill in the form below.

Name _____

Address _____

_____

Send to: Star Books Cash Sales, P.O. Box 11, Falmouth, Cornwall. TR10 9EN.

Please send a cheque or postal order to the value of the cover price plus:
UK: 45p for the first book, 20p for the second book and 14p for each additional book ordered to the maximum charge of £1.63.

BFPO and EIRE: 45p for the first book, 20p for the second book, 14p per copy for the next 7 books, thereafter 8p per book.

OVERSEAS: 75p for the first book and 21p per copy for each additional book.

While every effort is made to keep prices low, it is sometimes necessary to increase prices at short notice. Star Books reserve the right to show new retail prices on covers which may differ from those advertised in the text or elsewhere.

*NOT FOR SALE IN CANADA